E S MOXON is of Anglo-Italian heritage, and her life has always involved languages and travel. Her parents love history and growing up she spent many family holidays visiting ancient burial sites and stone circles, exploring Britain's multi-cultural past. Her Italian grandfather, somewhat of a rascal in his youth, would regale her with his roguish adventures. This oral storytelling, akin to old sagas told around fires in Saxon and Viking mead halls, fuelled Elaine's passion for writing from a young age and she's loved it ever since.

E S MOXON

WULFSUNA

THE WOLF SPEAR SAGA · 1

SilverWood

Published in 2015 by SilverWood Books

SilverWood Books Ltd
30 Queen Charlotte Street, Bristol, BS1 4HJ
www.silverwoodbooks.co.uk

ISBN 978-1-78132-273-4 (paperback)
ISBN 978-1-78132-274-1 (ebook)

British Library Cataloguing in Publication Data
A CIP catalogue record for this book is available from
the British Library

Set in Sabon and Stonehenge by SilverWood Books
Printed on responsibly sourced paper

For Nonno, the greatest storyteller I ever knew

Þy wæs sweart land. Her fuhton wigendas here.
It was a dark land. Here warriors fought an enemy army.

E S Moxon

DRAMATIS PERSONAE

Wulfsuna of Germania

Brithwen – a lady
Chapper – Heahstan's cnapa
Ealdwig – a thegn of Germania
Frithbert – a thegn of Germania
Frobe – Sieghild's cnapa and Lorri's friend
Geldhere – a thegn of Germania
Heahstan – a thegn of Germania
Ianbert – a thegn of Germania
Leofgist – a thegn of Germania and friend of Sieghild
Lorri – Wulfgar's cnapa
Sieghild – a thegn, Wulfgar's lifelong friend
Stubb – a young Saxon
Tortsig – a thegn of Germania
Wulfric – warrior lord of the Wolf Sons
Wulfgar – Wulfric's son and ealdorman

Hwychas

Acgarat – Huweyn's wife
Anwen – a seer
Clodri – a wool tucker
Gwidol – a preacher
Huweyn – leader of the Hwychas tribe
Morwyneth – a seer, daughter of Anwen
Turpilos – Hwychas elder
Vendognus – Hwychas elder

Wulfsuna of Bryton

Brunbard – a farrier and blacksmith
Cwenfleda – daughter of Brunbard and Estelflead, friend to Morwyneth
Estelflead – wife of Brunbard and mother of Cwenfleda

Godelina – a seamstress
Osmund – a thegn of Bryton
Radliffe – a thegn of Bryton
Shepherd – a Seaxan
Skinner – a Seaxan
Trunhild – a thegn of Bryton

Other People, Places and Things

Aberhabren – fictitious village near River Severn
Afon Habren – sub-Roman term for River Severn
Angon – javelin-type spear used for throwing
Angulus – Angeln in modern Schleswig-Holstein, Germany
Aquae Sulis – Celtic name for Bath pertaining to water Goddess Sulis
Bathumtun – Saxon name for Bath
Bryn Hwychas – fictitious hill on which village of Prenhwychas is built
Bryton – Britain
Brytons/Brytonic/Bryttas – British people of Sub-Roman Britain, Britons
Burrium – Welsh tribe
By Ceastre – village of Bicester, Oxfordshire
Byrnie – hip-length chain mail shirt with sleeves to the elbow
Caernwealas – Saxon term for south-west Britain, Cornwall
Clann mhic Ailpein – archaic term for McAlpine Clan
Cnapa – Saxon term for knave
Cruithnii – Celtic term for Picts
Dobunni – tribe of native Britons inhabiting what is now Gloucestershire, North Somerset, Herefordshire, Oxfordshire, Wiltshire, Worcestershire and Warwickshire
Dudley – a travelling scop/bard
Eadmaer – Lord of the Angle Boars
Etocetum – sub-Roman town, now museum in Wall, Staffordshire
Fosse Way – major trade route
Frigg – Saxon goddess attributed to motherhood and marriage
Geats – Jutes
Glevum/Gloui Ceastre – Gloucester
Gobannus – Welsh tribe
Hig – a young Angle
Hildwaeg – Saxon ship, the Battlewave
Holig Monath – Holy Month, Saxon for September
Humbre – River Humber
Hwychas – fictitious tribe based around location of the real Hwicce

Ingui – early representation of fertility Goddess Freyr
Limitanei – mercenaries hired by Rome to bolster the armies
Lindum – Lincoln
Menapii – Welsh tribe of the mountainous north-west coast
Metaris Estuary – the Wash, north of Norfolk
Oceanus Germanicus – Germanic Ocean (North Sea meets English Channel)
Peanfahel – archaic name for Kinneil near Bo'ness, Scotland
Pictii – Romanised term for Picts
Prenhwychas – fictitious Welsh village near home of the Hwicce tribe
Sabrina/Saefern river – River Severn
Sachsen – in Germania, home of the Wulfsuna
Saehunta – Angle ship, the Sea Hunter
Saeson – Welsh form of Saxon
Seax – 6–12 inch dagger, symbol of freedom
Seaxan – variant of Saxon
Silures – Welsh tribe
South Fosse – a major trade route
Taranis – Celtic Thunder God
Thegn – variant of thane, a Saxon duke
Thunor – Saxon God of Thunder
Tiw – Saxon God of Justice and War
Vambraces – iron splinted wrist guards on leather backing
Vindolanda – Roman fort at Hadrian's Wall
Waeclinga Street – Watling Street, a trade route
Wealas – Saxon name for indigenous settlement in the west
Wealh – Saxon term for foreigner
Wealisc – Saxon term for indigenous Britons
Weod Monath – Weed Month, Saxon for August
Wimme river – River Witham
Woden – Saxon God of War, Chief of all the Gods
Wulfsuna – Saxon tribe of the Wolf Sons
Wyndrysh river – River Windrush

CHAPTER ONE

AD433,
Germanic Ocean, East Coast of Bryton

Sieghild had never seen the land of his mother. He wondered if there could be others the same as he, a man born of two lands. Soon he would know. Leaning out starboard from the long ship *Hildwaeg*, he scratched his week-old beard. A south-westerly breeze tossed surf off the waves and lifted his brown hair from his back; a welcome reprieve from the warm summer afternoon. Gulls cried as they circled overhead, having smelled the cured fish stowed on board, which mingled with the stench of sixty sweating men and damp wood. Behind him, the main sail billowed on the central mast, the grey wolf thereon appearing to jump and pounce as each gust of wind punched the hefty fabric.

"You were right, my friend. Our crossing has been protected by the gods."

Wulfgar sauntered down the deck, blond hair whipping his bare arms. Sieghild had known Wulfgar, their lord's only son, since birth. Sieghild nodded an acknowledgement as a heavy hand slapped him on the back.

"What ails you? Missing the fatherland already?" Wulfgar leaned on the side of the boat, his iron-splinted vambraces winking in the sunlight.

Sieghild sighed. "This journey unsettles me. No Wolf Sons have been back since your father brought them home."

"Twenty years." Wulfgar shrugged. "A little more than our lifetimes."

Sieghild shook his head and smiled, wondering how Wulfgar could dismiss eighteen years so lightly. "They became men in that land, under the Empire, our fathers and other Wulfsuna."

He looked to the bow where Lord Wulfric stood. The leader of the 'Wolf Sons', regal with his white beard clipped neatly about his round face, in wolf furs and a gold embossed helmet, stared out to sea; the weight of his convictions a heavy burden on his posture. Standing alone, where once he had stood abreast with Sieghild's father, he bore a sombre image: a man without his friend and battle brother. Wulfgar, seeming unable to watch his father long, turned back out to sea feeling his own beard, clipped short like that of his father's. Sieghild watched his friend lose his thoughts to the sea. Eventually Wulfgar spoke.

"It is several years since Aelfsieg's passing and yet my father carries the grief still."

"It is not only Lord Wulfric who feels as though my father fell recently in battle," Sieghild replied.

Wulfgar straightened his arms, knuckles turning white as they gripped the side of the lapstrake vessel. "Yes. It was a fearsome fight we struggled to win against those savage Geats." He spat phlegm into the water, as though uttering their name had caused a foul taste in his mouth. "And here we sail with another pack of brutes."

Sieghild followed Wulfgar's nod to the second long boat sailing an arrow's reach behind them. Known as the "sea-hunter", she carried two score and ten men of Angulus. Their leader Eadmaer, ten years their senior, had more than once delighted in reminding Sieghild and Wulfgar they were mere 'bearna' in comparison. He had oiled his sword arm a decade longer, and this, in his eyes, made him a better warrior. Wulfgar emitted a low growl that resonated in his chest, reminding Sieghild of his friend's hatred towards their uncomfortable ally.

"There was one man my father did not bring home from Bryton after the Empire fled." Wulfgar jabbed a thumb in the direction of the *Saehunta*.

Sieghild nodded. "Eadmaer's father, Maerard."

"Maerard," Wulfgar echoed, shaking his head. "What makes my old man believe the Angles will not take revenge?"

Sieghild rolled his hip along the boat, turning his back on the ocean and the Angles, elbows resting on the side. "They have never sought revenge. No blood can be shed between our tribes. Lord Wulfric and Maerard's widow swore an oath in Maerard's name."

Wulfgar stood proud of the side of the ship, jabbing a thumb towards the Saehunta. "Yes, but they swore it over the soil of Sachsen, and Eadmaer's mother no longer lives. I do not trust them."

Sieghild laughed. "You do not trust anyone."

Wulfgar smiled briefly, patting Sieghild's chest with the back of a hand. "Only you, brother. We are as though blood links us."

Lord Wulfric's order to lower the sail brought the young men's gaze back to the bow of their own ship, known proudly as the "battle-wave". The ships had reached the mouth of the Metaris, the estuary that would lead them inland up the river Wimme to Lindum. They had arrived. Sieghild felt the power of the goddess Frigg thump his stomach, churning it over inside and sending his heart into a fast beat. Breath caught in his throat and he coughed to disguise it. Oarsmen leaped over ropes and wagon wheels that were tethered to the mast, hurrying to their rowing chests. Many of these men had never sailed, while for others it had been many years since they had guided a vessel through water. Lord Wulfric rated land above all else. Voyages overseas to plunder wealth were forbidden, especially to the island of Bryton, a land that had provided coin and shelter in his youth. As mercenaries attached to the Twentieth Legion at Gloui Ceastre, Wulfric and Aelfsieg had defended Bryton from the Pictii at Vindolanda and then against raiding Angles on the east coast. The men of the blue designs had viciously defended their own land north of the Humbre with fierce vigour. It had been easy to fight painted strangers. Battling kin from Germania had been too much for the Wulfsuna to suffer though. When Wulfric declared the Wolf Sons were to return to the fatherland, Maerard and his Boars had argued against it. Like their Angle cousins raiding the east coast, Maerard and his men had wanted to remain, to befriend the Pictii and fill their purses with coin from Bryton. Wulfric's deadly encounter with Maerard on the shore of the Metaris sealed the decision to return to Germania.

As forty men aboard the *Hildwaeg* drove their oars into the last of the deep, dark Germanic Ocean, they glided into the fens, the *Saehunta* in their wake. The view held Sieghild in a hex, his eyes unable to blink as he drank it all in. Immensely open, a marsh filled with oyster-catchers and terns, plovers and gulls, the wide landscape threatened to swallow them up. To the north, shallow chalk cliffs with red strata formed an unusual and colourful coastline. Grey clouds, like boulders in the sky, hung above them with stormy intentions, devouring the sun. The flat expanse of wetland beckoned the vessels into its shallows and sandbanks, beautiful and treacherous; almost bewitching. Salt-water whipped Sieghild's face and he inhaled the air of the motherland; it was sweet.

Lord Wulfric walked down the ship, a heavier gait to his son that rolled with the *Hildwaeg*, seamless and omniscient. Sieghild straightened and Wulfric smiled at him, though directed his words to his son.

"These waters are dangerous. We are fortunate there are higher tides this year, here and at home. We must thank the gods."

Wulfgar shrugged, indifferent, and so Lord Wulfric turned his attention on Sieghild. "We will soon discover if this mystical isle has changed since we left her. Do you have your father's map?"

"Yes, My Lord." Sieghild patted the leather pouch hung from his war belt, feeling the roll of paper inside spring back from his touch.

"Good. Your father had great patience, Sieghild, and a good eye. He drew that map when we served here at Rome's pleasure, and when we left the island to return home, he charted our route. It is how we will find our way back in." Lord Wulfric cast an arm towards the shore, which they approached with painstaking accuracy.

Sieghild looked past his gesture to where the land rose up northwards in the distance. Sheep scattered the hillside; clusters of white woollen shapes. To the south-west a modest settlement clung to the sloping ground, puffs of grey smoke rising from its thatched conical roofs. Several streams, fed by the estuary, twisted and wound around small oblong fields of crops on the fringe of the Fens.

"Are you sure we'll be welcome?" Wulfgar asked.

His father laughed; a gentle sound that conflicted with his size. "We shall know soon enough, eh?"

Sieghild stifled a smile at Wulfgar's derisive snort, which he made no attempt to hide. His father ignored him and instead gazed landward once more.

"Heahstan is a master helmsman, do you not think, my son?"

"Yes, father." The quiet reply preceded a heavy sigh.

Sieghild felt compelled to interject, if merely to counteract his friend's obvious lack of interest. "My Lord, he is a helmsman to be proud of. The *Hildwaeg* shall not falter in these sandbanks at his hands."

Lord Wulfric winked at Sieghild. "No, she shall not, son."

As their lord returned to the bow, Wulfgar groaned, depositing a heavy arm onto Sieghild's shoulder. "He loves you, more than he does me. I'd swear we were swapped at birth. Ah, Sieg, my loins would kill for a good woman right now."

"One day soon, brother. You hope," Sieghild replied, his mind lingering on the unknown land they approached.

"I hope." Wulfgar gritted his teeth in mock frustration, hissing as he drew in breath. "I've had my fill of all these wise old men and their war tales."

"One score and ten miles to go. At least that's what your father tells me."

Wulfgar laughed. "That old cockerel? He has the stars in his eyes. I'm sure he expects an Emperor to welcome him with gold and maidens when we reach the Fosse."

"Well you take the maidens to your loins and I'll take the gold, eh?" said Sieghild, tapping a finger against his chest.

Wulfgar waved a dismissive hand. "I have enough gold. Besides, you wouldn't know what to do with a maiden." He tilted his head to one side. "One score miles and ten. You believe that?"

Sieghild nodded. "He is our lord. Yes, I believe him."

"He is your lord. He is my father." Wulfgar stabbed his chest with a forefinger. "I can doubt kin."

Sieghild shook his head. "Don't let Thegn Heahstan hear you say that."

"Get dressed, weaner," shouted Thegn Heahstan. An ageing warrior, built like a mighty stone wall with white hair and a long beard, he resembled Woden himself. Wulfgar raised a threatening fist to Heahstan's back, leaving reluctantly to find his tunic. Sieghild choked on a laugh, watching his friend hail his cnapa, Lorri; a thin weed of a youth responsible for carrying his war gear and never where his master wanted him to be.

"Lorri, bring me war-face and my death-light." Wulfgar twisted in all directions. "Lorri?" Wulfgar looked back at Sieghild, who grinned at his friend's servant dilemma. Wulfgar shook a playful fist in response. "So help me, I'll hang that lad before he reaches fifteen."

Sieghild cupped his hands over his mouth, needlessly amplifying his voice. "How can you lose a man on a boat?"

Wulfgar's arms spread wide in disbelief. Finally the scrawny-faced boy appeared, skulking out from behind a group of warriors who were lowering the main sail. Sieghild joined them in laughter while watching the oarsmen guide the *Hildwaeg* to moor at a jetty protruding out into the fens. This was where the vessel would rest until next high tide. As the *Saehunta* drew up several yards behind them, out in the marsh Sieghild saw Lord Wulfric raise a hand to Eadmaer to signal that they should disembark.

Under Lord Wulfric's orders, Sieghild and Wulfgar organised the departure of the Seaxan warriors onto the jetty. Sieghild and another young man called Leofgist jumped onto the wooden walkway to tie off the long ship on one of many vertical supporting timbers. Wulfgar, helmet in one hand, had finally dressed and was fidgeting under padded shirt, tunic and byrnie. He counted heads as other men followed, ensuring they had all secured their oars and collected their round shields. Some local villagers, wading for cockles, were eyeing the arrival of the Seaxans curiously. Unsure whether to remain or flee, they paused in their work and observed the strangers until they were satisfied they posed no threat. Warriors who had disembarked stretched stiff limbs and swapped jokes, passing round water from an animal bag. The last taste of home, thought Sieghild, recalling his instructions to the men to fill the hide bags from the well before they had departed. Sieghild watched Wulfgar trying to hurry the last few men.

"Give an old man chance," joked Tortsig, a thegn no more than five years older than Wulfgar.

Wulfgar dodged the shield that narrowly missed his head. "If you were my thegn, I'd leave you at the rear."

Chapper, a trader with a weathered face like oak bark and a shaved head, waved a hand. "Out the way, baby warrior. Does your father know you're not on your mother's tit?"

Giving up on the stragglers, Wulfgar joined his friend on the jetty. "Is it how you imagined?"

"I do not know." Sieghild pondered. "It smells different."

Wulfgar laughed. "That's the natives, Sieg."

Sieghild elbowed his friend in the ribs, only to have a hand shoved into his face in response. Wulfgar aimed a playful fist at his stomach, which he deftly avoided and bent over. Never as quick to move, Wulfgar felt his stomach collide with Sieghild's head and shoulders and the pair grappled arms. Unable to contain a laugh, Wulfgar lost his balance first, taking them both down onto the jetty. Wulfgar's helmet rolled from his hand across the planks as he fought to hold on to Sieghild. He lost, and Sieghild rolled and stood, readying his fists.

"You're losing, weaner," Heahstan called, grinning.

Sieghild raised his head to grin at Heahstan as Wulfgar made to continue the friendly brawl. All but a few Wulfsuna were now on the jetty, Lord Wulfric and two of his thegns remaining on the *Hildwaeg*. By comparison, only a handful of the Angles had disembarked from the *Saehunta* with Eadmaer and made their way through the fens to meet with them. Sieghild put a restraining hand on his friend's shoulder.

"Why did the *Saehunta* not dock behind the *Hildwaeg*?" Sieghild asked.

Wulfgar shook his head. "Perhaps there are obstructions beneath the water."

The small group of warriors loitered close to one another. A dark-haired young man Sieghild knew as Hig smiled at one of his Seaxan friends, Stubb. However, his smile faded intermittently, his gaze drawn to Eadmaer. The Angle leader was lurking nearby amid a circle of large warriors. Hig shook hands with Stubb, the latter attempting to lure his companion over to a jug of ale being shared round. More than once, Sieghild noticed Hig held back, his eyes darting to Eadmaer as though checking his actions.

Sieghild looked around them and tapped Wulfgar on the arm. "Why have all the Angle Boars not joined us?"

"They will, soon enough," his friend replied, ambling off to retrieve his helmet.

Wulfgar's disinterest troubled Sieghild. He expected him to be more alert considering his intense hatred of his father's choice of ally. Sieghild checked the *Saehunta*. Two-thirds of the Angles remained aboard her, all gathered backboard facing those on the jetty. A frown creased Sieghild's brow as fear began to swell within him. He did not like this. He looked at Eadmaer and caught him sliding a tongue slowly across the front of yellow teeth. Stubb once again asked Hig to take a drink with him and the young Angle hesitated.

Worrying about the five burly warriors surrounding Eadmaer, Sieghild gripped the leather handle of his death blade and swung round to search for Wulfgar. In that brief moment he despaired at the Wulfsuna around him, relaxed and oblivious. The warrior Boars moved into a horseshoe around their leader. Eadmaer lifted his chin, a minute response, though enough to rouse Sieghild's full attention and witness the Angle's hand slide round his scabbard, releasing the peace ribbon off his sword hilt. He had to warn the Wulfsuna. The fates, however, would not allow it. Hig drew his dagger from his belt and thrust it into Stubb's abdomen, gripping the shoulder of his friend as Stubb collapsed onto the jetty. Hig's face contorted in agony at the outcome of his orders, youthful tears breaking down his cheeks. Sieghild cried Wulfgar's name, though Eadmaer's bellow drowned his call.

"Kill the wolves."

A roar erupted from the few Angles surrounding them, who killed and gutted as many as they could before the Seaxans overcame their surprise. Wild fowl scattered and the cockle waders ran for their lives. Sieghild yelled instructions as Wulfsuna leaped for weapons, drew axes or fought with fists. Before he could lick blade with blade against their foes, combat had ceased. The Angles drew back.

"To sword."

Even before Lord Wulfric yelled the order, Wulfsuna ran for the pile of spears and angons on the jetty. Soon after, the deck of the *Saehunta* released an arrow shower, dispersing men from both sides. Sheltering behind the bow of the *Hildwaeg*, Sieghild dared a few glances. The remainder of the Angles were joining the battle. The *Saehunta* spewed her men from the deck. Like honey drops down string, men slithered down a rope into the water and ran across the marshes. In response, the Seaxans jumped down into the muddy wetland and charged the enemy, calling out the tribe's name in three guttural syllables: "Wulf-su-na, Wulf-su-na." Those who had their shields formed a wall of wooden circles intersected by protruding blades. They continued to shout their name, axe hafts and sword hilts drumming a din against the backs of the shields, a fearless invite to the first wave of Angle Boars. Sieghild gripped the hilt of his sword tightly, issuing a prayer to Tiw as he fetched an abandoned shield and ran into battle.

*

19

Beyond the jetty, a safe distance behind the shield wall, a second line of attack prepared for battle.

"Haven't you put that helmet on yet?"

Wulfgar ignored Heahstan's jibe, sliding the leather strap into the buckle, securing his helmet under his chin. The bowmen ran past them on their way to the *Hildwaeg*. He doubted they would be ready in time. He turned to Heahstan, who was swinging his axe to warm his arm muscles.

"Where is my father?" he asked the older thegn.

"Dressing for battle."

"It will be over by the time he arrives," Wulfgar spat.

"He is a true leader," growled Heahstan.

Wulfgar had never understood the ways of his elders; the ritual formalities they clung to. "You mean he lets his men fight his battles for him?"

With the back of a hand, Heahstan slapped the cheek flap of Wulfgar's helmet. The metal smarted against his face and Wulfgar rounded, axe raised.

"There are no Wulfsuna without their headman," Heahstan told him, chest thrust forward in defiance of the younger man's response. "He will fight when he is suitably protected. Meanwhile, his loyal warriors will hold the fighting back."

Wulfgar checked his helmet, scowling at Heahstan and calling to Lorri, "My shield."

Heahstan added, "Being a headman's son does not exclude you from showing loyalty."

Lorri handed Wulfgar the 3 foot lime wood circle. Painted blood-red, three snarling wolves' heads chased one another round the iron boss that protruded from its centre. Wulfgar gripped the leather-bound handle in the shield's back, checking his splinted iron vambraces were secure on his wrists. Thirty yards off, from the deck of the *Saehunta*, a second wave of arrows began to fly at the Seaxan wall. Heahstan rallied those around him.

"Into the wall. Get down."

Wulfgar followed as they ran up and over the jetty and through the marsh to bolster the shield wall. Dead men bobbed in the tide, arrows or spears rammed into their flesh, the shafts of the weapons waving to and fro. Wulfgar braced shoulders with Heahstan and the other warriors, overlapping their shields like fish scales. Men's sweat and fear mingled with the salt and seaweed of the cold water round their shins. Wulfgar held his battleaxe tight at the shoulder of the handle. Arrows reached them; hard pelting shards of death falling from a high arc off the *Saehunta*. Thudding into helmets and shields, they battered the wall. Men without mail cried out as arrows shot through their shields and tore into their bodies. Wulfgar jolted from arrow hits to his helmet, bouncing his head into his shield. Another glanced off the shoulder of his byrnie, knocking him off-balance. He stumbled into Heahstan, supported by the man's large frame. Above their heads, a gull screamed and fell between them, an arrow through its wing, and was quickly trampled to death under their frantic feet.

The familiar sound of an arrow storm came from behind them, like a great gust of air. Wulfgar imagined the bowmen on the *Hildwaeg* pouring a barrage over the Angles' shield wall and into the *Saehunta*. The lethal distraction would momentarily weaken them. As he felt Heahstan move, Wulfgar also lifted his head. The arrows from the *Saehunta* had ceased. Treading clumsily over dead men sunk beneath the shallows, they pushed their wall nearer the Angles. Men at the rear launched more angons, the long spears graceful in the air. Their death blows were less graceful, pinning men into the sand through guts, eyes or legs.

Wulfgar and Heahstan pushed into the front wall, closing up danger-ous gaps where men had fallen. A weaker youth, who was struggling in formation, seemed to gain renewed strength seeing the son of his lord beside him. Finally, the walls met and it began. An axe blade caught Wulfgar's helmet, jarring his whole body. He slouched further down behind his shield. He didn't fancy having his neck broken by an axe-beard tugging his head off. He slid his hand to the end of his axe handle to swing it. Thrusting the blade up and down, he sliced into arms or face plates of helmets, fending off the enemy. Fellow warriors dealt him punches as their elbows and axe hafts were drawn back to strike opponents, Wulfgar doing the same, unable to avoid bruising fellow Wulfsuna as they fought like trapped animals. Now separated from Heahstan, he continued to hear him yelling abuse.

"Die, you motherless sons of hairy pigs."

Wulfgar would have laughed, but for the gruelling fight to remain on his feet and safely behind his shield. When the Wulfsuna had faced the Geats he had not entered the wall. Having been returning home from trading, he had joined his kinsmen late in the battle. The walls had long fallen and he had instead faced individuals, fighting man-to-man and blade-to-blade. He asked Woden to deliver that moment, knowing he could fight better that way.

Blood lashed Wulfgar's helmet, the young boy beside him crying out. He spat the blood from his lips and cursed as the youth dropped onto his right leg, pinning his foot. The offending Angle came at Wulfgar, roaring. He slung his axe into the man's chin, cleaving his lower face in two. As the body reeled backwards, Wulfgar grasped the tunic of the dead boy and heaved him off his shin. Heahstan shouted, nearer this time.

"Rot, you smelling turds."

Heahstan rammed his seax under Angle shields, probably having lost his axe in one of the enemy. He skewered one warrior in the gut, releasing his innards into the wash. Then, swinging his blade downwards, Heahstan removed the forearm of another Angle who was unfortunate not to be wearing a byrnie or vambraces. Wulfgar could see the gaps in the enemy wall widening. They had to keep pushing. He shoved his shield into oncoming Angles, the iron boss denting an Angle's helmet and fending off the downward strike of another's axe. He raised his own battleaxe, securing the beard of the blade over his opponent's shield. Yanking down hard he revealed the Angle and hit him in the face with his shield boss. The man staggered back from the blow and Wulfgar jabbed him in the throat with the butt of his axe. His air supply cut off, the Angle began his descent. As he fell, Wulfgar dealt him another blow on the rear of his helmet. Woden had answered his prayers.

Deep in the throes of blood rage, Wulfgar did not know how long they had fought for. He could only judge by the men he had slain and, being as they were Angle Boars, he had not killed enough of them. His shield lost to the bloodstained water behind him, he had drawn his seax. A familiar voice cried out. It was Lord Wulfric. Wulfgar prayed the scream was a call to battle and his father had not been taken by Woden's death maidens. Trapped and tangled among the putrid mess of lost souls and clashes of death-lights, he struggled to writhe free. Wielding axe and seax, he tore away from the edge of the battle he was defending, twisting to try and see aboard the *Hildwaeg*. Over battling helmets he made out the carved dragon head prow of his father's vessel. Bowmen hung dead over the sides, their limp bodies staining the wood with their blood. Wulfgar scrambled over bloody cadavers, straining to see more. Eadmaer appeared starboard, the tusks on his menacing boar-skin headdress making the dead pig appear to grimace. Wulfgar started running through the tide of death. Making it to the jetty, he clambered up. Two men held Wulfric's arms taut as they tethered him to a wagon wheel. His father's helmet and byrnie had been removed. Eadmaer grinned, tossing a command to a third man who raised a sword into the air.

Ice claimed Wulfgar's heart, as cold as the waters surrounding them, and he screamed "No", chasing down the jetty towards the *Hildwaeg*. He went unheard above the noise of the marsh war in progress, though Eadmaer heard him, narrowing evil eyes and once more revealing yellow teeth in a grin. Light glinted off the blade as Wulfgar helplessly watched the warrior drive it into his father's chest. As though stopped by a shield boss in his gut, Wulfgar halted abruptly. Frigg yanked on his heart, her fists clenched round the sinews of his innards like reins on a horse. He felt the muscles clench in his face, drawing up his lips in a snarl as he looked to Eadmaer. The Angle pointed a finger at Wulfgar then drew it across his throat, intimating the ealdorman would be his next target. Emitting a roar, Wulfgar checked the grip on his axe and seax and ran for the ladder connecting the *Hildwaeg* to the jetty. As he reached the top of the ladder the last of Eadmaer's men were escaping starboard down a rope. He beat the haft of his axe handle against the ship and swung round. Frantically his eyes searched for one of the thegns and found Heahstan nearby, beating down a shorter man with the butt of his axe. Wulfgar shouted to him over the battle din. Heahstan took a moment to find him, other Wulfsuna relieving him as he withdrew to the jetty.

"Wulfric is dead," Wulfgar told him, gasping from his exertion.

"Eadmaer?"

"Yes." Wulfgar descended the ladder and hurried back along the jetty, leaping into the water.

"Angle pig-swill."

Heahstan looked back towards the fighting, as though contemplating what it was they were fighting for. Wulfgar had not known either, until witnessing his father's murder. He expelled air through his teeth, wincing at Frigg's relentless and hellish grasp on his heart. She refused to allow his pain to subside. He choked away tears, arms agitated and weapons desperate to seek Angle flesh. A false alliance made and an ocean sailed, all discarded by one man's revenge.

Wulfgar shoved his axe into his war belt and grabbed Heahstan's arm. "We did not come here for this."

Heahstan shrugged him off. "Swallow it. We're here now."

Wulfgar contemplated the older man's abandonment of his hand. "Swallow what?"

"Your pride and your fear," the thegn told him.

Fear? He was not afraid of Eadmaer. He wanted to kill him. He thrust his seax towards Heahstan's face.

"I have no f…"

"Lead us," growled Heahstan.

The thegn's searing stare through his metal mask was all that was needed to propel Wulfgar into the fray; to find the head of the battle. Drawing his axe from his belt again, he went in search of his friend. He found Sieghild, knee deep in blood and marsh, battleaxe locked with an Angle sword hilt, baring his teeth with the force required to overpower his enemy. He won, pushing the man away for long enough to slice the warrior's groin with his axe blade and drive the butt into the man's helmet as he went down.

Wulfgar inhaled deeply, and bellowed, "Wall."

Free men fell in where they could around him, the Wulfsuna rallying one another as they tightened the gaps between their shields. They hammered the wood with their axe handles, pommels and spears; a deafening drumming accompanied by their tribal chant. He looked at Sieghild standing beside him, and no words found him. Sieghild began shouting with the rest of them, compelling Wulfgar to join in. Behind their single line Angle stragglers met their gods at the hands of Thegns Ianbert and Geldhere, who were leading a pincer formation. One by one, like sheep, they herded the enemy into a pen of death. Fearing some of the Angles would board the ship to steal or mutilate his father's remains, Wulfgar instructed "Secure the *Hildwaeg*" to Sieghild, who did not hesitate.

Leaving the wall, Sieghild shouted for Leofgist and they left immediately. At once the Angles retreated across the marsh towards the *Saehunta*. For a brief moment Wulfgar imagined them to be drawing back to rebuild their own shield wall. They did not halt, however. Unable to believe it was a full withdrawal, Wulfgar left the wall, launching himself onto the jetty for a higher vantage point. As his feet landed on the wooden planks he rounded quickly. Eadmaer had returned to the *Saehunta* and Angles were making off with supplies they had stolen from the *Hildwaeg*. Sitting further out in the fens, the *Saehunta* had not yet been abandoned to the mud flats by the tide. Wulfgar grappled with the leather chin strap and ripped his helmet from his head, wiping damp hair from his face with the back of his hand.

Filling his lungs, he shouted after Eadmaer, "Traitor."

Eadmaer waved politely, like some relative leaving after a familial stay. The accursed wretch had no manners as well as no loyalty. So, Eadmaer had come to finish what his father had started. He had come all this way only to betray the Wulfsuna, as Maerard had intended nearly twenty years previous. Wulfgar wanted to spit, but his mouth had become dry and he could not swallow his disgust.

"I will not forget this, Eadmaer," he called, whether the Angle leader could hear him or not. He needed to say it aloud, as a personal promise. He would never forget.

CHAPTER TWO

Fen Marshes,
Metaris Estuary, Mouth of the River Wimme

Sailing northwards out of the estuary, the *Saehunta* appeared but a minute speck in the distance when Sieghild joined Wulfgar on the jetty. The ealdorman had not moved. Hesitant to come between his friend and that which his eyes would not relinquish, Sieghild hung back slightly.

"Wulfgar?" he tendered.

Wulfgar swallowed hard, angry eyes welling, his voice unusually deep. "We should not have come."

Sieghild grasped his shoulder and shook him fondly. "Come to your father's side."

Sieghild enrolled Lorri to walk ahead and clear the way for them. Escorting Wulfgar, whose feet were reluctant to follow, Sieghild noted that the view continued to hold his friend under a spell, his gaze unable to leave the expanse of the fens. Leofgist lined up the men, who all bowed their heads as Wulfgar passed along the jetty. Sieghild ushered him onto the deck of the *Hildwaeg* and over to his father's body. He remained close by as they watched Heahstan and the remaining thegns paying their respects at their dead lord's side. Heahstan picked up a discarded helmet with its full face plate, ornate gold eyebrows and beard in relief on the metal. He held it out to Wulfgar, who tensed at the offering.

"Lord Wulfric always told me you should have this."

Wulfgar shook his head. "I do not want it."

"It was your lord and father's wish." Heahstan shoved it into Wulfgar's stomach. "It is yours."

Wulfgar rolled the helmet in his hands. "I will not wear it."

Heahstan exhaled loudly. "As you will. It is in your possession. I have done as Lord Wulfric asked of me."

Thegn Tortsig leaned forward. "We have lost Thegns Ealdwig and Frithbert. What now, My Lord?"

Wulfgar did not answer. He stared vacantly at the body of his father at his feet, drawn inextricably to the fate that had found him in this wasteland. Crimson stained Lord Wulfric's noble tunic, blood and sinew splattered across his chest and white beard. At his wrists, the rope bindings the Angles had used to tie him to the wagon wheel remained. Seagulls screamed above them, ready to scavenge upon the wrecked and torn flesh of the fallen, crows drawn from inland to join the feast on the dead.

Thegn Ianbert spoke, repeating Tortsig's question. "My Lord, what now?"

Sieghild sent a hand to Wulfgar's arm, causing him to turn finally. "Wulfgar? They ask of you. You are now our lord and headman."

By the look in Wulfgar's eyes, Sieghild knew his friend was bereft. Wulfgar stepped back, seeming to pull away from his responsibility. Sieghild tightened the grip on Wulfgar's arm, lifting his free hand to his chest, palm pressing firmly against the links of his bloodstained byrnie.

"Lord Wulfgar."

The thegns showed their allegiance, echoing the title. Down on the jetty the foot soldiers recited the tribe name, as they had done during the battle, the vehement chant fighting against the call of carrion overhead. Wulfgar looked at Sieghild, half shaking his head in refusal of the fervent cries filling the air around them.

"I think we have company."

Heahstan's knowing voice dimmed the celebrations. Wulfgar removed himself, leaning on the side of the ship, his back to everyone. Sieghild followed the older warrior's pointed finger, leading to a small group of local men marching with purpose through the village. They were heading for the jetty. Heahstan turned to Sieghild, unable to hide the fact his eyes had sought out their absent young headman.

"Dress down and take Leofgist and a few men. Subdue the natives."

"Make them believe we're friendly?" Sieghild smiled wryly.

"We are." Heahstan spread large hands. "We only fought brothers here today, or what we assumed were kin. I want to collect my land gift, and don't want some farmer with a fork up his backside to be in the way of that."

Sieghild grinned. He knew what to do. Removing his byrnie and helmet, he encouraged the same of Leofgist. After much persuasion, they convinced half a dozen foot soldiers to leave their shields and spears behind, and ambled off up the jetty to meet their visitors.

Leofgist nervously scratched the stubble on his chin. "A good time to try out your mother's tongue. Do you remember?"

Leofgist's troubled enquiry brought a smile to Sieghild's face, ruddy cheeks rounding beneath blue eyes as he shrugged. He did not know if the words of his mother's people had changed in all these years. Even if they had not, it was possible his Germanic accent would smother her language. Leofgist began to fidget, his hands shuffling about his clothes where his axe and sword had been, emphasising the fact his clothes appeared too large for his bony frame.

"Be still," Sieghild whispered, "you have your seax."

Within a few yards of the visitors, Sieghild grinned and waved, calling out a greeting in the native dialect. They halted in surprise. Sieghild put an arm out across Leofgist's chest, bringing him to a stop, and turned to address the foot soldiers.

"Say and do nothing. Well, smile. Look friendly."

"We are friendly," Leofgist replied.

Sieghild laughed. "I know that. They do not."

Facing the bewildered villagers, Sieghild walked slowly towards them. There were less than a dozen men, all ages, sizes and shapes; elderly, and youngsters not even men yet. The mature among them wore moustaches, and their tunics were pinned on one shoulder with enamelled brooches. All of them carried farming implements, Sieghild conjectured as weapons. Again Sieghild called to them, smiling and showing them outstretched arms. One of the older men cast his friends a wary glance and moved forward, shortening the distance between him and Sieghild. He gripped a wood axe.

Sieghild made a third attempt to communicate in their language. "Hello. I am sorry if our skirmish alarmed you."

The native forced words from his mouth through clenched teeth, pushing his axe towards Sieghild. "Who are you?"

Sieghild gambled on the truth being best. "We are Wulfsuna tribe of Sachsen. We are sailing to meet our Brytonic kinsmen near Lindum. We come for settlement."

"You are Saeson? Warriors?"

"Yes." Sieghild nodded. "Some of us were once Limitanei." He hoped it had not been too long ago for the old man to remember.

"You speak our tongue." The man lowered his axe, examining Sieghild through a squint.

Sieghild could not stifle a smile, pride swelling in him. "My mother was Dobunni."

The man relaxed his stance, his face softening. "You mean us no harm?"

Shaking his head, Sieghild gestured to the *Hildwaeg*. "Our lord has been murdered. We wish only to rest and deal with our dead."

The man cast looked at the strangers before him and their anchored ship in the distance. "Men will be on watch until you leave this place."

Sieghild nodded. "We understand."

"Go in peace."

"We shall."

The villagers departed, those at the rear remaining unsure of the foreign warriors standing fast on the jetty. They did not believe him, Sieghild knew that. For now, though, he felt confident these people would keep their distance and cause no trouble. Sieghild waved his soldiers back to the *Hildwaeg*, and they fell in behind him and Leofgist.

"Did it go well?" Leofgist asked.

For a moment Sieghild frowned, then laughed. "Forgive me, Leofgist. I forgot which tongue I was using."

"You appeared to speak it well."

"Yes. I think I did." He patted the back of his hand on Leofgist's chest. "All is well, my friend."

"Thank the gods."

Sieghild smiled and thought, Yes, that would be wise. It would do no harm to have someone watching over them. It was likely Eadmaer was sailing north into the territory of the Pictii. It was what Maerard had wanted to do, twenty years ago: to ally with the blue painted men and ravage the lands south of the Humbre. However, nothing appeared certain now. After a betrayal by brethren, negating a sworn oath between two tribes, he could not say what awaited them.

Further up the beach, out of the marshes, the Wulfsuna gathered their dead and made a funeral pyre for a mass cremation. The fire brought curiosity seekers from the local village, eager to glimpse the foreigners who had overtaken their shoreline. In reverence, some sat at a distance atop the hill with small torches, which they staked into the sand and left to burn into the night. Rows of blazing light threw dancing shadows on the beach below, sinewy plumes of blue smoke filling the sky. Earlier, Lord Wulfric had been buried in all his noble regalia on the headland facing Germania. His son was not among the men that bid farewell over the grave, leaving Heahstan and Ianbert to quell ripples of discontent among the thegns and their men. What ale had not been stolen was opened to toast the warriors' passage, and enemy weapons were claimed as added wealth for the new headman. After a modest feast of dead fowl, fresh fish and cockles, the Wulfsuna retired to the *Hildwaeg* to wait for high tide.

Sieghild sat on the most inland section of the jetty, watching Wulfgar drink. His friend, slouched opposite him, seemed eager to avoid for as long as possible not only the long ship, but also the rest of the tribe. Wulfgar downed a cup of ale in one swig and picked up his father's helmet, examining it thoughtfully. Light from the burning torches winked off a small silver wolf's head protruding from the crown. He spoke quietly.

"I loved my father, but I did not understand him."

"That is the curse of each new generation, my friend," Sieghild replied, wondering if he had known his own father that well.

He certainly knew very little of his mother, except her foreign words and odd images that clouded the back of his mind; fleeting shadows that were hard to hold on to. She had died young, although she lived long enough to teach her son the language of her native people. To Sieghild it was strange and beautiful, and he had embraced it with fervour, using it to create a striking family emblem. As a man of two tongues, like the serpent, his war gear bore two entwined snakes. He ran fingers over his belt buckle, lingering on the garnet eyes of the snakes which were in relief of the gold knot work serpents.

"I was fighting Boars while he was being dressed like a fowl for banquet." Wulfgar let the helmet tumble from his lap onto the jetty.

"He is, was, a warrior of the old times of honour and discipline," said Sieghild

"You understand him more than I, then." Wulfgar turned to face his father's burial site that lay behind the uneven row of torches on the headland. "I would run at the enemy with only my anger, if that was how a fight found me."

"That seems a foolish sentiment to have," Sieghild told him with a smile.

"Hah. Sieghild: the wise."

Sieghild tilted his head to one side. "The wise outlive the foolish."

Wulfgar rounded with an angry glare, refilling his cup with ale and setting the jug aside, out of Sieghild's reach. He returned to his copious drinking, which Sieghild knew to be out of character. Wulfgar enjoyed his ale, but he never attempted to drown in it. Sieghild leaned forward.

"You are the headman of the Wulfsuna now. You have no freedom to be a fool. You are bound by the bonds of your ancestry. You must be the wise leader."

Wulfgar stood and tossed away his half-full cup. "I am not Wulfric."

Sieghild gave his friend time to come down from his outburst before continuing. "No. That man is dead, but must his vision for this tribe die also?"

Wulfgar looked at the floor, idly kicking the ale cup with the toe of his boot. Behind him on the sand, warriors collected byrnies they had left to dry in the sun and knelt to run the mail tunics through the dry sand to remove rust and grime. Later they would grease them in preparation for the next battle, if and when that came. Sieghild inhaled, filling his lungs with courage before he spoke.

"Consider it," he said to Wulfgar's back.

Wulfgar emitted a growl, and barely turned as he replied, "Consider becoming my father?"

Sieghild held a hand out to his friend. "You know what you must do."

Wulfgar turned, stabbing his chest with a finger. "I do not want it, but I am warrior enough to know it."

"To be it?" asked Sieghild, raising eyebrows.

A wry laugh escaped Wulfgar as he looked away. "It disturbs me that you know the truth in such matters."

Sieghild smiled. "I shall accept that as a compliment."

"It pleases you that you are always right."

"Not so." Sieghild shook his head. "I should like someone else to be right occasionally."

"As long as it is not I?" Wulfgar asked.

"I am your friend. Why would I think that?"

Wulfgar stared from beneath a furrowed brow. "I see it in your eyes, Sieg." He retrieved his cup from the deck and tossed a second at Sieghild.

Sieghild caught it before it hit him in the face. "You want me to drink with you now?"

"Would you rather a fist in your gut?" Wulfgar waved the aforementioned fist, frowning when his friend laughed.

"Wulfgar, always the bruised man."

Sieghild silenced as gestured by Wulfgar's raised finger, and did not refuse the generous drink he was poured. His cup brimming with amber liquid, he watched Wulfgar settle himself opposite, his expression contemplative. Calm once more, the young lord's gaze never left his ale while he spoke.

"How long have we known each other, Sieg?"

Sieghild tasted his ale, smacking lips in satisfaction. "Since birth."

"You know me. You know who I am," Wulfgar replied, placing a palm on his chest.

Sieghild licked ale from his lips, replying, "Better than anyone."

Wulfgar's grey stare pierced the space between them. "Then tell me. For I have lost who I am. It was all so clear in Sachsen, even as I stood on the shore and watched the *Hildwaeg* riding the tide. We were meant to bring the Wulfsuna here and find new land. We were to plant crops, build homes and find ourselves good women to wed."

Sieghild settled his back onto a vertical post supporting the jetty. "That is still possible."

"Is it?" Wulfgar's searching eyes seemed desperate to find an answer. "I do not see it so. Not with Eadmaer lurking at our every turn, following our every footstep with his Angle dogs intent on killing me."

Refusing to allow his best friend to retreat from his new responsibilities, Sieghild gave what encouragement he could. "You will find a way."

Wulfgar gritted his teeth and waved his cup threateningly, the contents leaping out and soaking his trousers. "I will find Eadmaer. I will kill him as he has killed Wulfric."

"Your father would not have wanted revenge," said Sieghild, leaning forward as he sensed the mood alter between them.

"I am not my father." Wulfgar hurled the cup and it bounced on the water, tumbling over once before landing and being taken under the foam of the incoming tide. He stood again. Sieghild sensed the furnace inside Wulfgar would continue to erupt wildly for a long time yet. It would take more than a few exchanged words to quell the burning within his lord's heart. He spoke quietly.

"We all thought a sworn oath would keep Eadmaer from killing your father, but Wulfric killed Maerard. As you know now, it is not easy for a son to forget."

Wulfgar's spit flew like sparks from a fire. "That lying whore's son broke his word. He betrayed my father and his fellow men."

Sieghild set his drink down and rose to his feet to face Wulfgar. "Rome left our fathers to defend a land they had not been born into. The Angles could see the isle breaking apart and seized on an opportunity to raid for wealth."

Lips revealing his teeth, Wulfgar shook his head in denial. "My father never wanted to fight kin. It was Maerard who wanted blood spilt."

"Maerard lost his life for his betrayal. Wulfric lost his life for Maerard's murder. Should it not end there?" Sieghild asked.

"No."

Sieghild ignored his friend's emphatic response. "If you continue the revenge, if you kill Eadmaer, you bring it down through further generations. It will never end, Wulfgar."

"No," Wulfgar said again, waving a dismissive hand at Sieghild. "Eadmaer has no heir, no kin. There is no one to continue the bloodshed on his side. I shall finish it."

It was disheartening to Sieghild that Wulfgar was so sure; that he was adamant revenge would cure the burning ache. He voiced his concerns.

"I hope so. I do not wish to witness it should the outcome be otherwise."

Wulfgar walked away, the ale-fuelled stupor undoubtedly clouding his rational thoughts and increasing the pain in his heart. Sieghild prayed to Woden for guidance.

Wulfgar woke, sweat-soaked and breathless. The roll and ebb of the ocean drew him gradually back to consciousness. The wild land was sleeping, as were the Wulfsuna. He licked dry lips, tasting the salty evening air, closing his eyes. He could still feel the naked wench draped between his thighs, could still see her pale body writhing against him. He groaned, pressing the heels of his palms into sore eye sockets, pushing the dream into a darker place where it would not reach him. It was the third time the nightmare had come for him since leaving Sachsen. He needed a drink. Opening his eyes he stood, inadvertently sending a hand to settle the erection in his trousers. Treading carefully over sleeping men, their snores and farts puncturing the silence, Wulfgar found Chapper. He was hugging a small barrel of ale, a smile branded across his face. Wulfgar prised the barrel from Chapper's arms then made his way down the jetty, halting after a few strides. He stared out over the low-breaking waves. At the edge of the earth, sea lapped a sunset of red, orange and gold hues sparkling like gemstones on the undulating surface. He drank the ale and thought of home. If it were not for his father's foolish dream, one day he would have been a lord in Sachsen; a lord over a land he knew and people he trusted. Now he was a lord over a divided tribe in a strange land. He prayed his mother would die peacefully, never knowing the heartbreak of Wulfric's murder. The news would kill her. It was better the sickness folded her into its deadly embrace and she fell asleep one last time, although he would not be there to kiss her forehead and sing her a song.

His eyelids dropped and once more his body felt the demon wench from his dreams, clawing at his body like a rabid vixen. He wanted her, all of her, but the nightmare was a frustration; an evil temptation never fulfilled. He could almost taste her. He threw ale in his mouth, letting it spill down his face. Her sweetness would not leave him. He could not rinse it away. As deep as the Angle blood that had stained his hands, so this hellish creature from his dreams was buried as densely into the cracks and fissures of his torn mind. He despised her as he despised the torment now engulfing him; his inherited responsibility a burden he had not expected to encounter for several years. He had envisaged many more adventures, women and battles before the yoke of leadership chained him to his father's people. Wulfgar hurled the empty ale barrel into the sea and strode briskly inland.

"Not so fast." Sieghild's voice was tinged with humour. "Do not leave me alone to face Heahstan."

Wulfgar barked over his shoulder. "Lie."

"You know I cannot" came the reply.

Wulfgar threw his words into the night air, his voice reaching out to the gods as well as Sieghild. "I will not be missed."

"Do you forget me, friend?"

The gently spoken words made Wulfgar turn, though his stance remained weighted by his burdened thoughts. "I am your headman now. How can we be friends?"

Sieghild spread out his palms. "You are both to me."

The ease with which Sieghild adapted unsettled Wulfgar, for he found their new relationship daunting: a path not yet trodden and fraught with obstacles. "I do not know if I can be both to you and be true."

Sieghild smiled warmly. "You are always true, Wulfgar. You can never be untrue. Your pride does not permit it."

With a tilt of his head Wulfgar gestured inland. "I was running away."

"I know."

He gazed at the waves, pouring his gratitude out to sea for he found it hard to tell his friend to his face. "I can see again, now you are here, Sieg."

"It fills my heart to know I am your eyes as well as your second sword. I shall try to do both, honourably."

Wulfgar held out his right arm, and smiled as Sieghild strode forward and clasped it strongly. "Your leader, your friend."

"My leader, my friend." Sieghild smiled.

Heahstan's gruff voice bellowed across the water. "Come on, you lovers. We have a ship to sail."

Raucous laughter from the men aboard the vessel momentarily dragged Wulfgar from his misery, a smile breaking his lips into a curl. Sieghild tossed an arm over Wulfgar's shoulders as they walked back to the *Hildwaeg*, a contented smile finding him as his friend's humour returned.

"Come on," Wulfgar said, "before I kiss you and tell you I love you."

Sieghild feigned disappointment. "You do not love me?"

Wulfgar took Sieghild's hand and removed his arm from about his shoulders, discarding it as though it was part of a rotting corpse. "I'm still not kissing you," he grinned.

Heahstan bellowed, "To oars."

Sailing through the night and into the next day, north then west through the marshes and wider aspect of the river Wimme, the Wulfsuna found the waterway diminished to fleets. They stopped near Lindum, once a Roman fort. Heahstan informed them it had been home to retired legionaries the last time he had seen it; a bustling inland port with a forum, basilica and public baths. It now appeared to be home to a mere handful of people, who were neither intrigued nor afraid of the Seaxan arrivals, appearing more interested in their daily work than visitors passing through. On a slope graced with lime trees a small hamlet of roundhouses led up to the east gate of the fort. On the riverbank several small jetties led into the water and, set back from the water's edge, there were working huts of various trades: pottery, metalworking and a livery business. Sieghild considered the inside stone wall of the town, higher up the slope, and thought he should perhaps send some men in to scout for possible trade. There could be a market in the forum, if they had happened upon the right day.

Chapper rose from his rowing chest and approached Thegn Tortsig, who leaned on the side with Sieghild. "I'll be glad to be off this ship, whenever that will be."

Tortsig rubbed a hand across the back of his neck. "I shall feel better when we have these on land and are on our way at last." He gestured to the stack of axles and wheels tethered to the central mast.

Chapper looked at Sieghild. "Do we have a long journey ahead of us?"

"I do not know." Sieghild shook his head. "Like you, I have never been here before."

Chapper screwed up his rugged face. "Heahstan says the wolds of the middle lands are a maze of winding ways and farmsteads."

Sieghild shrugged. "The only man left who knows this land as well as Wulfric did is Heahstan."

Tortsig nodded to the shore with his long nose. "I wonder if the beorgh at Gloui remains occupied?"

"Why did we not sail up the Saefern?" Chapper asked. "There's always been good trade there, and the estuary is a breeze to sail, we know it so well."

Tortsig, seeming wary of others listening in, leaned in towards the other two men and lowered his voice. "It had something to do with Wulfric's arrangement with Eadmaer."

Sieghild agreed, "Eadmaer obviously had his own reasons for using the Metaris."

"Huh, we found that out," said Chapper, screwing up his face as though a foul smell had met his nostrils.

Tortsig nodded. "If we had sailed up the Saefern, we could have docked at the harbour market in Caernwealas and then made Gloui."

Sieghild saw Heahstan approaching and fell silent. He knew the older thegn would not take kindly to the conversation they were having.

Unfortunately, it swiftly became apparent he had overheard. Heahstan barged in past Sieghild, shaking a finger at Tortsig.

"Eadmaer forced Wulfric's hand in his choice of estuary. We would not be here if it were not for that Angle pig."

Only Chapper was brave enough to reply to the old warrior. "This is where we hope the messenger reached the Wulfsuna of Bryton."

Heahstan stiffened, appearing to grow even taller. "We agreed it would be seven days before Weod-Monath. They will be here."

It had been arranged for a young thegn named Trunhild to bring what remained of the Brytonic Wulfsuna to Lindum. Likely to be farmers of animals and crops, mostly young or old civilians, they were Wulfric's heart of his vision for a unified Wulfsuna settlement on the island. Sieghild watched the reaction of the other men as Thegn Heahstan walked away. Chapper spat phlegm over the side and raised a pair of eyebrows at a frowning Tortsig before wandering off. Tortsig faced Sieghild and shook his head. He was not convinced either, it seemed. No one believed these Brytonic Wolf Sons would appear after the betrayal in the Metaris by their Angle cousins. Who could blame them? However, Sieghild knew it would fall to him alone to convince Lord Wulfgar this help would arrive.

Shortly after docking, Sieghild stood on the river bank south of the town, idly watching a few farmers mingling near the outside fortifications. Their voyage by water ended here, and the *Hildwaeg*, now obsolete, would have her clinkered remains used to assemble wagons, the wheels for which they had brought from Germania. Once reunited with the Wulfsuna of Bryton, they would begin their journey by road. Where the middle lands rose into duns and clops of which Wulfric had spoken, the Wulfsuna would join the Fosse Way and make for the harbour market in Caernwealas, before searching for land. Sieghild as yet was unsure whether their new headman would honour his father's dream. If the Brytonic Wolf Sons did not appear, he reckoned Lord Wulfgar might divert from the plan and head after Eadmaer. He inhaled deeply, a discomfort in his abdomen creasing his brow.

Leofgist poked his head under Sieghild's nose, narrow eyes darting, never still. "How long do you think it will take us to build these wagons?" he said, scratching his head.

Sieghild scanned the vicinity, looking for Wulfgar whose absence became increasingly noticeable among the tribe. "I do not know."

"It makes me nervous, lingering here," mumbled Leofgist.

Sieghild looked around them. "Because Eadmaer could find us?"

Shuffling his feet uneasily, Leofgist said, "No. Because I do not trust these Brytonic Wulfsuna."

Sieghild smiled and placed a hand on his companion's shoulder. "In time, you will see they share our path."

Leofgist emitted a false shiver. "I wish I could be that sure."

Sieghild felt the familiar heavy hand of Heahstan slap his back.

"What worries you ladies?" Heahstan asked, a rare grin breaking through his beard.

Leofgist jerked his head towards the Fosse Way in the distance. "New arrivals."

Heahstan looked at Sieghild, patting his shoulder. "We need to build these wagons, or it will soon be night. Where is our headman, Sieghild?"

The morning had barely begun, but daylight was precious and Sieghild was forced to agree, nodding and again searching their surroundings with a furrowed brow. "I have been wondering the same, Heahstan."

Heahstan's laugh was like a rumble of thunder. "He will not come on his own. You will have to drag him from his bed."

"Why me?" said Sieghild, pointing to himself.

"You are his trusted friend. He listens to you," said Heahstan.

Sieghild frowned and gestured to Heahstan. "He listens to you also."

Again, Heahstan's thunder roll echoed over them. "He does what I say, but he does not listen to me."

Sieghild sighed and nodded, acknowledging that it was he alone who could rouse his lord.

chapter three

Lindum,
River Wimme, Near the Fosse Way

Wulfgar was aft, hoping he would be left alone. Sitting in his trousers and boots, using the remainder of his clothes as a bed, he had not moved all night. Everyone believed his mind was clouded by grief. It was not. It was consumed by treachery. *How had his father not seen through the lies of that Angle Boar Eadmaer? How had the rest of them missed that?* For years now, Eadmaer had been courting the Wulfsuna, cradling their trust in a cloak of falseness. He was no better a man than his father, Maerard. Many times had Lord Wulfric told the story of his best friend's betrayal; how Maerard had believed an alliance with the Pictii to be opportune after Rome's withdrawal. His father had not wanted to discard a decade of loyalty to the emperor simply because their services were no longer needed. Neither had he wished to fight kin who had chosen to invade. The Pictii had indeed become a strong force, evident by several attempted invasions south, but they were simply that: attempts. Lord Wulfric had stood by the claim that he had never wanted to kill his friend. However, loyalty meant more to him than the blood of his kin. He had made it clear on his return to Sachsen that it should be his duty to inform Maerard's widow and young son. He did not want a war with the Angles. And there had never been a war, until now.

Unable to function with his emotions swilling round his heart like wine turned to vinegar, Wulfgar pushed them down into his gut where they could do him no harm. He stood, pulling his padded leather tunic from the crumpled pile of clothes and tugging it over his head. He would not be his father and spend half the day dressing. If only they had sailed up the Saefern. He wanted to be at the harbour market on the south-west peninsula, where there were fine wines and women, and daggers of gold. He had spoken out against Eadmaer's insistence that they could sell wares and buy essentials at Gloui. Many other travelling warriors had told of how trade at the beorgh had been declining since Rome's departure. Wulfric would only listen to Eadmaer, perhaps out of fear that the younger man would suddenly accuse

Wulfric of his father's murder and turn his Angle tribe on the Wulfsuna. Still, here they were. There was no going back. He threw on a new face, one he had become adept at hiding behind, and went to join Sieghild.

"Here he comes," Leofgist shouted with a smile.

"Ah, the weaner is up." Heahstan raised his loud voice even more, calling over sarcastically, "Good afternoon, My Lord."

Wulfgar trudged slowly towards them with his head down, yanking on leather ties to tighten the vambraces on his wrists. As he reached the three attentive men, he raised his head, running a hand through unkempt hair. Sieghild smiled at him, though Wulfgar refused to be convinced. He knew well his friend's methods in attempting to break a sombre mood between them.

"I thought you entered battle equipped merely with anger, My Lord?" said Sieghild.

Wulfgar flashed narrow eyes at his friend, unwilling to be swayed by his humorous comment. He would drag himself out of the darkness for no one.

"Didn't you know?" Heahstan slapped one of Wulfgar's wrists. "He sleeps in these."

Ignoring the folly being played against him, Wulfgar stared at them each in turn. "I do."

Heahstan shook his head, laughing, his long beard waving from side to side. "Sieghild, for the sake of all women, talk to your lord."

Leofgist stared at the splinted metal wrist guards. "You sleep in those?"

With the same disdain as he would observe horse manure on his best boots, Wulfgar sent Leofgist running with a single look, the thegn murmuring something inaudible as he cantered off after Heahstan.

Wulfgar faced Sieghild. "Where is Trunhild with the horses and oxen?"

"Patience." Sieghild smiled. "They will be here."

Wulfgar dismissed his friend's confidence with the toss of a hand, snorting through his nostrils. "They should have been here waiting for us. They knew when we were coming."

Sieghild spread his hands. "Who can say what trouble they may have come across?"

Sieghild whistled to Leofgist with a wave, beckoning him to assist in organising the men as they disembarked from the *Hildwaeg* for the last time. Wulfgar felt jealousy twisting his stomach, observing Sieghild taking command so readily. It came so easily to him. He was brave enough to have men heed his words. Wulfgar did not feel so brave. The power of having all men heed him, the immensity and weight it posed, seemed to him an unbearable burden. Eyes wandering to the outskirts of Lindum, Wulfgar's concern grew. When his father had left these mercenaries to forge lives and families on the island, had they remained true to the Wulfsuna or had they chosen Maerard's way? He doubted the Wolf Sons of Bryton would ever arrive. He felt his anger rise like bile in his throat. When Sieghild returned he did not hide his frustrations.

"We should never have trusted them, Sieg." Wulfgar stepped agitatedly from side to side, fiddling once more with his vambraces. "That little wealas runt, Trunhild, has no right to call himself Wulfsuna."

Sieghild seemed to bristle. "He has every right. Heahstan fought alongside his father. That 'runt' was sired by a Wolf Son."

"His father did not return home. Trunhild, Wulfsuna by blood or not, has never set his feet in Sachsen." Wulfgar waved an arm eastwards in the direction of Germania.

Sieghild shook his head. "That is not reason enough to doubt his loyalty. They will be here."

Wulfgar wandered off, pacing in a circle before coming back to stab a finger near Sieghild's chest. "If you are so confident they will arrive, why are we not building these wagons? We need to move on from here as fast as we can, otherwise Eadmaer or the locals are sure to force us to. I thought you would have begun by now."

Sieghild turned away briefly, his back tensing like a board as he muttered, "We were awaiting your orders, My Lord."

Wulfgar stared at Sieghild, unwilling to admit he had been too immersed in his own thoughts to give an order. His previous frustrations spewed forth, bringing a bitter taste to his mouth and a clench to his jaw. He looked down finally, trying to secure his belt more firmly although it was already well fastened. He mumbled a reply.

"Build the wagons." Looking up, "Those are my orders, Ealdorman Sieghild."

Wulfgar strode off, catching Sieghild's shoulder as he passed, knocking his friend roughly aside. He marched off towards the fray of disorganised warriors, scattered between wheels, axles, rowing chests and weapons. Attracted by the chaos, which seemed to fit his mood, he went to lose himself once more.

The middle of the day passed by and nourished men returned to work. Sieghild stood watching them as they broke up the *Hildwaeg* and built wagons with her wood. It seemed strange to imagine the long ship riding over land instead of sea, segmented and fractured, fulfilling a new purpose for the tribe. She had been a proud vessel. Pride: Sieghild wished he could feel that about his new appointment as ealdorman of the Wulfsuna. Instead, he felt only humiliation. The gift had been given, however, and it was considered dishonourable to refuse one's lord. Wulfgar's demeanour since the Battle of the Fens troubled him. Their headman obviously did not wish to take his father's place at the head of the tribe. Sieghild understood loss; he had buried both his parents and an infant sister. He could not understand his friend's disregard for his new responsibilities, and could not forget their last conversation. They had argued before, though not like this. There had never been such acridness between them.

Wulfgar caught his eye, lugging a wagon wheel onto its edge so he could roll it towards a wheel-less wagon supported by two soldiers. Mud and grass marks scored his bare arms, his hair slick to his head with sweat. He shouted instructions at another group tackling a second wagon, thereby delaying his own progress. The two soldiers lowered their side of the wagon onto a boulder, having tired of waiting for him to secure the wheel in place. Wulfgar finally turned his attention to his own wagon and noticed the men at rest. He stopped, features scrunched by anger, and yelled at them.

"Lift it up, you lazy hogs."

The soldiers looked at one another with raised eyebrows. They paused briefly to attain a better grip, before taking hold of the wagon again. Sieghild turned to a tap on his shoulder. It was Heahstan.

"He should hold council," the thegn said.

Sieghild shrugged. "I have tried, Heahstan. He will not heed me."

"Make him."

Heahstan departed as swiftly as he had arrived. Sieghild hung his head, feeling the intensity of all that was happening pushing down onto his skull. Ten times heavier than his helmet or his byrnie, it tugged like a relentless burden at his shoulders. He lifted his chin and walked over towards the half-assembled wagons. As Sieghild drew near, Wulfgar's shouting continued.

"Lift it up."

"Lord Wulfgar." Sieghild's call distracted his headman.

Wulfgar halted and looked over as his ealdorman approached. "Sieg, give me a hand."

Sieghild reached his friend and took a few moments to survey the situation. He gestured to the two soldiers buckling under the weight of the wagon.

"Take this wheel from Lord Wulfgar. Find Thegn Tortsig and gather more soldiers to have these wagons built. I will return to check your progress." He turned to Wulfgar. "We are going for a walk."

Sieghild did not wait for him. He wandered over to the river's side and waited on the bank. Wulfgar's heavy footsteps arrived behind him soon afterwards. A heavy sigh and agitated feet preceded his lord's words.

"Why did you take me away from my work?"

Sieghild watched as a moorhen guided her chicks to the water, three little black blobs plopping onto the rippled surface of the river. "Heahstan says you should call council."

Wulfgar threw his arms up. "Is that all you can think of? We will never be on the road unless we build these wagons. The Wulfsuna need to be moving before the Angles return for more blood."

Sieghild faced him. "Your work is to lead the Wulfsuna."

Wulfgar exhaled loudly and walked further up the bank. "You sound like Heahstan."

"He is right," Sieghild replied, "We need a new headman, which you cannot be by doing everything yourself. What are you trying to prove? The men can do this work. It is your duty to hold a council. Your thegns will want to know where they stand under your leadership."

Wulfgar swivelled round, a thick finger stabbing his chest. "My thegns will do what I demand of them because I am their leader. They know it will be a dishonour to refuse me. When we take revenge against Eadmaer..."

Sieghild shook his head gently. "That is not what your father would have wanted."

Wulfgar straightened. "My father is dead. I am Lord of the Wulfsuna. It is my decision to make."

Sieghild held a palm out towards camp. "It is the decision of council to go to war, not yours alone. You must not dishonour your thegns by not seeking their support."

"I shall not hold council when our Brytonic brothers have not yet shown their faces."

Sieghild nodded, knowing Wulfgar would not fold, regretful that it had not gone well. "As you will, My Lord."

Walking off to find Heahstan, Sieghild looked back at Wulfgar who remained by the river, pacing, tethering his wild wolf nature. It would not last long. At least his headman would not return to wagon building. If he did so, it would appear he had taken orders from his ealdorman, and Sieghild knew that was the last thing Wulfgar would want.

He found Heahstan breaking up wood with a group of other men, venting their obvious frustrations on the salt-worn keel of what remained of the *Hildwaeg*. The scent of cut wood mingled with the smells of the river: leather-working and smoked fish from small businesses along the bank. Horses from a livery neighed intermittently, unsettled by the unfamiliar and continual loud noises of the Wulfsuna's efforts. The thegn's face was expectant when he saw Sieghild, who shook his head in disappointment. Heahstan smiled and threw his axe into a plank, leaving his work momentarily.

"He would not?" Heahstan asked, flexing aching hands.

"No. He will not. Not without our Brytonic Wulfsuna."

Heahstan's eyebrows lifted. "Hah. The weaner is learning."

Sieghild frowned. "It was a test?"

"Ealdorman Sieghild, I fought alongside Lord Wulfric and your father. I was witness to a bond that went deeper than brothers, more kin than blood alone. Worry not. He is learning."

Sieghild removed his helmet to rub sweat from the back of his neck and nodded thoughtfully. "Progress will not be swift. He is not the headman I thought he would become."

With a shrug, Heahstan said, "The poor cannot choose their meals. Give him time, your time, and your shoulder to lean on."

Heahstan returned to his axe and the crowd of men, ferociously hacking at the blessed vessel that had brought them here, which would never sail again. Shards of wood lay scattered over the ground like bodies in battle, criss-crossed and tumbled. Gazing at the patterns, Sieghild felt a rush of blood to his head; a dizzying, stifling experience. He felt taken by the gods, Tiw's hands firmly grasping the sides of his head. He was shown a vision, brief and bloody: horses whinnying frantically and men dead on a battlefield. It ended as quickly as it had arrived. Sieghild did not know what he had seen, or how he had been able to see it, but as he blinked, his eyes returned to the real world around him. Moving away, Sieghild paused by Heahstan.

"How did you know he had made me ealdorman?"

Grinning, Heahstan said, "I did not, though if he is a true leader you were his best choice."

The afternoon began falling into dusk. Soon the men would be hungry again. Wulfgar had been scanning the western view all day, eyeballs twitching with every glimpse of wild rabbit or farmer on his way to market at the fort. More than once he had contemplated marching to the Fosse Way in search of the elusive Brytonic Wulfsuna to drag their lazy bones across the broken earth. He began to doubt they existed. A gang of men had hauled the main sail onto the bank, unfurling it and holding it taught, while others took their daggers to it. Wulfgar winced as he saw blades cutting through the three wolves' heads that formed the circular design in red ochre. It was as though they were taking their blades to his heart. He looked away, glimpsing Sieghild in casual conversation with Thegn Leofgist. Tired of waiting, Wulfgar strode over, speaking in ignorance of them and their current discussion.

"Where are half my men? They should be building wagons."

Sieghild's shoulders rose and fell, his chin dropping into his chest, before raising scornful eyes. "Chapper and a few others are at the market in Lindum, trading for some supplies."

Wulfgar huffed air through his nose. "I was right about one thing. There was no emperor with gold and maidens."

Sieghild remained quiet, shifting gaze to Leofgist who nodded knowingly and parted company. Wulfgar went back to scanning the Fosse Way and finally his eyes were rewarded. Small silhouettes appeared, breaking the line where land met sky.

Wulfgar turned and shouted to anyone who would hear him. "They are here." He pointed a long arm towards Lindum. "Fetch the men from market."

Leofgist ran past, confirming he would carry out the order. "My Lord."

Sieghild shook his head at Wulfgar. "How do you know it is them?"

"If it is not, it is time to move on."

"You will not wait for them?" Sieghild asked.

Wulfgar faced his friend, a palm outstretched, enunciating, "I have no mind to waste another day."

"Yes, My Lord."

Wulfgar frowned, a grin playing with the side of his mouth. "You do not challenge me?"

Sieghild smiled, eyes darting to the floor. "You are my lord and headman. I give heed to your wishes."

Wulfgar considered this briefly, not wanting to dwell on the discomfort he felt. "And what as my friend?"

"I agree. Another day here would cost us more than to move on without our brothers."

Wulfgar, satisfied with the answer, thought aloud. "We should be ready to go with what wagons we have. Remaining wood can be carried with us for more wagons, tents or kindling."

"Yes, My Lord."

Wulfgar returned his attention to the approaching figures in the distance. Two men rode in front, accompanied by a gaggle of civilians, horses and sheep. A couple of carts, drawn by oxen, followed, accompanied by one small wagon covered in tarp. Was this it? Was this the Wulfsuna of the Isle of Bryton? One of the horse riders quickened pace and began a canter aimed directly at Wulfgar. He stiffened and called for his helmet.

"Lorri, war-face."

His cnapa, for once not far from his master's bark, came running with his helmet. Wulfgar took it, holding the cheek flaps and sinking his head into the suede lining, securing the leather buckle under his chin. The simple nose plate partially disguised him, though the ornamental wolf's head on the crown identified him.

"What now?" Wulfgar asked of Sieghild, who stood abreast with him as Aelfsieg had for Wulfric.

Sieghild raised his chin to the unknown horseman and sent a hand to his sword. "They will meet their headman."

The rider eased his mount into a walk and halted within a few yards of them. He wore no helmet or byrnie. He had not come to fight, nor come from a place where fighting was needed. Eyes roaming over the young man, squat and stocky in build with shorn hair and no beard, Wulfgar realised they were of a similar age. The new arrival shuffled in his saddle, desperate to look back to his tribe, although visibly afraid to remove his gaze from the strangers standing before him. Heahstan cleared his throat, announcing his arrival. Wulfgar ignored the prompt. Sieghild looked behind them to acknowledge the thegns who had assembled with Heahstan, and nudged Wulfgar's arm. He knocked it away. He had waited years for this moment, expectation gorged by a lifetime of his father's grand tales. The auspicious moment left him wanting. These peasants could not help them fight Eadmaer. They should have remained on their simple farmsteads. They did not even know how to behave before a headman. Wulfgar felt Woden release the cork that had thus far stemmed the keg of his anger.

"Where have you been?" Wulfgar demanded, giving the stranger no time to answer. "It was agreed the seventh day before Weod-Monath. That day is almost at an end. Where were you when we needed you? Lord Wulfric is dead, and I stand here before you as headman because your band of little runts could not make good time."

The young man whimpered, "Lord Wulfric...dead?"

Wulfgar inhaled, shouting, "Do you not dismount to honour your new lord and headman? Have you Brytonic pigs forgotten all your fathers brought with them from the fatherland? What world is this, where respect and honour lie dead on these green lands?"

In his haste to dismount, the visitor caught his sword hilt in the reins. He attempted to bow, half standing, half hoisted to his horse. With clumsy hands he fumbled to untangle his war belt. Wulfgar growled and turned away, fists at the end of stiff arms feeling every word.

"It is no good. We cannot receive these useless whores' sons into our tribe. They are not real Wulfsuna. They have not been forged in our homeland, grown with swords in their hands before they could even walk. They have not seen blood and iron."

The man freed himself and stood proud. "My Lord, we share fathers who were Wulfsuna together under Rome and her great legacy. We have seen blood and iron, not through battle it is true, but through the hard work of daily life. We have carved..."

Wulfgar rounded, his lips drawn back over his teeth in a snarl. "A grave! A stinking empty hole where the gods have sworn never to tread, and if you join us you will bury us with you."

The man's half-step backwards revealed his inability to withstand the tirade that had greeted him. His mouth opened and closed without speech, confusion twisting his features. Wulfgar thrust two palms into his chest, once, twice, a taunting offence.

"Where were you? Why did you not meet us as agreed?"

"Lord Wulfgar." Heahstan's quiet warning rumbled between the men.

"No, Heahstan," Wulfgar bit back, "as lord and headman, I have a right to know why Wulfsuna failed me. I demand an answer."

The man looked at Heahstan and Sieghild in desperation. Wulfgar could not bear the apparent ignorance. Again he smacked him, pushing him off balance with a glancing hand to one shoulder.

Sieghild went to move. "My Lord..."

Wulfgar withdrew his seax. "No. This man will answer me or I will cut out his tongue from his head with my own blade."

The young man dropped on to one knee, quivering and bowing his head, voice high and broken. "My Lord. I, Thegn Trunhild, accept all responsibility. Shepherd's mother died and we had to bury her."

Wulfgar pressed the tip of his seax into Trunhild's throat, his chest expanding in satisfaction at the intense fear he had instilled. "You should still have been here. You should have left Shepherd to bury his mother and been here to meet me." Trunhild attempted to swallow without forcing his neck onto the blade that Wulfgar refused to remove. "Forget to bow before me again and I'll cut your legs off at the knees."

Wulfgar strode over to Sieghild, behind him Trunhild collapsed onto both knees, exhaling loudly. Sieghild straightened to attention, though

Wulfgar chose to ignore the scorn his friend's eyes held for his actions. Satiate with calm, his anger fading swiftly as the sun behind a cloud, Wulfgar sheathed his seax.

"Now," he said to Sieghild, "I will hold council."

Sieghild nodded curtly. "My Lord."

Wulfgar, now without a vessel in which to find solace, wandered off down river to find somewhere to breathe. These people, these events and the world around him were stifling him. He sent shaky hands to unbuckle his chin strap and hurled his helmet several yards along the bank, screaming in fury. Small birds scattered from among nearby trees, and in the distance, wood-cutting halted momentarily. He closed his eyes, inhaling deeply and calling on Frigg to temper his rage.

"Wulf?"

Sieghild's calm voice, warm as a mare's breath on a winter morning, eased his anger. He was soothed. Wulfgar kept his back to Sieghild.

"You did not address me."

"I come as your friend, not as your ealdorman," said Sieghild.

Wulfgar turned his head slightly. "I need my friend more than I need my ealdorman."

"Thegn Leofgist agreed to introduce Thegn Trunhild and his people to the rest of the Wulfsuna. Heahstan is herald for council. Your thegns will be assembled soon."

Wulfgar finally met Sieghild's drawn face. "You are doing my job."

Sieghild smiled. "I am doing my job, as ealdorman."

Wulfgar shook his head, resting his thumbs in his war belt. "I did not ask it of you. You are acting on what you believe I want."

"I know you well enough, Wulf."

"It is wrong. You share too much of a burden, which I should be carrying alone."

Sieghild waved an arm towards the camp. "You are not alone, as you will see when in council. The whole tribe will be behind you."

"Will they?" Wulfgar asked, steeped in self-doubt.

Sieghild went to answer and bent over, pushing a hand into his gut and inhaling sharply. Wulfgar approached hurriedly, a hand resting on his friend's back.

"Have you sickness, Sieg?" he asked.

Sieghild's mouth pulled wide. "No. Some strange ache I have had only since my feet landed."

"The land of your mother speaking to you," said Wulfgar, having heard the island to be drenched in magic.

"Perhaps," said Sieghild.

"Is it passing?" Wulfgar gently shook Sieghild by the shoulder.

Sieghild took in air, finally able to stand upright. "It has left me."

Wulfgar clasped Sieghild round the face with a firm hand. "You are grey as a stone. Let us sit."

Forsaking the fact Heahstan would have assembled the thegns for council by now, Wulfgar made Sieghild join him on the grass. He examined his pale ealdorman, waning from his afflictions. Having left his dying mother fading from a great sickness in Sachsen and his father buried on a hill above the fens, Wulfgar did not want to lose Sieghild. He refused to believe the gods would take his friend from him. Having no other kin, Sieg was the hammer that made his heart beat. He was Thunor's strength in his blood.

Wulfgar grinned, idly playing with grass in his hand. "You must come find me again, as my friend. It is like old times."

"Not so old," said Sieghild.

Wulfgar gazed out along the river. "Yesterday feels a lifetime behind me."

"I am behind you, Wulf, always." Sieghild clasped Wulfgar firmly by the wrist, making him look round.

Wulfgar returned the grip, each man grasping the other's forearm. "I thank you for your loyalty, though I fear I have made enemies after my attack on Thegn Trunhild."

Sieghild, noticeably refreshed, vehemently shook his head. "Do not concern yourself with things you do not know for certain. Thegn Trunhild may not have taken kindly to your words, yet your words were true."

"True?"

Sieghild gestured back to the tribe. "It is Thegn Trunhild's lack of experience that prevented him from recognising you as lord and headman. Even once he knew, he had to be reminded to pay his respects." He leaned forward. "Neither did he announce himself. He has much to learn."

"As do I," Wulfgar said.

Sieghild grinned and slapped Wulfgar on the leg, jumping up. "Come. Give council. The way to learn is to do."

ChApTER FOUR

Lindum,
River Wimme, Near the Fosse Way

Without a long hall, Wulfgar was forced to consult his thegns in a wooded copse beside the river. Heahstan had organised two groups. One side was strictly for thegns in their red Phrygian caps, coloured ribbon attached to them denoting what region each man was from. Congregated together in council, it was clear to see many wore the same ribbon. It was a close gathering of true kinsmen. The second group, all free men and some of them warriors, gathered opposite the thegns. Nervous coughs and shuffling feet punctured the serenity of leaves hissing in the breeze and wild fowl clucking on the river as night drew in.

Scanning the faces of all the men, half in shadow by the light of burning torches, Wulfgar knew instantly those who had joined them that day. The foreign stood out from the familiar, to his mind ticks in an otherwise healthy tribe. Expectantly the men looked on. Wulfgar knew what he must do. He had seen Wulfric give council since his first childhood memories could recall; men gathered with ale in a dark, smoky hall filled with laughter and song, arguments and brawls. Now, though, he could not find the words to begin. He leaned into Sieghild, their shoulders brushing, and felt Sieghild's body rise as he inhaled. His ealdorman had not forgotten, nor lost his courage.

"Be you hale," Sieghild called.

The Wulfsuna replied likewise, and the roll call filtered down the line of thegns, Heahstan, being the first and oldest member among them, commencing the count.

"Thegn Heahstan, first council."

"Ealdorman Sieghild, second council."

"Thegn Geldhere, third council."

A moment's pause was held to remember Thegns Ealdwig and Frithbert who had fallen at the Battle of the Fens. By Sieghild's nod, the calls continued.

"Thegn Ianbert, sixth council."

"Thegn Tortsig, seventh council."

"Thegn Leofgist, eighth council."

Sieghild waited for Trunhild to acknowledge him before speaking. "Those Thegns of the Brytonic Wulfsuna will give their council numbers and take their new ones behind the Sachsen Wulfsuna."

Hesitantly, Trunhild nodded. "Thegn Trunhild, first council, now ninth."

"Thegn Radliffe, second council, now tenth."

"Thegn Osmund, third council, now eleventh."

As all eyes rested upon him, Wulfgar knew support from the thegns was paramount. They had a promised proportion of any wealth the Wulfsuna received and a percentage of land when they reached a settlement. They were also capable of using an agreed number of men, should there be any battle they felt required to attend. If Wulfgar could not convince a majority of them, he would have to allow the council decision to overrule him. He inhaled deeply and used volume to hide the unease in his voice.

"Give council."

Asking those present was but a formality. It was customary for the headman to speak first, and so, in response to their lord, all men replied in unison.

"We abide."

They waited for Wulfgar. He shifted stance, resting a hand on the gold pommel of his sword. Thinking better of it he let his hand swing down to his side and straightened his back, chin raised in challenge to any who would oppose him.

"We are a day behind. We must work harder, together, to finish these wagons and be on our way."

Tortsig stepped forward, waving a casual hand towards the Brytonic thegns. "We could have used their numbers at the Battle of the Fens."

Thegn Osmund, one of the newcomers, stepped out abruptly, brow furrowed. "We were never to meet you at the coast. Lindum had always been the agreed location."

Tortsig looked Osmund up and down, the one side of his mouth curling in disdain. "What if we had walked into trouble here? How can we trust men who know not the value of a day?"

Osmund turned, hand steadying his sword and shrugging Thegn Radliffe's restraining hand off his arm. He was a short though strong man, with chin-length black hair and a sturdy jaw line. He prodded his broad chest with an extended finger.

"We had dead to bury, as did you. Is a wife and mother of the Wulfsuna counted for so little as to have no right to a proper funeral?"

Chapper broke rank as a foot soldier, and jeered across council at Osmund. "How do we know you are not allied to these Pictii, the same as Maerard?"

Heahstan barked Chapper's name, bringing his man in line, and glared at Sieghild, trying to communicate with waggling eyebrows and nods. Osmund, meanwhile, snarled like a wild dog at Tortsig, temporarily tethered by two of his companions. Sieghild nudged his headman, who had lost all thought listening to the debacle.

Wulfgar raised both arms. "Hear me."

For a brief moment, disgruntled murmurings among the tribe settled. Wind hissed through the birch trees above them. Wulfgar scanned the council, his confident scowl belying his bewilderment. Thegn Geldhere raised a hand and Wulfgar's stomach ceased rolling over. He recognised his third council.

"Thegn Geldhere."

"Lord Wulfgar."

Geldhere nodded his gratitude, the long fringe of his pale brown hair bowing over his eyes, before acknowledging Osmund.

"If I may speak for the Wulfsuna of Germania, I believe what my fellow Thegn Tortsig was implying is that we have all travelled far. We are none of us accustomed to one another, and have not yet had time to build trust between our people. Yet we are one people. We are all Wulfsuna. We have all lost kin. I lost my younger son at the Battle of the Fens. Nothing will change that."

Geldhere, noble in all but birth, pulled his russet cloak around himself and sat down on a fallen log. Osmund nodded by way of thanks, and Geldhere bowed graciously to him. Radliffe released Osmund's arm and looked round all the men of Sachsen, eyeing them closely. He raised a hand, only looking to his new headman when he had been recognised.

Wulfgar called, "Speak."

Radliffe faced him. "Lord Wulfgar." Addressing the council, Radliffe said, "We are not Angle pigs. Thegn Geldhere speaks the truth. We are all Wulfsuna. We are here, now. Our presence is our show of loyalty. We need shelter for the elderly."

Heahstan grinned. "Help us with the wagon building and your elderly will have shelter."

Sieghild intervened. "My Lord, I can organise the wagon building if I may have Leofgist and Tortsig at my disposal with their men."

Leofgist nodded eagerly. "Yes, My Lord."

"I want no part in the wagon building," Tortsig declared.

Wulfgar caught Trunhild watching him closely, eyes narrowed. It reminded him of Eadmaer's evil stare as he had threatened to slit his throat. He knew he was responsible for how Trunhild now felt towards them all. However, Tortsig's bitterness did not help matters. Wulfgar removed his eyes from the former Brytonic headman and glared at Tortsig.

"You will work with Ealdorman Sieghild, Thegn Tortsig, and surrender your men to help build the wagons." He looked at Leofgist. "Work with Thegn Trunhild and any able men he can spare."

Trunhild nodded at Wulfgar, his resentment seeming partially assuaged as he replied quietly, "Yes, My Lord."

Wulfgar turned to Heahstan. "Meet with the rest of my thegns and organise the remainder. I want the Wulfsuna out of this town at dawn and on our way. It's summer, so there'll be early light."

Heahstan bowed. "Yes, My Lord."

Men dispersed in all directions and thegns called for their men, rallying the workforce that Wulfgar hoped would deliver them inland to find their land gifts. Sixty men had left Sachsen. Thirty-eight had sailed out of the fens to Lindum. Those lost had almost been replaced in number by the Brytonic Wulfsuna, except in addition they had gained about twenty non-fighting citizens, comprising women and the infirm. Those twenty, Wulfgar knew, would slow them down and increase their journey time. Adding to that the livestock, which needed to be grazed and watered, Wulfgar was unsure they would make the harbour market on the south-west coast without falling under attack from Eadmaer.

For five days they travelled the Fosse Way, catching only glimpses of rural life clustered near to abandoned Roman forts, or ensconced behind more ancient fortifications. Natives ignored them or kept to a safe distance, herding their livestock further afield. Wulfgar could not understand those who fled. The ambling wagon train, led by a score of ragged warriors and followed by Brytonic Wulfsuna and their bedraggled animals, hardly constituted a formidable invading army. If Eadmaer did find them now, they would be easy pickings for sure.

Sieghild tapped Wulfgar's arm, pointing ahead. On the brow of the windswept hill they neared a crossroads. Wulfgar consulted Aelfsieg's faded map and put an arm up.

"Halt."

He rode ahead a few paces to examine the landscape. Aelfsieg had written of a high crossing near to a farm. The farm still existed, the tribe having passed it on their climb uphill. A stiff breeze lifted his hair from his shoulders, whistling past his ears as he gazed round. He listened to the whispering of the gods, hoping for a message, a sign. Farm and forest lay beneath them, fertile land stretching as far as one could see. Magic lingered all around them, the power of the gods seeping up from the earth and bearing down upon them from the sky. Wulfgar felt it, and did not wish to stay too long in such a place. He turned to acknowledge his friend and companions as Sieghild brought his horse up beside him with Heahstan, Osmund and Trunhild walking behind. His least favourite Brytonic thegn was swift to speak up.

"Lord Wulfgar, we should take Waeclinga Street. It will take us further west, and there is an inn at Etocetum."

Wulfgar discarded Trunhild's suggestion with a scowl, rendering it a turd tossed to the ground. "We will follow Aelfsieg's map."

"But Lord Wulfgar, I have lived here all my life. I know these trade ways. At Etocetum there is a bath house, we can rest and…"

"A lifetime to know how to lead us astray, or into a trap. We stick to the map." Wulfgar waved the piece of paper at Trunhild.

"I object, Ealdorman Sieghild," Trunhild gave Wulfgar his back, "to the way your lord disparages my tribe."

As he was filling his chest to respond, Wulfgar caught Sieghild's wary glance towards him. He paused, knowing Sieghild would fill the air between them.

"I am sure he means no ill will, Thegn Trunhild," Sieghild said.

Wulfgar's face curled in a snarl and he prodded Trunhild on the shoulder. The thegn turned slowly. "Do you forget," Wulfgar demanded, "I am your lord and it is my tribe?"

Trunhild glared back at him. "No, I do not forget, Lord Wulfgar. I regret it, but I do not forget."

Sieghild sidled his horse between them, sensing the fight that Wulfgar could smell brewing in his nostrils. He could not believe the insolent runt had voiced his thoughts. He may have been elected leader of the Brytonic Wolf Sons, however Wulfric had always been their rightful headman. Trunhild was no lord.

"Can we not send two men ahead to verify Thegn Trunhild's suggestion?" Sieghild suggested.

"Lord Wulfgar," Heahstan interjected, "Ealdorman Aelfsieg and I drew this map during our time here as young men. Much may have changed in twenty years."

Wulfgar paused and could almost hear everyone holding their breath. He sighed, hoping his frustration would leave him. Every small step had to be a council meeting. Why could he not speak and men do as he ordered? He lifted his face to the sky, adding another sigh for good measure.

"Who is the lord of this tribe?" he asked. Dropping his gaze upon his captive audience, he saw eyes shifting sideways, no one willing to respond. Eventually, Sieghild found voice to answer.

"You are, My Lord."

Wulfgar glanced at Sieghild and smiled before addressing those surrounding him. "We are here following Lord Wulfric's dream. Now he is dead, I must help the tribe to follow this dream, and all we have is Aelfsieg's map."

Sieghild released a rather false cough, darting his eyes to Thegn Trunhild. So, his ealdorman was agreeing with the Brytonic runt, as well as Heahstan. If he did not know better, he would have thought they were conspiring against him, forcing his hand. Wulfgar took another look at Aelfsieg's map.

"Very well," Wulfgar conceded, "send two men with horses ahead along Waeclinga Street and two more down the Fosse. I want them back by nightfall. We will rest here."

Watching Trunhild 'the runt' wander off with a grin of satisfaction, Wulfgar overheard Thegn Osmund talking to Sieghild. He kept his eyes fixed on Trunhild as he listened.

"We would do well to head no further west, Ealdorman Sieghild. The Pictii often invade Wealas from the north."

"Thank you, Thegn Osmund." Sieghild leaned over his horse to speak to Wulfgar. "Do with that news what you will, My Lord."

"Sieg?" Wulfgar pretended to be lost in the map.

"If you want to find Eadmaer, we might do well to continue west. If you do not want to find Eadmaer, we should follow the Fosse south."

Wulfgar was aware Sieghild would know he was lying, but he said, "Eadmaer's whereabouts will not sway me."

Sieghild smiled. "Are you certain of that, My Lord?"

Wulfgar shook his head at Sieghild, trying to hide a grin as he turned his horse away. "You know me well enough not to have asked."

By dusk, Wulfgar stood over a modest fire with Sieghild and Heahstan, mesmerised by the flame-bitten logs. He recalled the pyre burning on the beach only a week ago; the corpses of the dead rising into the sky through dust and flame. He had been unable to see his father laid to rest. Even knowing the resentment it would breed, he could not bring himself to see Wulfric in that way. Neither had he been ready to face the Wulfsuna. They wanted another Wulfric. He could never be that kind of man. They wanted a man like Sieghild: young of mind and body, though amenable to the old ways. Wulfgar wanted revenge. He could admit that to himself. He wanted to kill Eadmaer and all his stinking Angle Boars. He would admit it to no other. He had hoped Sieghild would understand, but Sieg had always been a peace-maker. As though his friend knew Wulfgar to be thinking of him, Sieghild spoke.

"Why did you not wish to listen to Trunhild, My Lord? He is a native, and if he says there is an inn why should we not believe him?"

Wulfgar rubbed a hand through his hair and checked Trunhild did not linger nearby. "You are too trusting. Perhaps it is the half-blood you have running through you."

"There is an inn. I have been to Etocetum," Heahstan mumbled into the fire.

Wulfgar frowned at the thegn, peeved he had not mentioned it earlier. "I do not dispute the existence of an inn." Wulfgar pulled at the neck of his tunic and took a step away from the fire.

Heahstan mumbled again, "Though twenty years is a long time." He looked at Sieghild. "Were you not expecting there to be more of them?"

The ealdorman shrugged. "I did not know how many there would be."

Heahstan nodded in silent acknowledgement. "I thought there would be more, remembering those we left behind."

"It is possible not all of them wanted to leave their homes and join us," Sieghild replied.

Wulfgar spread his arms between the men, seeking eye contact from them both before saying, "That is why we need to be certain the road is in use and there are no traps. What if a disloyal few remain at the Brytonic homestead and have laid a trap with Eadmaer?" He folded his arms and stared into the fire. "We will wait for the scouts."

Both pairs of men returned, thankfully without incident. So too did Trunhild, eager to have his say in the findings. It seemed the south Fosse would be more suitable for the wagons, being of a sturdier construction. Waeclinga Street, an older trade route native to the island, would pass through smaller settlements and would be less favourable to the wagons. Wulfgar felt his chest swell, feeling the gods were with him and had answered his concerns. Trunhild, however, was hungry for the kill and again harangued him.

"It seems Aelfsieg's map will add several miles to our journey, Lord Wulfgar."

"We have no need to lengthen our route," said Heahstan.

"Yes, think of the elderly," said Trunhild, nodding and making suggestive noises.

Wulfgar stared at Trunhild. "You brought them, you think of them."

"Though a short, poor road will be no quicker than a longer road in good condition," Heahstan added.

Sieghild waved an arm towards the line of vehicles and kinsmen. "We want to reach the harbour market in Caernwealas. The faster route is better when we have all these wagons and civilians."

Wulfgar exhaled loudly and paced in a circle. "Elderly, wagons, civilians: sacks of stones weighing us down."

Trunhild frowned. "We are here for Lord Wulfric. Not all are warriors, though we are all Wulfsuna."

Sieghild intervened once more. "My Lord, it would be better to head south. Do you not agree, Heahstan? Especially if Thegn Osmund is right?"

Trunhild's shoulders sank as he gazed at Sieghild. "Osmund?"

Heahstan nodded. "I'm in no hurry to march into Wealas territory. I've seen my fill of Pictii."

Trunhild's brow creased with worry as he wrung his hands. "But we have seen no Pictii for a long time."

"We have," Heahstan told him, scowling down at the young thegn and sniffing loudly, clearing phlegm from his nostrils.

For all Trunhild's apparent plotting, Wulfgar was pleased to know his own men were with him. The harbour market in Caernwealas was a large trading port with foreign produce. They would be able to fetch good prices for their own wares as well as purchase much needed commodities.

"Let us remain on the south Fosse. Mark on the map where it will take us to." He turned to Trunhild. "Assist Ealdorman Sieghild."

Trunhild grinned. "My Lord, I can draw…"

"No." Wulfgar held up a hand. "Ealdorman Sieghild will mark the map. You can point."

Wulfgar handed Aelfsieg's map to Sieghild, who took it with great care. After examining it himself, Sieghild held it out to Trunhild.

"Where will the south Fosse bring us to?"

Trunhild looked at the marks on the map, tracing his finger along an imaginary line parallel to Aelfsieg's route. "We head for the town in the marsh and over the place on open upland. After the beorgh at Corinium Dobunnium, we cross the river and there will be another beorgh, a spring and the dark wood. We join the west Fosse once more at Bathumtun, the spring of Sulis."

Wulfgar met his friend's eyes over Trunhild's shoulder, eager to learn of the consequences of altering course. Sieghild had a second glance at the map and addressed Wulfgar.

"We will not see Gloui. It takes us directly to Bathumtun." Sieghild looked at Trunhild. "You had better be right."

"I'm right," Trunhild replied, leaving them.

Heahstan elbowed Sieghild in the arm. "I wouldn't worry. Aelfsieg and I couldn't draw if our lives depended on it. We're following the place names, not the lines."

Headman and ealdorman waited for the thegn to leave them and drew closer beside the fire. Both men regarded the thick flames devouring the wood with amber tongues, each lost in their own thoughts. The night air caught the sounds of the tribe, lifting them into the dark blue sky: laughter, playful banter, bleating sheep and a lilting saga song. The never-ending landscape surrounding them became a black sea, homesteads and villages marked by flickers of golden light, like shimmering stars reflected on a great ocean. After a while, Sieghild returned his father's map to Wulfgar, who took it silently.

"Osmund says there is little trade at Gloui," Sieghild began.

Wulfgar exhaled, watching his breath swirl like a ghost from his mouth. "We will not know now, will we?" He looked at Sieghild. The ealdorman never lifted his gaze. Wulfgar rolled the map and pushed it into his leather pouch.

"Wulf?"

Wulfgar twitched at the unexpected hand on his shoulder. "Yes?"

"My father drew that map twenty years ago. The map is not my father. The map is not all you have left of your father. If we do not follow it we are not dishonouring those good men."

Wulfgar pinched the bridge of his nose between thumb and forefinger. "It feels that way, Sieg."

Sieghild gently tugged on his shoulder. "I did not believe we should have risked taking the tribe further into west Wealas. We are right to alter our journey, for the sake of the Wulfsuna."

Wulfgar inhaled deeply, his hand dropping from his face as he straightened his back. "I fear Eadmaer's treachery has poisoned my heart, that I distrust all my kinsmen."

Sieghild took him by both shoulders. "Believe me, Wulf, the south Fosse is best for our kinsmen, for all Wulfsuna."

Wulfgar clasped one of Sieghild's arms and smiled. "You have good reason to favour that route." Sieghild withdrew, frowning, and Wulfgar continued, "Did I hear Trunhild mention Corinium?" He regarded his friend who silently observed the fire.

After a long pause, Sieghild replied, "Yes. Corinium Dobunnium."

"Your mother's tribe." Wulfgar took a step closer to Sieghild.

His ealdorman turned, voice low. "I did not know we would pass that beorgh until it had been decided, Wulf."

Wulfgar grinned, grasping Sieghild by the back of his neck with one hand and patting his cheek with the other. "You have good reason to favour the route. You shall see the home of your mother."

Sieghild smiled at last, though his eyes remained thoughtful. "Do you think her land will speak to me more strongly as we near it?"

Wulfgar recalled Sieghild's sickness by the river bank in Lindum. "Who can say?" he replied, squeezing his friend's shoulder and releasing him. "Come. I do not wish to remain here. I feel the gods too closely in this place. We will travel through the night."

CHAPTER FIVE

Village of Prenhwychas,
North-West of the River Saefern and the Fort at Gloui

Taking up a small wooden pail and a stool, Morwyneth smiled as she heard her goats bleating. They knew it was almost time. She stepped outside her home, greeted by the warmth of the new morning breaking through a cloud-filled sky. It would be a good day. Smoke rose from the thatched roofs of her neighbours' properties, grey spirals reaching up like long fingers. Hens clucked nearby, searching for grit and spilt grains among the cluster of roundhouses perched on the slope. Hoisting the skirt of her sage green woollen peplos over a short willow fence, Morwyneth waved her pail at two men. They grinned broadly, waving their crooks in response. They were on their way to the croft, shepherds for Lord Huweyn's sizeable flocks of long-horn sheep. Walking briskly down the hill, two dogs chasing their heels, they shouted to one of the guards to open the perimeter gates. Rubbing sleep-heavy eyes, a guard unlatched the gates.

Dropping her skirt, Morwyneth greeted each eager goat by name and set her stool down to milk the first. She milked them in the same order every day and they knew their place. As she warmed the cold teats in her hands, extracting the milk into her pail, she looked uphill. The noble residence of Lord Huweyn sat atop Bryn Hwychas, shielded from wind by a horseshoe of birch trees. Morwyneth felt the villa looked down upon them as a wise guardian. Certainly Huweyn's successful wool trade had secured wealth and stability for Prenhwychas. Their village had been allied to Rome, and even when the Empire left it continued to trade with them. The Hwychas were proud of their fine cloth, which they made into peploses, tunics and underwear mostly for their own uses. For export they made a very fine birrus Britannicus, a hooded cloak favoured by the Romans, as well as saddle blankets. Tuckers tucked the raw wool with their feet, washing it to be later combed, spun and woven by the women.

Morwyneth patted the first goat and it wandered off, allowing its companion to move in for milking. She settled the animal with a fond caress between the ears, its body rubbing against her knees as it made itself comfortable. Again she warmed the teats and set to filling the rest of the pail. The early light caught the low honey-coloured dry stone wall that embraced the villa. Smiling contentedly, Morwyneth adjusted the cloth cap that had slipped from her head and threw her long brown hair back over her shoulders. Her pail full, she petted the goats and went inside.

A fire burned in the central hearth, bright orange flames flicking sparks onto the circle of stones around it. Hanging over the fire from an iron tripod, a cauldron warmed water. Morwyneth set the pail on the floor and reached for a clay cup from her small table. She dipped her cup into the pail and sipped the tepid milk, pondering whether Lord Huweyn had risen. She wondered, almost daily, whether the rumours of love between their lord and her mother were true. Her mother had never spoken of any love and, when answering queries about the origins of her father, Anwen had always told Morwyneth she had met a man when on pilgrimage, spirit walking in the south.

Setting down her half-empty cup, she felt the world spin violently. Morwyneth closed her eyes, disorientated. She fell onto her bunk, kicking over the pail of milk. Behind her eyelids, dark ethereal clouds rolled over themselves. She heard the screams of dying men and smelled the stench of blood mingled with moss. Iron weapons clashed in the distance. Opening her eyes, Morwyneth gasped. No longer in her home, she inhabited a dark place where she could see nothing except rolling black cloud. Screams grew louder and heavy breathing crept up on her from behind. As she turned, she only encountered the darkness, ever-folding, consuming. A face appeared in front of her. She screamed. The blue-painted face held wide black eyes, glaring wildly. Tribal drawings, burned into the skin, ran in designs down the face and neck onto a body obscured amid the gloom.

As swiftly as the vision had captured her, it released her, and Morwyneth's eyes shot open to see the roof of her home. Safe at last, she clutched her abdomen where the ache of her menstruation had intensified with the experience. Her mother, Anwen, had warned her of such visions. Prior to Anwen's death, Morwyneth had known of the possibility she would inherit the seer's way. It had been so for hundreds of years. However, the arrival of the gift varied between individuals. Her mother had 'seen' for the first time at Morwyneth's birth, and yet her grandmother had not 'seen' until the death of her husband, fifty years into her life. Reaching for some dry herbs she kept by her bunk, Morwyneth held them to her nose. She inhaled long and deep, the scent of them stemming some of her pain. It would be a day of great portent.

Acgarat stood in the main hall admiring frescoes of old and new deities. Orange beams danced over the artwork from lit braziers. She raised a delicate hand to the image of a dying Christ in the arms of his mother, inhabiting the wall beside older non-Christian imagery. Her touch lingered on his naked legs and she licked her lips, her fingers hovering over the muscular calf of the reclined martyr. Footsteps interrupted her lustful examination. As she turned swiftly, tight russet curls hanging from her forehead bounced, gold embroidery on her peplos reflecting light from the brazier. She held her breath. Hearing her name whispered from the rear salon, she knew it to be Turpilos, one of her husband's elders. She found him loitering in the back room, almost bouncing on the spot. When he saw her he strode over, grabbing her arms. He held her tight to his robes, kissing her fervently. She pushed him away, eager to speak.

"He was up all night again, buried in scrolls."

Turpilos shook his head. "He will not find it. I have hidden it well among his accounts."

"Do not be so sure. I am certain he has found something."

Moving nearer, Turpilos swept aside the stern finger pointing at him. "Did he tell you?"

"Is it not why he has called for you this morning?"

"No. It is a meeting of the elders. Gwidol will be here also."

Acgarat paced, chewing a nail on her thumb. "That does not mean he would not reveal your treachery. He mentioned a discrepancy."

"My treachery? We are both involved in this, Acgarat." He smiled at the scowl she gave him. "Your beauty fades when you frown, my sweet."

"My patience is fading...with you and that man."

"Your husband."

She waved a dismissive hand, moving to lean on an ornately carved armchair facing the internal courtyard. She smoothed dainty fingers idly over her peplos, adjusting its fall from her shoulder into neater pleats.

"You know I despise any reminder of my marriage to that old goat. He dotes on me and I loathe it." She gazed out through the courtyard to a lavish garden with tall trees beyond.

"Come now..."

"He is a tired old man. He only took me as his wife because his heart was so heavy from the death of that wretched seer. He loves me merely as a distraction."

Turpilos approached her, cautiously glancing back to the main hall to ensure they were still alone. "He will not find my calculations. I will show him today where his weary, ageing mind has made a mistake and we can persuade him he is too old for his work."

She sighed heavily. "Huweyn could be the father of Anwen's daughter."

Turpilos laughed wryly. "Why do you suspect that?"

"Something…words uttered in his sleep, I…"

He reached for her wrists, drawing her up off the side of the chair. She placed her palms on his chest, resting her forehead against him. Murmuring into the thick cloth of his blue-dyed tunic, her voice fought back emotion.

"He calls her name in his dreams. Had I not demanded separate bed chambers…" She broke off, gathering herself. "I cannot bear him calling out to that dead woman, that peasant."

Turpilos stroked her hair. "These are only suspicions. Not facts."

She withdrew, slapping his chest with both hands. "How can we persuade him to relinquish control, that he is an old man with no heirs? If the seer's child is his, he will have an heir and will not consider you as his replacement."

"If it were true," Turpilos replied, "we could use it to damage his standing within Prenhwychas."

She considered him for a moment. Returning to his embrace and caressing him, she slid her hands down to the belt at his hips. He held his breath, trying to resist her. Her hands gripped his belt tightly and she pulled him harder against her, whispering seductively up to him with heavy eyelids.

"Come to me tonight."

He cupped her buttocks firmly in his hands. "I love it when your eyes sparkle like flames in a brazier."

"Acgarat?"

Huweyn's call roused them from their passions and they immediately separated. Acgarat smoothed her hair, removing wayward tendrils from her forehead, and moistened her lips. She called out light-heartedly, "Turpilos is here."

She glanced back. Turpilos wiped the back of his hand over his mouth as though eradicating Huweyn's wife from his lips, tidying dark hair with his fingers. She smiled and walked gracefully off in the direction of the main hall, hearing him follow at a distance. At a long table, draped in white linen, Acgarat settled her slim figure elegantly into a vacant chair and waved a servant girl to fetch refreshments. She watched Turpilos enter the room and meet eyes with Huweyn.

"My apologies, Turpilos, I did not hear you enter." Huweyn took his elder's hand firmly.

Turpilos smiled. "I was out walking and saw your wife enjoying the morning sun in the rear salon."

"Come, take a seat." Huweyn gestured to the chair beside him as he sat down.

Servants arrived with trays of goblets, flasks of wine, bread rolls and goats' cheese. Huweyn leaned a weary head on one palm, slim fingers playing with the grey hair that streaked his natural brown at the temples. Turpilos leaned over.

"You seem tired, My Lord. Perhaps I should accompany you when next you trade?"

Huweyn laughed. "And in whose care should I leave my beautiful Acgarat? I am always confident of travelling knowing you are here for her."

Cutting a small piece of cheese, Acgarat smiled coyly. "I have assured you, on many occasions, I am never fretful in your absence."

Huweyn swirled his red wine round his goblet. "Because Turpilos is here to watch over Prenhwychas and all her treasures."

Sitting back in his chair, Turpilos checked Acgarat's expression before he spoke. "Your lady wife says you need my help with a problem?"

"Yes," Huweyn confirmed, "there is a discrepancy from my last trip to the fort at Gloui. I wondered if you would help me locate it. It is a small sale, but nonetheless important."

Before speaking, Turpilos again glanced at Acgarat who lowered her head, concentrating on her cheese. "I shall try, My Lord, though you should not concern yourself with such small things."

Huweyn frowned. "The Civitas has collapsed. Those, as I, who were magistrates now look inwards to their own small worlds, rather than outwards towards trade in the Empire. That is a mistake."

"We remain a municipium," Turpilos replied, leaning forward and raising his voice. "We are a self-governing community, answerable only to ourselves now. We are free of Rome and her taxes and legal constraints. Our men can carry weapons, for the first time in several generations."

"You believe that to be a force for good?" said Huweyn, spreading an open palm before the younger man. "Coin is becoming scarce and is worth so little. Our lives are changing and not at all for the better. Soon we will be forced to barter in goods. Every ounce of coin we make is precious. You will help me find that discrepancy, Turpilos."

Acgarat watched Turpilos regard the finger Huweyn pointed at him and settle his back into his chair. It was not going as well as they had planned. After a long pause, Turpilos responded meekly, "Yes, Lord Huweyn."

A knock on the door preceded Gwidol the preacher's entry in a flurry of gesticulations and breathless grunts. A heavy man of medium years, he had more fat about him than he could carry, despite having been a tucker before finding Christ. Spiritual life was more sedentary than treading wool. The preacher waddled over to join them. With a nod from Huweyn, he took a seat next to Turpilos, hungrily eyeing the bread and cheese.

"Good morning, My Lord."

"A setting for Gwidol," Huweyn ordered.

A plate was delivered and the preacher filled it eagerly. No sooner had the wine entered his goblet, he took several large mouthfuls. "Please accept my apologies for my lateness, My Lord."

"It is of no matter, Gwidol," replied Huweyn. "Turpilos and I, we were simply discussing some accounts."

"Yes. This discrepancy you speak of." Turpilos finished his wine. "If I may be permitted to say, perhaps My Lord is weary of mind as well as body. A sign that it may be time to retire from office? I am more than capable..."

"Yes," Acgarat chirped, "allow a younger man to carry the burden of your accounts, Huweyn."

Gwidol chuckled. "You need an heir, My Lord."

Turpilos glanced at Acgarat, whose hand tightly clasped a knife hovering over her plate, large round eyes glaring at Gwidol. The heavy entrance doors flew open and a small figure stumbled inside. Acgarat sprang from her chair emitting a mouse-like squeal. The fires in the braziers billowed wildly and two servants darted forward to catch the wayward doors, one of them kicking out a chicken that had inadvertently flown inside. Gwidol snatched his plate from the table as a breeze buffeted the cloth, threatening to hurl his meal on the floor. Huweyn pushed his chair away to stand. The intruder threw back long hair and straightened.

Huweyn gasped. "Morwyneth?"

"I have the sight." Her breathing was ragged from her dash up Bryn Hwychas.

Huweyn met her across the room, pulling her tightly into his arms. "Sweet wonder. After all, you are Anwen's daughter."

She writhed free of his embrace, eager to speak. "I had a vision. I saw blue painted faces. I sense evil."

Huweyn looked round sombrely. "It could mean an attack on Prenhwychas."

Turpilos laughed through his nose. "Cruithnii? They would never dare attack this far south."

Morwyneth cast worried eyes around the room, as though only now realising others were present. She smiled nervously at them. "Forgive me for having brought this upon you, Lord Huweyn."

He cupped her hands in his own. "You should be proud that the spirits of your ancestors have honoured you in this way and you can continue your mother's work. Go home and worry no more of this. I will speak with you again soon."

Morwyneth glanced round the hall a second time, eyes lingering on the statuesque guests; Acgarat and Gwidol frozen by her sudden entrance, and Turpilos idly poking at breadcrumbs on his plate. She padded quietly to the doors, looking up sharply as a servant pulled them open for her. Pausing on the threshold, she cast one last look at everyone and left. Huweyn smoothed a wrinkled brow with a thumb and forefinger. Turpilos's eyes flickered in Acgarat's direction as she hovered over her seat, her usual elegance thrown into disarray as she hesitated. She looked at Turpilos, then Huweyn, eventually sinking back into her chair, hiding shaky hands in her lap. Huweyn regarded them all.

"I must ask you all to guard this as a close secret. We must avoid panic."

Acgarat smoothed her hands over the table. "Panic?"

Huweyn nodded solemnly. "Not all are open to communion with the spirits. Her mother was forced to deny her own gift in order to remain here and care for her daughter."

Turpilos shrugged. "What bearing does this have on us?"

Huweyn approached in long strides. "The torment of that denial drove Anwen to take her own life, feeling she could better serve Morwyneth from the spirit world."

"Do you believe this?" Turpilos asked Gwidol.

"They may linger in the old ways, Turpilos, from a time before Christ illuminated our lives, yet they are people with faith." Gwidol chewed on a crust of bread. "I am more concerned with those without faith."

"That is my fear." Huweyn took his seat once more, "that there will be those among us who will not trust someone of the old ways."

Acgarat leaned forward. "How can we trust the word of a so-called wise woman, and a new one at that?"

"What if we distrust her and this vision is true?" said Huweyn, ushering a servant out of his way as they came to pour him more wine.

Acgarat shook her head. "People will fear her, mistrust her, as they did her mother. This could bring us all kinds of trouble."

Turpilos tapped Gwidol on the arm. "What do you say about this?"

The preacher scratched his stomach through brown wool. "If the villagers discover her gift it is safe to say she would be forced not to use it."

"You see, Huweyn?" Acgarat intervened. "She cannot stay."

Gwidol held up a restraining hand. "There may be a way. Let us think." He sipped more wine, sucking it over his teeth. "We could ask her to swear an oath to Christ, never to use her powers."

Acgarat smiled wryly. "She would not live her life fully. As a consequence, she could take her own life, as Anwen did."

Gwidol nodded, a single plait of long hair bobbing on his shoulder. "Yes, if faith is strong in her."

Huweyn left the table, turning his back to look quietly into the leaping flames of a nearby brazier. His gaze followed smoke plumes, rising at random, spiralling up to where borders of symmetrical patterns interlaced on the ceiling.

"Acgarat may be right, My Lord," said Turpilos. "We would not want the death of a young woman on our hands. We must think of the health of the entire village. If she will not swear an oath, it may be best to expel her, for her own sake as well as ours."

Acgarat approached her husband, reaching a tentative hand to his shoulder. "Huweyn? Send her away, before our people force her to leave. It is best for her, for everyone."

Gwidol agreed. "It could save her life."

Huweyn's head dropped. "I promised the girl's mother I would watch over her." After a moment's pause he rounded on them. "What of this Cruithnii evil that is on its way? We must prepare."

"We can, My Lord." Turpilos joined Acgarat at Huweyn's side. "That does not change our current problem. This village will not tolerate another seer."

Huweyn dismissed the suggestion with the wave of a hand. "We need to give the people a chance. Since Anwen's death, many of those against her have left or died. Now we have Gwidol. Perhaps with his guidance, she may be able to remain?"

Gwidol smiled, raising his goblet as though giving a toast. "You have hope, My Lord. That is good."

Acgarat shot a look to Turpilos, a shaky hand hovering near her heart. She could feel her composure fraying, her threadbare patience unravelling with every statement her husband made. She had to do something.

"Please excuse me," she whispered, wilting sideways as she staggered to the rear salon.

*

On her hands and knees, Morwyneth felt beneath her bunk and withdrew a cloth bag. Opening the drawstring neck, she slid a hand inside. With closed eyes she pulled out a handful of small carved objects. She tossed them over the table, oblivious to one piece that fell to the floor. Two figurines presented themselves to her: a bone carved as a cow and a wooden piece fashioned into a crow. Morwyneth picked up the totems and felt their curves and indents, listening for a spirit to inform her of its message. As she received the purpose of each piece, she acknowledged it aloud.

"Cow: nourishment...crow: magic."

Feeling warmth pervade her home, Morwyneth knew she had been joined by a comforting spirit. She turned to see her mother's face rounded in a smile. It was a mirror of her own and told much to anyone who had looked upon them together, sharing the same eyes and hair. Anwen spoke.

"I have been waiting for this time. Now you share the seer's gift. You will bear the same burden for the rest of your life as did I, and countless generations before. From the first root of our ancestors on the isle, we have guarded the wisdom and mystery of our land. So much has been forgotten, so many words lost. Words, like a hot poker, burn eternally into the flesh of the deepest part of spirit. Remember, Morwyneth: when wind spoke and horsehair told of whom to wed; when dancing cured the sick and caves were the creators of the world."

Before Morwyneth could ask any questions, her mother had gone. Angry shouts permeated the familiar noises of the village. The voices were female and recognisable. Morwyneth replaced the carved totems into the bag and hid it under her bunk. She stepped out of her home to take a look. A throng of women marched towards her. They were friends and neighbours; wives, sisters and daughters of farmers and herders. They came for her; a pack of hungry she-wolves baying for blood, faces contorted in hatred. Fear held Morwyneth captive.

"Gouge out her wicked eyes," one of them screamed, wielding a small knife.

"Yes," cried another, "they are a beacon to this evil that comes. Cut them out."

They grabbed her roughly, a mass of hands smothering her, hungry, feverish. Morwyneth shrieked as her outer garments were torn, her peplos ripped from her shoulders. They yanked her hair, bringing her head back sharply. It stung like a thousand wasps biting her scalp. They tore her cap from her head, along with some of her hair. Morwyneth winced at the pain, tears stinging her eyes. The woman waved her handful of prize in jubilation. Immediately the rest of the gang began to chant.

"Cut it off! Cut it off!"

As Morwyneth writhed and bent, trying to free herself, she pulled further against their grip. She resisted, pulling her wrists and legs from clawing hands. It was all in vain. There were too many of them. They continued to jeer and shout cruelties at her.

"Kill her, before she leads the evil here."

"She sins against all of us."

One of them hissed in her ear, "It is said you will bring us ides of rain. Fifteen days of rain. What of the crops?"

Morwyneth heard the slicing metal sound of a pair of sheep shears. Cheers erupted and the frenzy continued. They removed the last of her peplos, taking her feet from under her. She landed heavily on the cold, hard earth, the women not caring to avoid her with their feet. Heels and toes collided with her face and body. She attempted to curl in a ball, but they would not allow it. Fighting against their fierce grip, Morwyneth felt her body ache and crack.

"Pin her down."

They sat on her legs and abdomen, and forced her arms into the dirt beneath her. Like pincers, thumbs and fingers dug into her flesh: the crooks of her elbows, her thighs and stomach. Two women took fistfuls of her waist-length hair and pulled it taught. She sobbed. They responded with cackles of pleasure, and Morwyneth shook with fear. The shears began to snap around her head, tangling in her hair for they were not sharp and oiled. Little by little, the tension on her hair receded as they cut it away. Like wicked banshees, they whooped and leaped about with her shorn hair in their fists.

Huweyn's voice invaded the hellish nightmare. "How dare you treat a fellow villager this way. I am ashamed to be Hwychas."

His announcement delayed the onslaught. However, it did not entirely placate the vile intentions of the angry women. Morwyneth lay on the ground weeping from her ordeal, streaking her face with mud as she wiped away tears. A handful of villagers came forward and formed a protective circle around Morwyneth. Huweyn spoke again.

"I feel betrayed by my own kin," he added.

The woman with the shears spoke out. "She'll have to go, Huweyn. Or we'll kill her." The omission of his noble title made her lack of loyalty obvious.

Turpilos intervened. "Let her go, My Lord. You cannot secure her safety if she remains."

Morwyneth blinked dirt from her lashes, watching Huweyn approach the circle of villagers. They parted to allow him through, remaining close to one another, constantly aware of the gang of women lingering menacingly close by. He crouched down to her, lifting her gently by the arms. Her feet were not sure and she was grateful when he steadied her. He pulled her tight to him, burying his face in her hair. He was warm and smelled of wool and wine.

"You must leave. I am sorry there is no time to find you food for your journey. I always knew, one day, I would have to lose you as I did your mother. I love you...daughter."

Morwyneth released a sob, clinging to his robes with grazed hands. It was true. Despite her mother's denials, Morwyneth had felt the truth in her dreams, inside the very heart of her spirit. The elation soon dissipated, however, with the sadness that overwhelmed her. She had to leave him. She pulled back, gazing into his face.

Shaking her head, she whispered, "Father..."

"You cowards."

Morwyneth and Huweyn looked up as the woman shouted out. On hearing their lord's admission, a few of the angry protestors had retreated, bringing the scorn upon them from their ringleader. This woman advanced, accompanied by the remainder who were in agreement with her, all waving shears and knives.

She continued, "So she is his child. It does not change anything. She will still bring evil among us."

Huweyn choked on tears, setting Morwyneth away from him. "You must go."

The ringleader snarled, "Hurry up, Huweyn, or we'll carve her where she stands."

With one final look into her father's eyes, Morwyneth tore out of Huweyn's grasp. As she ran down to the village gates, chickens jumped and flapped out of the way of her bare feet. The path was cold and stony against her skin. A shrill cry ignited the savage women to action and she heard them give chase after her. Morwyneth ran as fast as she could, the incline increasing her descent so that she stumbled. Her heart leaped in her chest, fearing she would not save herself from falling. She did. Two spearmen stood aside as she passed beyond the village perimeter, running down the hill path. From the village she heard Huweyn bellowing to the guards.

"Close the gates!"

Morwyneth braved a final glance back at Prenhwychas. Men on the watch towers turned on the village with bows drawn taught. Below, the two spearmen stood firm while two more pushed the heavy gates shut. The entrance barred, Morwyneth heard the gaggle of women land against it, beating and cursing the wood. Relief became grief, Morwyneth unable to understand why friends and neighbours had turned against her. She had lived here her whole life with no enemies. No more it seemed. Pain from her abdomen caused her to clutch her stomach. Though searing, it did not suppress the even greater pain that now owned her heart. No longer needing to run, though hurrying nonetheless, Morwyneth retreated, knowing she may never return.

CHAPTER SIX

Afon Boughs,
Near the Town in the Marsh, West of the South Fosse

The summer air, thick with heat, made it hard to breathe while walking up a small knoll. In the grass ragged robin wilted in the humidity, its fragile pink petals closed tight, as those wary of the gods close their doors when a rainstorm is due. They were in Samhradh, the light half of the year. Morwyneth raised her head to the grey belly of the sky. Slow-moving formations of teal clouds revealed a storm on its way. It would be wise to leave the pasturelands and seek shelter. She made her way to a gnarled apple tree, huddling under its sacred branches. The thunder god Taranis hurled his first strike and lit up the sky. Immediately a thunder roll swooped down over the brow of the knoll, growling and punching the warm air overhead. Cradling her knees into her chest, Morwyneth watched Taranis scorch the hill above her, the bolt fizzing and crackling as he tore his bull-drawn chariot across the sky with another loud thunder roll.

Torrential rain fell, pounding the leaves and fruit on the tree. Filtered by the heavy laden branches, a lighter shower soaked Morwyneth beneath. She reached a hand up to wipe droplets from her face and push long hair back. Instead she found the ends of her short sheared hair. It felt unfamiliar, *salw*: ugly. Rain landed on her discoloured under-gown, creating moist circles on the sorry cloth. Memory of her expulsion returned. By attempting to eradicate her existence, she presumed the women had imagined they would be safe from their own possible gifts of sight. For although many would refute it, there were others in Prenhwychas with ancestors who had been healers and wise women. Her mere presence, reminding them of the possibility, must have been too much to bear. Whether it be through fear or hatred, Morwyneth prayed no others were suffering the same torment elsewhere.

Believing Taranis had appeared to express his anger at how she had been treated, she found a fallen twig and drew a cartwheel in the damp ground in his honour. Wet, though grateful to be free and alive, Morwyneth closed her eyes for a moment's sleep. She hoped the rain would soak away her sorrows and that her scarred thoughts would evaporate into the verdigris branches above.

When she awoke, the rain had ceased and the clouds had paled to lilac, casting a pink hue over the knoll. The sky had risen again allowing the lungs of the earth to breathe, leaving the air cool. Morwyneth wanted to bury her face in the meadow to inhale the tantalising aroma of sweet, sodden ground. The fleeting repose had been her first rest in a long time. She stretched aching arms and winced in pain as paralysed ankles refused to move. Although the discomfort brought tears, she stood gingerly. Looking downhill to the west, she knew there would be a water source on lower ground to bathe her ankles, and perhaps some healing foliage.

A light breeze lingered, and near the base of the knoll the air was fragrant with a myriad of wildflowers. Oak, ash and hawthorn led into a small valley where the faint trickle of water heralded a narrow brook. Its pebbled shoreline ran through the small wood. Morwyneth picked her way down to the water's edge through tree roots and rocks, looking for comfrey. On the bank she found a profusion of the creamy-white flowers and set to work, ripping two strips of cloth from her undergarment. These she wet and set on the grass while she plucked generous handfuls of comfrey. She rubbed the roots against her ankles to release the healing oils from the plant, mashing the remainder of the roots between two large pebbles. Smudging the paste onto the strips of cloth, she secured a compress around each ankle.

On the warm side of the bank, Morwyneth gathered a handful of fruits from a wild blackberry bush. The juices stained her hands and lips deep purple and she rinsed them in the brook, the cold water reviving her face. Basking in the sun on a sorrel-laden bank, Morwyneth allowed herself to daydream. Her mind wandered to better times when her life had been sweeter; sweet as the blackberries, not dark and black as their colour, as her life had become. She tried to recall the message from her mother. Disconnected remnants floated round her mind. Anwen had spoken of the burden of her gift, which she had been quick to discover at her expulsion from Prenhwychas. It seemed she had but two choices: to deny herself the seer's sight for the comfort of community, or accept her powers and spend a life in solitude. Yet her own lifetime felt a mere glint in time when compared to her many ancestors who had suffered the same through countless generations.

"*Remember,*" Anwen had said. Morwyneth remembered the dress her great-great-grandmother had made. It had been passed to each daughter on maturity. Her mother had worn the lavender-blue robe when performing rituals inside their home. The hem, cuffs and neckline were decorated with un-dyed woollen knot work, a tangled growth of embroidered foliage, acorns, oak leaves, holly and mistletoe, creeping over the shoulders and down the bodice. Each new wearer added their mark to the magical garment. A light breeze whispered the word again, "*Remember*", carrying it across the brook. Assuming the magic gown to have some importance, Morwyneth could see no safe way of retrieving it now. Trying not to be disconsolate, she stood and prepared to recommence her journey. Something drew her onwards; something she knew would be of learning, though where she was heading and why remained a mystery only Spirit knew for now.

As dusk approached with a warm golden light, Morwyneth shortened her strides and her thoughts turned to a bed for the night. She had been following the bend and twist of the brook. The land to either side was open and there were no hills with caves or sheltered indentations. Needing to rest her ankles, she reached a large rock and threw herself heavily onto it.

"Argh!" the rock yelled.

Morwyneth leaped up with a high-pitched scream as the brown mound began to roll and stand, finally towering above her some six and a half feet. A pair of grey eyes scowled at her from beneath swathes of long grey eyebrows and matted grey hair hanging in plaits and twists over wide shoulders. She noticed bird feathers and fine strands of different coloured cloth woven into the ends of the plaits like charms. A long brown cloak hung over his purplish-grey cloth tunic and trousers, with sheepskin bound by leather around his calves.

"What means you?" the human rock demanded in a low, rounded tone.

Morwyneth trembled, having seen nothing like him before. He spoke her words but rearranged them, as though his own tongue ordered them differently. She could not place him by accent.

"I thought you a rock, good sir," she stammered, taking a few steps back.

"A rock," he considered, then bent backwards and threw his head far back, letting out a huge roar of laughter.

Morwyneth stared in shock. As the laughter subsided, the human rock stepped forward with a pronounced limp in his left leg. He held out a gnarled hand.

"I be Dudley. Local scop."

She nestled her small hand in his large one. "Blessed be you, Dudley. I am Morwyneth of Prenhwychas."

He shook her arm energetically, bouncing her up and down. "Of Prenhwychas? Far have you come." Releasing her, he added, "Be well."

"I was hoping for shelter to sleep."

He gathered his belongings: a large sack cloth tied into a ball with rope that he slung over one shoulder. He used a tall branch of birch, retaining its bark and adorned with charms from nature: shells, feathers, tiny animal feet and pieces of fur, as a walking staff. He hobbled over and glanced at her bandaged ankles.

"There'll be shelter in Aberhabren." He tilted his head to one side, smiling through a grey beard. "You are travel worn, little peace maiden."

Morwyneth half smiled, tired and, of late, unused to care from another. Dudley crouched down and beckoned her to him for a piggy-back. She accepted, bemused. As he stood, Morwyneth gasped at the height she had become, but settled her arms around his neck, thankful for her saviour in sheepskins and sack. He began walking.

"You are named well, for you are a maiden who will bring peace to those who need it."

"How will I bring peace? To whom will I bring it?"

He chuckled. "You will know when the time appears."

"How do you know so much about me? Are you a seer?"

"I am a storyteller, a bard. I wend through kingdoms old and new, telling tales of heroes and gods. I speak of your gods and mine."

Morwyneth wondered whether this chance meeting had been the reason for her wanting to come this way. Perhaps this would be her learning and she would become a scop like Dudley. How he had come to be here and in this profession intrigued her.

"Where are you from?" she asked.

"I come from the meadow."

Morwyneth did not feel he had answered her, however she felt it impolite to push her enquiry any further. A vixen called out nearby, her haunting cry floating across an orange sky, and in some bushes, badgers fought.

Morwyneth woke to sounds of hilarity, unsure for how long she had been asleep on Dudley's shoulders. Jovial voices grew louder and she rubbed sleepy eyes. He strode confidently into a village enclosure she assumed to be Aberhabren. Clusters of thatched roundhouses sat about a central courtyard, in the middle of which a large fire burned. Children, chickens and dogs darted between adults busy with giant cooking pots or making unleavened bread. It reminded her fondly of Prenhwychas. Several people waved with familiarity at Dudley, one man shouting out, "Have you brought us a virgin sacrifice?" Dudley's laugh rang through his body, vibrating on Morwyneth's chest. Near one of the houses Dudley set her down, pointing for her to sit still as he wandered off to greet the tribal leader. Without request, a woman ran over and threw a blanket over Morwyneth, smiling broadly as she tucked it in around her, asking if it was an improvement. Morwyneth nodded and smiled gratefully. Somewhere, the other side of the giant fire, drums beat loudly, silencing the village.

Dudley's booming voice rang out as he shouted, "*Hwaet.*"

People sat down or leaned against the houses, attentive. After a long pause, Dudley spoke again, loud enough for all to hear plainly.

"Be well, Aberhabren, for my return is showered in warmth and well-come."

Momentarily the drumming continued as women handed out garlands of vine leaves. Morwyneth decided she would see better if she stood. Wrapping the blanket around herself like a cloak, she moved forward slightly to view the proceedings. Morwyneth recognised the festival for August Eve, marking the last day of July and the start of the vine harvest. She waited expectantly for it to begin. It had been some time since she had been privy to one. Prenhwychas had long abandoned such rituals.

Dudley announced, "*Calan awst, Lughnasadh.*"

The whole village responded likewise. The drums continued along with singing, and people danced clockwise round the huge fire, carrying bunches of grapes or sheaves of corn. Several women carried a large cauldron filled with warm wine, ladling it out to onlookers. Morwyneth sipped from the ladle as they passed, thanking them. The line of dancing villagers dwindled, and a man leaped out wearing a deerskin and a pair of stag horns, his face made green by a smearing of moss. He pranced and twirled while Dudley began a rite.

Harvest, draws near,
At this, the height of the year,
The Sun King has brought us the corn,
And now as he dies back to the earth we mourn,
May the bounty of this rich season us sustain,
So having given all he doth not die in vain,
The Mother Goddess is now whole,
In spirit, in body, in soul.

The villagers repeated in unison, "In spirit, in body, in soul." The antlered man continued to leap around the fire as children formed a line and took turns to place whole apples in the forming embers to bake.

The leader of the village approached Dudley and shook his hands firmly in both of his own. Morwyneth guessed he would be thanking Dudley for coming on this special night. Then the tribe leader turned round to the boisterous scene and cupped his hands over his mouth to announce supper.

"*Bwyta!*"

There was much shuffling of feet and jostling of elbows as villagers queued up, each with their own bowls, to partake in the festival meal: a rabbit stew. Unsure of local custom, Morwyneth withdrew slightly into some shadows and waited for Dudley to return to her. She did not wish to assume that she would be fed. Sure enough, Dudley made his way back towards her, albeit slowly. At almost every other step, well-wishers and children stopped him, all most happy to see him. He gave each in turn his full attention, until finally he reached Morwyneth.

"Are you hungry, little peace maiden?" On seeing her nod, he winked. "Then fetch some of this rabbit stew. Shallots, wild garlic, carrots, cabbage – the women cook well here."

A small boy about four years old, himself with a limp like Dudley, brought them both a wooden bowl. Dudley ruffled the boy's hair and slapped his own bad leg. The boy slapped his bad leg in response and grinned, forming some symbols with his hands. Dudley roared with laughter. Morwyneth's quizzical expression led Dudley to explain.

"He has no speech with his mouth, he speaks with his hands."

"What did he say?"

"I'm lame, not limp, and my mother's cooking stinks." Dudley grinned. "I taught him that when last I came."

Morwyneth suspected Dudley to be a giant sprite in disguise, playing his naughty tricks wherever he went. Two women passed by with the pot of stew. Dudley and Morwyneth helped themselves to a large ladle each, and took a piece of plaited unleavened bread from another woman's large basket. The stew was hot and indeed delicious. Singing arose from the far side of the campfire as the energetic entertainment recommenced. The antlered man had stopped dancing to have his stew, while the maidens in the green continued to swirl clockwise around the fire. Each with a tree branch in their hands, they spread out like the spokes of a cartwheel. Turning round, they took hold of each other's sticks to form a moving circle, dancing faster and faster. From the fire, grey smoke rolled and danced, ebbing out into the community. Drums beat a rhythm all hearts recognised, throbbing, igniting ancient memories.

A single thud of a solitary drum dropped the dancers to the floor in untidy heaps. They leaped up after a momentary pause, reaching their sticks up and inward to form a roof, chanting the name of the goddess. The antlered man, realising he had almost missed his cue, wiped stew from his mouth with a sleeve and ran to the centre of the sticks, accompanied by raucous laughter. He crouched low, the maidens keeping face as best they could while he readied himself. Withdrawing their sticks, they all dropped onto one knee, bowing before him. He stood and raised a large wooden plate that had been painted to represent the sun above his head. Morwyneth and Dudley joined in the final applause.

"I must begin." Dudley stood, stretching a moment to regain his balance. Taking his staff, he hobbled over to the dwelling of the village leader. A man stood guard outside, counting in a small group of people after which he closed the door. The festivities continued round the campfire. An older woman approached Morwyneth with a bowl of hot water and a rag. She gestured to Morwyneth's ankle compresses, which by now had withered. In response to a nod of agreement from Morwyneth, the woman gently removed the old pieces of cloth and bathed Morwyneth's ankles. She patted the skin dry with the hem of her gown and deftly applied some new, thicker cloth. The bandages formed simple socks, and although they were not shoes, they would suffice for a few more miles.

A while later, the first group of people emerged from the roundhouse and a second group were ushered in. As before, celebrations went on, and so this continued several times throughout the evening. Eventually, most of the villagers had been in. The doorman beckoned Morwyneth over, gesturing inside. She entered nervously. Everyone sat in a circle with Dudley at the far side of the house, facing the doorway. The leader sat next to him. Dudley gave her a relaxed smile and she took a place near the door. A polite hush fell on the room and all eyes turned to Dudley. He spoke firmly but quietly, forcing all to listen hard to hear every word. Morwyneth noticed a different tone in his voice as he told of times past; of heroines and heroes great; of long ago stories, before the Romans, before the first memories of time. Some of them were rhymes, jaunty and fun. Others were sagas with happy or sad endings. As he told them all, Dudley waved his staff in various ways, or drew pictures in the dirt on the floor, enchanting his onlookers with vivid images. When he fell silent his enthralled audience begged for more. A stiff palm faced them. He had finished.

The aura of mystery that had been created within the circle had distracted Morwyneth. Although she dared not admit it, she had not heard the content of the stories. She had been too deeply enthralled in Dudley's voice. The atmosphere had overpowered her concentration. The leader held up his hand as Dudley bowed his head, and it was their signal to leave. Each guest laid an object at Dudley's feet in thanks: bread, sack cloth, ribbon, wooden beads. Being by the door and last, Morwyneth had nothing to offer except her blanket – she draped it over Dudley, pressed her palms together and backed out of the house, bowing her thanks to the tribe leader.

Outside, a friendly young girl took her by the arm and led her to a nearby dwelling. Inside, the family had made up two extra beds of straw and cow hide. The young girl showed Morwyneth to one of them. Exhausted, Morwyneth sank into her bed, practically asleep when Dudley joined them a short while later.

"Night, Dudley," she murmured.

"Goodnight, little peace maiden," Dudley whispered, covering her with the blanket she had gifted to him.

The following morning came all too soon for Morwyneth, who had hoped for a few more hours. They ate some warm milk and bread, before the tribe leader took them to the gates of the village where they made their goodbyes.

The leader smiled, offering a friendly hand. "*Diolch*, Dudley."

Dudley shook his hand firmly. "*Fárwel*. Until the darkness lengthens."

"Honoured will we be for your return."

Dudley nodded and started walking, Morwyneth following. A small group of villagers, mostly children, gathered to wave them off. Dudley and Morwyneth kept waving until they rounded a bend out of sight. In the distance, a cockerel in the village began his morning lament. Morwyneth wanted desperately to talk about the wonderful evening they had shared with Aberhabren, but Dudley did not look to her for discussion. They journeyed in silence for some time until they reached a main roadway under a great oak. Dudley stopped. Morwyneth knew it was too early for lunch.

"Are we resting?"

He smiled. "I must leave you here, little peace maiden."

"I thought we would journey together," she replied, unable to hide her disappointment.

"My path is not yours. Your path is not mine."

Dudley leaned his staff against the magnificent trunk of the oak and swung his bag off his shoulder. He pulled out the blanket and approached Morwyneth, placing it round her shoulders.

She shook her head. "You will need it."

His loud roaring laugh echoed around the empty landscape. "I am accustomed to sleeping outside, remember?"

"You never told me from where you really came," she said.

He spread his hands. "I am from the meadow."

"But the meadow is no particular place," she argued.

"I was born in a meadow, in no particular place, and I shall die in a meadow. I am as my name suggests."

She smiled. "I shall miss you very much, Dudley."

For a brief moment, sorrow passed across his eyes. "And I you, little peace maiden. Perhaps we shall meet again."

"In the meadow?" she proffered.

"I expect so."

He clasped her to him with such a force as to break her in two. Morwyneth clung to him as long as possible, trying to breathe him in enough so that she would remember his smell: a musty, warm aroma that she found comforting. He let her go and took up his belongings.

Adjusting his sack bag, he said, "*Fárwel*, as they say here."

"Be blessed in your travels, Dudley."

"Bless you, little peace maiden. And have hope. You will find those that will help you."

He turned north and did not look back, Morwyneth watching motionless until he became a haze in the distance. She pulled the blanket closer round herself, inhaling his scent from the cloth. Surrounded by open grassland and the majesty of the single oak, Morwyneth felt bereft. Having met Dudley she had thought he would be part of her lifelong journey; someone on the earth plain to watch over her for all her days. Knowing he had been a brief interlude, an experience for her to savour only for a moment, saddened her. Strangely she felt no tears this time, merely a heavy sensation in her stomach, a weight that slowed her progress as she set off in the opposite direction.

Not long into her day the sky again became full and black with cloud. Morwyneth looked for shelter as the first rumble passed overhead. The land sensed her need and she found some beech trees, running over to sit beneath them. The growing intensity of thunderclaps went on for a long time, at first with no rain. Fiercer than the storm she had encountered at the Afon Boughs, this one made her tug her blanket over her head, imagining Dudley's large arms around her, shielding her from danger. When the rain did fall the trees offered little protection. Soon her blanket was sodden and Morwyneth along with it. The downpour seemed eternal, and with it a high wind arose. Morwyneth began to feel cold, her body shaking uncontrollably. However much she wanted to move, she felt pinned down by the rain.

She yelled at the sky, "Away."

The dark clouds rolled, the wind howled and the rain hammered. She dug her heels into the soft soil beneath the trees and threw her arms out to the sides, palms forward. Closing her eyes tight, she lifted her face to the heavens, the rain pelting her skin. She imagined a wall that she could push back to send the rain off over the hills ahead of her.

"Stop."

Her feet pricked with the pain of several knife stabs and the power of Taranis ran down her arms, as though his lightning had struck her. Anwen breathed her name and she opened her eyes.

"Mother?" Anwen stood before her, a willowy apparition distorted by the falling rain. "Why are you here?"

"You called upon your gift when you raised the power from the earth. You are part of the storm, my watched one. We are one with the elements."

Without realising, Morwyneth had manifested a great power, for what intention even she did not know. She shook nervously as the full portent of her gift became clear to her.

"Forgive me," she whispered.

Anwen laughed gently, her voice bubbling. "I am not here to chastise you. I am here to guide you." Holding her hands out, she said, "Breathe gently and deeply."

Morwyneth closed her eyes and inhaled, taking in the scent of the wet ground and the air still alive from the storm overhead. Although rain was falling, Morwyneth felt as though she were inside a cocoon, sheltered from the elements. The rain continuing to fall on her face, became warmer, more palatable. A bright blue tunnel opened up behind Morwyneth's closed eyelids; a long crystal corridor running forever, passing through the real landscape ahead of her.

"Do you see it?" Anwen asked.

"I see it."

"This is your path, Morwyneth."

"Forever it moves, on and on."

"That is because you have not embraced your destiny. Once you have chosen your path, the end will appear."

A tall figure filtered into the tunnel, the image slowly clearing. It was Dudley.

Morwyneth gasped. "Is he dead?"

Smiling, Anwen confirmed, "He has appeared for he has already been a part of your journey. As you seek your true path, others will appear. Craft parts of your journey, imagine what you wish for, and you will find it here."

"I should like to see Dudley again." She pictured his vision once more, further along the tunnel. "And you, many times."

"Do not remain long here, Morwyneth," Anwen warned. "The storm has aroused your gift. Do not allow it to consume you."

The warmth of the rain disappeared and the air once more became cold and windswept. Morwyneth opened her eyes and her mother was gone, from sight though not from sound. One last message lingered on the wind.

"When you meet the wolf, let him into your life." Anwen's voice echoed and faded. "Let him in."

Scanning her surroundings, Morwyneth cried, "Where will I find this wolf?"

There was no response. She would have to find the meaning on her own. Curling into the wet blanket that had lost all scent of Dudley, Morwyneth felt devoid of comfort. She closed her eyes, fighting back uncontrollable shakes, and conjured up an image of the scop in her crystal tunnel. I will not stay long, she told herself.

ChAPTER SEVEN

South Fosse,
South of the Town in the Marsh

Wulfgar rode his brown mare ahead of the wagon convoy, side-by-side with Sieghild, oblivious to the foot soldiers behind them. He could not hear the rattle of spears and shields, the clunk of wood and metal as they marched along the stony road. The scent of the horses and the chatter of small native birds darting through rosehip and hawthorn beside them did not register. His thoughts had been abducted. Since the *Hildwaeg* had beached the fens, his dreams had been invaded by a maiden with blue crystal eyes. She had come for him again last night, during the heavy storm that had rattled the wagons. The ground remained soaked, sweet from the sky's tears. He only knew the scent of his damp wolf-skin cloak, arousing him for it reminded him of the naked wench he had taken on a bed of pelts.

He could tell no one about her, not even Sieghild. "Dreaming of maidens?" he could hear Sieghild say. "Where is the misfortune in that?" He glanced sideways at his ealdorman, who once again appeared to be suffering from the ache Wulfgar had witnessed overpower him by the river at Lindum. Sieghild twisted his leather reins around a clenched hand while forcing his other knuckle into his stomach, pushing hard into his byrnie. Men shouting and a woman's scream punctured the serenity, and Wulfgar twisted in his saddle. He could not see past the first few wagons and cursed in frustration. Lorri appeared on foot beside him, breathless from his dash down the convoy.

"What's the noise?" Wulfgar demanded.

"Shepherd is fighting a thrall."

"A Seaxan thrall, or a Brytonic one?"

Sieghild put a hand out to Wulfgar. "What does it matter?"

Lorri paused, then told Wulfgar, "One of ours, I think, Lord."

Emitting a loud growl of discontent, Wulfgar pulled the reins tight and turned his horse towards the back of the wagon line. Cantering past oak and ash trees, he spied a buzzard riding warm air above him, circling for prey. Lagging several yards behind the last wagon, Wulfgar found Shepherd wrestling with a man taller than him but half his weight. Bringing his horse down to a walk, Wulfgar monitored the brawl for a short while. Shepherd, whose nickname was Mountain, seemed more than the skinny thrall could handle. Grimacing beneath his helmet with every blow Shepherd threw, Wulfgar felt certain it would soon be over. However, when the thrall managed to bring Shepherd to the ground it became clear that the match proved more than even.

"Enough," Wulfgar yelled. "Chapper, break them up."

In desperation, the thrall made a grasp for Shepherd's seax, only to be thwarted by Shepherd who rolled to his feet and faced his leader for instruction. A servant had tried to remove his dagger, a symbol of his free status, and use it to kill him.

Wulfgar searched the faces of onlookers. "What is the meaning of this?"

Chapper, gripping the thrall's arms behind his back, answered, "This louse was trying to make off with one of Shepherd's flock. The ewe at the rear." He nodded to the modest herd Shepherd's son was guarding stalwartly.

Wulfgar addressed Shepherd. "Is this true?"

"Yes, My Lord."

Wulfgar rode over to the thrall, who strained against Chapper's grasp. "Do you deny it?" The thrall merely scowled. Wulfgar turned his mount to leave, tossing a command over his shoulder. "Thrash him."

Scuffling feet accompanied cries, and Wulfgar looked back to see the thrall make a second lunge for Shepherd's seax. This time succeeding, the thrall went to stab him. Chapper intervened, with the help of two other men who rushed to detain the prisoner before he delivered the blade. Wulfgar swung down from his horse and strode over, facing the accused. Grasping the thrall's tunic at his right shoulder, Wulfgar tightly gripped the fabric in his right hand. In an instant, he swung the thrall round, bringing the man's back sharply against his chest. His right arm secured around the man's throat he drove his seax into the thrall's back, puncturing his lung. Throwing the gasping body away from him, he did not linger to see the discarded corpse reach the floor.

Steadying his horse to mount, Wulfgar yelled, "Clean it up."

Sieghild held up a hand, halting his two mounted companions and the marching men. On the roadside, smothered under a sodden wool blanket, lay an unknown writhing shape. Dismounting, he collected his shield from one of the men and approached the round wet lump with caution.

It could be a lure to some deadly ambush, or a trick played against them by the gods. He tightened his hand around his sword handle, feeling the lattice leatherwork pressing deeper into his palm. Warriors of the Wulfsuna readied themselves on all sides, raising their round shields warily to their chins. Within a step of the strange sight, Sieghild paused, beads of sweat trickling down his neck beneath his helmet. Midsummer sun broke through grey clouds as the rain-soaked mass turned over, revealing a head of shorn hair, the ends blunt and staggered.

Sieghild reached out a hand. "*Ic bidde thu, becumen.*"

A buzzard cried out overhead while the creature on the ground rolled and croaked deliriously. Hair still drenched from heavy rain fell aside to reveal a young female face. She had skin as pale as the moon and lips of pure garnet. The warriors around him shuffled uneasily, their eyes and ears remaining alert to attack from the surrounding landscape. A few civilians left their wagons, some brave enough to walk down and glimpse the spectacle, others merely straining their heads to look down the road. Two words filtered into the air, shouted by onlookers.

"*Wealh.*" Foreigner.

"*Nix.*" River witch.

Sieghild set aside his shield and leaned over, one hand secured tightly on the hilt of his sword. He wondered who she could be and how she had come to be here. Bright blue eyes opened wide, crazed, trying to hold him steady in their gaze. She went to scream, finding herself mute. He stumbled backwards, as though her eyes had stabbed him with an invisible blade. What was happening to him? He grappled for his balance, losing grip on his weapon, glancing round fearfully. In response, Wulfsuna readied stance for battle; spears resting on top of shields, senses locked on an enemy they believed would soon appear. Regaining his composure, Sieghild stared at the small-boned woman in a ripped and marked under-gown. He wanted to know more about her; wanted to know how she could move him by mere sight.

Chapper and two other men removed the dead servant to store him for cremation when they next stopped for camp. Wulfgar secured a foot in the step rope that hung from his wooden saddle and noticed the wagons were no longer moving. Hauling himself onto his mare, he went to direct her back to the head of the convoy when he heard two shouted words that made him still.

"*Wealh.*"

"*Nix.*"

Wulfgar's throat constricted uncomfortably. Could Eadmaer have sent a river temptress to fool them into an Angle trap? His eyes darted all around them, ears suddenly alert for the slightest sound. He tried to shake the fear from his shoulders and rode at speed past the wagons. Arriving at the scene, Wulfgar immediately became aware of the bizarre contrast between battle-ready warriors and civilians loitering casually to view the excitement. Heahstan and Sieghild were unusually at odds in a lively altercation, the old warrior the most animated Wulfgar had ever seen him. Heahstan's wide eyes revealed the pink flesh around his eyeballs, his arms taught with clenched fists.

"She is Nix. She is death. Kill her now, while you can, Sieghild."

The ealdorman shook his head vehemently, a straight arm pointing ahead to something partially concealed in the undergrowth. "She is a young woman who needs our help, or she will die."

Heahstan spat with rage. "She is not one of us. She is no one we can trust."

A deep frown concealed beneath his helmet, Wulfgar demanded briskly, "What goes on?" His sight followed that of the assembled crowds. "Is she *Wealisc*?"

Sieghild stepped forward. "I saw her at the side of the road, all wet. I fear she has the fever."

"You know how I feel about collecting waifs and strays, about wasting time when we have yet to reach our intended destination."

Sieghild pressed him. "She might die if we do not aid her."

The crowd had fallen silent around them, watching and waiting for their headman to make a decision. Sun burned through grey swift-moving clouds, breaking the coolness created by an intermittent August breeze. The wilderness around them was moving and whispering. Red squirrels chattered in the pine tops. Blackbirds sang in the hawthorn. Angons and chain mail were still and silent by contrast. Wulfgar rode his horse forward to look at the sodden creature, speaking more to himself than to those around him.

"She must have been here all night."

The body rolled, revealing the face beneath dishevelled wet hair. Wulfgar's breath caught sharply in his throat. The wild visage staring up at him was the maiden from his tormented dreams. She was here, at his feet. He turned to view his mounted thegns, the foot soldiers, wives, children and others. All waited expectantly. Whether she was woman or nix, he could not now abandon the face from his nightmares. He had too many questions unanswered. For that he hated himself. Where was his fortitude? He sighed heavily, head dropping briefly before he stared directly at Sieghild.

"Put her in the last wagon."

"Yes, My Lord."

Two men carried the young woman to the last wagon and the onlookers dispersed. Sieghild mounted his grey stallion and caught up with his headman. For several strides they rode in silence, the gait of their horses finding a common rhythm. The further they went, the closer the animals walked until the men's boots brushed each other's. A loud exhalation from Wulfgar split the silence between them. He spoke so only they could hear one another.

"Sieg, Sieg. Why are we now one body heavier?"

Sieghild drew in a large breath, and replied, "She would have died had we left her."

"Like scores of others we have passed along some of these forsaken roads."

"Most of them were already in Hel."

"Not all." Wulfgar glared at his friend.

Sieghild read and understood the pain in Wulfgar's face. They had discovered, in isolated regions, a troubled country where fighting and famine were spreading out like the icy fingers of death. People had begged and died around them since they'd joined the South Fosse. They had travelled through many tuns filled with their own wealth of stock and grain, trading with any who would acknowledge them. However, a contingent also existed who felt abandoned by the security the Empire had given their lives, many turning to crime. Neither had he forgotten that evil lurked on their tail in the guise of Eadmaer. Any pause to collect unwanted cargo put the entire Wulfsuna in jeopardy, allowing that known evil to gain ground on a more heavily burdened wagon train. Besides which, they did not know this young waif. She could be a trap laid by the Angles.

Wulfgar continued, "I shall pray to Woden to instil some sense into your head."

"For why?" Sieghild frowned.

"Can you be sure she is not nix? She was wet."

"Thunor broke the clouds last night."

"We are near many places of water, including Bathumtun, the spring waters of Sulis." Wulfgar gazed ahead. "Does the land of your mother still trouble you with an ache?"

There was a long pause before Sieghild replied, "Yes."

"Did it speak to you when you found the nix?"

When Sieghild did not reply, Wulfgar glanced at his friend who idly fingered his horse's silver mane. Wulfgar knew there to be more to this waif than Sieghild had revealed. Wulfgar himself knew it, for he had been dreaming of a stranger who they had now found on the roadside.

"Did it?"

Sieghild sent him a sharp stare. "Yes. What of it?"

Wulfgar returned the ferocity of the gaze, competing until he felt justified to answer. "I think it spoke to me also."

Wary of the proximity of listeners, Sieghild glanced behind them, leaning closer. "How?"

Having stumbled into this ravine of truth, Wulfgar saw no way out except to tell his friend what he had experienced. He inhaled at length, preparing for the taunts he imagined would follow his admissions.

"Her face, I have seen the nix in my dreams."

"In truth?"

"Since we left Sachsen. I could not tell you. I am a fool, yes?" He faced Sieghild.

"As much a fool as I, Wulf. I saw her, and the ache in my gut left me. Is that crazy?"

"No more than this strange land, my friend."

The jostling of the wagon on the chalk road woke Morwyneth abruptly. Her head felt full of wool. She had no idea how long she had been unconscious. Her face lay in soft sheepskin and a heavy blanket covered her now dry body. Her slumber had not been a pleasant one. She had been plagued by nightmares of fearful monsters with metal faces and leaping snakes. Hearing soft singing, she turned over. A large built woman with an ample bosom and long brown plaits sang a pleasant ballad in a soft voice.

"*Godne mergen.*" The woman nodded curtly and reached over to pass Morwyneth a generous lump of bread and a cup of ale.

Morwyneth thanked her, eating heartily, her last meal having been at Aberhabren. The woman sat stitching hides together, all the while singing. She looked up when Morwyneth passed her the empty cup, and Morwyneth caught her attention, drawing her hands away from each other to symbolise distance.

"How long?" she asked, laying her head on her hands to suggest sleeping.

The woman rested her head in a palm and held up a thumb and forefinger. She had been asleep for two nights. Morwyneth had no idea in which direction they had been travelling, or where they were heading.

She did not even know if her presence among these strangers would be welcomed. Listening to the woman's calming song, Morwyneth felt that if she were a prisoner they would not have cared for her and fed her. She had her conclusion confirmed when the woman stopped sewing to press a hand to her chest.

"Godelina."

Morwyneth repeated the gesture with her own name. The wagon came to an unsteady stop and countless feet rallied to the side of the road. Godelina said a word Morwyneth did not understand, and so she moved to the back of the wagon to try and see out. A helmeted warrior with long brown hair instructed a group of men to form a line facing the wagon convoy. All were armed with spears, and their trousers were held tight to the leg below the knees with diagonal binding, Morwyneth wondered if they could be the Saesnig mercenaries she had heard stories of. Huweyn had spoken of them from his travels, telling her how some had worked for the Romans at trading outposts such as Gloui. More recently, some had looked to them to assist in their battle against the raiders of the north, whom Morwyneth and her people knew as the Cruithnii: the people of the blue designs she had foreseen would sack Prenhwychas.

Almost hanging out of the back of the wagon to see the proceedings, Morwyneth felt Godelina's large but gentle hand on her shoulder, easing her back inside. Godelina shook her head in disapproval. Morwyneth sighed heavily and sat down. An ill-tempered male voice called to Godelina and the older woman rolled her eyes, reaching for some of the finished cow hides. A tall, thin man met her with a furrowed brow, complaining in his own tongue as she waved his words away with a disinterested hand.

"*Yea, Yea.*" She sighed, climbing out of the wagon.

Morwyneth waited to be sure Godelina was not returning too soon then ventured outside, keeping close to the large wheels. The grey day with a heavy mist made it difficult to see very far. The lack of visibility made her all the more eager to know her location. She crept further along, attempting not to alert the pairs of warriors who had been stationed either side of each wagon. She did not succeed. One man saw her, alerting the helmeted warrior she had glimpsed earlier. He neared her apprehensively.

"*Eala.*"

Morwyneth attempted to respond with his native word. "*Ella.*"

Two serpents with garnet eyes entwined over the brow pieces of his helmet, their tails trailing down onto the cheek flaps. Several days' worth of black stubble darkened his angular chin. Hypnotised by his intense gaze, Morwyneth sensed they had already met. He shook his head from side to side.

"You are not allowed outside."

Hearing her native tongue caught her off guard. The blend of her words and his accent sounded familiar, though she could not place it at that moment. The warrior put a hand on his chest.

"Sieghild."

Morwyneth, still entranced by the design on his helmet, reached out to feel the snakes, whose tongues overlapped intricately and whose red eyes shone, even in the weak light. The heel of her palm accidentally brushed his mouth and he stepped back abruptly. He repeated his statement to her.

"You are not allowed outside."

His hand moved to grip the handle of his sword, and Morwyneth saw two more entwined snakes on his belt buckle. She tried to look further down the convoy and he sidled in front of her, stepping closer. He warned her once more in her own language, "I do not want to hurt you, little girl."

She was confounded as to how he knew her words and why the way he spoke them sounded so familiar. An image of Dudley flashed through her mind: the hut, the sagas, the mellow voice. It was the same combination of lilting accent blended with her native words. She realised Dudley could have been Saesnig.

"I must know where I am," she pleaded, moving as though to pass him.

Sieghild grasped both her arms firmly in his hands. "You must stay in the wagon until we reach camp."

From amid the fog came a gruff bellow. "What takes so long?"

In fear of the venomous voice, Morwyneth recoiled, trying to attach herself to Sieghild. He pushed her sideways behind the wagon next to them. A rider on a chestnut mare appeared through the fog, commanding a devastating presence in pale garments beneath well-polished mail. Long hair, gold as wheat in the sun, curled out from under a gold and silver helmet, settling on powerful shoulders wrapped in a sumptuous grey pelt. The young man scowled fiercely when he laid eyes on Morwyneth, as though it were no surprise to find her there.

"*Thu.*"

Morwyneth held onto the back of the wagon she had been thrust behind. Sieghild stepped away from her to face the rider, conversing in their own words. She saw him gesture to the rear of the convoy, perhaps suggesting she had been about to return there. The mounted warrior, seemingly of a higher rank, was unconvinced by Sieghild's statement, his tone harsh in response. Sieghild bowed his head briefly. Morwyneth watched the interaction. They were but a few years older than her. Although the words exchanged between them were unknown to her, she nonetheless felt the tension and became fearful a fight would erupt. The leader locked his pale, wild eyes upon her, gripping her heart in frost. She felt her palms throb, a pull on her chest as she fell into a vision. She saw him as a child: blond, stocky, tumbling across the ground with a brown-haired boy, perhaps Sieghild.

"*Thu.*"

She froze, her stomach sick from the strength of the vision, arms shaking. She clutched the wagon tighter. His horse stamped impatiently at being held stationary, her hooves unsteady on the chalk. He turned his attention back to Sieghild, appearing to ask a question, lifting his chin in Morwyneth's direction. Sieghild took an age to respond and Morwyneth's throat constricted with terror. His leader snarled more unknown words, and his horse reared her front legs as he yanked her about and cantered back down the convoy.

Morwyneth sighed with relief when Sieghild took her by the arm and led her towards the last but one wagon. Huddled inside were mostly elderly and infirm tribe members. She lifted a leg to climb up. Sieghild roughly pulled her back down, shaking his head. He took her wrists in his hands and pulled a length of hemp rope from the back of the vehicle. Her eyes bulged in horror and she tried to twist free. Her distress made him angry and he gripped her more firmly, winding the rope round her wrists. She tried to make eye contact. Sieghild hid beneath his helmet, his gaze lingering down and away from her. He tethered the other end of the rope to the rear of the wagon, pausing with his hands wrapped around the rope. He buried his face in his shoulder, hissing what she presumed to be a profanity. When he brought his head up, she stared at him in dismay. His face was contorted in contempt of his orders and he released the ropes, grappling with his chin strap and ripping his helmet from his head. Revealed, he allowed his emotions to pour over his face, attempting to relay all his feelings to her with a small shake of his head. *He did not want to tie her.* He slowly walked away.

A gouge from a battle-axe would have befitted the physical agony Sieghild felt, deepening the further he walked from the nix. She remained silent as he departed, silent and strong. A weaker woman would have pleaded to his disappearing back as he made his way to his horse. He managed to keep his face free of the pain until Lorri had handed him the reins to his grey, Harsteda. Hiding behind the stallion's thick neck, he grimaced, bearing teeth and hissing through them, eyes tight shut. What cure did she possess that his pain subsided in her presence? Or worse, what hex could she wield to torture him for his absence? She laid his gut to rest, settled his blood whenever he neared her. A peace existed between them, however dark their current situation seemed. As he made to mount, Thunor made threats with his hammer across the heavens, and Sieghild began to wonder if their suspicions of her being nix were true. Their enemies could have summoned her to detain them; distract their tribe from their journey enough for an ambush. Or perhaps even the power of Sulis lingered still over her native magic spring? Allowing the idea to filter through his mind, Sieghild would not relinquish that first feeling on finding the waif. Although mad with exposure, she had held him with her eyes not as a captive, but cradled as a child in her arms. She had seen through him into his deepest flesh. He had felt her in his blood, twisting and winding round his body, knowing him from the inside even before she knew his face. She had certainly drawn him into her spell. She had caught him: a herring in a net, writhing in vain.

Before Wulfgar had given the order to bind the nix, Sieghild knew his lord would be unhappy she had crawled out of her wagon and interfered with the proceedings. Large towns were particularly dangerous places to pass. Bathumtun, not as bustling as it had been under the Romans, remained a major town. Law enforcement existed, although it was not of the calibre and speed of response as it had been under the Empire. Therefore local thieves and roving bandits alike made lucrative livings selling stolen stone or attacking foreigners heading there to trade. However, right now Sieghild would rather sink a fist into Wulfgar's face than take any more orders from him. Lucky for his headman, a lifelong friendship and close childhood would not allow him to make good the threat.

"Ealdorman Sieghild."

He stood to attention, swinging his helmet back onto his head to hide his anger. Wulfgar calmed his horse with a few pats on its neck and tightened the reins.

"As it is your doing we have this stray, I am entrusting you with the job of keeping her in line. Can you do that?"

Sieghild refrained from making eye contact. "Yes, My Lord."

The public admonishment was a tactic Wulfgar was using more and more frequently, proving outwardly to the rest of his men he held no favours. Privately, they would have a different conversation, on more equal terms. For now, Sieghild took the verbal punishment and wondered how, in Frigg's name, he could justify the latest addition to the Wulfsuna.

"To your places," Wulfgar cried, hauling his mount round sharply as he turned and rode back to the front of the line.

With all the guards assigned to their wagons, the convoy set off again.

Sieghild rode to the front to join Wulfgar. He felt eyes boring into the side of his helmet, his lord using the power of the gods to cleave his skull open and see into his thoughts.

"You should not have ordered her bound, Wulf."

"She could be a runaway bride with a tyrannical nobleman hunting her down as we speak," Wulfgar warned.

"Or a slave. Did you see the cloth bound around her feet?"

Wulfgar considered the suggestion and shook his head. "Abandoned cargo? Slave traders sell at the harbour markets, not inland."

Sieghild leaned over his horse's withers, not trusting the ears around them. "Whoever she is, she has not wronged us. You cannot treat her as a thrall. We do not know her status."

Wulfgar stiffened, facing his ealdorman and dropping his voice to a low growl. "She disobeyed the headman of the Wulfsuna. I did as I would have for any of our own who refused to yield to me. She had a lesson to learn."

"She may be of service to us. She may possess skills we can put to good use."

Wulfgar adjusted his seat in the saddle and looked away. "On your head let it rest, my friend, if you are proven wrong."

Sieghild did not linger, pulling sharply on the reins of his horse to head aft up the convoy to the sixth wagon. Slowing from the brief canter, he caught the surprise in the face of the nix. He hailed a thrall as he dismounted, handing over the fiery animal and his discarded helmet. He fell in beside Morwyneth, matching her pace. Trying to keep a detachment, he asked his questions firmly, in her language.

"Have you a craft?"

She replied hesitantly, "I do not understand."

"What were you where you came from? A spinner? What?"

"I kept goats and chickens. At harvest I helped in the fields."

Sieghild cast his eyes around the vicinity for inspiration, hoping to find something she could do whereby he could visit her often. He knew Shepherd would not allow her near his flock. Superstition was rife, and Shepherd would strongly object to a river siren tending his animals. Godelina's singing echoed out over the convoy.

"Can you sew?" he asked quickly.

"Yes."

"Then you may help Godelina. She sews for the tribe."

She watched his every move as he untied the uncomfortable hemp that had dragged her thus far down an unforgiving road. Once freed, she rubbed her sore wrists and stared into his face expectantly.

"I thank you."

"It is nothing," he told her. A lie for sure, for her words were everything to him at that moment. She moved past him and he grabbed her by the top of her arm. She calmly regarded the white-knuckled hand holding her firm. Raising her eyes she met his. Struggling with unfamiliar emotions he uttered his words coarsely, jaw stiff.

"I would have you know, I am glad you had a craft."

Her brief smile heralded the sensation of a thousand spiders engulfing his arms. His head filled with imagery; fleeting, brief scenes of places he had never been. Were these places not yet seen, a vision of the future? Were these places she had been? Her smile left her and she closed her eyes quickly. The images were instantly extinguished and he saw no more. He released her. Watching as she walked swiftly to Godelina's rear wagon, his mind begged her to look back. She did not. Considering the images he had seen, he began to wonder if she could reveal things to him, perhaps about his mother. Passing Corinium Dobunnium, he had felt the ache in his gut, its power increasing as they travelled through his mother's tribal home. He considered the nix might be Dobunni. She possessed an essence, a way with her that spoke to a part of him he had not hitherto known existed. The last wagon trundled past him and he had to resist the desperate need to look for her. Something held him shackled to this creature's every movement, her every word. It was not love. Neither was it lust. Whatever it may be, he had to fight it, for it had already brought him trouble.

Lorri appeared beside him. "Ealdorman Sieghild?"

"Yes?"

"You are wanted by Lord Wulfgar."

"I come."

CHAPTER EIGHT

South Fosse,
Passing the Dark Wood

An orange ember filtered through the sides of the rear wagon, sending golden motes swirling across Morwyneth as she reposed. Having taken all day to warm away the fog, the sun, now at its lowest point, could barely be seen above the land. Godelina had been still for some time, dozing intermittently, her sewing complete. Morwyneth sensed the entire convoy had tired of travelling. They had not stopped in a long time and, from the noises her stomach was making, she knew they were long overdue for a meal. She had not even heard the warriors, who periodically sang as they marched.

Morwyneth found herself thinking of Sieghild. When she had touched his helmet, somehow she had been able to sense him through the metal, knowing his heart was beating at the same time as her own. Then when he had untied her, his grip on her arms had set her gift alight, burning through her. Her own power frightened her. Anwen had been right in her instructions not to linger in the tunnel. Morwyneth had realised it almost at a cost to her life. She felt it was time to add some further pieces to her journey and summoned the long blue crystal corridor with caution. Imagining the soles of her feet were the roots of a tree, she drew on the power of Mother Earth, calling it up through magma and stone, tree roots, soil and the floor of the wagon. A deep pulse began throbbing in the soles of her feet, moving and growing until it encompassed her entire body in a basal rhythm. Gradually the sounds around her dissipated. With the outside world muffled, she could concentrate fully, rocked gently in the arms of Gaia.

Behind her closed eyelids the tunnel opened up in her seer's vision. Dudley's image remained, smiling back at her. Next she added Sieghild as he had stopped to save her. Wondering if her powers would help find some answers, she asked, "Where are we heading?" She heard an echo of Sieghild's voice from earlier and his mention of Bathumtun. She concluded it must be Aquae Sulis, the Roman Bath town. She had heard stories, but never been. She then asked, "Where am I now?" She found herself flying high above the wagon convoy, as though she were a bird looking down on their location. As mist lifted she could clearly see a forest behind them, and ahead a large river broadening out towards the sea. They were south of the uplands and west Gymraeg, heading towards the southwest coast. Once they passed Bathumtun they would soon be nearing south Gymraeg, the land of the lizard. She imagined her last question would be the hardest. She asked it nonetheless. "What do I need?" Another vision sprang up in her mind's eye: two people entwined passionately. As she watched it unfold, shock overwhelmed her. She wanted to deny the blond hair she saw and cast the vision out. It persisted. Undeniably, before her lay the Saesnig leader over her very own body. She immediately cut off her connection with Mother Earth, dragging herself back to reality with a bolt. She had no intention of such an alliance with that man. His gaze and manner made her fear him. She did not trust him. What shadowy influences had worked their way into her mind to conjure up this lie? Each time she drew on her gift, a brutal reminder befell her of the dangers it held. She picked up the sewing in front of her as a distraction, disheartened by the whole experience.

A short while later, a galloping horse broke the quiet progress of the convoy. Morwyneth envisaged its nostrils flaring as it snorted and slowed to a walking pace next to a nearby wagon. She heard the leader talking to some of the rear guards, mentioning Sieghild's name. The horse galloped away to the front of the line, and after several more yards the convoy came to a halt. The sound of many pairs of feet leaping from wagons signalled a large falling-in of warriors. Scabbards and angons clanged against shields, and someone dropped a helmet on the road – Morwyneth smiling to herself as she heard hurried footsteps and imagined the soldier chasing after it. All feet fell silent and still, then Sieghild's voice gave instructions to the men. From the sounds of yet more feet, it seemed groups of warriors ran off in different directions to perhaps act as perimeter guards. Morwyneth met eyes with Godelina, who seemed excited by the activities outside and started rubbing her hands together in anticipation.

Morwyneth pressed a palm down on the floor of the wagon. "Stop?"

Godelina's confirming nod cheered Morwyneth. The constant buoyancy of the wagon had begun to take its toll on her, unaccustomed to incessant movement. Godelina rifled around beside her intently, searching for something. She muttered inaudible phrases, tutting until she found what she had been hunting for. She pulled out a thick bluish cloth which turned out to be a man's tunic and handed it to Morwyneth. For the first time since leaving her village, Morwyneth changed out of her worn undergarment and into clean clothes. The comfortable tunic, which reached well past her knees, had long sleeves and a round neckline.

They did not have to wait long before a warrior poked his head round the back of their wagon and beckoned that they could exit. Morwyneth climbed out. A flat landscape confronted them, with the west coast and the long estuary before it some way off to the right. Morwyneth could hear another water source nearby, perhaps a smaller river coming in from the estuary. To the right, hills rose in the distance. She had been right about perimeter guards. At key points, where the land dipped and peaked, small groups of men were positioned facing out towards any approaching enemy. Remaining warriors unloaded equipment into a central area, where it looked as though there would be some accommodation built. Under guard, several older men left the camp area, presumably to search for firewood. Light was fast sinking. The thin, angry man that had called for Godelina earlier came trotting over to them. In a more affable mood, he exchanged a kiss with Godelina, and Morwyneth imagined him to be her husband. He motioned them towards a wagon nearer the front of the line.

Following them, Morwyneth remained conscious their leader could ride past at any moment. After her awful vision, she had no wish to meet him, and kept her gaze low, asking those that watched over her to protect her from the torment. A welcome aroma of hot food permeated the cold dusk air, and eventually they came to rest at the cook's wagon. As he was busy cooking onions and wild mushrooms, his wife handed out pieces of bread and cheese. A young woman interrupted Morwyneth as she ate her bread. About Morwyneth's age, the woman had brown eyes, a round face and fair hair, like many within the tribe. She showed Morwyneth her piece of bread, out of which she had eaten the soft centre, retaining the crust as a shallow bowl shape. The girl queued up to collect some of the onions and mushrooms in her bread bowl, and brought this back to show Morwyneth so that she could do the same.

When Morwyneth had fetched her own onions and mushrooms, the girls exchanged names. Her new helpful friend, named Cwenfleda, seemed excited at having found a companion. She escorted Morwyneth around the camp, showing her the ongoing preparations, chatting happily in her own tongue. Morwyneth understood barely a handful of words and only made partial sense of the rest from sign language. However, she found it relaxing listening to Cwenfleda, and briefly had thoughts of remaining with these Saesnig people, learning their words and ways. As quickly as her mind had settled on the idea, so it left her. The tribe leader walked casually towards them. A formidable sight in full battle gear, although without a helmet, as he neared them Cwenfleda swooned. Morwyneth hung back, turning away from him. She stared at the ground and attempted to find a distraction. He stopped within a few strides of them and spoke to Cwenfleda, who became coy and falsely bashful. Morwyneth found his deep, calm voice unnerving in comparison to the immense anger she had previously witnessed. After several exchanged phrases, Cwenfleda's voice became terse. She gestured to Morwyneth that they were to move back to the area by the cook wagon. Following Cwenfleda, Morwyneth cast a look back. The leader stood fast, as though ensuring they returned as obviously instructed. His legs were set apart, and his arms folded drawing attention to some intimidating iron wrist cuffs. Morwyneth whisked her head round smartly and caught up with Cwenfleda.

On a fallen tree they sat and drew in the soil for each other's amusement. Trying to understand her new friend's scrawls and monitoring the activity around her, Morwyneth began comparing the Saesnig tribe to Prenhwychas. Over her lifetime there had been many squabbles in her village. Huweyn's position had been in jeopardy on several occasions. And not only men had fought for power. Under the Romans, women were subservient and prevented by law from taking positions of leadership. Since the departure of the Empire, however, there had been a matriarchal uprising. The power of the Brytonic female had returned to her village with a warped purpose. Flouting the old title 'head of the household', they had rallied to overthrow their men. Unease had come to rest on Prenhwychas long before Morwyneth's untimely departure. She wondered if Huweyn and his elders would discover the ringleader. She did not even know if her father had retained control following the outbreak of violence at her expulsion. Looking around, Morwyneth realised how far removed her background appeared from the close-knit community with distinct hierarchy she now found herself among.

Sieghild removed his war belt, setting his sword down carefully, and shrugged out of his padded leather tunic. Seated on one of several pieces of log arranged around the giant camp fire, he watched the tall flames that seemed to lick the stars, just missing the glowing crescent moon suspended in the evening sky. Other thegns gathered by the seating, dispensing with their own war gear. A substantial tent made of hemp sail sections and wooden poles stood behind them. Wulfgar joined them, closely followed by two men serving out ale in horn cups.

A vehement discussion erupted between Wulfgar and some of the younger thegns eager to know their lord's thoughts on the tribe's progress and the whereabouts of Eadmaer. Sieghild nudged his friend's arm to alert him to a cup of ale being offered. Sieghild waved the thrall away, Wulfgar being too involved in the heated conversation to respond. Listening to the sea of overlapping voices, all vying for their lord's attention, Sieghild knew Wulfgar would not hear all that had been said. Intermittently, Sieghild intervened, repeating pertinent words or phrases to Wulfgar.

"Enough words. Let us drink."

Heahstan halted all talk, and horn cups were raised jovially, the thrall returning at Sieghild's beckoning to provide Wulfgar with a full cup of ale. Wulfgar elbowed Sieghild and waved his cup towards the grassy incline where the rest of the tribe had gathered.

"It swells the heart to see Wulfsuna together like this."

Sieghild looked up. Everyone sat in groups laughing, reclining outside their parked wagons, to some of which hemp awnings had been added. Their happy faces were illuminated by the huge fire. He grinned.

"Indeed, My Lord."

"Wulfgar."

Sieghild tipped his ale cup. "Wulfgar."

"Welcome to the west, weaner." Heahstan's thunderous laugh engulfed them all as he poured his ale over his young lord's head. Wulfgar laughed, licking the ale as it dripped from his beard.

"Thank you, Thegn Heahstan."

Amid raucous laughter, they both held out their empty cups to be served more ale. Sieghild followed the frivolity as it spread through the men, mingling with the heart-warming sounds of a tribe having fun at last. The distraction led him to look at the slope leading up from the left-hand side of the camp fire. His sights rested on the nix, and the noise surrounding him ebbed away. She sat watching him, knees drawn up and arms wrapped around her legs. He continued to gaze at her and she did not look away; did not, or could not. Feeling caught by an invisible thread, knowing each intrigued the other, Sieghild did not care if she could be nix. He believed it. Her eyes called to him, the skin on his hands and arms rippling with the sensation of a thousand scurrying spiders. When Godelina appeared, draping a blanket over Morwyneth's shoulders and ushering her out of sight, Sieghild blinked. Facing his companions, he found all eyes were on him, including a stern pair from his best friend.

Wulfgar lifted one eyebrow. "You left us, Ealdorman Sieghild. Where were you?"

Sieghild saw Leofgist walking back from the slope to take his seat. Wulfgar had sent him to have the nix removed. An unfamiliar anger arose within him, which he tried to restrain as he replied.

"Forgive me, My Lord. Please excuse me."

Sieghild stood and walked some distance away, busying himself sipping his ale. Never had a woman's eyes eaten into his soul in such a way. It intrigued him how she could hold him in her power so strongly with look alone. Leofgist interrupted Sieghild's silent contemplation grasping his forearm. He had expected Wulfgar to tap him on the shoulder.

"Sieghild."

Half-turning, Sieghild eyed the hand on him with acridity. "Leofgist?"

Leofgist released his hold. "Sieghild, be wary. You do not want to bring the wrath of our new lord down on you."

"I am well aware of Lord Wulfgar's temper," Sieghild told him.

"If the nix does have a hex on you, I shall let it be known I warned you," said Leofgist, tip-toeing agitatedly from one foot to the other.

Sieghild raised an eyebrow. "Thank you."

Leofgist left him. The immense orange light of the camp fire played shapes over his trousers and cast a long shadow of him across the grass. The spidery ripples returned to his skin and he flexed one hand to erase the sensation. It strengthened. He thought he heard Wulfgar's voice whispering, "Look at me." He rounded. Wulfgar scowled at him from his seat outside the tent. It could not have been his voice. Perhaps the gods played tricks on him, whispering through the trees.

The following morning the convoy moved on, trundling south-west, aiming to pass east Bathum and turn west towards Bathumtun and the spring of Sulis. They travelled for two days, resting only in their wagons for a night. Occasionally they paused to alleviate weary feet and hooves, although no sooner had men and beasts been fed and watered they took to the road once more. When rumours of a camp were suggested, word spread fast. People hurried between wagons passing on the news, animals and equipment moving around even before the wagons had come to a complete stop.

Sieghild wandered up the line of wagons, all parked at odd angles. Running children, a dog and some wayward sheep crossed his path, while elsewhere he heard raised voices, no doubt frayed tempers from travelling. He passed some people attempting to light a fire in the fine drizzle, eager to warm some ale. He ran two hands through his loose hair, tucking it behind his ears, and slid a hand over his chin. He had a beard, not having shaved since they landed. He made for the last wagon, for the nix. He wanted to know more about her and why he felt as though he had known her in another time. Arriving, he leaned on the back of the wagon, arms folded. Godelina nodded a greeting. The nix, not having seen him arrive, jumped, so he gave her a welcoming smile.

"Hello."

He waited for an answer, which never came. Instead, large round blue eyes hauntingly stared through him. He turned to converse with Godelina.

"Shepherd has some sheepskins for you, if you go and see him." He gestured in the direction she might find him. "Here, let me help you."

He reached a hand out to her and aided her jump down, a supportive hand to her elbow. She grinned broadly, eyes twinkling.

"Thank you, Sieghild."

His attention returned to the nix, whose gaze had not left him. He gave her a broader smile, tempting her to talk. She remained mute. Placing a hand inside the wagon, he checked her response as he slid himself onto the edge to sit. She recoiled, backing into a dark corner.

"Am I forgiven for tying you to the wagon?" She tendered an almost indiscernible nod, and he reciprocated. "Good. I have found a family who will look after you. You have met their daughter, Cwenfleda?"

She licked her lips. "How was it you saved me from being bound? I thought I was to become a slave."

His head dropped, an exasperated sigh escaping him. "You disobeyed our lord. It was a temporary punishment." He looked up. "I persuaded him to release you, that you could perhaps be useful to us."

There was a hint of a smile, and then she drew herself into an even tighter ball. He decided it would be best to leave. Dropping down off the wagon, he wandered back to the front of the convoy. Unanswered questions filled his head, and strangely he believed the nix held the key to the answers; that she could unlock the mystery he found himself cloaked in. Men addressed him as he walked past in his emotional stupor. Ordinarily he would have given them a cursory nod of acknowledgement. Eyes cast to the ground, he had his deep thoughts interrupted by the forcible thrust of a helmet in his stomach; his own helmet, handed to him by his headman.

"This should be on your head, Sieghild."

Slightly winded, Sieghild solemnly accepted it as Wulfgar continued silently in the opposite direction.

Cwenfleda had brought Morwyneth to the cook wagon where apples were being handed out. She bit a chunk out of her apple and offered it to Morwyneth, who refused kindly, pointing to her own apple. Cwenfleda shook her head and proffered the chunk a second time, pushing Morwyneth's apple to her mouth and signalling to bite a piece. Morwyneth took a chunk of apple and they exchanged pieces.

"*Hlaefmass*," Cwenfleda said, holding up a single finger for first and pulling up some grass to simulate harvest.

Morwyneth nodded that she understood it to be their harvest festival. She remembered fondly the harvest celebrations at Aberhabren with Dudley.

"*Lughnasadh,*" she told Cwenfleda.

Cwenfleda pointed to the ground, then to the moon that had appeared early in the cloudy August sky. "*Theos niht.*"

Morwyneth thought once more of staying with the Saesnig. Cast out of Prenhwychas with the wilderness her only other option, Morwyneth felt compelled to admit they were her last hope. The leader's scathing bellow halted most of the tribe as he arrived to drag away several footmen who had paused by the cook's cart to eat. Her dream evaporated. She could not stay when such a ruthless tyrant, who found her presence abhorrent, existed. Her vision of him writhing naked over her lingered in her mind; festered and irritated her in a way she had never known before. She almost hated him because of it, and she had never held hatred for another living thing in her life. Despite the ferocity of the women at Prenhwychas, her heart could not hate them. Led by narrow minds and hearts, they knew no other way to respond in such chaos. Anwen's wise words from a recent dream came to her: "We must have compassion for those who do not see as clearly as we do. Their minds are blinded by fear and mistrust." And so she had forgiven the women; pitied them. The leader bellowed a second time, pausing on his horse to scowl in her direction. She could not pity him.

Cwenfleda took Morwyneth by the hand and led her to her family's wagon. Along the way she talked incessantly, though Morwyneth felt in no mood to listen, instead smiling and nodding politely. Cwenfleda's home consisted of two vehicles, the first full of tools belonging to her father, the farrier and sword smith. They found him hard at work under shadow of an overhanging awning, a brazier alight next to his anvil, smiting a sword badly bent in battle. Other implements lay in orderly piles around him, newly-made or repaired pieces and objects waiting to be seen to. The second wagon housed the main living area created by an awning staked out from the side of the rear wagon. An older woman appeared, undoubtedly Cwenfleda's mother. She beckoned the girls inside, offering them each a wooden stool. The mother placed a graceful hand on her chest.

"Estelflead."

Morwyneth repeated the gesture with her own name. A fleeting smile lifted the older woman's mouth and she peered outside their home, as though searching for unwanted onlookers, then instructed her daughter to retrieve a comb from a nearby chest. Estelflead excused herself, leaving Cwenfleda to do obediently as she had been asked: to brush Morwyneth's hair. Many rainstorms and nights under the elements had not been kind. At its longest, her hair sat no further than her chin, while elsewhere it remained short and wayward. Cwenfleda teased out the tangles one by one, restoring the hair to a short, layered style. From the same chest, Cwenfleda found a necklace made of wooden beads from an assortment of trees, their varying colours forming a design. She handed it to Morwyneth and gestured that she should put it on.

"*Giefu. Giefu.*"

Come the evening, the young women left for the celebrations. The drizzle had ceased, and the friends found a comfortable viewpoint from which to watch the activities: atop one of the wagons with its tarp pulled up on one side. As at Aberhabren, everyone positioned themselves around the camp's central fire. All the women gathered on the outskirts of the camp, whereas all the men congregated in the centre. It being difficult to see individuals among the uniform-clad warriors, Morwyneth could not find Sieghild or his leader in the throng of rowdy men. To their right a man blew an animal horn, and the tribe fell silent. Morwyneth and Cwenfleda settled themselves on a bed of skins.

Cwenfleda gasped, gripping the edge of the wagon in earnest, stretching up to see over heads of bystanders. Morwyneth followed her friend's gaze to find the leader moving through his men into the open. He began a speech, barking over the hush around him; strong-felt words emphasised by vigorous gesticulations. Morwyneth assumed it to be an invocation to their harvest gods. Lit from behind by the giant fire, the leader himself evoked the vision of a god. His last words faded on the night air and all the men answered with a roar, raising weapons and fists. Following the rite, they parted to form a horseshoe. The women, who had been standing to one side, moved in a procession into the horseshoe. They bestowed a kiss on each man, causing much hilarity. Some clutched the women in strong embraces, rousing husbands who shouted in jest from across the semi-circle.

The amorous procession soon ended, and women brought out a large cauldron Cwenfleda called *freols aeppel ealu*. Morwyneth understood it to be some form of spiced apple ale. When it reached them, they each took the small cup offered. On tasting it, Morwyneth found it to be sweetened with honey and flavoured with spices that warmed the tongue. A few men took up song while the ale was passed round, and this soon grew to encompass most of the camp. Some leaped up to dance round the fire. Morwyneth sat back and watched the joyous frivolity, fondly reminiscing about Lughnasadh at Aberhabren. As the evening wore on beer replaced the spiced ale, and a session of games began with wrestling, sprint racing, high jumping over swords and sword fights. Cwenfleda made no attempt to hide her immense pleasure when their leader stood up to challenge his ealdorman. Morwyneth, however, could not remove her eyes from Sieghild.

Beads of sweat ran down Wulfgar's face, his helmet pressing damp hair to his scalp. His sweat enhanced the sweet odour of the suede lining beneath the iron. He had already competed in several of the games, though his thirst for fighting had not been quenched. The camp fire burned into the side of his face, Tiw's hot breath spurring him on. Opposite him, Sieghild prepared to tackle him in friendly combat. He had other ideas. He intended to use the game to have some questions answered.

Sieghild gave a shallow bow, retaining eye contact. "Lord Wulfgar."

Wulfgar circled his friend. "Ealdorman Sieghild."

"Shall we draw?"

"When you like."

Sieghild drew his sword. "How about…"

"Now." Wulfgar unsheathed his sword and brought it up to block Sieghild's down blow. They pulled each other close, hilts tangled, and Wulfgar read the challenge in his friend's face.

"Leofgist says the Brytonic Wulfsuna are concerned about your behaviour."

Sieghild stepped back, disengaging the fight, dropping his sword. The crowd released their verbal disfavour with him. Wulfgar charged him, sword held with both hands, forcing the ealdorman to clash blades once, twice, and again they were leaning their bodies onto their hilts. Wulfgar remained unrelenting in his insistence to turn their friendly duel into a battle of words.

"I have never known you so lost in a maiden, Sieg. You are under a hex, friend, and I will not allow a woman to break us."

Sieghild replied through gritted teeth, "She is no ordinary woman."

Wulfgar found himself pushed into retreat, stumbling backwards from a forceful thrust by Sieghild. The crowd cheered loudly, no doubt enjoying seeing their headman overpowered. He had won almost everything else that night. He did not intend to give up now. He readied his stance and withdrew his seax in his right hand for good measure. Sieghild's eyebrows lifted. Humour: so, his ealdorman still existed inside the shadow. Wulfgar ran at him with two blades, only to be dashed away in a clash that sparked into the camp fire. The cheers of the crowd mocked his failure and he ran his dagger towards Sieghild's gut. Sieghild thwarted him, snatching an axe from his war belt and tearing the seax from Wulfgar's grasp. His glances to find the dagger were halted when Sieghild came back at him with sword and axe. Wulfgar grinned, knowing the game had at last begun.

"I know," said Wulfgar, "she has you sleepwalking when awake."

Wulfgar weighted his sword in his hand, taunting Sieghild. As his ealdorman charged him, he dived sideways. Their blades met, reflecting the fire out into the excited audience. Sieghild swung his axe down in a high arc. Wulfgar raised an arm to shield his face, the beard of the axe glancing off his wrist guard. He felt the blow reverberate from his elbow into his shoulder. Moving swiftly, he used his free hand to twist Sieghild. He locked him in an embrace, Sieghild's back landing against his chest. He brought the tip of his sword up beneath Sieghild's chin, grinning when the ealdorman released his axe onto the damp grass.

"Admit it," Wulfgar murmured in a growl, "she has swallowed your soul and you are bound to her every word."

Sieghild gave a false laugh. "Hah. You are worried that the Brytonic Wulfsuna will sense the unrest between us, not that a maiden has me in a hex."

Wulfgar shrugged. "I can worry about both."

"As you will," Sieghild replied, thrusting an elbow backwards and winding Wulfgar.

The headman inadvertently lowered his blade, reeling from the stomach punch to which his friend had given full strength. The following head butt was unexpected too, the clash of helmets stunning Wulfgar. He took several steps back to regain his footing. Sieghild rounded on him fast, advancing smartly with an upwards cut of his blade. Forced into a retaliating descent with his own sword, Wulfgar tried to fend off lingering dizziness with a shake of his head. Their weapons barely scraped, the crowd jeering at the near miss. Wulfgar stumbled again, pivoting on one foot to bring himself back around for a possible second attack. Sieghild paused.

"Enough talking," Sieghild ground out. "I had a mind to fight you when you made me tie her to the wagon. Let's have it."

Wulfgar laughed. He should have expected Sieghild to take the fun out of their friendly game. "Ah, Sieg, you are a man at last."

Sieghild unleashed a roar, and Wulfgar braced his feet into the ground. The ealdorman swung at him, their blades locking once again. Circling his sword, Sieghild prised the hilt from Wulfgar, who lost grip of his weapon and watched it tumble through the air behind his friend. Wulfgar pulled his axe from his war belt in time to meet eyes with Sieghild's turning back from watching the sword land on the grass. By Sieghild's frown, Wulfgar knew his friend had not finished with him. He stood fast as Sieghild ran at him, confident that he knew an axe better than a blade. As they met, Wulfgar hooked the beard of his axe over Sieghild's blade, twisting it from his hand. Sieghild drew his seax in haste, and they began a dance, waiting to see who would dare make the first attack.

Never one for waiting, Wulfgar lunged first. However, Sieghild proved the better judge of distance between them and swivelled away. The punch to his forearm shook the axe from Wulfgar's grip, his last weapon gone. Before he could respond, Sieghild grabbed him by the arm and used his back to roll Wulfgar over onto the ground. Landing heavily on his back, winded, Wulfgar knew he had lost when Sieghild's seax met his throat. A standing ovation poured round the camp fire, shouts and whistles reverberating off the trees. Wulfgar stared up at the face in shadow hanging over him, chasing away a fleeting concern that his friend intended to maim him.

"Let the Brytonic Wulfsuna wonder," Sieghild told him. "Let them all wonder about the nix. I will speak to her because she is of my mother's people, therefore she is part of me and I am part of her. Do you deny me that?"

Wulfgar swallowed, the blade pushing against his skin as he did so. "I would never deny you anything, brother. I would gift you my blade and my life if it meant you lived, but..."

"But what?" Sieghild asked.

Wulfgar smiled. "Can I stand now?"

Sieghild withdrew his seax and extended an arm, pulling Wulfgar to his feet. Wulfgar retained the grasp and hoisted Sieghild's arm in victory, standing back and allowing his ealdorman to take the applause. Sieghild removed his helmet and took a bow. When he turned to walk back, Wulfgar clasped his friend round the neck, shaking him affectionately.

"You know I do not deny you access to your mother's people, eh Sieg? We are here, in her land. You are here."

Sieghild dropped his gaze. "I know."

Wulfgar squeezed Sieghild's shoulder. "I have concerns because you are drifting away. I no longer know all of you, and it worries me. You have been different since we left Lindum."

Sieghild stopped, searing blue eyes alight. "I am not the only one."

"Yes." Wulfgar's grin faded briefly. "We'll do this again tomorrow, yes?"

Sieghild's face finally broke into a smile. "I need some ale first."

Sieghild gratefully received the cup of ale a male thrall brought him. He sank it fast and ordered another while he shrugged out of his padded leather tunic. Heaving his byrnie over his head, Sieghild caught the arm of the thrall as he moved away.

"Leave the jug."

He sat himself on the hides that had been tossed on the ground as makeshift seating and drank his ale, watching Wulfgar retrieving his lost weapons. Heahstan shouted as his lord came back over to them.

"You lost, weaner."

Ruffling sweat-soaked hair with his free hand, Wulfgar smiled. "Only the last event."

Heahstan roared with laughter. "Only the most important."

Sieghild caught his friend's sideways glance and continued to sip his ale. While Wulfgar set his sword and axe down and removed his byrnie and padded linen tunic, Lorri appeared with a cloth and started to clean his lord's blades of mud and grass. He had another young lad with him: a tall boy with strong arms for his age and a warrior's scowl beneath a long brown fringe.

"Ealdorman Sieghild," Lorri tendered nervously.

Sieghild spoke over his cup. "Lorri?"

"You have no *cnapa* to clean your blades, and I was wondering, my friend…"

Sieghild saved the young man torment and examined his friend, who scratched the back of his neck where newly shaved hair irritated him.

"Do you have a name?"

The boy straightened, arms stiff at his sides. "Frobe, sir."

"Frobe, you may clean my weapons and be my *cnapa*."

Sieghild hid a smile as Frobe's scowl lifted into a boyish grin and he began his duties earnestly. Meanwhile Wulfgar, inserting his clean seax into its leather scabbard on his belt, twisted and turned.

"Where do I get a drink round here?"

An empty-handed servant pointed to Sieghild, sitting with the jug beside him.

"Winner's privilege?" Wulfgar asked, sitting next to the jug and taking the handle.

Sieghild slammed a hand on top of the jug. "That is my jug and you must ask."

Wulfgar rolled his eyes. "Please, Sieg, may I have some of your ale?"

Sieghild mulled over the request for too long and Wulfgar snatched the jug, pouring himself a generous cup. "You owe me this ale. You almost broke my wrist with your battleaxe."

Sieghild coughed. "A scratch."

Wulfgar huffed through his nostrils.

"I was aiming for your head," said Sieghild.

Wulfgar rubbed the beard on his chin where Sieghild's seax had left a small nick in his skin. "Yes. I thought you had some kind of death wish on me."

"The feeling is mutual."

Sieghild gestured to a thin red mark on his neck made by Wulfgar's sword and caught the nix's eyes upon him once more. She sat alone in a wagon with neither Cwenfleda nor Godelina nearby. Wulfgar whispered in his ear.

"Caught in a hex."

"Intrigued," Sieghild corrected, emptying his ale cup and standing.

Wulfgar clutched his friend's ankle. "Remember our discussion."

"I am going to talk to her. You said you would not deny me that."

Released, Sieghild made his way deftly through seated groups of people, dancers and excited children. A power seemed to be guiding his feet, saving him from misfortune even though she had captivated him. He reached the wagon and she shifted anxiously, brushing strands of short hair from her face. He placed both hands on the side of the wagon as he greeted her.

"Hello."

She dissected him with her eyes. He did the same, drawn in to her dark blue eyes, much darker than his. The light from the fire picked out red flecks in her brown hair, which framed an impish face. As a nix, she had taken the guise of a pale and alluring goddess.

"You are alone." His voice brought her out of her fixation and she jumped slightly.

"I am fine."

She became unsettled, moving restlessly and looking for a way out. Sieghild caught the fleeting glimpse of fear in her eyes and immediately changed his approach. Leaning further into the wagon, resting his arms on the side, he put a hand out and caught her by one arm.

"Do not be afraid, little girl."

She frowned and pulled herself up, indignant. "I am woman."

In one swift manoeuvre, Sieghild made a foothold on the wheel and levered himself in beside her. She went to dive away from him and he caught her, his hands round both her arms.

"Hey, little woman."

His comment made her still for a moment so he released her. Her slim hand fondled the shorn ends of her hair, and he recalled how she had reached out to the serpents on his helmet. It struck him it had been four days and he did not yet know her name.

Unprompted, she said, "Morwyneth."

"Morwyneth." He smiled.

She returned the smile, settling her back against the wagon. He made himself comfortable and found he could think of nothing to say. The spider sensation, beginning in his fingertips, travelled up his arms and into his chest. With it came a thousand whispering voices in his ears, an army of spirits murmuring a forgotten language. He tried to focus his thoughts elsewhere in the hope the voices would leave. She spoke.

"Your name, what meaning has it?"

Her personal question caught him off guard and he answered after a pause. "Victory in battle."

She tilted her head to one side. "Has it been so?"

Stiffening, he replied, "Thus far, and many more will there be."

The crawling sensation increased, the rhythm of his heart leaping round his ribcage so that it rang in his ears. He began to believe Wulfgar, that the nix had him in a hex. He regretted diving so quickly into the wagon. His eyes narrowed to slits as he wagered whether she would become demon before his eyes and devour his head.

She countered, "You are so sure."

"The only sure thing is battle. That and death," he told her.

She stared at him for a long time, then said, "In future you may meet both on the same day."

Sieghild put a palm to his chest, his voice rising slightly in volume. "Then I shall join Woden, ruler of all, on the wild hunt."

"I shall wait for the Summerlands," Morwyneth told him calmly. "When I arrive I will be old and at peace."

He went to laugh and was restrained by her serious expression. Quietly, he asked, "How do you know this?"

"I see it," she said, shivering and wrapping her arms around herself.

He leaped up to pull the hemp tarp back over the one side of the wagon. As he did so he glimpsed Wulfgar staring back from beside the fire. His friend would not believe they had simply talked. Shrugging off his resentment, he finished securing the cover and sat back down, slipping on a cowhide. He landed in an ungainly way with his face next to Morwyneth's and an unfortunately placed hand on her upper thigh. She stared at him. His unfathomable discomfort multiplied, as did the thousand spirit voices eager to deafen him. In the distance the huge fire crackled and tribe elders continued their lamented singing. Her eyes had not left him. He withdrew his hand.

"What are you?" he asked. "Are you Dobunni?"

"I am Hwychas," she said, her expression hopeful as though the statement would tell him everything about her.

His mouth was gripped by a thirst, as though he had walked a hundred miles on a hot day, and the confines of the wagon enhanced the sweet smell of her. He licked dry lips and swallowed. "When you are near me, when you touch me, it is the strangest thing. I can feel things and see…"

She leaned towards him, bringing that delightful sweetness with her. "What do you see?"

Fighting to keep his eyes from her garnet lips, he murmured, "That which my own eyes have not witnessed."

She reached out her hands and he instinctively allowed her to take his. The energy that crawled through him surged in ferocity, physically jolting him. She gasped and released him, tumbling away from an invisible force that almost propelled her across the wagon.

Sieghild's eyes widened. "What?"

"You…" she stammered, crawling back to him on shaky hands and knees.

"I did nothing."

"No, wait." She reached out a hesitant hand to his face. No sooner had their skin touched than the power returned, concentrated. Morwyneth closed her eyes and Sieghild felt it ebb, as though she were controlling it. Memories, lost and dormant, rushed forward and met him; words and images buried for more than a decade. Tears welled in his eyes as he inhaled sharply, choking on a sob.

"*Mōdor.*"

Morwyneth went to withdraw her hand. Sieghild prevented her, a firm grasp on her wrist maintaining the connection.

"A moment," he begged. "A moment longer, please."

She snatched her hand from his face, ripping herself free of his tight hold. He felt the spiders leave his body and finally the spirits were silent.

"Why?" he asked.

"It is not safe to remain for too long. I learned that at great risk to my own life, the night before you found me."

He took both her hands in his. "Whoever you are and whatever you are, I am glad I found you."

"I am grateful to have been found."

She smiled and did not resist when he pulled her towards him to lie down, curling his body behind hers and settling an arm round her waist. He nestled his face in her hair and they drifted off to sleep.

CHAPTER NINE

Fosse Way,
Entering Caernwealas Along the West Coast

Walking past an enthusiastic Frobe holding Harsteda in check for him, Sieghild tried to erase thoughts of Morwyneth from his mind. Since their shared experience at Hlaefmass he had been unable to sleep. She haunted him. She bred a yearning he fought against every waking moment. The trundle of the wagons along the stony road would have been intolerable after so many miles had his thoughts not been bound to the nix. Quilted cloud hid screeching gulls from view while morning mist gradually revealed their surroundings. It seemed as though the gods were shrouding the real world from him; the gods, or the nix. Brawling men and the calls of local traders to view their goods for sale were but whispers in the distance. Even the clash of metal on anvil was a mere hint of a smithy at work. Visitors of many regions and dialects filled the approach to the market, a cacophony of words barely heard by Sieghild. He did not smell the stall selling the morning's fresh haul of pilchards, releasing its pungent aroma into the air in contrast to the sweetness of exotic fruits, wines and spices being plied by foreigners.

Guided by the strength of her power through his arms, Sieghild fell into a steady pace behind the last wagon. Morwyneth, hanging eagerly out of the back to witness the bustle of the market, did not see him approach. He relished the surprise he caused as she finally noticed him. Godelina immediately excused herself, gratefully receiving his assistance to aid her from the moving vehicle. He smiled from beneath his helmet, conscious he had duties to perform. He would not linger long.

"Some of us are heading for the harbour market to trade with the locals," he told Morwyneth.

"Can I go with you?" she asked. "I would love to see the market."

He tried to sound firm. "No, there are many bandits on this route. You will be safer here in camp with everyone else. Stay here with Godelina and I shall see you tomorrow."

Leaving her tore at his gut and brought back the searing pain. He stifled a grunt, hoping his grin would hide his agony from her as he turned away. Lord Wulfgar had sent for him, and he did not want to delay his duty further. He headed for his lord's wagon, currently fifth in the convoy. To confuse any enemy that may be watching, Heahstan had suggested they move Wulfgar's wagon regularly. This amused Sieghild as Wulfgar could rarely be found inside it. He used it for weapon storage more than he slept in it. When Sieghild found his headman the convoy had halted. Wulfgar was rummaging around in the back of his wagon, examining a collection of daggers. He had laid them out by blade shapes, handle materials and designs, inserting them into his war belt in turn.

"Sieg, come tell me what I am missing."

Sieghild shook his head. "No more daggers. If you possess any more, I fear you will stab me when next we embrace."

Wulfgar ignored his friend's refusal to assist him. "Have you organised the men for the harbour market?"

"Yes, My Lord."

Wulfgar selected a dagger with a carved deer's horn handle and engraved blade. Sieghild recognised it as Lord Wulfric's seax. Silence cloaked the air around them as both men recalled the Battle of the Fens and the Wulfsuna's great loss.

"Your father's," Sieghild murmured.

Wulfgar did not reply. He tossed the dagger between his hands. In his left he swung it from tip skyward to the floor, his hand deftly changing grip on the intricate handle as he made stabbing movements downwards. After several thrusts he stilled the blade, opening his grip to examine the design of wolves chasing and eating each other's tails.

"This is the death-light that will bring Eadmaer his final breath," Wulfgar hissed, sincerity in his promise. "That whore's son is lurking somewhere."

Sieghild made to leave and Wulfgar called to him over his shoulder.

"Sieg? Do you know what you are doing?" Wulfgar idly tossed pebbles with the toe of his boot.

"With the men?" Sieghild asked, shielding the fact he knew very well what Wulfgar meant.

"You know with whom I mean."

"I do not know. Do you?"

Wulfgar's shoulders rose as he inhaled deeply and held onto his breath for a moment. "As headman, I still do not know what I am doing. But with Eadmaer, all I know is that I cannot rest until he is dead."

Sieghild left Wulfgar to his thoughts and daggers, and returned to his men to finalise their visit to the harbour market. Half the thegns remained with their foot soldiers to guard the civilian wagons from local threats. Sieghild divided the remainder into groups, each with specific wares to acquire. He put Chapper in charge of a wagon to carry goods back to camp, while the cook and ale carts followed to obtain food and drink. Waiting until Wulfgar had appeared beside him, Sieghild gave the command for the civilian wagons to head off and make camp. Staring at the back of the wagons as they ambled down the road, Sieghild felt Morwyneth was thinking of him. A hand on his shoulder broke his thoughts.

"Come. Let us enjoy some wine." Wulfgar slapped Sieghild's arm. "There are figs here too, I hear."

Reluctantly Sieghild fell into step with his friend as they sauntered through the throng of traders and buyers. Unfortunately his mood did not match his location. It was an excellent market and he wanted to enjoy it. All manner of edible sea creatures were on offer, delicacies local to the south-west coastline, as well as more exotic finds. Armorican ships from the Gaul shores had brought spices from the East through Mediterranean seas, plus wines, fruits and slaves. A burly man dragged a chain of bound women up onto the harbour, a mixture of females from all continents: olive beauties from the East, fire-haired natives from Ierne Lande and ebony warrior maidens, tall and firm of skin.

Although Sieghild had witnessed similar, the scene distracted him. Morwyneth entered his mind. It had been fortunate he had found her, or else slavery may have been her fate. His gaze wandered out to the cool ocean billowing against the rocks, ships moored at the quay bobbing on the tide, including a passing Roman trade ship perhaps not long out of Tintagel. His gut wrenched, his heart becoming the victim of Thunor's hefty hammer, battering and bruising him from the inside out. He imagined he had heard his name, Morwyneth calling it. He instantly dismissed the notion, a sharp tap from a strong finger on his shoulder alerting him back to his duty.

"Here." Wulfgar thrust a fig into his hand.

Sieghild took it, watching Wulfgar tear open the fruit and devour the sweet flesh inside. Wulfgar winked, fig juice running down his bearded chin.

"These always remind me of women."

Receiving a jovial shove on his shoulder, Sieghild smiled at last. Wulfgar laughed, tossing the fig skin on the floor and wiping his chin with the back of his hand.

"Now you are with me, friend. Come, you can help me choose metal."

Sieghild allowed Wulfgar to drag him to a stall selling blades of all descriptions, unsure he should be encouraging the acquisition of yet another dagger. Wulfgar immediately found one he liked and picked it up, confidently turning the long knife in his hands to examine the craftsmanship. The narrow blade, as long as a forearm with a slight curve, ended in a blunt shape rather than a point. The hard, pale bone handle, faultlessly carved, sat well in the hand.

"What say you to this one?" he asked Sieghild.

"It is the blade of a king, My Lord."

Wulfgar ran a thumb down the edge of the thin curved blade and tightened his grip on the intricately carved ivory handle. "Then I shall have it."

Sieghild thought he heard a voice on the wind for the second time. He swung round, looking back in the direction of the road. Again he heard it and turned back to Wulfgar, wondering if his friend had spoken.

"You called me?" he asked Wulfgar.

"No."

He would have sworn on his life he had heard someone speak to him. Sieghild tried to convince himself it had simply been other voices raised in the market. Wulfgar showed him the hilt of his new dagger, a mystical animal with flaring nostrils and a long scaly body winding round the hilt.

"Ealdorman Sieghild."

The call to attention yanked Sieghild from his daydream. "Did you hear that?"

"Hear what?" Wulfgar asked.

"I heard my name."

"Yes. I called it."

"No." Sieghild glanced round feverishly. "Another spoke it."

"It is the wind."

The voice reached Sieghild's ears a fourth time, and on this occasion he knew. It was Morwyneth. He twisted on his heel, shouting over his shoulder as he departed at speed.

"The slave market."

He ran as fast as he could, a hand holding his scabbard from swinging against his leg. He knocked into customers and tripped over eel creels. He collided with a pottery stall, several pieces shattering as they hit the floor in his wake. Angry cries and profanities chased the air behind him as he neared the slave area and picked up speed. Finally he shoved through a line of people, including a Roman noble. The burly slave trader had the hair of a young woman in one hand, her small body writhing in his grasp. Sieghild tempered his pace. He had to be certain who the man had in his grasp. When the woman screamed, he knew instantly.

"Sieghild," Morwyneth cried once more.

The trader raised his free hand ready to strike her. Sieghild drew his sword and surged forward. He skewered the man under his right arm, the blade puncturing lung and heart before appearing through the front of his chest. Passers-by dispersed into a wide circle, gasping in panic. The large merchant choked on his final breath and collapsed, his knees breaking with a loud crack when they hit the cobbles. Posthumous blood spat over Morwyneth's tunic. She tore his hand from her hair, shuffling away from the dead man. Sieghild faced the crowds. The Roman noble shouted with raised palms, retreating backwards.

"Peace. Peace."

Sieghild peeled the merchant off his sword with his foot, chest still heaving from his run. The fat body landed with a slap on the floor of the dock. He looked at Morwyneth, her face drenched in tears. She sat transfixed, watching the trickle of blood from metal to stone.

"You killed him," she whispered.

The circle of interested public grew into a huge crowd. Sieghild knew they had to go. He held a hand out to Morwyneth, instinctively replying in Seaxan.

"*Ic bidde thu, becumen.*"

Morwyneth found strength to look up. "You killed him."

Sieghild heard Wulfgar calling him. He looked up to see his headman waving his drawn dagger, signalling they should leave. Sieghild beckoned the frozen Morwyneth a second time, taking her by the arm.

"*Giese. Becumen.*"

He led her at speed back towards the main road where they met with Wulfgar and a handful of warriors. Morwyneth flung herself behind Sieghild for protection, though Wulfgar paid her no heed. Dismissing the men at his side, he approached Sieghild.

"You could have been killed, Sieg."

Sieghild cast his eyes down briefly. "I knew the danger."

Scoffing through a wry laugh, Wulfgar's arms spread wide. "You were surrounded by Gauls."

"They were heavy with wine. We passed them on the way into the market."

"That may be. But why risk your life for her?" Wulfgar tossed a hand in Morwyneth's direction and she cringed further behind the ealdorman.

"She is travelling with us and as such is one of us. I defended her as I would any other member of the tribe."

"Pig shit." Wulfgar paced, pushing fingers into the hair at his temple and clutching a handful of curls. "What was she doing back here?"

"She must have followed us back and was taken as a slave."

"So you killed him?"

Sieghild looked away to the roaring sea, pulling Morwyneth's shaking body round into his embrace, resting his chin on her head. Wulfgar sighed, shifting his feet and glancing up the road to where camp had hopefully been constructed. Strumming fingers on his seax scabbard, he quizzed Sieghild again.

"She is just a Wealas, a stray. They could have had her. Why did you kill him?"

"He was going to strike her," Sieghild told him.

Wulfgar closely examined his seax blade for a moment. When he again looked up, Sieghild gestured to the road with a small lift of his chin.

"Go on ahead. The Gauls may send someone after me."

"Do not be too long," Wulfgar warned.

Sheathing his dagger, Wulfgar ran off. Sieghild released Morwyneth. Without words, he took her by the arm and approached the tree line. Dragging her behind him, he seethed at what trouble would await them. Torn by friendship, honour and his uncontrollable draw to the nix, Sieghild did not know where to direct his anger. He hurried Morwyneth along under the trees where she tripped over stones and protruding roots. With little time to catch up, the further they went, the heavier she became. The more she resisted his grasp, the angrier it made him. At some point between the market and camp, Morwyneth managed to disentangle herself from his hold and stopped dead. He marched back for her. She riveted herself to the spot, refusing to move as he tugged on her arm. She yelled at him, eyes searing with volcanic intensity.

"No."

Morwyneth rose up, trying to be as tall as she could be. Sieghild froze, sensing something. In the distance the sea rolled gently, while around them the trunks of the trees began to sway towards them, the branches shaking in a violent hiss of leaves. Morwyneth started to shake. The lower the trees bent, the more she shook. Her arms thrust forward, palms outermost. Sieghild found himself lifted from the floor by an unknown power. Like the giant hand of a god, it threw him against a tree. His sword fell from his grasp with the force. A moment later the invisible hand released him. He dropped to the floor, his lungs bereft of air. The hiss of leaves and creak of branches had ceased. He opened dazed eyes, rubbing a hand over the back of his head. Morwyneth ran to him, collapsing at his side, her cheeks burning crimson.

"Sieghild?"

"Who are you?" he asked, bewildered.

She smiled. "Morwyneth of Prenhwychas, forever in your debt."

Sieghild stared at her, reaching out a shaky hand to stroke her face with his knuckles. "No debt is owed."

"But you killed him."

He sat up. "He would have hurt you."

"You will not."

He knelt over her, lowering her body into the moss and fern of the forest floor. One of his hands reached for the nape of her neck, holding her prisoner to his enquiring eyes. She placed her hands on his byrnie and his chest leaped at her touch, as though she had burned him directly on the skin.

"Do you feel that?" he asked.

She nodded. "Yes, but I do not understand why."

"Do we need to know why?"

She shook her head and he bent down, running a quivering hand through her hair and down her cheek. He paused, unable to go on until he had shared his thoughts and feelings.

"I do not know if I love you," he told her. "I do not know why I want to do this. All I know is that I need to be part of you."

"I understand," she whispered, "I am not afraid. It was meant to be."

It was a spiritual union. Through the physical bond, they would know one another; questions would be answered by the gods and spirits they communed with. Sieghild captured her mouth, softly tasting her warm lips. Morwyneth sank into his embrace, wrapping her legs round him, her magic power humming through their bodies.

When they arrived in camp, the sun had dropped below the land, draping a gold tinge across the grass, the trees throwing long shadows. Emerging from the coppice, they were spotted immediately by a lookout whose hand signal drew two men on horseback into the open: Trunhild and Leofgist, galloping out to meet them. Sieghild felt Morwyneth's hand close more tightly round his, and he pulled her close. The thegns halted their horses. Leofgist spoke quietly, his face drawn.

"Morwyneth must go with Trunhild. You must come with me, Ealdorman Sieghild."

Sieghild lifted Morwyneth onto the rear of Trunhild's horse and watched them ride to the wagon village several yards in the distance. There were perimeter guards hidden everywhere. Under watchful eyes, Sieghild walked beside Leofgist as he rode towards the headman's residence. Wulfgar had once again had a large tent erected as his lord's hall. At the entrance, two pairs of guards stood aside. Unsure what to expect, Sieghild sent one hand to his baldric to steady his scabbard. He paused with a hand on the tent flap, taking a deep breath. For the first time in his life, he did not know what would confront him when he faced his lifelong friend. He entered.

Wulfgar sat motionless at the back of the tent on a generous mountain of straw and hides, his face unreadable behind the small fire burning in the centre of the room. Swirls of smoke rose through a hole in the top of the tent. On the opposite side of the fire lay a smaller pile of straw and hides. Sieghild stepped forward and stopped short of the seat provided. The scent of ale lingered thick in the air. Wulfgar hung his head low, shaking it. He released a long sigh and spoke in a low voice that had been glazed in sweet alcohol.

"We have known one another since birth, shared mother's milk, ale, fights and women, and yet I do not know the man who stands before me now. There is time enough to commune with the otherworld. Death in battle will send you into the arms of Hel swiftly enough, without tempting Her by allowing dark spirits to draw you into their bosom."

"She is no dark spirit, Wulfgar."

"*Lord* Wulfgar," his headman corrected sharply.

"You have not asked me here as your friend?"

Wulfgar stood to pace. "I cannot deal with you as my friend. And I cannot convince everyone she is not a dark spirit. So, for your own safety, you must distance yourself from the nix."

"Her name is Morwyneth."

Wulfgar pinned Sieghild to the spot with a searing grey stare. "The nix. You will stay away from her."

"I feel that will be difficult now, My Lord."

Wulfgar walked round the fire and stood in front of Sieghild, who turned his face away from his lord. Wulfgar grabbed him by the chin, pulling his head round.

"You should be happier than that after making love to a woman."

Sieghild stepped back a pace, eyes flying wide open. Wulfgar wandered over to a table where a jug stood with two cups. He hurled one at Sieghild and it landed on the floor. Sieghild picked it up.

Wulfgar poured himself a drink, attention focussed on his cup. "As I said, I have known you since birth. It is written across your face as though the scribe used charcoal. Besides, you have moss in your hair."

Sieghild ran a hand through his hair and took his cup to the table, filling it. It was mead. He took a large mouthful of the honeyed alcohol, closing his eyes as its warmth slid down his throat. For a brief moment his thoughts returned to Morwyneth's arms and her sweet body. His lord continued, breaking Sieghild's contemplation, and he opened his eyes.

"You know you have brought this trouble upon yourself," said Wulfgar, pointing at him with cup in hand. "If Gauls catch up with you, they are yours to fight. I can lend you no men."

Sieghild watched the hand Wulfgar dashed aside to emphasise his point. Yes, it was true. A lord could not lend men for a personal fight such as would find him if the Gauls tracked him down, though it was unlikely. Most of them were drunk, and it had all been over too swiftly for anyone to make sense of it. He realised he had not answered. He replied quietly.

"I understand."

Wulfgar threw the last of his mead into his mouth and looked at Sieghild, clearing his throat of trapped emotion. "Your nix is now a prisoner. She cannot wander freely through the tribe."

Again Sieghild answered, "I understand."

Wulfgar set his cup down loudly, straightening his back, trying to look down at his ealdorman with authority. "And you are not to see her. Is that clear?"

Sieghild could not agree. "No, My Lord. I do not understand."

Wulfgar's mouth tightened. "You are not to see her."

Sieghild stepped backwards, hand moving to the hilt of his sword. He had to see Morwyneth again, and he would not allow his friend, or his lord, to prevent that. He watched Wulfgar's eyes narrow, fingers on his left hand twitching near his scabbard. Sieghild ran a finger and thumb over the peace ribbon slung around the hilt, pausing to rub the amber bead used to weight it. He realised then how friends became enemies; how allies became foes, recalling Eadmaer on the jetty removing his peace ribbon prior to the attack on the Wulfsuna.

"Why can I not see her, My Lord?" he asked.

Wulfgar, too, had noticed the minute move and flexed his sword arm in response, his tone stern. "Because, my dear Ealdorman, any wrath you have brought upon yourself I consider you have also brought upon the Wulfsuna. It cannot happen again. This confirms my suspicions that the nix has you in a hex. You do not know your mind."

Sieghild's jaw tightened. "Her name is Morwyneth."

With a loud roar, Wulfgar tossed the small table over, splashing mead into the fire and igniting tall flames. Sieghild flicked the peace ribbon off the hilt of his sword and prepared for his lord to draw his weapon. He did not, instead turning, yelling and waving his arms.

"In Frigg's name, forget her! You've had her. Do as I command."

Sieghild caught Wulfgar glancing at his sword, the hilt hovering proud of the scabbard, almost drawn. His friend's nostrils flared like a stallion's after the scent of a mare, eyes narrowing. Disbelief crossed Wulfgar's features, and Sieghild knew he had made a mistake. Slowly he sheathed his blade, securing the peace ribbon once more. However, he feared it was too late. Wulfgar ran a hand across his mouth, biding time, turning it into a fist and chewing on his knuckles.

"Sit," Wulfgar said eventually. "We've a way to go yet. I have more mead and three kegs of ale."

The corner of the wooden table crackled in the fire. Wulfgar kicked it free of the flames and wandered off to rummage in a chest. Sieghild sank onto his seat, removing his baldric and war belt. He caught a fresh cup Wulfgar threw at him and sat in silence. Wulfgar brought over a keg of ale and offered him the first pour. Accepting it, Sieghild saw Wulfgar attempting to hide a smile of satisfaction.

"You won the battle of words. You are happy," said Sieghild.

Wulfgar's expression regained a serious demeanour. "I should not have to win it. You should obey me."

Sieghild gestured round the tent. "There are no thralls present. I thought you had asked me here as your friend."

Wulfgar lowered his voice and glanced at the doorway. "I could not have witnesses to what we discussed. That is why there are no thralls. You are here as my ealdorman, Sieghild. An ealdorman who endangered his tribe for his own desires."

Sieghild returned to silent contemplation, drinking his ale and losing his thoughts to the fire. Wulfgar removed his weapons and tunic, as always keeping his wrist cuffs on. He slumped onto the floor, swigging copiously from his cup and refilling it immediately. Neither man spoke for a while.

"If we drink enough, will it help?" Sieghild asked, a few cups later.

"Yes." Wulfgar smacked his lips as he finished another cup, reaching for the keg. "It will help us forget that I am a lord and you are an ealdorman. It will help me forget that if you disobey me again, I will have to punish you and I do not know if I can do that to my friend."

As Wulfgar looked up, face stony, Sieghild knew their friendship had reached a place it could not come back from. The boundary had been set, and to infringe it would hold consequences, for both of them.

chapter ten

Wulfsuna Camp,
Caernwealas, South-West Coast of Bryton

Morwyneth sat alone in the back of a wagon. She had been tossed off horseback and bundled in like a sack of raw wool. Outside stood a guard, his hand on his sword. Since falling asleep in Sieghild's arms two nights ago she had slept soundly, unmolested by nightmares, no longer plagued by vivid images of her departure from Prenhwychas. She believed she had him to thank. Mother Earth's energy had coursed through them that night. Only with her mother had she previously felt such spiritual power. Addictive, like an herbal drug, she had yearned to be with him, to explore their connection.

Today that had happened, though not as she would have envisaged. She had not meant to lose control. Panic had gripped her though, ribbons of colour transcending her vision. She had felt her feet sinking into the earth, her hands heavy with a crushing force. Anwen had answered her call, as she had during the storm after leaving Aberhabren. "Take heed. Release the earth and be freed," her mother had told her in a whisper breathed above the waves. Her gift had receded, the energy leaving her limbs, though too late to save Sieghild from injury.

Too distracted by emotion, she realised she had had her first sexual encounter. There had been no love, although they shared a common love to unite. Both of them had wanted to join, to explore the spiritual power that appeared to constantly draw them together. He had smelled of wood smoke and his breath had been sweet from fruit he had eaten. She recalled his mail shirt chafing her breasts through her woollen tunic. In response her gift had erupted in her abdomen, her hands and feet becoming hot as stones in a fire. Although the union had been brief, the uncomfortable ride on the horse had exacerbated her swollen flesh and she had begun to bleed. She could find nothing in the wagon to aid her and so continued to wait silently.

Since leaving Prenhwychas she had done no more than survive on a journey with no ending, no purpose. She began to wonder whether she had found her purpose, with Sieghild at the core of it. In his position, perhaps he could persuade their leader to return to Prenhwychas. They were a tribe of many strong warriors who could save her village from the descending blue north men. She did not know when this invasion would occur, although she had confidence that those who watched over her would assist. In the confines of a tent, the raised voice of the tribe's leader chastised Sieghild. She burned with shame that she had once again been the cause, and felt her plans to save Prenhwychas slip away with the last of the sun's rays.

She began to cry. She missed the comfort of Godelina's singing. The older woman had a varied repertoire and always chose the appropriate melody for the mood, though she also knew when to leave a moment's quiet. A curt whistle from the guard made her look up. Bewildered, and attempting to curb her tears, Morwyneth crept over to see what he wanted.

"I am Trunhild," he announced in her language, taking a second glance. "Are you crying?"

She shook her head, not wanting to appear weak to these savages. Looking warily around him, the soldier climbed into the wagon and drew her into his arms. His presence brought with him the stench of boiled cabbage and sweat. He rocked her gently, his warmth comforting and the bristles on his shaven head tickling her brow.

"Do not fear. It will be fine," he assured her, releasing her.

"I have bled," she told him, blushing in the darkness.

"I will fetch one of the women."

He left her for a while and she realised the shouting had ceased. The camp had fallen into silence, leaving merely the sounds of nature in the moonlight. Trunhild returned with Estelflead, who brought cloth scraps and a small posy of chamomile to infuse in hot water, which she held out to Morwyneth in a small pail. Morwyneth smiled at the chamomile. Menstrual cramps were not the cause of her bleeding. She smiled gratefully and they left her alone to wash. Morwyneth considered escaping, though Trunhild returned all too soon. He leaned into the wagon.

"Do not fear," he whispered. "It will be fine. It will be."

He resumed his guard of her, and she stared at the back of his head. Unable to wholly trust these people now, she forced her heart to believe he spoke the truth. Eventually sleep claimed her.

Deep into the night Morwyneth woke, roused by the heat of another body behind her and a soft kiss on her neck. She sat up with a start. Sieghild placed a finger over her parted lips.

She whispered frantically, "The guard."

He stroked her arms. "We are safe."

She frowned and refused to lie back with him, pushing his hands from her. "I have brought you trouble again. It is not safe for you to be here." Her chest constricted in pain, searching the darkness for Trunhild's shadow and realising he no longer stood guard. "What if your leader should find out? I heard him, shaming you."

"Trust me. All is fine." He attempted to fold her in his arms.

She fought him. "Do not deny it. I heard him. How can you stand by him?"

"I trust him as my friend." Sieghild's words did not placate her.

"I do not understand. How can he be your friend and speak to you so?"

Firmly he replied, "Because he is both to me, my leader *and* my friend, and as my leader I must pay him respect."

Shaking her head, she said, "You should not have saved me."

He grasped her shoulders. "I had to. There is more for you in this life. You have not lived yet."

She sank into a deep pile of sheepskins which had not been there when she fell asleep, the weight of his body over her resonant of their elopement in the forest. He took her open mouth in his and pressed her hips into his body with one of his large hands. She felt slender in his muscular arms; a fine thread in the hands of a giant. He released her lips.

"Your eyes...when you look at me, I fear I shall never find my way out of those blue depths."

He came back to her and she opened up to him a second time. An image of blood running from the tip of a sword pierced her thoughts. She closed her eyes tight, not wanting to relive the murder on the dock, and abandoned herself to pleasure.

In the morning Sieghild had gone. However, Trunhild gallantly stood guard. Bright and chirpy, he whistled happily, waving when he heard her move. His whistling continued while Morwyneth stretched languorously on the sheepskins. The bright day came as welcome relief from the recent bad weather. Free from the mist, birds sang loudly in celebration. On hearing footsteps she sat up, hoping it would be Sieghild. A thin warrior came bearing a plate of bread, berries and cheese. Trunhild greeted him with a grin, pretending to take the plate as his own. The skinny man sidled past Trunhild and handed it to Morwyneth, secreting a few berries for himself first.

"When can I come out?" she asked of him.

The warrior spoke, and Trunhild translated, "You cannot."

"Not at all?" she gasped.

The man clasped his hands, pretending to pee, imparting more instructions that Trunhild relayed to her. "If you need to go to your toilet I am to call Estelflead, but you must return immediately."

Distracted by a slap on his arm, Trunhild turned to listen to his companion. He waited until the man had left them before speaking to Morwyneth.

"When you have eaten I am to tie you to the back of this wagon as they need the storage inside for supplies."

Trunhild did not return to his whistling. Morwyneth chewed slowly on some bread, growing ever more tortured from her confinement. Her mind turned once more to thoughts of escape. She knew they were in South Gymraeg, and that the convoy could move on again any day. Sieghild had mentioned his people were looking for land to settle, though how long they intended to spend searching for it she did not know. Desperate to ask for assistance to return to Prenhwychas, she did not feel it would be possible to approach Sieghild, not now that he had fallen from favour with his leader.

A warrior's voice bellowed. They were on the move again. Trunhild hurried her out of the wagon, carrying out Leofgist's request and tethering her by her wrists to the rear of the wagon. Men loading boxes and sacks into the empty wagon knocked her sideways with their broad shoulders as they swung sacks of grain. A couple of them elbowed her out of their way, their fierce scowls confusing her. She could not imagine what she had done to earn their disfavour. With the loading almost complete, the same two men spat on the floor near her feet, muttering a small word at her she did not understand.

"*Nix.*"

Dusk fell on a long day's stumbling behind the wagon, and Morwyneth hoped her agony would end. Her wrists were sore and her feet blistered. She visited her crystal tunnel to ask her watchers for guidance. The spirits were unnaturally silent. She took it to be a test of her capabilities to find her own path. She would have to read her own destiny, revealed through dreams and omens; through glimpses of particular animals, the cries of birds or objects discovered on the ground.

Trunhild rode beside her, occasionally whistling to break his own boredom. When he could be certain there were no eavesdroppers, he taught her Saesnig. A few simple terms were easy to remember, partially resembling her words. Others were completely foreign to her, though she tried her hardest to memorise them.

Trunhild looked around them again, ensuring no one was within earshot. "*Ic thonc thu.* I thank you."

Morwyneth repeated the words cautiously.

Trunhild smiled. "Good. Remember it thus, *thonc* as the sound at the end is similar to your word, *diolch*."

"*Thonc, diolch.*"

He grinned broadly. "Good."

She smiled. "Sieghild will be happy to know..."

"Tell no one," he interrupted, his brow creasing into a deep frown. "You will be safer if you can speak their language, but do not trust them."

"Are you not one of them?"

Trunhild straightened in his saddle. "I am born of this isle. My loyalty is first to this land that has cradled my ancestors. Second is my loyalty to the Wulfsuna."

He rode off, and soon after the convoy came to a slow stop at the roadside. Morwyneth feared Trunhild's convictions would not be well received by their leader. She did not understand why he felt it dangerous for her to share her knowledge of Saesnig, though she adhered to his warning. She could trust very few around her and Trunhild seemed to want to assist her, albeit at a risk to his own safety. Born a Bryton as she had been, they shared a birthplace. Trunhild returned on foot with some cold mutton, resting the plate on the back of the wagon. Morwyneth's hands, having been tied separately, gave her some freedom of movement and she fed herself. Though tough and cold, she ate the mutton hungrily, tearing and chewing on it like a vixen at a kill.

"How are your wrists?" Trunhild enquired.

Morwyneth dropped her meal and looked at her skin after a day's imprisonment. Red and broken, in some places the rope had almost cut her to bleeding. Trunhild left a second time and brought back two pieces of linen. He untied one hand at a time, wrapping each wrist in linen and replacing the rope over the fabric to reduce further chafing.

"I'll have Estelflead look at them later."

"Why are you helping me?"

He looked warily round before replying, "I am Wulfsuna, but of Bryton."

"Wulfsuna?" she repeated.

It being the tribe name, Trunhild realised he had not thought to translate it. "Wolf Sons," he told her.

Many images and words rushed forth. Morwyneth closed her eyes to examine them all individually: Dudley's parting phrase that she would meet someone who would help her find peace; Anwen's advice to let the wolf in. Causing a gasp, her seer's sight took her to a battlefield, the debris of strewn bodies decaying into bloodied soil beneath. Sun haze obscured a coppice from out of which came a creature of the night. Across the mortality ran a grey wolf. Morwyneth cut herself abruptly from the vision and opened her eyes. Trunhild rested a warm hand on her bound ones, attentive.

"Morwyneth? What is it?"

"I saw battle," she said.

"I am certain you are right." Trunhild pulled his mouth tight. "We are here to find land to settle together, we Wulfsuna of Bryton and those from Germania. Our lord was uniting us after twenty years."

Morwyneth looked towards the front of the wagons. "Your lord? The man with pale hair who is…"

"Not him," Trunhild snapped, immediately softening his tone and his expression for Morwyneth's sake. "He is no leader I recognise. No, his father: a great man of whom my father spoke constantly and revered in our Mead Hall."

"Where is he?"

"He is dead, murdered by a friend who betrayed us all. It is not a good omen that such a great warrior was lost before his feet could touch the soil of this land."

"Is Sieghild a Wulfsuna of Bryton?"

Trunhild shook his head. "No, though I believe his mother was of this isle. I pity him for having befriended the son of our lord, that wild devil-warrior…"

"Thegn Trunhild." The wild devil-warrior glared down at them from atop his horse, iron wrist guards glinting in the last of the light, bare-chested beneath a grey wolf pelt and without helmet. "You are to feed her, not tell her sagas."

Trunhild fidgeted with his belt, scratching the back of his neck with shaky fingers. "Yes, Lord Wulfgar."

Morwyneth's hands began to burn, not from her wounds but from her gift. She could not remove her gaze from the muscled torso under the wolf skin. He *was* wild: a fearsome beast; a wolf in a man's body. He lingered, restraining his horse each time she made to leave. She exhaled, snorting noisily through grey velvet nostrils. He leaned forward to rub her neck, soothing her. Morwyneth tried to push her energy back into the earth, to quell it. Daring to face his intimidating eyes, once more she found herself on the bloody battlefield, staring at an advancing grey wolf. She glanced away from Lord Wulfgar, shaking her head to dispel the vision, and heard him ride off.

"Say nothing of our conversation, I beg you," Trunhild implored her. "He would have me beaten for the words I have spoken against him."

Morwyneth reassured him with a smile. A man approached the rear of the wagon and hauled out a barrel of ale. Trunhild eyed it enviously and made an enquiry; Morwyneth guessed for whom it was intended.

The man replied, "Lord Wulfgar." He eyed Morwyneth for a moment, before hoisting the barrel onto his shoulder and hastily retreating. Reminded of the men who had loaded the wagon that morning, she queried their behaviour.

"Trunhild," she asked, "what is *nix*?"

"Where did you hear that?" He searched the vicinity again, checking they were alone.

"This morning," she told him, "two men loading the wagon said it to me and spat on the floor. What were they calling me?"

Trunhild, seeming unable to face her, sought solace in the ground. "It is a river witch, a beautiful maiden who lures men into water to meet their deaths."

"Why would they think that of me?" she asked, a frown creasing her smooth forehead.

Trunhild looked up. "You were wet when we found you. Many suspect our enemies summoned you to lure us into danger."

Morwyneth swallowed tears, refusing to be disheartened. It appeared she had left Prenhwychas only to be found by foreigners who viewed her with equal contempt. She called on her mother silently, wondering why Anwen had sent her into the lair of these wolves.

"Take heart." Trunhild rubbed her arm gently. "All will be well."

"Do you think I am a river witch?" she asked plaintively.

He grinned. "If you are, maybe you can take Wulfgar and leave the rest of us?"

He went. She did not know where. Alone, surrounded by people who did not trust her, who feasibly hated her and would kill her if she posed such a threat, she did not feel safe. The waxing moon had risen in the sky, allowing the sun to rest until morning. It burned amber in the dying sunset, the tops of the trees ablaze with fire. It reminded Morwyneth of home, the many times she had witnessed the day's end on the brow of Bryn Hwychas, Huweyn's villa painted with auburn light. Tiredness drew the last strength from her and she sank to the ground, her ties only long enough for her to sit with her arms held in front of her head. She leaned her forehead on her bound wrists and closed her eyes.

A while later she stirred. Night had fallen and the moon's blue light bounced off leaves of nearby trees. Snores and the low murmurs of horses intermingled with an owl's cry and scurrying nocturnal mammals. A hand closed around her mouth and she tossed violently on her ropes. Behind her muffled squeals she recognised Sieghild's whispered voice.

"Be still. It is me, little woman."

He released her mouth and she gasped his name. "Sieghild."

He placed a finger on her lips and searched the shadows around them. He untied her wrists, leaving the ropes attached to the wagon, and led her into the woods. After two dozen or so paces he halted and pulled her into an embrace. He had removed his chain mail and weapons. She clung to him, burying her face in his tunic. At that moment he represented all she had; one of few she could trust.

He set her away from him, hands on her arms. "Has Trunhild cared for you?"

She nodded. "He was talking of your leader."

Sieghild's eyes darkened. "My leader, my friend."

Morwyneth continued, "He seemed angry with him, yet afraid of him."

"Come." Sieghild gestured to a moss-covered log and they sat. "When we met Trunhild and his warriors, they were late by a day. Lord Wulfric had been killed by our supposed Angle allies and Wulfgar was angry. He did not receive Trunhild well and it has not made for a good friendship between our people."

"I do not think your people like me either."

"What?" His face contorted in disbelief.

"I know that they fear me, that they believe I am *nix*." In using the Seaxan word she could see she dug a deeper wound in him.

He gazed back towards the road. "The day we found you, you were wet…"

She placed a finger on his lips. "The day you found me, a new friend had left me for his own journey. He was a *scop* and he told me I would meet someone who would help me bring peace."

Sieghild removed her hand from his lips, placing a kiss in her palm. Solemnly he said, "To have peace, first there must be war."

"War is coming. I have seen it, and that is why I need to return to Prenhwychas with warriors who will bring peace to my village once more. That same day, my mother came to me in spirit. She said I would find a wolf."

He grinned, moonlight reflecting off his teeth. "I would say you found many wolves."

"You found me."

His smile waned, eyes searching hers. "I believe you found me. And your eyes could see so much more than war alone. Your eyes could see all worlds, all beings, all things." He caressed her cheek with the back of his hand as though she were fragile pottery.

She closed her eyes to his touch. "I only see that which is necessary for my path. I cannot use it selfishly." His hand dropped and her eyelids shot open.

"You cannot show me my mother?" he asked, sliding off the log to his knees and taking both her hands.

"No, Sieghild. I would want nothing more than to please you, but your path is written. It is different to mine. The loss of your mother, your life here in the Wulfsuna, all of this is your journey."

He considered what she had told him, expression briefly becoming bleak at her refusal. "I understand," he said finally.

He slid his arms behind her, pulling her onto him. She straddled his thighs, winding her arms instinctively round his neck. He gripped her buttocks, bringing her hips closer to his.

"Then I will simply be with you, for you are part of my journey also."

She smiled as he took her in his embrace, resting her down upon ferns and pine needles. Without further words he pulled her into the curve of his body, a warm hand resting on her abdomen. The comforting rhythm of his breathing lulled her to sleep.

Morwyneth opened her eyes and found herself alone. A bright full moon illuminated the silent night. She heard breathing; not the slow breathing of a man asleep, however, but the fast panting of a four-legged beast. Nearer and nearer it came. Paralysed by fear, she held her breath. In an instant a wolf leaped upon her. Mouth snarling and drooling, its front feet pinned her shoulders to the ground. Sharp teeth glistened bright white in the moonlight, and hostile grey eyes froze her heart. It drew back, ready to lunge at her throat.

She woke in a cold sweat, panting and trembling. Behind her, Sieghild lay in a deep sleep. She knew the image to be of her own creation, a message from the Dark Mother who inhabits all souls. Anwen had often spoken of She who knew the innermost fears and desires of all men and women. It would seem her fear of Wulfgar had transformed into a vivid nightmare of a real wolf. Morwyneth knew the nightmare held an important message, although she did not wish for her thoughts to linger on it. As dawn broke into a cold, dry morning, Morwyneth made a deal with herself. She would become Seaxan in every respect. She would use all her time, all her confinement, to secret away this learning, for it would save her and help her to save Prenhwychas.

CHAPTER ELEVEN

The Fosse Way,
North-East of Bathumtun and the Spring of Sulis

They made camp and remained there for many days. A quarter-moon passed by Sieghild's reckoning. He continued to see Morwyneth during snatched moments and felt a small victory in providing her with the brief interludes of freedom from her tethered existence. Morwyneth possessed a gift that he wanted to understand, for it soothed the ache of the Motherland in him. He did not understand why Wulfgar could not see how valuable she could be.

Wulfgar's mind rested on other things. Their headman had decided the Wulfsuna were short of trained warriors. Civilian camp had become a training camp, the constant clash of sword on sword and the bumps, grunts and punches of hand-to-hand combat now familiar background sounds. Another day of training lay ahead of them, with Sieghild wishing he could spend it with Morwyneth rather than a score of sweating novices. He watched the jumble of thralls and farmers as they gathered under an oak, arguing over wooden swords and an assortment of reclaimed foreign shields.

Leofgist wandered over. "I prefer it when our wagons are moving."

Sieghild sighed. "Yes. We have stayed in camp far too long for my liking."

"Can you not tell him? He is your friend."

"Lord Wulfgar?" Sieghild shrugged. "I have told him. He knows my thoughts."

"So why all of this training? Is he afraid of meeting Eadmaer?"

"He does not want to encounter Eadmaer without enough skilled warriors to hand."

Leofgist laughed. "There is no telling when we will meet the Angle Boars. We may never be ready."

Sieghild was going to reply when Heahstan walked past him without acknowledgement. He fell into step behind the eldest thegn, calling after him. Heahstan halted abruptly though did not turn round. Sieghild caught up and came round to face him. Leofgist approached, seeming as curious as Sieghild to know why the thegn had ignored him.

Sieghild asked again, "Heahstan?"

A deep frown preceded a huff of air from beneath the big white beard. "Do not waste your breath on me."

"Waste my breath?"

Heahstan glared at Sieghild. "After the mess you left at the harbour market, we had to persuade some local muscle you had scarpered. It seems you scared some wealthy customers away. They were not happy."

Sieghild spread his arms. "I only wanted to protect one of our own."

"You mean one of *your* own." Heahstan pointed a large hand at him. "I thought you a wiser man than that, Sieghild."

Sieghild stepped forward, chasing the thegn as he made to walk away. "We are here to settle in these lands, the land of my mother. Should we not consider them fellow kin?"

Heahstan considered his ealdorman with a deep frown. "By all means, though you could have saved her without murdering a Gaul slave trader with half an army wandering round the market."

Leofgist interjected, "They were drunk, Heahstan."

Sieghild laughed derisively. "I do not think he would have listened with simply a blade at his throat."

Heahstan smiled wryly. "We will never know now, will we?"

"How else could I have saved her?" asked Sieghild, uncertain of how to placate the older man.

Heahstan waved a large hand. "If this nix means so much to you, I am sure our lord would have paid a thrall's price for her had the trader resisted your suggestion. Me," he prodded his broad chest with a thick finger "I would have left her to her fate and then perhaps you would be free from her witch's hex."

Both men watched Heahstan walk off, contemplating the old man's mood. Leofgist slapped Sieghild on the arm.

"He is sore. It will pass."

Sieghild shook his head. "He is right. I did not have to kill the man."

"It is done," Leofgist told him, grinning. "Come. Let us batter some volunteers. That always makes me feel good."

Almost a full moon hung in the clear sky. Morwyneth nibbled at the remnants of some bread she had been given for supper, wondering how she could be so hungry from sitting idle. She sipped from the small portion of sweet ale she had been given to wash down the dry crumbs of the old bread. Trunhild appeared. He seemed more hurried than usual. He tossed an armful of clothes inside the back of the wagon and showed her some brown horse hair.

"I cut this from my mare's tail. It is a similar colour to your own. I have seen other women use it to lengthen their hair for rites and festivals." From the back of his belt he pulled out a small dagger with a blade the length of his palm, and handed it to her. "I have this for you. It is a symbol of freedom. You deserve it, but tell no one you have it."

"Can I show Sieghild?" she asked smiling, eyes widening expectantly.

"He may not come tonight," Trunhild informed her.

"I know." She dropped her head. "He has not visited me every night."

Trunhild shuffled round, leaning past the side of the wagon before speaking. "He is wary of discovery."

"Yes." Morwyneth examined the small blade. "I expect it must be difficult, trying to visit me at odd times and on odd days so that he is not discovered."

"Yes, difficult and dangerous." Trunhild took the dagger from her hands and leaned towards her, waving it. "Tell no one you have this. Understand? Or it could mean punishment for both of us...or worse."

Removing an empty sack from the wagon, which he must have hidden previously, Trunhild stuffed it full of the clothes and slipped the dagger inside also. He slid the sack behind some barrels, and with a brief smile handed her the horsehair and left. Morwyneth fingered the horsehair, remembering her mother's words "When horsehair told of whom to wed". A sickening pit opened up in her stomach and she felt as though part of her had been torn away. She fell into a vision and saw a warrior lying dead, slain in the back by the sword of another. Morwyneth cringed from the image and tossed the horsehair into the wagon, extinguishing the vision.

She looked around her quickly. Shepherd's modest flock huddled beneath trees, each with a leg tethered to the next and finally secured to a trunk. They were quiet and resolute, much like Morwyneth. The foxes began their cries, screams resonant of strangled women echoing around them. The sheep became restless at the sound, their sleeping canine companion waking instantly. The dog growled a low and hardly audible rumble. Morwyneth rose to her feet and carefully stalked the tree line. An owl hunting overhead startled her as it rustled leaves landing on a high branch.

Watching the animals intently, Morwyneth likened herself to the sheep. Sieghild, her trusted guard, watched over her at night and protected her from fiercer creatures, such as prowling wolves. She remained fearful of Lord Wulfgar, refusing to acknowledge either he or the Wulfsuna was the wolf Anwen had advised she let into her life. Her thoughts returned to the brief vision she had experienced while holding the horse hair. Reluctantly, Morwyneth slid her hand into the wagon and withdrew the clump of hair. Rubbing it between her fingers, she closed her eyes. Inhaling deeply, she felt the cool night air and the scent of the trees tease her senses. The sweet ale lingered on her breath and she thirsted for more.

The vision returned, embellished. Iron clashed in the distance, overlaid by the cries of men at war. The ground, soaked crimson, lay wrecked and dug into with battling feet. She heard Wulfgar's name called. Morwyneth tried to view him in the throng of men and beaten bodies. The vision broke briefly, dragging her to face a warrior's chest. She gasped as a sword came through it. Blood dripping from the tip of the blade ended her glimpse of the violent scene.

Morwyneth opened her eyes, trying to swallow with a dry throat. She wiped moisture from her eyes and replaced the horse hair in the wagon. The foxes had ceased their calls and the dog had settled back down beside the flock. She heard footsteps. Sieghild appeared, his face grey revealing tension as well as bruises from training. He untied her ropes.

"It was a longer day than I had thought it would be. Wulfgar wanted me to repeat some training with two of the men who are struggling."

"It is of no matter," she told him, stroking his face with one of her freed hands, lingering on a graze on his cheekbone.

Sieghild smiled weakly. "Something is different this evening. I can see it in your eyes."

She did not want to share the battle vision with him. Their time together being so brief, she refused to spend it discussing something so bleak. What could she share? She had seen a battle. She did not know when or where it would take place. She had seen a warrior slain, though she did not know who he might be. She had heard Lord Wulfgar's name, though that did not suggest nor preclude him as the victim. She tried to smile.

"I am tired, that is all. It is hard to sleep when I am shackled to the wagon."

He took her by the hand and they ran into the woods, finding one of several places they favoured among the dense collection of trees, and sat down behind a bank of ferns.

Wulfgar woke, sweat-soaked and breathless. He had been dreaming of the nix again, of crawling into a dark tent to devour her garnet lips and milky breasts. He shoved both hands into his hair, clasping them into fists.

Licking his lips, he found her sweetness lingered in his mouth, so real had the dream been. Countless times had she invaded his sleep and the dream had increased in frequency, and with it the sensations. Wulfgar sat up, his belly aching from his unquenched nightmare. He slid his baldric over his naked torso and pulled on his boots.

His guards leaped nervously, trying to look alert when they saw him emerge from his tent. Their slouched stances and heavy eyelids gave them away. Wulfgar nodded at them and wandered over to the thegns' tent. Inside, he scanned the sleeping bodies for Sieghild and could not immediately see him. He took to checking each slumbering man with dark hair. Unsuccessful, he found Leofgist, waking him with a boot in his backside.

"Leofgist," he hissed in the dark.

A pair of wide eyes gawped at him. "Lord Wulfgar?" Leofgist reached for his weapons, seemingly in panic of some imminent attack.

Wulfgar crouched and settled a firm hand on Leofgist's shoulder. "Where's Sieghild?"

After a brief look round the tent, Leofgist shook his head and whispered his reply. "I do not know, My Lord. He was here when I came to sleep."

Wulfgar pressed his lips together tightly, not liking the thoughts that were forming in his mind. He stood abruptly and marched out of the thegns' tent, heading for the nix. Passing the wagons of Brunbard the farrier, he noticed Trunhild's horse tethered outside when it should have been with its master, guarding the nix. He shook more doubt from his mind and continued. Nearing the last wagon, he slowed. He had intended to confront the cause of his nightmares and to enrol his best friend in communicating with the nix. Not having Sieghild beside him, he worried his fear would be too immense for him to carry out the task. Checking his iron wrist guards, he took a deep breath. Rounding the wagon, he saw the untied ropes hanging loose. No nix, no Trunhild and no Sieghild. He did not like it. Sensing he had been made a fool of, Wulfgar ran back to the thegns' tent and roused Leofgist and Heahstan.

"Come with me," he ordered.

They did not question their lord's request and dutifully followed him into the night. He walked briskly, looking back often to encourage the other men to keep up with him. Only as they neared the perimeter of camp did Leofgist raise a query.

"What are we looking for, Lord Wulfgar?"

Wulfgar stopped shy of the last wagon and spoke in a low voice. "Not what, Leofgist, who."

"Who?" Leofgist scratched his head, yawning.

"Sieghild," Heahstan announced knowingly, drawing a frown from Wulfgar, "and the nix. I told you to kill her the day we found her. She has our ealdorman in a hex, Lord. She is nothing but a danger to us."

"We do not know that, Heahstan," Wulfgar challenged.

"Then why are we here?"

Wulfgar shuffled his feet, looking between Heahstan and the woods beyond camp. They had found nothing yet which would raise suspicion. Sieghild could be pissing up a tree for all they knew. He dared not reveal his dreams of the nix purely to make them believe in Sieghild's disloyalty.

"I have a suspicion."

Heahstan voiced what Leofgist's wide-eyed stare attempted to communicate. "That your ealdorman has disobeyed your orders and is with the nix. What is your intention?"

"If we find that he has been disloyal?" Wulfgar looked briefly to the ground, head tilted. "I shall punish him."

He walked towards the trees, his steps heavy as he trudged through broken fern leaves and over mossy twigs. Led by a strange knowing that he could only attribute to twenty years' experience of his friend's habits, Wulfgar found his way to a fern-laden bank beside a dense collection of trees. About to move on, Wulfgar almost missed them until he caught sight of the nix. In repose across a sleeping Sieghild's abdomen, she too slept. They resembled a human knot of arms, legs and torsos.

Wulfgar lifted a hand up and his companions halted. Anger rose in him, mixing with the lust from his dreams. A silk thigh gleamed under the full moon, pulling him into his nightmare once more, reminding him of the warmth of her body connecting to his own. He tore his gaze from her. First Eadmaer's betrayal, and now this. He had warned Sieg; he had told him there would be consequences, and yet his friend had ignored him. His anger grew. He motioned to Leofgist, making no attempt to whisper.

"Lift her off him."

Leofgist secured his hands under Morwyneth's arms and hauled her roughly to her feet. She gasped, dragged from slumber into a firm grip. This woke Sieghild, who lurched forward to save her. He jumped to his feet as Leofgist removed her further.

"Heahstan," Wulfgar barked.

Sieghild ceased his advance as one of Heahstan's large hands locked round his arm. He met Wulfgar's glare and stumbled in response. Wulfgar found his speech had left him. He could only shake his head, teeth clenched, bidding his anger to subside. It would not. He paced, shaking his arms to remove his emotions. Frigg's grip on his heart tightened issuing pain, and he could no longer remain silent. He ceased pacing and faced Sieghild, his words weighted with anguish.

"I warned you. I told you not to cross me again, for I would have to act upon it. Damn you, Sieg." He paced once more, no longer able to look his friend in the eye. "We will do it at dawn, Heahstan. We will need the light."

"Do what?" Sieghild demanded.

"You will find out at dawn," Heahstan informed him grimly.

Wulfgar looked at Morwyneth and saw nothing but her open mouth. "Tie her back to the wagon," he told Leofgist, "and bring a long rope to bind Ealdorman Sieghild."

Leofgist struggled to hold her as she objected violently. After several scuffles he managed to restrain her. She began shouting, her demands a mix of fury and trepidation.

Sieghild glared at Wulfgar. "She asks what you will do to me."

Wulfgar closed his eyes and turned away from her, blocking her out. She continued to scream her question until Sieghild spoke to her. Although Wulfgar had heard it before, the Brytonic sounded strange coming from Sieghild's mouth. He spoke it more softly than he ever had. It calmed the nix sufficiently for Leofgist to drag her back to camp, though she did not cease her yelling for some time. It fell silent shortly before Leofgist returned with the lengthy piece of rope looped over his shoulder.

"How did you silence her?" Sieghild ground out.

"I did not strike her," Leofgist was quick to inform, handing Heahstan the rope. "I simply gave her some examples of punishment a lord can demand be carried out."

"Tie his hands in front of him," Wulfgar instructed.

Heahstan paused with Sieghild's hands drawn behind his back. He nodded and released Sieghild, who cast a worried glance at Leofgist. Heahstan shoved the young ealdorman roughly on the shoulder to swivel him round. Sieghild held his arms in front of him. Heahstan tied them, yanking the rope tight and securing the other end around a nearby tree. Heahstan and Leofgist joined Wulfgar sitting on the floor, waiting for dawn to appear. The men did not speak. Heahstan appeared to sleep sitting upright, while Leofgist watched Wulfgar whittle a branch. Eventually, Sieghild sat also, resolved to whatever fate awaited him.

Lady Moon had not fully slipped from the sky by the time the Sun King had broken free of his slumber. Wulfgar stood and examined the land around them. Finding what he wanted, he called to his companions.

"Bring him."

Leofgist untied the rope from the tree and, with Heahstan, led Sieghild after Wulfgar. Stopping by a tree stump about two hands high, Wulfgar pointed to the floor beside it, looking at Sieghild.

"Kneel."

Sieghild did not respond immediately, realising what may be to come. A weighty shove from Heahstan forced him to his knees. Wulfgar barked instructions, his anger barely concealing his regret and pain.

"Heahstan, hold him. Leofgist, take up the rope slack."

Heahstan crouched behind Sieghild, a pair of strong arms going round his waist. Leofgist knelt opposite Sieghild, winding the rope round his wrists to form a better grip as he leaned back on them. Wulfgar stared at Sieghild, whose hands were held firm over the tree stump. Sieghild did not move, though his eyes revealed his thoughts and fears. Wulfgar could say nothing. He could not be Sieghild's friend at this moment. He had to be his lord.

"Tighter," Wulfgar shouted.

Leofgist leaned back further and Heahstan pulled on Sieghild's torso, tightening the rope and making the ealdorman's arms taught. Tight-lipped, quelling his emotions, Wulfgar drew his battleaxe. Sieghild leaned his head back, eyes tight shut. Wulfgar fought back tears, looking up quickly into the branches of the trees above to dispel them. Readying his stance, he held his axe aloft and emitted a loud cry as he swung it down.

The blade sank into the stump, severing the ropes. With the tension released, all three men fell over. Heahstan shoved Sieghild off him, cursing at his lord. Wulfgar let out an immense roar, tossing his axe into the forest. When he had expended all the air in his lungs, he stumbled backwards, wiping sweat from his upper lip onto his arm.

Leofgist murmured, "What?"

"Leave us," Wulfgar growled.

Heahstan stood and fetched a bewildered Leofgist, tugging on his clothes. "It is over, Leofgist. Come."

Wulfgar watched the others leave, listening to his and Sieghild's rapid breathing. Their fears lingered among the trees with every breath the only sound. When they were eventually alone, he looked at Sieghild. Confusion contorted his friend's features. Sieghild stood to face him.

"Wulf, I..."

Sieghild's jaw, harder than he imagined it would be, left a sting on Wulfgar's knuckles as he watched Sieghild roll to his knees, lifting tied hands to rub his chin.

"I wanted to do that before you thanked me for sparing your hands." Instantly recognising the look in his friend's eyes, he knew Sieghild clever enough to remain silent. He continued, "When I shared mead with you after the Battle of the Fens, you spoke of honour and discipline. You said the wise outlive the foolish. It seems you have become the fool, Sieg, and it saddens me." He spread his hands. "Has the nix stolen your mind? Is it a hex? Is it love?"

"It is not love." Sieghild rose to his feet, freeing his wrists of the last of the rope. He thumped his stomach. "I have this ache, this hunger, as though the land is calling to my body and I do not know what it wants from me."

"Do you think she holds the answer?" Wulfgar tried to remain aloof, while knowing deep down Sieghild spoke the truth. The land did seem to be calling to them: Sieg's ache, his own nightmares of the nix. He had reacted to ancient fears from men like Heahstan. He should have had more faith in his lifelong friend. After all, half of Sieghild belonged to this strange land through his mother.

Sieghild waited for him to make eye contact. "Yes. When I am with her, the ache stops."

Wulfgar walked away. "You should not have betrayed my trust in you."

"I did not intend for it to become a secret."

Wulfgar laughed. "Rot. You have been skulking round like a ferret."

"I need to be with her."

Wulfgar strode over, grabbing Sieghild by the tunic with both hands and shaking him. "You need to obey me. You need to stay away from her."

Sieghild snatched Wulfgar's hands off his clothes. "You should have gone through with it, Wulf."

Wulfgar watched Sieghild walk away from him, wondering how it had come to this. He glanced at the cracked tree stump, mirroring his failings as a headman. He spat on it. Sieghild had spoken true again. Had he dealt the punishment, the Wulfsuna would have known him to be a man of his word; that he held true to his threats. His failure had made him no more than a strutting cockerel, fluffing its chest feathers at any who opposed him. He did not feel strong enough to lead these people, and prayed to Woden none of them would realise that.

He hunted for his battleaxe and found it embedded in the roots of a tree. Cleaning moss from the blade, he inserted the handle into his war belt and headed back to camp. As he neared the edge of the forest, the sounds of camp coming to life for the day greeted his ears. Emerging from the tree line he found Morwyneth huddled on the floor. When she saw him she stood hastily, pressing her back into the wagon. Wulfgar approached her, determined at least to utter one word to her. Standing within a step of her, he looked into large blue pools that blinked frequently, hiding from him.

She whispered a single word in her own tongue "*Anifail*" and turned away. It was one of few he understood. She thought him a beast. He grasped her small chin, forcing her to face him, her tears running over his fingers. A strange sensation crept through his hand and up his arm. Frigg grabbed his lungs, squeezing the last breath from them. While he fought for his breath, the nix writhed like a wounded deer pinned by an arrow. He forced her shoulder against the wagon with his other hand.

"Be still," he croaked, coughing.

She did so, glaring straight at him. His nightmare haunted his waking moment as Frigg released him. He inhaled deeply, his gaze fixed on his prisoner. Mesmerised by images of ecstasy, he desperately wanted the dream to complete itself. It did not. It ended as it had done in his sleep, unresolved. The sensation in his arm subsided and he knew she had released him from her hex.

Shaking her head, the nix mumbled, "*Na, na.*"

He frowned, angered by her bewitchment of him and her obvious refusal to grant him fulfilment in his dream. Now he knew the power Sieghild fought to resist. If he could not make Sieghild stay away from her, perhaps he could scare the nix into releasing his ealdorman. He spoke, regardless as to whether she would understand his Seaxan tongue.

"Sieghild, make him stay away from you." He dashed a hand aside to emphasise his words and grabbed her by the wrist. Unsheathing his seax, he held the blade to her skin, pressing it into her soft wrist. He wanted to show her what he intended to do if she crossed him again. "Or I will cut off your hands as well as his."

Wulfgar replaced his seax in his war belt, watching her as she looked intently at the indentation his blade had left on her arm. She trembled. Walking briskly down the road, he left her. Threatening her had not given him the satisfaction he thought it would. Instead, it had rekindled his desires from the dream and made his gut sick from his actions. The nix had been right to call him an animal. He did not recognise the man he had become. He had allowed old witch tales and ageing men to sway his mind. He did not hold dear to these ancient ways, never had. He would not become his father, or another Heahstan.

chapter twelve

Sieghild released the reins on Harsteda to adjust his padded leather tunic, the grey stallion continuing to amble along a muddy path baked dry by the summer heat. Sieghild had dressed in a hurry to arrive earlier for training, donning the quilted leather to protect himself from friendly weapon blows. Without his byrnie he could move more freely when instructing the men. Lord Wulfgar had become obsessed with training, imposing longer days and tougher exercises on them all. Sieghild did not relish the day's task of teaching novices to ride horses.

Several days had passed, the event in the forest remaining unspoken of by all involved. Sieghild wanted to be with Morwyneth. However, at every opportunity she shook her head at him, fear in her eyes. Knowing what Wulfgar had contemplated doing to him, although he had not carried it out, Sieghild did not wish to consider what things his lord would do to Morwyneth if they betrayed him again. The caw-caw of a crow drew his attention to the sky. The warm day, unmasked by clouds for once, did little to lift his spirits. Sieghild watched the bird take flight, its silhouette a fitting omen for the shadow that hung over him.

The volunteers gathered in front of Lord Wulfgar's tent: some young foot soldiers who had only fought at the rear of the shield wall thus far, as well as civilians of various ages: Lorri, Frobe, Cook, Shepherd, Brunbard and Chapper among them. Sieghild intended to use two horses: his own grey and a pony for someone to accompany and emulate him. He knew many of the men had never ridden, and the Wulfsuna did not possess enough horses for all of them. Nevertheless, he began the morning teaching basic riding skills, the men aiming to stay in the saddle at various speeds. Come mid-afternoon, they combined riding with fighting, learning how to wield swords or axes while mounted. Sieghild shouted to Chapper, "Grip with your thighs."

"That's easy for you to say," Chapper complained, dropping his axe as the pony leaped into an impromptu canter.

Watching the stocky man bounce around on the small animal, arms flapping, those looking on fell into uncontrollable laughter. Sieghild joined in with the hilarity. The laughter increased when Cook, who ate as much as he handed out to others, started to run after Chapper and his mount.

Sieghild gestured towards the wayward pony, and said to Frobe, "Catch her, will you, before the men rip their guts laughing."

The muzzle of Lord Wulfgar's mare appeared beside his head. "Seaxans do not fight on horseback," said the headman.

Sieghild did not turn. "The knowledge and experience will prove useful, even if rarely used."

Frobe caught the pony and tethered her to a tree, her ears pricked and her back legs kicking up dust. Chapper hastily climbed down. Sieghild thanked his cnapa and turned round, squinting into the sun. He tried to read his lord's expression, for Wulfgar's voice had been stern. They had not spoken directly to one another since the failed punishment, orders coming to Sieghild through Heahstan or Leofgist. Unable to tell his friend's mood, Sieghild shouted to the men.

"Take an ale break."

Eager feet scuffled round a fallen tree log to fight for turns from the solitary keg. Another of Lord Wulfgar's impositions while in camp had been rationing of food and drink. Sieghild did not understand why they had remained in camp for so long. Gloui lay but a couple of days away and the Wulfsuna needed fresh supplies, which they could obtain from one of the beorghs along the Fosse.

He addressed Lord Wulfgar's silhouette, reminded of the crow he had seen. "Some of the men are slow, My Lord, but they want to learn."

"Are you not brave enough to teach them the axe race?" Lord Wulfgar's challenge held a tinge of humour, and Sieghild suspected his headman had come to amend their faltering friendship. Hiding in his tent and sending scouts to search for the Angles had obviously worn thin as a pastime.

"My bravery is intact, My Lord. All I require is a worthy opponent."

He and Wulfgar had played the axe race for many years, and he always won. It would certainly make for some competitive entertainment. Wulfgar ruffled the mane of his mare and walked her around Sieghild. Eyes alleviated from blinking at the sun, Sieghild could see his headman clearly and he was smiling.

"Will I do?" Wulfgar asked.

Sieghild regarded his friend, half-naked in trousers, boots, war belt and vambraces. "You are not dressed," he grinned.

"I told you once before, Ealdorman Sieghild," Wulfgar pulled his axe from his belt, "I will face battle with only my anger if that is how the fight finds me."

Wulfgar hurled his axe into the ground beside his horse. Sieghild hailed Frobe to bring him Harsteda, embedding his own axe in the soil beside Wulfgar's. He found a stick and drew lines in the earth between their axes and a few paces either side. Frobe appeared with the grey and Sieghild mounted, lifting his chin to Wulfgar.

"Are you ready for defeat?"

Wulfgar grinned broadly, ordering two pails of water. These he had placed alongside the outer marks drawn by Sieghild. With their horses facing in opposite directions, Sieghild and Wulfgar each readied themselves to race towards a nearby tree.

"Ready?" Sieghild asked over the ears of his eager horse.

"Ready."

They set off at a gallop, turning when they reached a tree and racing one another back to their axes. Sieghild arrived first, hanging skilfully off his horse to lever his axe from the soil. He had already used the beard to hook one of the pails of water when Wulfgar reached his axe. His headman yelled an obscenity, having to dismount to yank his axe out of the ground, aware he ran a poor second. Sieghild hung the pail on his arm and turned for the final run: to hurl the axe at a tree trunk. Wulfgar had settled back onto his saddle, trying to hook his axe beard under the handle of the water pail. Sieghild tossed his axe into a tree, the rowdy audience erupting in cheers.

Sieghild halted Harsteda at the half way marks, meeting Wulfgar who had not completed the race. He did not seem to mind and smiled at Sieghild.

"You are too good, my friend. How can that be so?"

"You never let me lose." Sieghild returned the smile, the game having reawakened fond memories of past races. Wulfgar winked, tossing the remaining contents of his pail towards Sieghild, who reared his mount in response. Hidden behind the horse's neck, he avoided the shower. He sat back up and grinned, lifting his pail off his arm.

"I would not do that," Wulfgar warned, a teasing smile playing with the corner of his mouth.

"I am not you," Sieghild replied swiftly, hurling the contents over Wulfgar.

Wulfgar swore, shaking the cold water from his face and hair, wiping it from his naked chest. The sharp thud of an arrow piercing the ground between them cut short the hilarity. Both men looked in the direction from which it had come: the arc of coppiced wood south east of the camp. The morning sun took away their sight. A second arrow took down Frobe in a swift and violent strike to the neck. He was dead before he hit the floor, and Lorri ran to him emitting a childish cry. Sieghild caught the axe that Wulfgar tossed to him.

"Go," Wulfgar instructed, yelling, "To sword."

Sieghild kicked his horse, the beast rearing on its hind legs before charging into camp. Quickly, he sought out Thegn Frithbert while repeating Lord Wulfgar's orders to any men he passed.

"Collect your men, Frithbert, and join with Ealdwig and his warriors. Set up a shield wall at the opening to the coppice."

Frithbert nodded. "Yes, Ealdorman Sieghild."

Frithbert called for his foot soldiers by way of his rank in council. The men gathered hastily, not all of them dressed for battle, although every man held a weapon. Sieghild followed them back to the training area where they soon formed an overlapping barricade of shields. They began the death rhythm, the echo of wood against shield pounding the air with their chants of "*Wulf-su-na*". Small birds scattered, screaming their fright first at the noise and then at the surprise of arrows joining them in the sky. Their shrieks mingled with the hiss of arrow fire from Ealdwig's archers, organised several yards behind the shield wall. Able civilians scrambled for piles of spears and shields previously set aside for training.

Sieghild met with Wulfgar, riding back to the training area with Thegns Geldhere, Osmund and Radliffe, their foot soldiers running behind them. "What now, My Lord?" Sieghild asked.

"I want Osmund and Radliffe to lead their men through the trees. Try and cut these bandits off from the rear. Geldhere and his men can ride with us." Wulfgar called to Lorri. "War-face."

Reluctantly leaving Frobe's body, the youth dashed to his master's tent. Meanwhile, Wulfgar rounded his horse to retrieve Sieghild's axe from the tree. Osmund and Radliffe departed when he returned. He offered Sieghild the handle of his axe. Sieghild exchanged weapons so they held their own battleaxe, for each had been weighted differently according to each man's preference. Thegn Geldhere brought his horse alongside his lord and ealdorman, and they waited abreast for Lorri. The cnapa reappeared, gasping, and threw Wulfgar his helmet. Securing the chin strap, Wulfgar locked eyes with Sieghild, bearing his teeth in a snarl. He inhaled sharply, bellowing the tribe name.

Wulfgar led the charge, riding off to the right of the Wulfsuna shield wall, dodging armed civilians with angons, scythes and knives. Sieghild headed into the left of the open landscape, Thegn Geldhere and his men tailing him. The foolishness of the opposing force revealed itself immediately. They had rushed from the coppice, doubtless assuming they would find a purely civilian convoy. They had not expected mounted nobles and organised shield walls.

Flooding into the open, the bandits initially fell in clusters. Pierced to the ground by long spears, those still breathing were swiftly delivered into the arms of Hel by Geldhere's men. Tortured screams resounded off the trees. Sieghild weaved Harsteda from left to right to avoid their weak, though persistent, responsive arrow fire, hugging the tree line of the horseshoe coppice. Lying behind his horse's ears, he smelled the animal's scent blended with the aroma of wood and leather on the field and the sweetness of grass that had been warmed in the sun.

Through the trees, Sieghild heard Osmund and Radliffe's men clashing with bandits as they tried to break in through the rear of the enemy. The Wulfsuna's arrows ceased and the shield wall progressed onto the open landscape with a formidable blade-studded fascia. An arrow shaft biting past his ear lifted his hair in its wake, and Sieghild heard Wulfgar calling for the enemy location. Glancing over his shoulder, he saw him and replied, "Main group south-east."

Sieghild's mind turned to Morwyneth, defenceless and tethered to a wagon. Distracted from his advance, he made his way towards Wulfgar. A couple of bandits wielding spears attempted to disarm him. He slid his battleaxe through his hand to grasp the throat of the haft, swinging it in a circle. The beard of the blade trapped one spear handle and Sieghild removed it from its owner. Another Wolf Son stabbed the man in the back. The second man lurched forward, his unprotected face meeting the butt of Sieghild's swinging axe. There was a loud crack as blood, teeth and butchered flesh splattered into the air, dousing Sieghild's leg in crimson sludge.

Sieghild demanded of Wulfgar, "Who guards camp?"

Wulfgar kicked a bandit off his sword that he had run through. "Heahstan."

An experienced warrior who would ensure a substantial defence, Heahstan had made clear his dislike and mistrust of the nix. Sieghild doubted whether Heahstan would keep Morwyneth safe if the bandits broke into camp. He had little time to worry. Thegns Osmund and Radliffe had forged entry through the woods. Discovering they were outnumbered and surrounded, albeit too late to do anything about it, the bandits had chosen to fight fiercely even if they left empty-handed. They focussed their efforts on lesser capable Wulfsuna who had so far survived on the outskirts of the skirmish.

Sieghild swung his axe backwards, catching an approaching bandit unawares with the axe blade, splitting his skull. Sieghild shook his head, not quite able to believe a man fighting on foot with no helmet. Too embedded in its victim to remove, the axe was abandoned, the bandit dropping heavily to the floor as Sieghild released the weapon. He drew his seax from his belt and charged Harsteda further into the centre of the battle. With the handle secure in his fist and the blade pointing down, he hacked at unprotected heads, necks and shoulders. The seax broke through weaknesses between byrnies, and delivered fatal stabs into collar bones or under arms for those without mail.

The air became putrid with the stench of blood and faeces, the long grass in the coppice flattened and stained. Through the killing, Sieghild's gaze darted round the field, trying to determine how they fared against the enemy. Warriors wielded hefty swords in deep swings, breaking ribs, severing limbs and crushing internal organs. Those naive enough to lay their blade against a wooden shield found out too late the sword embedded in the grain. Judging by the falling numbers, Sieghild reckoned the bandits would soon withdraw.

Harsteda whinnied loudly, his front legs buckling as a man rammed a spear into his chest. Lurching sideways, the horse tumbled to the ground. Sieghild landed hard, his right foot trapped under the belly of the beast. A bandit dived over him. Freeing his foot, Sieghild rolled onto his back, skewering his enemy on his upturned seax. Sieghild grunted under the full weight of his victim on the handle of the dagger, the man's contorted, stinking face drooling over him. Blood ran out of the limp body onto his hands, covering his white knuckles as he fought to keep the handle of his dagger from sinking into his own gut under the pressure. With a heave, he threw the dead man to the side and stood up, eyes and ears scanning all directions.

Now a foot soldier without a helmet, the irony did not escape him. Instinctively seeking out his friend, he saw Wulfgar running towards him, also on foot. Sieghild twisted left and right, catching glimpses of Wulfsuna guarding his back, pushing the bandits back to the trees. Across the field men from both sides lay dead; more villains than Wulfsuna, though still too many kinsmen for Sieghild's liking.

Sieghild's attention returned to an approaching Wulfgar, making haste across the bloody ground. His bare arms and torso were dashed with crimson and his hair hung like red rats' tails beneath his helmet. Behind him, an unchallenged bandit saw him pass. The foe began a pursuit of an oblivious Wulfgar, who had no warriors flanking him as they should be. It would be pointless to shout for no one would hear amid the din of clashing metal, and the distance was too far to make it in time on foot.

Passing his seax into his left hand, Sieghild searched for his axe buried in the skull of the dead bandit. He scoured the carnage for the carved handle, asking Tiw to guide his eyes. He found it and ran over. With a boot on the head of the cadaver, Sieghild took the belly of the axe haft and set the weapon free. Turning, he ran towards Wulfgar at full pelt. Luck placed the bandit behind Wulfgar, though to the side of him. In a few paces Sieghild knew he would have a clear shot. It came, and Sieghild lifted his axe, yelling his headman's name.

"Wulfgar."

Alerted to their headman's predicament, Wulfsuna who heard ran to protect their lord. Sieghild hurled his axe towards the bandit. It tossed over in the air and Wulfgar slowed down, inadvertently closing the gap between him and his advancing opponent. Sieghild held his breath, uncertain if his weapon would hit the foe in time. While the remaining bandits tried to leave the field, finding themselves surrounded, Wulfgar spun round. He spied his attacker as Sieghild's axe reached the pursuer. The blade penetrated the man's unprotected chest, sending him reeling backwards, his back landing before his feet and legs. Wulfgar looked back at Sieghild, grinning broadly and waving his sword in the air victoriously.

Sieghild smiled. He had saved his friend. He jolted forwards, cold sweeping beneath his right arm. Pain surged through his ribcage and warm fluid rose in his throat. He coughed, excreting warm blood down his chin. Looking down, the tip of a sword protruded through the front of his leather tunic. A breeze filtered past his ear: Leofgist's blade, swinging down to kill the bandit who had struck him from behind. He heard Wulfgar screaming his name as he sank to his knees, hitting the ground with a thump. Coughing again, more blood spewed from his mouth, dropping in red threads. As he fell back, Leofgist caught him and the world became a haze above him, the tree line swirling in slow circles. Wulfgar's face came into view.

Sieghild tried to laugh. "I was wrong. I lost today."

Wulfgar gritted his teeth, withdrawing the blade from Sieghild in one swift move, though Sieghild did not feel it. His friend dropped to the floor, laying Sieghild across his lap. Pain and confusion filled Wulfgar's eyes. They had been at odds, their friendship torn apart by this foreign land and its magick, and by the nix. Wulfgar always struggled to find words, even in their best moments. Now, Sieghild knew his best friend would be unable to find many with confidence. Wulfgar's weak smile did not last the length of his words.

"You have won. You will join Woden before me."

Sieghild tried to laugh again and coughed, spitting more blood. "I was always first at everything."

Wulfgar attempted another smile and winked. "At everything."

Sieghild closed his eyes, comforted by an image of his mother lingering behind his eyelids. Her land had been calling him since he arrived and he began to wonder if this had always been his fate. Morwyneth appeared also, her tender features stirring his heart. In the forest, he had spoken the truth. He did not love her. He loved what she meant to him, that she represented his mother's people. Her gift, a strong one that he knew she would one day master, made her all the more alluring. Opening his eyes, he found Wulfgar staring expectantly at him.

"Wulf?"

"Yes, Sieg?"

"Morwyneth." The cold overcame the pain and he knew he did not have long. "Take her as your own."

"But Sieg..." Fear crept into Wulfgar's eyes.

Sieghild lifted a limp hand to clasp Wulfgar's arm. "Take care of her. Swear you will do that for me."

Sieghild felt Frigg clutch his heart, which struggled to keep him alive as well as talking. His journey to Woden's hall drew near. Coughing, he winced, feeling his life essence sliding down his face. He needed his friend to answer.

"Wulf?" he pleaded.

"I swear, Sieg," Wulfgar replied hastily.

"All she is feeling – it will be in her eyes. Look nowhere else."

The day turned black, shrouded by death's dark cloak as She came to collect him. Sieghild went willingly, content that he had left Morwyneth safe.

Wulfgar watched Sieghild take his last breath, falling still in his embrace. The land became cold, the trees in the coppice silent. A hush fell on the men. With a shaky hand, Wulfgar caressed the side of Sieghild's face, his fingers lingering in the slow trickle of blood emanating from his friend's lips. His hand slid down onto the quilted leather, examining the tear made by the cut of the sword. Wulfgar fought back sobs in his throat, face contorted in anguish behind his blood-stained and matted hair as he bent over Sieghild, eyes screwed shut. *It could not be.* He would not let it be. Sieghild dead had to be a dream, a nightmare. It had to be. He inhaled and opened his eyes onto the face beneath him, marked by death: gaunt, grey and motionless. He lost a tear and watched it land on Sieghild's cheekbone and slide down into the blood now drying on the ealdorman's face. Once, he had refused to believe the gods would take his friend from him. At Lindum he had denied the thought life. The gods had taken Sieghild; taken him when Wulfgar needed him most, cutting away the ground beneath his feet. His faith had been tested and he knew not why.

Leofgist's voice broke the grief-stricken silence. "Lord Wulfgar? Sieghild's final request – someone should tell the nix you mean to honour it."

Wulfgar's head twitched. How dare anyone stab the solemnity? However, Leofgist spoke true. The nix would have to be told. He could not deny what he had sworn in front of his thegns and their warriors, even if he felt otherwise. No other man spoke.

Leofgist placed one foot before the other. "Lord Wulfgar?"

The single step taken towards him raised Wulfgar from his stupor. A pair of wolf's eyes reached Leofgist. Wulfgar did not reply until he had glanced down at Sieghild once more and laid him on the ground as though he were a fragile bird's egg, whispering his lamentation.

"Wish it I that were slain and not you, my friend." Rising to his feet, fists clenching, Wulfgar held in his sorrow as best he could and replied tight-lipped, "Well then, Ealdorman Leofgist, you may tell Thegn Trunhild to inform the nix of Sieghild's death. He is a fellow Bryton she will understand. Tell her not what I have sworn. I shall tell her that myself when I am ready."

Leofgist paused, astonished by his unexpected promotion. "Yes, My Lord," he said quietly and departed.

Amazement on the faces of those around him made Wulfgar realise, perhaps too late, that he had made the decision to promote Leofgist without thought or consultation. He should have considered it carefully first. However, no other warrior had been brave enough to interrupt. The crows had already arrived to take the flesh of the dead to the otherworld. They could waste no more time on sorrow. He decided, finally, that Leofgist deserved the promotion, for his boldness if nothing else.

Someone called out, "The battle is over. The only enemy is dead enemy."

Wulfgar scanned the field, fresh with the dying and already dead. For him the battle had ended as the sword of the enemy had plunged through Sieghild's breast. Never mind that men had still fought around them as he had run to his falling friend.

Geldhere spoke. "The Wulfsuna fought bravely and fiercely at the end after our Sieghild's murder. He was popular with the men, My Lord. He shall be well remembered and sorely missed by us all."

Wulfgar had only eyes for his friend once more, and nodded. "We will bury him as though he were my blood brother. He will have a noble journey."

Thegn Trunhild scanned the battlefield. He had volunteered to assist in the search for corpses of fellow Wulfsuna. Heahstan had instructed they be brought back to camp on a cart. Bodies lay prostrate on the sodden ground, or twisted and tangled in pieces amid weaponry too stubborn to be removed. Surviving Wulfsuna hunted for their swords and axes lost in the fracas, each of them seeking out their handle designs protruding from some foreign flesh. Leofgist arrived, his posture uncomfortable as he addressed Trunhild formally.

"Thegn Trunhild."

There had been a change of rank. Fellow thegns did not often use one another's titles. Trunhild had seen Ealdorman Sieghild slain and the mourners gathered round their headman. He pulled his shoulders back, expecting trouble.

"Yes?"

"Lord Wulfgar wishes you to tell the nix of the death of Ealdorman Sieghild." Leofgist's eyes revealed the pain his orders would place on their new friendship. Trunhild felt his chest tighten with the impending agony he knew he would have to bestow upon Morwyneth. It would devastate her. He nodded, unable to speak for choking back his own emotions. Leofgist left hurriedly, betraying his awareness of how unpleasant an order he had given. Feet weighted by the immensity of his task, Trunhild slowly made his way into camp. His mind a barren wasteland, he trusted in Woden that he would find words on his arrival. He found Morwyneth crouched behind the wagon, looking eagerly for anyone to approach. She called to him desperately the moment she saw him.

"Trunhild."

He slid down the mossy incline from the coppice, thinking Woden, guide me.

"Trunhild," she cried again in a fervent whisper, "have we won?"

He found strength to move forward several paces, his smile not entirely convincing. "We have won."

A small frown creased her brow and she stood. "There is other news," she said to him.

Her knowing statement should have halted him. Trunhild's determination to do his duty by her, even if not by Lord Wulfgar, forced him to continue. As sure as Woden ruled the sky and bade all other gods obey him, so he would tell her. He reached her, his heart knowing there would be no need to say it.

"Yes. There is other news."

She took Trunhild's outstretched hand in her own bound ones and stared wide-eyed. "No." She shook her head, trying to hold back tears. Trunhild was unable to respond except for a shallow nod.

Her lips curled in disbelief. "Oh, say it is not true. Please say it is not." She closed her eyes to stem a flow of tears, her body wracked with sobs. "I saw a vision. I imagined it to be Lord Wulfgar."

Trunhild felt his face breaking apart with grief, watching her do likewise. Her mouth scrunched into a twisted grimace and she released an unholy scream that tore down the sky. This was Lord Wulfgar's doing. These had been his orders. Her bright blue eyes flung open and burned into Trunhild. Wrenching from his grasp, she landed fists on him, fast and unremitting. He wound his arms about her, silently weeping beneath the pummel of knuckles. He received the punishing blows without resistance and with the utmost compassion. He wanted to relieve her of her agony. He wanted to receive all that she could hurl at him because he believed it to be part of his duty, not simply as a Wulfsuna, but as a Bryton.

Everyone froze with the nix's cry. No souls moved. Like victims of Medusa, the Wulfsuna became statues. Wulfgar ceased even to breathe. Transfixed in the direction of the grisly sound that cut through his heart as easily as a scythe cuts into wheat, he felt guilt permeate his entire being. It should have been me, he thought, praying Woden would guide Trunhild. His new ealdorman interrupted him and the lingering thegns. Leofgist had been overseeing the collection of fellow men in Trunhild's absence.

"My Lord, some of the men were killed by spathae."

"The short sword favoured by the Romans? Could they be former Limitanei?" Geldhere suggested.

Wulfgar frowned. "Maybe, or their sons. They could also be stolen."

Leofgist waved a hand. "Probably no more than local criminals out to snatch wares from passing traders. They did not expect to meet the Wulfsuna."

Wulfgar's ears could not ignore the wailing still to be heard from camp as he muttered under his breath, "Collect all the weapons you can."

Wulfgar returned his gaze to Sieghild on the ground beside him. His friend had not drawn his sword in the battle. Crouching down, Wulfgar slid his hand around the intricate lattice-work hilt, the diagonal pattern of leather strips moulding into his grasp. He took it from the scabbard. The bronze pyramid pommel was well-worn from a thousand passes through the hands of its owner. Wulfgar turned the weapon over. Bronze snakes chased one another around the base of the hilt, their tails pointing down the well-kept blade. One's offspring usually inherited their ancestors' weapons. If his friend had wed the nix, she would have taken it. Sieghild had not, however, and had instead made Wulfgar swear to it. Wulfgar could not take the sword as his own. No one would. It would be buried with its master, as equally worthy of a place in Woden's hall as the warrior who had wielded it.

His gaze returning to his surroundings, Wulfgar failed to see his men carrying out the orders he had given Leofgist. Warriors staggered aimlessly round the blood-sodden field, their eyes wild and unseeing. One man stood, head back, staring at the sky, an axe in his limp hand at his side.

Wulfgar inhaled and shouted for his ealdorman. "Leofgist! Move these men. Leofgist?" Heahstan ambled over and Wulfgar greeted him solemnly. "Heahstan."

Bending his head sharply in respect, Heahstan said, "My Lord."

Wulfgar swung his head round in search of his absent ealdorman, exhaling with impatience. "Leofgist?"

"You must pay the living the same respect you pay the dead."

Heahstan's quiet statement, unexpected and without mention of his title, caught Wulfgar's attention. "What?"

Heahstan continued, "My Lord, many of these men never met battle until today. They are drunk from the killing. The fight in their blood will take time to ease. Give them that time."

Wulfgar recalled his first battle, against the Geats in Sachsen. He had never taken the time to remember. Allowing himself that time the memory returned, along with the feelings. He had felt it, the hunger and the want, the need to kill and kill until there was no enemy left standing. And afterwards, as Heahstan had described, yes he had felt drunk from the killing; a glorious stupor drowning him for an unknown length of time. He cast eyes downwards at his friend's body.

"I did not believe Woden would take him from me. A part of me died with Sieg on this battlefield."

"You are lucky it was not all of you." Heahstan slapped Wulfgar's bare arm with the back of his hand. "Enjoying some fresh air?"

Looking down from behind his helmet, Wulfgar examined himself, silently acknowledging his naked flesh painted with the spent crimson of the enemy. Exposed, except for wrists secure beneath iron vambraces and his head beneath a helmet, he had indeed been lucky today. To have survived with only minor scratches proved his skill as a warrior, and ordinarily he would have given a smug smile. He had remained true to his rule. A fight had found him and he had answered its call. He had wasted no time dressing in regal robes.

"There was no time. I took no blades," he replied finally.

Heahstan prodded his lord's bicep where a glancing spear had narrowly avoided him, leaving a shallow cut in his flesh. "There were several whistling past your ears." Wulfgar started to walk back towards camp, assuming Heahstan's lecturing had finished. Heahstan showed no sign of giving in and followed him.

"There is always time for a headman to ready himself for battle. Your thegns will start fighting while your thralls bring your battle dress."

"I am not my father," Wulfgar protested. "We had this argument at the Battle of the Fens."

"It has nothing to do with your father," Heahstan cautioned. "This was how your grandfather died. He was a young fool who wore nothing but a sword and believed the gods would guard his flesh."

Wulfgar strode faster in the hope of leaving Heahstan behind. "If the gods are strong enough…"

Heahstan ran after Wulfgar and halted him with a firm hand on his chest. "The gods have plenty to do. The best defence for the flesh is a shield, a sword, a shirt of mail and a helmet."

Wulfgar felt anger ripple through him. He glared at the hand holding him back and followed the arm that led to the wall of a warrior before him.

"Why call on the gods at all if they have so much to do?"

"The gods help more a man who can help himself." Heahstan smacked his hand sharply into Wulfgar's chest. "Feel it, here. Know it. Be at one with all who went before you."

Heahstan departed, requiring no response and leaving Wulfgar motionless. Wulfgar did believe he had known it, felt it. His swiftness to abandon the past had let him down, not his weapons. He had not wanted his people to expect to wait for him in battle. He had been determined to show them his eagerness to be first on the field of death, however unprepared. For what heroism would it be to show you could survive with blade alone? Today, though, he had been warned, and not merely by Heahstan. Sieghild's death and what remained of his closest kin seemed a potent message from Woden. For the first time, Wulfgar considered his mortality. To earn respect, he would need to retain his thralls more closely and accept that there would be no Wulfsuna without their headman; no Wolf Sons without their wolf spear. His people needed him alive. As Wulfric had often said, "Only a fool enters battle without his armour," and the Wulfsuna would follow no fool.

CHAPTER THIRTEEN

The Fosse Way,
Heading North Towards the Ceastre of Gloui

The convoy moved along sombrely as dusk closed in around it, grief pouring from every wagon. The submerging sun dipped below the land as night chased away the day. An unearthly silence pervaded, no man or beast uttering a sound. Certain the nix had cast a spell with her chilling scream, Leofgist felt uneasy even though she remained in the rear wagon. Trunhild rode beside him, the horses' bellies closely nestled, their riders' legs pressed between them. The horses smelled of sweet hay, their bodies warm from riding in the afternoon heat and their heads hung low with fatigue.

Giving Leofgist the task of leading the wagon containing Ealdorman Sieghild's body, Lord Wulfgar had decreed they were to travel through the night. Until a suitable resting place could be found for their ealdorman, they were road-bound. Trunhild had not spoken since leaving camp. Indeed, there were no words to say; none that would bring back a friend or make either of them feel any easier about their loss. Four horse lengths beyond them rode the surviving thegns with Lord Wulfgar at their head, alone.

Leofgist had to speak. He needed to reveal his thoughts before the day ended, or else he would never utter them at all. He looked over. Trunhild's face bore the result of his duty. Mauve and ochre stained his face, evidence of the fevered hands of the nix as she had fought against the news, refusing to believe Sieghild's death were true.

"If only I had moved, or turned," Leofgist began, "I would have seen the bandit behind Sieghild sooner. I could have stopped him."

Trunhild kept his eyes ahead. "You did as well as any warrior could have."

Leofgist adjusted his seat on his horse. "I shall attempt to be a worthy replacement, both in Sieghild's honour and for my lord."

Trunhild released a snort through his nostrils. "You have not replaced him yet. Your headman rides alone without an ealdorman at his side, while you sit here with me."

"He is a proud man…"

Trunhild laughed bitterly. "Lord Wulfgar is a half-hearted warrior. He should have finished the fight Eadmaer began on the east coast." He turned to Leofgist, brows low over dark eyes. "Wulfgar should have pursued the Angles and disposed of their leader before bringing the Wulfsuna south-west in search of land. He should have avenged Wulfric's murder."

Leofgist cast worried eyes around them, lowering his voice. "Do not speak ill of Lord Wulfgar. If it is true as the scouts have told us and Eadmaer is content raiding in the north, our time training extra men will have been worthwhile. When we do meet the Boars we will be ready."

Trunhild rubbed his bruised chin. "He should still have delivered that news to the nix himself. I shall not forget the look in her eyes. Besides, we could have avoided the attack if we had not stayed in camp for so long."

"Villains lurk in every pore of this forsaken land. Any man worth half his hidage should expect an attack sooner or later."

"Yes, but now we are off to bury Sieghild with Eadmaer on our tails." He nodded ahead. "Now we are like hares trapped in briar with Angle dogs baying at our backs."

"Sieghild did right by our lord," Leofgist defended. "He sacrificed himself for his headman. Without a leader there is no tribe."

Trunhild leaned closer to Leofgist, mouth curling in derision. "And neither will there be for much longer, you'll see. Who can say now who is with Lord Wulfgar and who is against him?"

Once again, Leofgist glanced round uneasily. "It was not a good council before we left, for sure. But it is merely old men grumbling about lost land gifts and young warriors showing their fear through anger and resentment."

Trunhild settled his gaze back to the road, his voice a deep growl. "Do not be so sure."

Leofgist stared at Lord Wulfgar, a solitary figure concealed beneath his father's helmet. While not the same kind of man as Wulfric, Leofgist believed him to be a good man, hindered by youth as many of them were. Leofgist felt he had no right being an ealdorman when men such as Geldhere and Heahstan lived. He suspected Lord Wulfgar held comfort in surrounding himself with men his own age, reserving the wisdom of the elders for council, though even then their headman seemed to fight against the advice of his older thegns.

At the Battle of Bathumtun they had lost not only Ealdorman Sieghild, but also Thegn Radliffe, Barker, Shepherd's son and several others. And of course poor young Frobe, whose death had marked the start of it all.

None had deserved to die. All had fought bravely and earned their place in Woden's Great Hall. Warriors of the Wolf Sons began to sing a new song as they marched; a new saga they were living and seeing with their own eyes.

Blown asunder by scowling skies of old,
Torn from life by enemies so bold,
Yet strong as bears in fight with dogs,
Brave warriors come with shield and sword,
In great ships built from the wood of the gods.

Morwyneth felt her time among the Wulfsuna had blurred into one monstrous moment. A waning moon cast its white effervescent light onto the world beneath, exaggerating the shadows and enhancing her pain. Leofgist had cut her ropes and instructed her to sit in the goods wagon she had spent a week tethered behind. She had been oblivious to the tribe packing their wagons and the bodies of the dead as they rattled past in a cart. When the camp disappeared under the warm veil of an early evening sunset, she had not revelled in its beauty. Her skin no longer felt the summer breeze and her ears did not hear the men's lament for a lost warrior. She felt like an old woman, her face marked with the cruel hand of fate, recounting long years and memories. Alas only weeks, not years, had passed, although the memories seemed as strong. Sieghild was dead. She had seen it and still he was dead. She could not accept her own failure, her own ignorance of her gift.

Morwyneth began to wish the Wulfsuna had left her on the roadside to wander forever, just as they had found her, as Sieghild had found her. The Seaxan clothes Trunhild had given her were safely stowed away in the rear of the wagon, awaiting such time that she felt she wanted to be one of them, if such a time ever came. Now in the company of the wolf, she had no intention of letting him into her life. The wild-wolf warrior Wulfgar only deserved her contempt. They had lost Sieghild because of him. Bereft, she wanted to dissolve into a ghost, an ethereal being amid the thick shadows of this pack of wolves.

Some time in the early hours, the convoy stopped. Morwyneth examined the dew-laden morn and saw a large lake, its expanse shrouded by a descent of mist. From experience she did not descend from the wagon. She would wait to be called. Despite her grief, she knew Sieghild no longer existed in the vessel of flesh they would be burying. They would be waving goodbye to blood and bone already decomposing, while Sieghild's spirit watched over them. He had a different afterlife to her own. That being so, she knew she may not meet him when her time came. The thought of finding him in her crystal tunnel remained her only comfort.

Men hauled planks of wood from a cart while Lord Wulfgar barked orders at them. Soon after, two warriors disturbed her to remove several spades from the wagon. Although they regarded her with wary eyes, they did not spit or curse at her as some had done before. Biding her time while they carried out some large task out of sight, Morwyneth considered what she might say over Sieghild's grave. With plenty of time to have considered a speech, now words were not forthcoming with the moment upon her. The mist had almost lifted from the lake entirely when the presence of Leofgist startled her.

He said simply, "*Cuman.*"

She found the seax Trunhild had given her, disregarding the fact he had warned her not to make public her possession of it. Climbing out of the wagon, she saw everyone moving towards the lakeside, including Lord Wulfgar and several other warriors in full battle dress. A procession of men carried Sieghild's body on a shallow bed of slatted wood. Panicking that they were taking him for burial and she had not said her farewell, she ran towards the procession. A hefty pair of hands caught her. Thegn Heahstan glared at her angrily from beneath his helmet and beard. She tried to wriggle free, but he held her fast.

"Nã," he instructed, gruffly.

She fumbled with the seax, twisting it in her hands. Some feet before the water's edge the procession stopped beside a large square dug out of the earth. A group of men finished work on the burial chamber, beating planks of wood into the vertical sides of the hole. Wulfgar turned to face the tribe and began a speech. Morwyneth attempted to keep up with her newly acquired Seaxan, catching odd words and phrases; he spoke of childhood, of games, of death, of father.

Wulfgar wore a silver helmet with ornate face plate that she had not seen him in before. With a lifelike image of nose and mouth in gold relief and two holes for the eyes, it obscured his face entirely. He wanted to hide from them, or from her. It pleased her not to be able to see him, else her anger would burn into his soul. In her mind she had condemned him already. Fate would assist her in her wish that it would not be long before he joined his friend. Harm none, she reminded herself. Finding an answer to suit her ends, she thought, I shall not be harming him; fate will be his judge.

Wulfgar knew the nix watched him, as well as the entire tribe. He could not have stood in front of his people with a naked face and shown them how he truly felt. His father's ceremonial helmet would shield him against any who now considered themselves his enemies. The council he had held prior to leaving camp had not gone well. He could perhaps count Heahstan, Geldhere and Leofgist among his supporters, though his confidence did not extend to any others. His new ealdorman had relayed to him the nix's attack on Trunhild and of Trunhild's anger towards him.

A disgruntled warrior he could handle, for he knew what lay in a man's mind. The nix concerned him most. He had been well aware that she would not take well the news of Sieghild's death. Their relationship had begun quickly and grown intensely over a short time. Sieghild's own behaviour at the market and willingness to lose his hands had been testament to how they had affected each other. Regardless of having sworn to carry out his dying friend's last request, Wulfgar could not face her. Myths of the nix lingered in his mind. How swiftly she had won Sieghild over, combined with the tribe's constant existence beside water, filled him with enough dread to remain distant. However, harbouring such fear would make it hard for him to take her as his own. To compound matters, he could not be seen by his people, as the son of a wolf, to fear a woman.

Drawing to the end of his speech, Wulfgar invited individuals to the burial chamber to pay their last respects and make offerings to the gods. He did not call the nix, preferring to keep her waiting at a distance. Warriors tossed swords, daggers or belts into the dark wood-clad hole, the thuds against earth echoing across the hush of the landscape. Wulfgar stepped forward to throw in one of his prized daggers and paused, staring into the oblong chamber. He retreated slowly, moving instead to Sieghild's body, kneeling down beside his friend. He slid the dagger beneath Sieghild's war belt and gave his final farewell. He prayed to Frigg that few heard him choke back a sob as he buried his face in Sieghild's, hugging him. Straightening quickly, he called the bed-bearers to load the body into the burial chamber.

Four warriors carried the bed and lowered the ealdorman inside the shallow grave alongside the body of his horse. Although having taken a spear to the chest, Harsteda had not died on the battlefield. Wulfgar recalled painfully how he had covered the animal's eye with his hand as he had put it to peace with his blade. Leaving the graveside, the bearers threw their precious objects into the lake. Wulfgar twitched when Leofgist caught him by the arm, whispering in his ear. Yes, he should really call the nix over. Wulfgar nodded his consent and Leofgist paused expectantly.

"Fetch her," Wulfgar whispered.

Leofgist approached Morwyneth and murmurs of discontent filtered through the Brytonic onlookers. An indirect request lacked respect. Also,

Sieghild already lay in the burial chamber. She could have no farewell contact with the body. Wulfgar stiffened as she made her way over to the graveside and knelt down. After a few moments of solace and whispered words, she stood and moved to the shore. With more whispers of reverence she took out a small seax. Wulfgar's eyes widened as he wondered how she had come into possession of such an object denoting freedom. He barely had time to contemplate the possibilities as she tossed it into the lake. It landed with a light plop and bobbed on the surface. He had heard Heahstan talk of the Wealas and their fondness for water offerings to appease river gods; more evidence she was nix as far as Wulfgar was concerned.

Coming back from his thoughts, Wulfgar saw that the knife had not sunk. It continued to bob on the undulating surface of the lake, tiny ripples caused by its entry. Murmurs spread among the Wulfsuna. Ignoring his earlier fears of nearing the nix, Wulfgar walked towards the edge of the lake. Halting a step or so from Morwyneth's side, he heard her incoherent mumbling and noticed her closed eyes. Whether they were prayers or spells he could not say, for he did not know the words she spoke. Finally the seax sank from view, slipping into the dark depths of the lake. Wulfgar exhaled loudly with relief, only to have his breath catch in his throat as the dagger resurfaced, blade first.

Gasps and cries of amazement merged with outcries from doubters. Air trapped in the bone handle or that it could be trapped in reeds were some reasons offered as the cause. Morwyneth opened her eyes and Wulfgar met her gaze, erasing the final step between them in one large stride. He followed her line of sight back to the water as they watched the seax return to the water's edge. People were running down to see the spectacle, jostling Wulfgar and Morwyneth as they tried to glimpse what was happening. One of the onlookers was Trunhild and he gestured to Morwyneth to retrieve her knife. Crouching slowly as Trunhild and Wulfgar held back the eager crowd with outstretched arms, Morwyneth reached for her seax. It promptly upended, presenting itself to her handle-first. Amid roaring cheers, she plucked it from the water and clutched it to her bosom.

Observing the nix, helpless as she triumphantly wielded her seax aloft to yet more shouting and whistles, Wulfgar felt his leadership ebb further away from his grasp. The pressure on his back receded and he turned to find Heahstan and other warriors had relieved him, holding back the exuberant crowd. He staggered, drunk from his own stupidity in not calling for her personally, drugged from the hex exuded by the nix. She had used the lake to work its liquid magick and lure the Wulfsuna into her confidence. Listening to his people revere the spirit worker, he had no doubt that a river witch stood among them. An icy shiver ran through his blood, the strength of Woden leaving him. He would not relinquish control to a Wealas hag. A day of reckoning between him and his people had arrived. Wulfgar filled his breast with air and clenched his fists, punching his way through the throng of people. Clear of them, he mounted the empty cart that had brought Sieghild's body and broke the chatter with a loud yell.

"Wulfsuna, hear me."

Most of the tribe heeded his call, though he noticed Trunhild lingered near the lake with Morwyneth. Having seized their attention, Wulfgar did not hesitate, launching into a speech.

"I know many of you are not happy. I know why you are not happy. As a ruler, I must say and do many things that do not make me happy. With this in mind, I tell you today that we are to hunt down Eadmaer. We are to hunt down the Angles." A great cheer arose, mostly from the Brytonic thegns and younger soldiers. Wulfgar continued, ignoring the solemn shake of Heahstan's head from side to side. "We will hunt him down and we will kill him, and bring vengeance on him for the death of our beloved Wulfric, your great former headman and my father."

It had become a day of retribution, like murky water dredging up the dirt of the past. Wulfgar knew Sieghild had not considered revenge a worthy course of action. However, Sieghild was gone and Wulfgar needed to appease those who might turn against him. A divided Wulfsuna would be a weak Wulfsuna. A show of strength against a sworn enemy would reinforce his leadership. Going after Eadmaer would also quell his own deep-rooted desire to avenge his father's murder. Vengeance was upon them and the wild hunt a warrior's breath away.

Listening to the declaration of war, Morwyneth felt vengeful herself. Lord Wulfgar had created an excellent opportunity for fate to find him on a battlefield. She remembered Sieghild's words to her: "Battle is the only sure thing. That, and death." When she had said to Sieghild that he may meet both on the same day, she had not truly felt it would have been possible so soon. She knew in Sieghild's eyes he had stood by his headman and friend in giving his life. To Morwyneth he had given himself unnecessarily. Wulfgar should have suffered whatever fate awaited him. Her returning seax had to be a message from Sieghild. Perhaps he wanted her, had invited her, to remain and become a Seaxan. Morwyneth felt her gift burn beneath her feet, her heart tugged into rhythm with Mother Earth. The surface of the lake broke into waves of ripples, fast approaching her as she stood planted to the ground. Anwen's voice came in a whisper across the water.

"Have faith, daughter."

Morwyneth answered in her mind, through her spirit voice. "Why was he taken, Mother? Should he not have helped me?"

"To find your true destiny, Sieghild could not remain in your life."

"Who will help me find my path now?"

"You and you alone will find your path. Have faith."

Her spiritual contact disturbed by Leofgist's hand on her arm, Morwyneth followed the dispersing Wulfsuna and returned to the wagon. They did not pause to make camp, instead travelling a few days north-east, for they had left the Fosse Way to bury Sieghild. They travelled east of the uplands, or *wolds* as the Seaxans called them, treading carefully through the White Horse valley. Morwyneth once more found herself in new territory. She knew the west side well, but had never been so far east. Morwyneth remained in her wagon, uninterested in the scenery. She did not consider if they crossed the uplands they would be nearing Prenhwychas. Death had drenched her memory, rinsing away all thought.

During a pause on the roadside for refreshment, Trunhild came to her wagon. "Now is the time for you to wear those clothes I found you and to braid your hair," he instructed her. "Warriors will not know or care. They are too stupid to see through tunics and plaits. But you must be protected from Lord Wulfgar."

Morwyneth sighed, reaching despondently for the sack Trunhild had hidden behind the ale barrels. She held it on her lap, eyes glazing over as she recalled Sieghild's visit to her after she'd received the items from Trunhild. Fingers from her right hand curled over her left wrist, caressing purple marks that lingered from the hemp ropes.

"Morwyneth," Trunhild prompted, grasping her hands in his and raising her attention to him, "I will only address you by a Seaxan name and we will have to work hard at teaching you to speak their words well. I shall ask Cwenfleda to practise with you."

Again she looked down at her wrists. She turned her left arm over to look at a small cut in her skin. It remained from where Lord Wulfgar had threatened to cut off her hands if she had contact with Sieghild. She faced Trunhild, frowning.

"Will Lord Wulfgar not wonder where I have gone?"

Trunhild shook his head. "He will be told that Morwyneth has left the Wulfsuna and returned to the wilderness."

She opened the sack and pulled some of the fabrics into view, pausing to rub her fingers over the cloth. "Who am I now?"

"Brithwen. Bright woman."

She nodded, biting her bottom lip as she felt tears swell in her eyes. "Fárwel, Morwyneth. Blessed be."

Trunhild gave a curt nod and squeezed her hands reassuringly. "Dress yourself. I will send Cwenfleda to assist you with your hair."

Wulfgar circled the interior of his tent, tugging off his baldric and throwing it at Lorri, who almost dropped it. Wulfgar glared at him, a warning stare.

"When was this?" he asked Leofgist, who loitered near the entrance, helmet in hand. Hauling his mail shirt over his head, Wulfgar shoved it into Lorri's chest while he shrugged out of his padded linen tunic, which he slung onto his nearby bed. He looked expectantly at his silent ealdorman.

"I said, when was this, Ealdorman Leofgist?"

Leofgist emerged from his trance, muttering, "I know not, My Lord."

"How can that be?" Wulfgar demanded, kicking his helmet across the floor.

"My Lord, your helmet..."

Wulfgar pointed a stern finger at Leofgist. "Do not tell me to guard my armour. You are not Heahstan. No helmet saved Sieghild." He dropped his arm and looked around the tent, eyes hunting. "When did she leave? Tell me."

"I know not, My Lord," Leofgist repeated, stepping back a pace.

Wulfgar continued to stride round the confines of the tent. "I must know everything that goes on in this tribe. Everything."

"I know..."

"You know not," Wulfgar scoffed, bringing two fists down onto a small table. "I know that. How can she have slipped past so many guards?"

Leofgist became mute once more. Wulfgar remembered the day at the market, how Morwyneth had left the wagon and found trouble for herself and Sieghild by the slave quay. She had shrunk from him, a small bird quivering in Sieghild's arms. He had scared her. She had reason to fear him, just as he had reason to fear her. They were alike in that regard.

"She is like an eel," he fumed, wandering over to a chest, hunting for his horn cup. He needed a drink.

"Shall I send some men on a scouting mission?" Leofgist suggested.

Wulfgar gazed at the floor, leaning on the chest with two hands. He had been foolish to be so afraid of a nix, a woman. He had been foolish to ignore her and wait to take action on his best friend's dying request. They did not know how long she had been gone, so there was no way of knowing where she might be. Sending scouts would be a risk. They may need the men, as word would soon reach Eadmaer that the Wulfsuna were on his trail. He had no choice though if he was to honour the oath he had sworn to Sieghild.

He whispered to himself, "I have been foolish."

"Lord Wulfgar?" Leofgist prompted.

Standing, Wulfgar waved a hand. "Lorri? I thirst for good ale. Find me some."

"Yes, My Lord." Lorri trotted out of the tent draped in his lord's battle gear.

Waiting until they were alone, Wulfgar said, "Leofgist, send as many men as we can spare. We have to find her."

He paced the tent, unsure what he was searching for; his mind a hoard of brambles. Leofgist had not moved and lingered, mouth moving without sound. Wulfgar thrust an arm towards the entrance.

"Now, Leofgist. What are you waiting for?"

"My Lord," Leofgist began, feet shuffling, the rim of his helmet passing through nervous fingers, "should we not wait until dawn, when we will have the light?"

Wulfgar stared at his ealdorman, knowing Leofgist was right. He did not like it though. The longer they left the search, the further the nix would be and less the chances of finding her. Frigg held his heart in a death grip, while Woden steadily drew the power from his limbs. He felt weak, as weak as the body after a fight once the battle-drunkenness has worn off. He refused to surrender to the gods' torments. With gritted teeth he unleashed a cry, arms raised above his head.

"Why? Why did she go?" He had not intended the question to be answered and Leofgist honoured that. Wulfgar looked round at his ealdorman waiting obediently, and partly in fear of his lord it seemed. Although with every passing moment the chance to fulfil his oath slipped away, it made no sense to send scouts out in darkness.

On a heavy sigh, Wulfgar muttered, "Send no men...until dawn."

Leofgist gave a curt nod and left the tent. Wulfgar collapsed onto some hides beside the fire, exhaling loudly and rubbing his face with his hands. Since war had been declared against the Angle Boars, most of the Wulfsuna appeared content. Meanwhile, Wulfgar was quickly losing himself, pieces of him splintering and falling, forever lost. He was a battle-worn shield, over-painted but still bearing the scars beneath. Wulfgar lost his gaze to the fire, trying to imagine what his father would have done after the Battle of the Fens. His father would have killed as many Angles as he could lay his blade to. He would have tracked the filthy Boars until the Wulfsuna were so hungry they would want blood on their hands so their headman would let them rest and eat. Perhaps it was a blessing from the gods that Wulfric had not lived to bear the weight of such treachery. His father's murder had left Wulfgar bitter, hatred burning within him. Since the loss of Sieghild, that hatred had festered and now spat flames. At the Battle of the Fens, every effort had been made to draw him and Sieghild away from Wulfric, and yet they had been blind to it. Heahstan and Sieghild had maintained it was a decisive strike to remove their headman, though Wulfgar never chose to believe them. The enormity of his foolishness made him all the more bitter. Eadmaer had waited twenty years to avenge his father's death, and Wulfgar had not seen it.

"Father?" he asked of the crackling dancing flames. "I knew you as a great headman, a great warrior. Help me understand my people."

A breeze lifted the flap on his tent and the fire was almost extinguished, except for a small flutter returning a moment later. He felt his father's presence sitting opposite him and closed his eyes. Through Woden, echoing from the Great Hall, his father's voice came to him, soft and deep.

"My son, you have made a bold and daring move to hound the one who took my life, but it is not of your choosing. You will have to fight, but you will fight a battle of your own choice. One who brings peace will come to you and you must help them."

The voice disappeared, as did the sensation of his father's spiritual company, and Wulfgar was left to wonder.

A four-man scouting group left the camp at dawn in search of the missing Morwyneth. Four days had passed since Sieghild's funeral, and although the Wulfsuna had been in camp for several days, there had been no central fire. Preparations for war had filled the camp and the lives of the people in it. Under duress from Thegns Heahstan and Geldhere, Wulfgar reluctantly relinquished the strict military training and organised some social distraction. He authorised the release of some ale from storage and allowed a modest fire, though not as large as the one they'd had for Hlaefmass. The Wulfsuna responded enthusiastically; the women prepared feast foods and a group of men hunted a boar to roast. Wulfgar scheduled the celebrations for the return of the scouting group the following night in the hope that they would bring Morwyneth with them, or at least knowledge of her whereabouts.

Dusk fell on the following day, and with it fell Wulfgar's hopes of seeing the nix again. Pacing inside his tent, he could not be certain he would ever have the opportunity of telling her of the oath he had sworn to Sieghild, though whether she would have believed him was doubtful. Part of him wanted to see her walk through the door of his tent, as it would mean he could attempt to do his duty for Sieghild. Another part of him wanted the scouts to return empty handed, so he would not have to face her. Maybe it was fortuitous she had left his life. He feared her; feared her powers, that she might have trapped him in a hex the way she had Sieghild, and he feared his lust for her. The nightmares continued to invade his sleep. Were they a hex? If so, he was failing his father and failing his tribe.

The aroma of roasting boar wafted in from the spit that Cook was supervising outside. Barrels of ale rumbled noisily out of the back of a wagon. The temptations of meat and alcohol did nothing to whet Wulfgar's appetite. He fidgeted with his belt, adjusting the latest favoured seax from his collection, checking it sat correctly in its scabbard. He had cleaned the blade more than once. It reminded him of the amazing scene at Sieghild's funeral when Morwyneth's seax had returned to her on the shoreline. What wild spirits had been on hand that day? At that moment he had feared her more than ever for the ways of the river witch, her unknown powers. On receiving it from the water, she had turned, like Boudicca, to present her prize to the Wulfsuna – his tribe.

"Be still," Heahstan growled from a corner by the entrance. "I feel as sick as a seafarer."

Wulfgar slumped, ungainly, onto his wooden chest, pulling at his tunic and shuffling his feet to adjust his boots to a better fit. "I cannot abide the waiting."

"Give them time. She is but one skinny Wealisc waif."

Eyes flicked up. "She is an eel."

Heahstan grinned. "You can eat eels."

"Hold your tongue, Heahstan."

The thegn turned with folded arms. "You should be glad that nix has gone. You should not be trying to find her."

Wulfgar left his seat with a hand on his seax. "I told you to hold your tongue, Thegn Heahstan."

Heahstan ignored the mild threat of his lord's weapon. "Wulfric would say the same, and he would also tell you to have patience."

"Patience?" Wulfgar replied, waving a wild arm. "We did not need patience when Eadmaer pounced on us in the fens."

"Your state of mind should match where you find yourself," said Heahstan, stabbing the air towards Wulfgar with a thick forefinger. "Now, here, you need patience. You need Sieghild."

Incensed his friend had been brought posthumously into the argument, Wulfgar marched up to his eldest thegn, holding a fist near his face. "You think I do not know this? As sure as Woden is the father of all gods, yes, I need Sieghild, here, now."

Heahstan replied quietly, "Then do as he would tell you."

With his forearm, Heahstan deflected the punch Wulfgar aimed at his face, ducking and bending to shove his shoulder up into Wulfgar's chin. The young headman reeled backwards and drew his left fist back a second time. Heahstan caught it in one of his huge paws as Wulfgar slugged him in the ribs with his right hand. The old warrior hissed through his teeth at the wild wolf fighting back at him. Wulfgar threw several quick punches into his thegn's side, jaw clenched tight in a fight to free his other fist from the iron grip of Heahstan's right hand. Unrelenting in his hold on his lord, Heahstan thrust the back of a hand into the young man's face, releasing the latter's left fist. Wulfgar flew back onto the ground, stunned, face stinging as though he had dived into nettles.

"Save it," Heahstan barked. "Save it for Eadmaer."

Rubbing a hand over his face as he watched the wiser man leave his tent, Wulfgar felt shame consume him. The gods had tied a rope to his arms, neck and legs and were all tugging in separate directions. He did not know what he had become, what ogre had been created. He did not know who to blame: Morwyneth for abandoning him, Sieghild for leaving him through death, or Eadmaer for killing his father. Perhaps he had only himself to blame.

Galloping horses arrived in camp. Wulfgar stood abruptly, holding his breath as he heard the riders dismount and hurry for his tent. Leofgist stumbled in, saddle-worn and weary. Wulfgar took a hesitant step forward. The men's eyes met over the hearth fire and Leofgist shook his head from side to side, breathing heavily. Wulfgar's head twitched as he fought against the truth. He had lost her; lost his chance to tell her of his oath sworn with Sieghild. He could not tell her that she had been Sieghild's last concern, the last one in his thoughts before death claimed him.

"No," he whispered.

Leofgist's face was drawn. "Forgive me, Lord Wulfgar. I wish I brought more favourable news."

"No, no." Wulfgar's head thrashed sideways once, twice, hurling his words into the fire. Wide-eyed he strode towards Leofgist. "No!"

His ealdorman did not wait to be excused, running out smartly before Wulfgar could grab him by the tunic. Missing Leofgist's arm by a hair, Wulfgar grabbed the fabric hanging over the entrance. His knuckles white and his teeth clenched, despair gripped him and would not let go of its deadly hold. He had failed Sieghild. He had lost the last thing that connected him to his friend. Tears threatened and Wulfgar let them fall, sobs wrenching his gut. He lifted his fists to his forehead, pressing the tent material hard into his temples. Loneliness came for him, dragging him down inside. No one could save him now. There was no consolation. Without her he had no oath, no honour, no outlet for the lust she had created within him. Like a hungry wolf scavenging for scraps of flesh on a dead carcass, Wulfgar looked round the tent, bereft, no arms of comfort to feed his soul.

He tore at the contents of his abode, throwing what he found around the tent: armour, skins, spare firewood. Anything and everything became his enemy as he tossed whatever he could claim, sobs wracking his body. Like a warrior on a war raid, he razed his surroundings, smashing, tearing and breaking what he could with his hands. His earlier conversation with Heahstan gnawed at his mind. "Wulfric...would tell you to have patience... You need Sieghild." It only sufficed to remind him that both men were now dead when he needed them most of all. Dead men were of no use to him.

Wulfgar stopped. He had not quenched the battle rage that throbbed loudly in his head. He had, however, exhausted stray items to hurl and destroy. The tears had abated and were replaced with anger. Sleep would be his nemesis, for if he slept the nix would invade his dreams, arousing him with no hope of feeding the hunger she unwittingly created. He could not even look upon her to partially dispel the craving the dreams evoked. He did not want it, but the need would be there, although she would not be. She had gone, and so had his chance to do right by Sieghild. He had failed. The devastation cut through him. He released a roar and drew his seax, slashing at the sides of his tent, opening up slits that cast shards of light into the descending darkness outside.

CHAPTER FOURTEEN

Fosse Way,
Middle Wolds South-East of Gloui

Sitting with Cwenfleda and her mother, Brithwen shared astonished looks with the other women at the commotion erupting from their headman's tent. Though they could not see it, they heard the roars and the ripping tarp. Having thought she would be happy to hear him in agony, Brithwen sobered at the reality. Guilt drenched her, knowing she was the cause of such anguish. She realised this was the result of Sieghild's absence, the overflow of Lord Wulfgar's emotion that had always been stemmed by his best friend's calm. He had lost his *irminsul*, the central pillar of life. She tried to imagine how he would feel if he found her now, or how she would feel. She had no answer. Thankfully she was in the company of the farrier's family, reassured by Trunhild that the Brytonic Wulfsuna would allow no harm to befall her.

A short time later Brithwen and her companions gathered on the outskirts of the camp near their parked wagons and small tents. Council members were gathering outside the headman's tent, which had fallen silent. The fire burned high and hot, a garnet and amber dragon twisting and lurching into the night sky, tearing the midnight blue with golden claws. The smoke from the wood and the scent of evening dew on the grass pleased Brithwen's senses, reminding her of happier times, of Aberhabren and Dudley. Stakes had been placed at intervals around the camp exterior, the heads wrapped in cloth doused in animal fat, lighting the perimeter. To one side of the fire a boar carcass was spit-roasting.

As they sat on low stools they had brought with them from the wagons, Cwenfleda's father Brunbard fetched ale for them all. Meanwhile, thralls passed by with platters of warm cinnamon bread, figs and lemons. Brithwen and Cwenfleda took some bread to try, though Brithwen did not feel hungry. She cradled it in her lap, watching the proceedings. The start of the evening was heralded with a horn accompanied by an animal skin drum, the jaunty rhythms of which encouraged singing. Laughter spread around the camp and several people began to dance. Their movement brought Brithwen's gaze round to see Leofgist walking towards them. He walked his sweat-stained horse over to a thrall who led the animal away to rest. Appearing from behind one of the stationery vehicles, Trunhild nodded at them with a smile.

Conscious that the new ealdorman would recognise her, Brithwen adjusted the hood of her green cloak over her head, her fingers feeling down to the round brooch that secured it at her chest. It felt strange to once again have long hair, the plaited horse hair extensions looking and feeling quite real. Her own hair had grown a little, and thick strands fell haphazardly across her temples. Trying to relax, she tossed the bread away and lay her hands in her lap, nestling her palms against the lattice leather belt on which hung her seax. Brunbard returned with their drinks and Trunhild tugged on the farrier's sleeve to draw him closer.

"Be wary to whom you speak. Seaxan Wolf Sons could plot against us."

Brunbard handed the rest of the drinks out and shook his head, smiling. "I do not believe they would dare, Trunhild, though I shall be cautious."

Heahstan strode over to Leofgist and the other scouts, who were removing their armour. Brunbard and Trunhild stepped away from their intimate discussion to overhear. Brithwen peeled back the side of her hood to listen more clearly.

Heahstan prodded Leofgist in the back and jabbed a thumb over his shoulder towards Lord Wulfgar's tent. "The wolf son of your founding fathers is having a bad day. As ealdorman, see the men are sure of heart in respect for their headman."

Open-mouthed, Leofgist shrugged. "I do not know if I have that influence."

"You must find it." Heahstan slapped Leofgist in the stomach and walked back to join the other thegns by the fire. Trunhild glared at them all and jogged over to accost an already stunned Leofgist.

"I told you. I said the Wulfsuna would rot from within. You shall see. This whole tribe will perish within the month."

Leofgist glanced after Heahstan, considering his advice. "You talk shit, Trunhild. Come and get some ale inside of you." He threw an arm round Trunhild's back and led him away to the ale cart.

Brithwen clutched her hood tightly in stricken fingers. What had she done? This imbalance, this doubt in their leader, had come from her selfish need to escape, to hide. Feeling more endangered than ever, she called on the Earth Mother to impart some of her magick. Drawing up energy through her feet, feeling it envelope her, Brithwen soaked herself in a spiritual veil. She hoped it would be enough; enough of a veneer to keep her identity hidden from eyes she did not wish to be recognised by.

Inside his draughty tent, Wulfgar sat in front of an extinguished hearth fire. Breeze filtering in through a dozen or more slashes in the tent lifted his hair. He did not bother to call a thrall to build a new fire. It had been some time since the horn had blown to start the festivities. By now the servants would either be drunk or seeking carnal pleasures in the woods. Shafts of light lay across the ground around him like golden blades, the fire outside revealed through the slits he had made with his seax. There was much merriment from the thegn's table outside his tent; toasting for new ventures, for old friends, for lost friends – Wulfgar wanted to believe in the last one: that what was lost would be found. However his heart hung heavy with concern that she had gone forever. He had made so many mistakes, with Morwyneth and with other things. No one had warned him on becoming lord and headman of the Wulfsuna that it would be so easy to make them. He regarded the chaos that surrounded him and spoke aloud, though no one was present to hear except perhaps the gods.

"What have I become?"

Sighing, he left his tent. Joining his men, he attempted to be mildly jovial and was glad when nothing was said of his tirade. He took a horn of ale offered to him and vowed to be consumed by alcohol so no woes could find him. After three ales, Wulfgar realised he was only half-listening to his peers. Most of his companions were inebriated while he had lost the taste for ale. He could not rejoice. He had no humour for it. He was saturated in guilt for losing the nix before he could do his duty by Sieghild. If only he had spoken to her, explained Sieg's intentions, she may never have run away. He cast an eye around the camp festivities. Men and women were cavorting round the fire, taking pleasure in food, ale and one another. He did not want to be here, among these people. Not tonight. He wanted to slip away, or slip into a warm woman. Perhaps that was what he needed. Maybe the arms of a woman would erase the guilt and set his thoughts of the nix on the wane. Tired of the frivolities, he held up a hand in farewell to the rest of the camp. Engrossed in their enjoyment, no one responded. Wulfgar took the opportunity and silently left the raucous throng.

Behind his tent, embraced under the darkness of trees, Wulfgar settled his back into a trunk. Dropping his head, he eyed a small grey stone and rolled it under his boot before kicking it away. Ordinarily this would have been a time where he and Sieghild would have played a dice game or sat across the fire from one another, swapping points of view. He pushed off the tree and began walking. To free his mind he had to liberate himself from the stifling presence of the Wulfsuna. No longer able to trust all who surrounded him, he kept moving so his heart was reassured. Keeping to the perimeter of the camp, he remained shadowed by the trees, avoiding twigs and cones underfoot, ensuring no one would be alerted by his approach.

Near a gathering of parked wagons, Wulfgar spied the "leech", Cwenfleda. He ducked behind a wagon. The farrier's daughter had been obsessed with him since the Brytonic Wulfsuna had met them at Lindum. She had a lofty ideal of becoming his bride. She repulsed him. Her lust was false, gorged by a greed for his noble wealth and a dream that she would represent the perfect high status female. He chanced another look. Cwenfleda was walking away from another young woman, and thankfully appeared to be heading for the ale cart. He did not recognise the friend she had left behind. Beneath a green hood, the woman sat gazing into the central fire, head tilted to one side. The ends of long brown plaits glowed russet in the firelight. She reached up a pale, slender hand, removing her hood. Her cheeks were tinted rose even though the night air contained a chill. He cursed silently that he was too far away to see her features clearly. She sat so still she looked immortal, a stone statue. Frigg had answered him. She had provided that which he had little energy left to pursue. Like a hunted deer, her bosom heaved rapidly with fright. Over what he could not imagine. Although he had not been running his breath caught in his throat, so thrilled was he at the sight of her. He needed to be closer. He rubbed the back of a hand across his lips in anticipation.

Estelflead appeared beside the strange beauty. Wulfgar managed in time not to reveal himself and shrank back. Laughter down by the camp fire took his gaze to Leofgist and some of the other thegns. Leofgist had grown to know Trunhild and some of the Brytonic Wulfsuna reasonably well over the last few months. He would ask his ealdorman. He picked his way back to the group of drunken men collapsed outside his tent, found Leofgist and tugged at his clothes, unfurling an arm in the direction of the mysterious goddess in the distance.

"Who is she?"

Leofgist squinted across the camp, eyes blurred by fermented hops. "I know not, My Lord."

Wulfgar tugged again on his friend's sleeve. "Then I would have you know."

Leofgist rolled his eyes and stood, a little ungainly. His precarious approach involved several near misses with fire and other bystanders.

Jeers rang out as a man dressed in women's clothing danced round the fire. Leofgist dodged him and fell into the arms of a nearby wench. She was overzealous and thwarted his attempts at freedom. He resolved to accompany her to the ale cart, their arms slung round each other. Wulfgar realised he would have to seek out this woman on his own. He had to know who she was.

He returned to the parked wagons, only further round. The young woman had not moved and he tried to observe her more closely. She had replaced the hood of her cloak, however. Cwenfleda arrived, accompanied by the young boy from the ale cart, who lingered only briefly then made his leave to continue serving. Cwenfleda's friend beckoned her closer and they engaged in hurried discourse, only some of which he caught.

"I cannot see Lord Wulfgar."

Cwenfleda twisted round, her gaze intense on the camp. "He was with Ealdorman Leofgist."

Her friend stood. "No more. Where is he?"

Wulfgar thanked Frigg for his fortune to have found a woman interested in him. He wondered why he had not seen her before. Being as she was with the farrier and his family, Wulfgar assumed she must be a Brytonic Wulfsuna. He had not yet set eyes on all the Wolf Sons of the isle, and some families adhered to the custom of keeping their young women of age hidden while preparing them for marriage. Brunbard's wife appeared, collecting the young woman and guiding her back to their accommodation. He had to know her name. After a safe pause, ensuring the object of his interest had gone, Wulfgar came out of hiding. He sauntered over to Cwenfleda, who caught sight of him leaving his cover and leaped with surprise.

"Lord Wulfgar?" Her shocked eyes struggled to focus from the effects of ale.

"Cwenfleda." He smiled, trying to be nice for once. "That woman who was with you, who is she?"

Cwenfleda tried to fold herself smaller, her arms curling into her stomach. "A friend."

"Why did she leave?"

Curtly: "She was weary."

"She went with your mother?" He asked the question although he knew the answer full well.

"Yes." Cwenfleda flushed.

Watching the leech quiver like a leaf in a storm, agitated and restless, Wulfgar knew he would not have long before she attempted to escape the situation. He could hardly contain himself as he asked the question to which he was burning to know the answer.

"What is her name?"

Cwenfleda hesitated, licking her lips. Wulfgar stepped impatiently from one foot to the other, a hand on his belt, using his authority unfairly to intimidate Cwenfleda. He stepped forward, a palm outstretched, about to bargain with her, and she fled.

"I must go," she threw over her shoulder.

Anger, frustration and disappointment all fought for space in his thoughts. He claimed one of the wooden stools the farrier's family had left, an elbow on one knee, resting his chin in his hand. His torment grew and he burned to know where she had been taken, even thinking so far as to have every wagon and every tent searched. He realised that would be disagreeable with the Wulfsuna. They would assume he was accusing them of harbouring Morwyneth and a revolt would certainly ensue. Unhappily he had to admit that the strange beauty was lost, for now.

He stood and meandered back to his tent. In the solitude of his vented abode, he unclasped his belt and tossed it to the floor. Throwing off his tunic, he collapsed onto his bed. The lethargy that had brought him in search of his bed did not lead immediately to slumber. Noise from the boisterous tribe outside lifted and fell in volume, intermittent surges of cheers erupting out of ale-induced singing. The cacophony of his fellow men seemed to rise and fall with his breathing. He observed his hands on his chest as they moved up and down in rhythm to the sounds. Eventually his eyes became heavy and the celebrations faded into the distance. Briefly before sleep came for him, he swore he saw Sieghild standing in the doorway, smiling widely before lifting the door flap and leaving.

In a small tent near to Cwenfleda's family, Brithwen had changed down to her linen undergown. She had imagined the excitement of her evening would have brought on sleep. She was wrong. Retreating from the festivities had cured her palpitations, though her thoughts still troubled her, preventing complete rest. Apart from Lord Wulfgar's vanishing act, which had sparked her anxiety, her evening had gone well. She and Cwenfleda had chatted in Seaxan, keeping her skills finely tuned. Occasional passers-by had addressed her as one of their own, no one seeming alerted by the sight or sound of her. It would appear her magick was working on those she wished it to. She chided herself for allowing the headman's disappearance to have affected her so strongly. It was quite likely he had been answering the call of nature, or was with people at the opposite side of the fire. It was not as though he were hunting her out in the undergrowth. She rolled onto her side, drawing her knees up and wrapping herself tightly in her blanket. She would try to sleep. She would need to sleep if each day in public were to be as traumatic as tonight... *In the faintest light of dawn, an owl signalled its hunt was over. A recurring breeze travelled through the nearby trees, the leaves rustling in waves, resembling the sea. Her eyes closed, Brithwen listened to the gentle hum of nature as she woke for the new day. An additional sound intruded: fast panting and the pad of four feet. She froze, unable to open her eyes. Eventually the sound stopped directly outside. She remained immobile, paralysed by the deep, rhythmic breathing of the beast at her door. A snarl rose up – she could imagine the lips curling, drooling, baring teeth. With a giant leap, the animal was inside and Brithwen's eyes flew open. A wolf it was, its large mouth growling at her in the half-light and boring into her soul, with pale blue-grey eyes. It lunged at her, her screams cut short as it tore into her throat.*

Brithwen sat up sharply in a cold sweat, her hands clasped around her neck. The profuse blood and pain fresh in her mind's eye, she had to blink many times to dispel it. Her heart pounded erratically in her chest; in comparison, her anxiety by the camp fire had been a mere flutter. Outside it remained the dead of night. Disturbed, she did not think she would return to slumber. She had not communed with Spirit for several days. With the full moon waning, any energy she put into her work required additional power drawn from the earth in compensation. She made a promise to call on Spirit at the first opportunity.

Wulfgar grew tired of the mood in camp. He had spent the last two days training for further manoeuvres the Wulfsuna had plotted to use next month, when they would be moving towards the north lands, nearing Eadmaer's southern troops. Trunhild called it *Yr Gogledd*. All the men wanted was to be at war – old men craving a new fight, young men craving their first. As for the women, from glances he received he knew Cwenfleda had found it hard to keep her tongue still in her head. Every brown-haired woman he stopped led to flurries of hushed laughter and many fingers pointing in his direction. The games of the leech merely aggravated him, gave him yet another excuse, one of a purse full, not to take interest in her as a possible wife.

Riding back early from an exercise, he had left Leofgist and Heahstan in charge of some new recruits. Long having lost his enthusiasm for any blade sport, he was returning to camp to shut himself away for further thought. All the great men in history had been deep thinkers. Scops told stories of intelligent heroes, scholars and strategists. He wanted to be one of them. Instead of the usual route, a well-used way now carved out of the perimeter of the whole settlement by horse hooves and the feet of many a passing warrior, Wulfgar chose to ride through the wagon village. Even he did not know why. A curious sensation had gripped his chest and his legs had compelled his mare in that direction. Cook threw back some dough on a flat stone, his large knobbly hands skilfully tossing and turning the soft, malleable mixture, the heels of his palms occasionally sinking into it. Brunbard was shoeing a horse, a perfect combination of strength and sensitivity; all beasts were calm in his experienced hands. Godelina was singing and therefore sewing somewhere, her powerful voice a melodic theme for the village to work by. Wulfgar recognised the song as an old tale he had heard his father sing, the words eerily poignant to him at that moment: "When a daughter loses her mother and when a son loses his father..." His mare shifted uneasily beneath him, creating deep hoofprints in the soft earth. A child's excited scream dragged him out of his daydream, children crossing in front of him chasing one another with bowls of cold water.

Looking up, he saw a still figure sitting on a stool next to a wheel, milking a ewe. He had found his goddess from the feast night. He halted his horse a dozen or so paces from her to admire her beauty, and the hubbub of the village seemed to subside. The young woman with russet hair sat slightly turned away from him. Experienced hands drew milk as she silently watched the people surrounding her. When the only sound audible was the farrier's iron on shoe, Wulfgar broke out of his trance. Nudges filtered round the onlookers who were watching their headman engrossed in the woman. At the first sign of his disapproving scowl, the village erupted into chaos, everyone once again busying themselves. He tugged his horse towards the farrier's wagons and rode over. He beckoned Estelflead with a wave of his hand. Tossing his head in the direction of his goddess, his terseness failed to cover his interest.

"Who is that young woman?"

Bowing her head deeply to hide a smile, the farrier's wife replied, "She is known as Brithwen, My Lord."

Wulfgar returned his gaze to the back of the woman, desperate to run his fingers down the pale skin of her neck that was visible beneath her parted hair, tied into two plaits over her shoulders. Not wishing to arouse suspicion with his enquiries, he avoided riding straight past her, taking a long way round to his tent. He was elated. He had her name. Tonight he would find the woman. Tonight he was going hunting. At his tent he shrugged out of his clothes and washed, pulling on clean undergarments and his best wool tunic and trousers. Digging around in his belongings, he found his dark wool cloak; a heavier one that he wore in the colder months. The darker cloth would be advantageous for slipping through the night. With it, he set aside his grey wolf pelt. Finding an appetite, he feasted copiously in preparation. He sent Leofgist to listen in at the wagon village, meanwhile engaging in obtaining liquid courage for his night-time ventures.

"Well?" Wulfgar ceased his drinking when Leofgist returned, throwing his horn cup down in anticipation.

"She is alone in a small tent, opposite the wagons of Brunbard the farrier. I overheard Estelflead taking her supper."

"Have you marked it?"

Leofgist nodded. "A small piece of fox fur is caught on the tent rope."

Wulfgar rose to his feet unsteadily, falling back against a wooden supporting pole and closing his eyes. Leofgist moved closer, arms half-raised to catch his headman.

"Perhaps you should consume no more ale, My Lord."

Wulfgar sighed. "Ah, you may be right, Leofgist my friend." He opened his eyes and addressed his companion more soberly. "For when I gaze upon her I shall be drunk with her beauty."

"Shall I come for you at nightfall?"

Wulfgar grinned. "In my present condition that may be wise of you."

Leofgist smiled as he said, "Yes, My Lord", turning on his heel and leaving.

Wulfgar slid down the pole to the floor, landing heavily. There had been many female conquests in his life, although none where he had been so intensely drawn in following such fleeting a glimpse of beauty. He did not know her voice, her eyes, her touch; he knew no more than her name. Even that he had not known when she had first attracted him like no other. He wondered if this was how Sieghild had felt about the nix: such intensity, such longing and agony, all at once. If it were, he envied his friend for having known it so. Also for the fact he had died and was no longer in pain for being distant from Morwyneth. He hoped she was still alive, out in the wilderness somewhere. She would be in her own pain without Sieghild. If only he knew where to find her, he would wrap her in his arms and take it away for her. I have been a fool, he thought, as drunken sleep claimed him.

At nightfall, Leofgist called for him. Bleary eyed, propped against the support pole, Wulfgar allowed Leofgist to assist him to his feet and into his dark cloak and pelt. Pulling back the entrance flap, Leofgist guided his headman outside. They stood still for a while, Wulfgar finding his feet after all the ale.

In a hushed whisper, Leofgist asked, "Are you sure you can do this?"

"I know my way around in the dark, Leofgist," Wulfgar hissed.

Leofgist released his arm. "Shall I wait for you?"

Wulfgar shook his head and skulked away, keeping to the perimeter of camp on his way round. Even in the dead of night, there was always a chance of meeting someone if he walked straight through the centre of the wagon village. As he made his way slowly and surely, an owl hooted and he heard its wings brush the leaves on a tree. There were other hunters out tonight. A breeze lifted shrubs and branches of trees, bringing the aroma of cabbage soup to his nose; someone's supper lingering in the cool atmosphere. His breath strained in his lungs as he became more anxious to lay eyes on his goddess. Feet sinking into the loose well-trodden track on the outskirts of the camp, Wulfgar finally spied the fox fur. He crouched low and paused. All was silent, except the laboured breathing that he fought to control. Luckily, there was no one around to hear him. He waited. Eventually his breathing calmed and he felt he could go on, the excitement of his pursuit sending shivers up his spine.

He peeled back the door flap and looked inside. She lay asleep before him, on her back, submissive and so tempting. She clutched a sheepskin across her stomach, her right hand curved above her head and nestled in a pile of clothes. He bent down and stepped into the low tent, settling on his haunches by her feet. She murmured, no doubt disturbed by the cool night air he had brought with him. He froze until he was certain she was again sleeping deeply. He stretched an arm out and eased the sheepskin from her grasp, setting it behind him. She was even smaller than he had remembered; a fragile, pale image in the moonlight, masked by his own shadow looming over her. The fabric of her undergown fell into every dip and curve of her, outlining her form. He reached out, intending to stroke her arm.

"Brithwen," he whispered.

Her eyes flew open and she gasped, "*Blaidd.*" She brought her right hand forward, lunging at him. Wulfgar saw moonlight reflecting off a blade too late. Retreating, his back connected with the tarp of the tent, trapped. Her dagger tore the clasp from his cloak and found his flesh beneath his tunic, the blade slicing him under the left collarbone. He rolled out of the tent onto the dew-sodden grass, shedding his cloak and the fur so as to make it fast to his feet should she come at him again. He did not recognise her exclamation though he had no time to consider it further. She scrambled out of the tent and ran for the nearby trees. He dragged himself to his feet in pursuit of her, unsure as to why she had attacked him. How dare she draw her weapon against her headman. He found her on the bank, wondering which way to run.

"Why did you draw your blade on me?" he demanded.

Her hesitation gave him time to catch up with her in the clearing and he soon had her by the arms. Enraged by her attack, he threw her to the floor and dropped to her side, his hands finding her shoulders. Both her palms connected with his chest, pushing him away. Meanwhile her legs flailed, catching him sharply in the side.

"Be still," he shouted. "Be still and answer me."

When she did not obey his command he tried to straddle her, cursing as she struggled more frantically, the front of her gown tearing amid their clawing hands. He found her wrists and pinned her arms above her shaking head. She writhed beneath him, eyes tight shut.

"*Na, na, ic bidde thu,*" she wailed.

She began to sob quietly and stopped fighting. Wulfgar's ferociousness ceased as he noticed his victim had surrendered. He sat back, ashamed to see he had torn the top of her gown, revealing lily-white breasts. His rage evaporated and he withdrew his hands from her body, examining the distraught figure beneath him. Tears fell from her face onto the ground and caught on strands of grass. He had never been so rough with such a tender flower. This was no warrior brawl, even though she had stabbed him. She was a woman and it went against all he believed. It would seem strange powers were at work on him tonight for he was not himself.

He whispered, "Little woman?"

She fell instantly silent, her eyes flying wide open. Wulfgar knew her immediately. Sieghild had been right: "You need look nowhere else". She was Morwyneth and she was not lost, she was here. Relief and ecstasy battled with anger and frustration at the woman he found between his legs. She had been among them all along. He crawled off her, rising up on his knees.

"By the gods," he swore, "you?"

Brithwen's tears soon left her, replaced by bitterness. She raised herself onto her elbows. "Is that all you will ever say to me? I have a name."

Her anger riled him and brought his own back to the surface. "Wrong. You have two names. Like a viper stalking mice in the grass, were you not sent by the Angle Boars to track us down before we could reach Eadmaer?"

Her face twisted, though her beauty did not lessen. "Do not be so foolish."

He threw a hand out at her. "I thought I had been coming to bed a woman who was interested in me, a Seaxan woman, and I find…"

"You find the nix," she spat, "the river-witch who serves you no purpose. It does not mean I deserve no dignity."

He pulled open his tunic to reveal his wound. "You were not so dignified when you stabbed me."

She looked away blushing, though her embarrassment did not last long. The heat in her cheeks fired Wulfgar's arousal when she turned back, trapping him with an intense gaze.

"I was saving my body from the uninvited ravishing of a wolf," she ground out, curling her legs to one side and rising to her feet.

Blaidd. Wolf. The meaning of the Brytonic word returned to him. Sieghild had taught it him over a decade ago. They had agreed to use it as a code name should they ever find the necessity. It had never come to pass.

Wulfgar shook his head, half laughing. "How have you hidden from me?"

"The Earth Mother provides me with her magick cloak, shrouding me from evil."

Wulfgar gestured to her nudity. "You have much less than a cloak to hide beneath now."

She raised her chin. "I no longer have a need to hide."

Brithwen ripped open her already torn undergown and threw it off her shoulders. The cloth dropped to her feet. For Sieghild's memory, for his friend's honour, Wulfgar wanted to look away. He could not. Her body was well-rounded and untouched by the heat of the sun. She glowed in the moonlight, creamy as polished bone and equally smooth. His nix dreams consumed him, ripping through the tattered shreds of what remained of his mind, lust and fear combining in a potent brew. She was not ashamed. She was filled with earth power and pulsing with magick. He noticed her tiny hands, vibrating beside her thighs and calling to the stream but a few feet away. The surface water rippled and curdled, bubbles spewing into the air as though stones were being thrown into its surface.

"Come," she invited icily, "come and take me."

"What?"

"Is it not what you intended?" she taunted. "Or do you no longer want me now you know I am the nix?"

He detested the way she spoke that word, *nix*, as though contempt formed it in her mouth. It was a trap, that much he knew. He had no intention of taking her body now he knew who she was. He wanted, needed, her to consent to him. He had to wed her. Whatever battle there was to be fought here, Wulfgar knew he would fare better on his feet. He made to stand. She thrust her palms towards him, knocking him to the ground.

All the warnings he had given his friend about the nix, warnings that had become mere jokes, now took on a sinister reality. He sat, paralysed by her invisible hex.

"Morwyneth…"

"I have buried that woman. She is dead. I am Brithwen."

Knowing his fate but persevering, Wulfgar stood again. Once more she knocked him down. Reduced to a pitiful pile of flesh upon the ground, Wulfgar lay still. His wound, which had been bleeding down his torso, now began to burn as the skin tore with every movement. He attempted to support himself on his elbows and the cut smarted. He hissed through gritted teeth and dropped back onto the ground. Brithwen rushed over, dropping to the floor beside him and leaning over, eyes wide with concern. He shielded his face with his arms, rejecting her approach. She ignored him, knocking aside his flailing limbs and tearing his tunic to eye his wound. She glanced around hastily and went hunting through undergrowth.

"I want no witch's remedy," he growled.

She returned, and before he could object she rubbed a handful of leaves over his beard. He blew down his nose and shook his head to dispel the pieces which had released a menthol aroma.

"Take in the scent," she instructed. Meanwhile she ripped a segment of her discarded undergown and left it to saturate it in the stream. She had forgotten she was naked. Wulfgar had not. When she came back and set to cleaning the knife wound, he could not help but be tempted by her. Guilt found him. He had almost taken his dead friend's woman, when what he had intended had been to comfort and console her. He winced as she pushed moss into the wound and he thumped his head against the ground as a distraction. He felt what he imagined was the jolt of Thunor's hammer, feeding through her hands as they touched him. His wound throbbed, his heart pounding in his ears until he was deaf. Thunor struck again through the nix's fingers and he growled in pain.

"I said I wanted no witch's remedy." He grabbed her wrist in his right hand, intending to tear her hand from his chest.

"It is not I," she informed him when he grunted in frustration, unable to remove her. "You are calling the power from me, pulling it from my hands."

Wulfgar's eyes widened. "Tell me how I stop it."

She hushed him, placing her other hand on his left shoulder, keeping her concentration on his wound as she worked in the remainder of the moss. The heat from her hands was immense, and Wulfgar felt shame burn him with equal intensity. He wanted her, though he would deny himself. But was it not what Sieghild had asked of him, to take her as his own? He looked up at her. She was silently crying, tears filling her eyes. She felt his eyes upon her and raised hers to meet them. Instantly he was aware of her innermost thoughts. She was thinking of Sieghild: imagining how she might have saved him on the battlefield. At the very least how she might have alleviated his suffering towards the end. He placed his right hand on hers, which still rested on his wound. They felt his heartbeat together for a while. Finally she composed herself and stood, gathering her clothes. Considering the torn garments briefly, she clutched the pile to her bosom and began walking back to the wagon village. She did not look back.

Wulfgar called out in a whisper, "Wait."

Although she stopped walking, she did not turn to look at him.

"There is much to say," he told her.

There was a long pause, until eventually she replied, "Not yet."

He watched her nakedness fold into the night and she was there no more. He rested his head back heavily on the floor and beat the ground with his right fist, cursing himself and his stupidity. The pain was subsiding and he slowly made to move back to his tent. He did not wish to be found out here in the morning. What a spectacle that might create – Lord Wulfgar discovered at the camp perimeter with a dagger wound. Now he realised he would have to conceal the injury, and the difficulties that would entail. He did not relish his next few days as headman.

CHAPTER FIFTEEN

Fosse Way,
Middle Wolds South-East of Gloui

It was morning. Wulfgar was considering the events from the night before, thinking back to how Brithwen had overpowered him with an unknown force and overwhelmed him with fear and lust. Her slight, pale body, so beautiful in the moonlight, belied her potency. Though physically she had brought him pain, her ethereal presence assuaged him. He would have to set eyes on her again, and soon. With this wanton desire for her image came renewed guilt. If he closed his eyes he could still see her lying beneath him, her tears stinging the ground. When he had called her Little Woman her panic had ceased, as though the phrase was familiar. Had Sieghild called her that? And Sieghild had spoken the truth when he had said her eyes revealed everything to you; like still water on a moonlit night, her whole being was mirrored in them. Wulfgar recalled her acrid comment, "I was saving my body from the uninvited ravishing of a wolf". It was not what his friend would have wanted. It was not what he wanted. He should apologise. There was much to say.

Say. He had not made the connection until now. They had conversed in Seaxan. Either she had known his native tongue before she had been found by them, or else she had learned their words from Sieghild, or possibly Trunhild. The guard outside announced Ealdorman Leofgist's arrival, and Wulfgar ceased his contemplations. Not as punctual as his predecessor, Leofgist nonetheless aimed to please his lord and, unlike many in the tribe at present, could feasibly be trusted.

"Good morning, My Lord." Leofgist grinned, too jovial for his headman.

Wulfgar frowned. "Hm. How goes it, Leofgist?"

"I bide fine, My Lord. And you?"

Wulfgar sat on a stool by the hearth fire and beckoned Leofgist with a nod of his head. "I have known it better. Come. Sit."

Leofgist sat and grinned broadly when he saw Wulfgar bring out some ale, though on seeing his lord use his right arm, he frowned.

"You usually pass with the left, My Lord."

Wulfgar paused in retracting his arm. "I do."

"How did it go last night?"

Briefly meeting Leofgist's enquiring gaze, Wulfgar knew he would have to reveal the cause for his actions. Not all of it though. He drew back his tunic to reveal the stab wound that he had had dressed in the early hours by a thrall. Leofgist spat his ale into the fire.

"She stabbed you?" he asked, eyeing the linen bandages wrapped over Wulfgar's left shoulder and under his arm, securing a compress over his collar bone.

Wulfgar sighed and refilled his cup with ale. "Yes."

"Not good then?"

Wulfgar's raised eyebrow was enough to silence Leofgist, though not for long enough. Leofgist smiled.

"The pain love brings."

"Leofgist," Wulfgar warned, his voice full of displeasure, "take it not so lightly. Word of this must not reach the tribe or I will lose any shred of leadership I have left."

"Forgive me, Lord Wulfgar." Leofgist bowed his head. "I forgot myself. I know I am not forged of the same steel as our beloved Sieghild."

Wulfgar nodded in silent agreement, refilling the ealdorman's cup.

"But I am worthy of your trust, Lord Wulfgar," Leofgist continued.

Wulfgar sat the jug of ale on the floor and considered his companion. How easily he had been available to slide into Sieghild's role. Conveniently, he was also the warrior who had brought Sieghild into camp after the murder in the market. The warrior he had sent to liaise with the Brytonic Wulfsuna. The same warrior he had sent to hunt for Morwyneth after her supposed escape from camp. He considered the possibility that Leofgist had known about the deception. He knew Trunhild and the farrier's family reasonably well. Whether he would confess was another matter. Wulfgar sank his ale to give himself a brief moment to compose his anger. He gazed into his empty cup, contemplating how to begin the interrogation. He would start by seeking reactions.

"Morwyneth is in camp."

Leofgist choked on his ale. "What?"

Wulfgar raised his head, fixing Leofgist with a steady stare. "She never left camp. She is in disguise as one of us and goes by another name."

"What?" Leofgist said again, eyes bulging.

Throwing down his cup and standing, Wulfgar yelled, "By the gods, man, know you no other word?"

"Sorry, My Lord." Leofgist dropped his eyes momentarily.

Wulfgar circled his subject, left hand hovering over his seax, eyes narrowing, doubting Leofgist's honesty. "And you did not know this?"

"I swear." Leofgist held out his hands. "I knew not she was still here."

Wulfgar gestured in the direction of the wagon village. "Have you not been keeping close company with those protecting her, such as Trunhild?"

He saw Leofgist's back stiffen as his ealdorman understood he was under suspicion. With a stern expression, Leofgist stood and kicked away his stool.

"Again I swear to you, My Lord, I have kept nothing from you." He threw his arms out. "I would not have ridden all day on a scouting mission to locate her had I known she was here."

Wulfgar felt Leofgist's response was genuine, though now he had opened himself up to possible danger if Leofgist breathed word of any of it. There was only one thing left to do. Marching at Leofgist, Wulfgar hauled him close by his tunic. He drew his seax, ignoring pain as it shot down his arm, and held the tip of the blade under Leofgist's chin.

"Wulfgar," Leofgist croaked, forgetting rank and noble titles in his alarm.

"Now take heed," Wulfgar ground out, pushing his dagger further into Leofgist's skin, "swear to me, on your honour, on your *life*, you will tell no one of this, or I will cut your throat while you sleep."

Leofgist replied swiftly, "I swear, I swear."

Wulfgar released his grip, the ealdorman stumbling back slightly. "Prove it," he challenged, his dagger poised for any retaliation.

Leofgist's eyes were glaring in the half-light of the tent as he withdrew his own seax. As Wulfgar readied his for defence, Leofgist turned the blade on himself, sliding it across the inside of his left wrist, drawing blood. He offered Wulfgar his hand. Wulfgar grinned, untying the leather on his left vambrace and letting the wrist guard fall to the floor. He cut his wrist and clasped forearms with Leofgist, sealing their bond in blood.

"I hope I have proven my honour?" Leofgist demanded. "Believe me when I say I would prove it to you again, with my life if need be."

Wulfgar exhaled, staring deep into the flames of the hearth. "You are a good man, Leofgist. A good ealdorman, and..." He looked at him, "a good friend."

Brithwen sat on a stool in the mid-morning sun, wondering about Wulfgar's infatuation with her when he imagined her to be a Seaxan beauty. His surprise to discover she was Morwyneth she had expected, for her earth energy had protected her from his eyes. However, the desire she had seen within him once he knew who she was had been unexpected. Still missing the warmth and companionship of Sieghild, Brithwen did not know how she would fend off Wulfgar's advances when she remained so emotionally vulnerable. Wulfgar had been right about one thing: there was much to say. There was also much being felt.

Watching people moving about in the breathtaking glow of the autumnal day, she could not help but remember Prenhwychas: the farrier beating his iron, another man scraping fresh hide, children chasing chickens. She recalled learning how to make a heather fire for cooking the unleavened bread, the first time she had milked a goat and the herbal lore and healing her mother had practised. She had heard Trunhild mention they had passed the valley of the white horse. From camp, Prenhwychas lay west across the hills. If only she could persuade Lord Wulfgar to head west instead of continuing north-east; to forget this enemy they were hunting. She did not know how far they had to travel before they caught up with this enemy, or what would transpire when they did. However, if there remained any chance they could pass her village first, they could help save her people. She thought of those people, the ones who had attacked her and run her out of the village. She doubted their worthiness to be saved, and yet knew they had to be. Harm none. She thought of Huweyn, who she had discovered too late to be her father. Lord Wulfgar knew the pain of losing one's father; maybe she could use that as a bargaining tool. She brought her thoughts back to the present, looked again on the people milling around the camp and felt she needed a place for quieter contemplation. She stood and wandered in the direction of the stream.

She meandered among the trees through which Wulfgar had pursued her the previous night. Her heartbeat quickened, remembering. The beeches opened onto the small clearing and she stopped for a moment to appreciate the tranquillity. Sun dappled the ground and a partridge flew overhead. The calm trickle of the stream bounced off the trunks of the trees. Anwen entered her mind, though she knew she did not need her mother at that moment and so her presence faded. She closed her eyes, waiting to see if visions appeared behind her closed lids. They did not. All was peaceful. She opened her eyes and sat cross-legged facing the stream, her hands loose in her lap. She was completely and utterly…

Not alone. She did not turn, though she knew Wulfgar stood behind her. His stealth was unmatched. Feigning calm she did not feel, she remained motionless as leather-strapped legs came into her view. Blond waves drew level with her as he sat beside her, crossing his legs in the same fashion.

After a while she cast a furtive glance sideways to find him watching the stream intently, as she had been. She returned her attention to the sunlight skipping on the surface of the water, glinting at them. As she contemplated whether she should break the silence between them, Wulfgar spoke.

"Good morning, Brithwen."

She looked round sharply to check he did not mock her. He watched the stream and did not turn to her. She faced forwards.

"Good morning, My Lord." A strained silence followed and Brithwen relented first. Turning part way to face him, though keeping her eyes on the stream, she asked, "How is your shoulder, My Lord?"

His head tilted a little in her direction. "I am grateful for your expertise."

She leaned round to glance at his shoulder and glimpsed a cloth bandage on his left forearm. She frowned. Had she been the cause of another wound last night of which she was not aware?

"You are welcome, My Lord."

He sighed loudly.

"Are you troubled, My Lord?" she prompted, again looking with concern at his bandaged forearm.

"I must apologise," he managed finally. "I am ashamed."

She kept silent, which seemed to help him continue.

"I should not have forced myself upon you. You were right to refuse me."

Confused by his openness, Brithwen tried to keep the discussion on less emotional matters. "Forgive me for wounding you, My Lord. You woke me from a nightmare. Does it trouble you?"

He reached a hand up to check his injured shoulder. "I cannot lie. You refused me only too well."

She hung her head. "For that I am ashamed, My Lord."

"We must talk of Sieghild," he stated firmly. His announcement alarmed her, causing her to twist round sharply.

"No."

Wulfgar shook his head at her. "Forgive me, but we must. I made an oath with him."

She tilted her head to one side. "An oath?"

"I must stand by it." He raised his left arm across his chest, clenching his fist at his shoulder as though crossing his heart in a pledge. The gesture brought him pain, which he refused with a tightened jaw. He proffered the same hand for her to take. She remained as she was, unable to comprehend what Sieghild would have held Wulfgar to. He let his hand fall to his lap, rejection evident in his eyes. She wanted to look away and found she could not for fear of abandoning him.

"What is this oath, My Lord?"

His gaze wavered, examining all of her before coming back to meet her eyes. "I am to take you as my own."

Brithwen allowed the words to sink in. "Take you as my own." *Take.* She was not to be given, or asked; not even cajoled, persuaded; merely taken? She held Wulfgar with a piercing stare, drawing her energy from the earth so that he would be unable to break away from her. She dragged him into her blue depths as she responded.

"Sieghild, victory in battle. He was not so victorious."

Wulfgar did not fight her and countered proudly, "He was glorious in battle. He saved my life."

She inhaled deeply, annoyed that tears were threatening. "But no one saved his."

"That is fate," he hissed.

She released her true feelings, let her blame shower him like arrows. "That is carelessness. Where were his men?"

He kneeled to reach some height over her, shoulders rounding in anger. Brithwen was swiftly transported to her nightmares of the wolf. She could imagine fangs beneath the curled lips as he ground his words into her heart.

"They were where he had told them to be, surrounding their headman, protecting me." He beat a fist on his chest. He reached out, a hand cupping the nape of her neck, drawing her to her knees. "You know not the battle-field. You know not its dangers."

Brithwen, hanging from his large hand, felt like a hare whose neck was about to be broken for the pot. She grabbed his forearm around the bandage and squeezed. He winced, frowning at her, though he did not release her. She seethed in his grip, fighting back sorrow that threatened to break her in two.

"I may not know of your battles," she bit back, "but I had fought many of my own before I met you and more hence. I still fight one now. I fight to remain who I am. I fight to survive in foreign company. I fight to keep breathing each day I remember he is dead."

Her voice broke as grief intervened and tears stained her pale cheeks. Wulfgar settled on his heels, backing down from the fight, his hand less firm on the back of her head. Brithwen did not notice immediately and fought on through her sobs.

"I fight not to be taken by anyone. Should someone ask me for my love, then that shall be given consideration."

He reached out for her and she dived away, leaping up and running back through the trees to her tent. She remained there until sundown when, under the blanket of night, she secured the flap of the entrance back to gaze at the sky. It had been a while since she had taken notice of the phases of the moon. The end of harvest would soon be upon them; the death of the Corn Lord heralding the arrival of the Winter Crone, her icy breath strangling the last life out of the landscape as darkness approached. There seemed to be no celebration preparations among the Wulfsuna for the festival. The tribe had been preoccupied with Sieghild's funeral and military training. She realised she had held no personal ceremony of her own for Sieghild's departure. She left her tent quietly, most of the camp sleeping, and made her way back to the stream. Among the beech trees she recalled seeing an alder. As she reached the bank, the tall deciduous tree faced her across the water. Turning for autumn, it was abundant with oval brown woody cones.

Brithwen could see several large stones just under the surface of the stream and used them to traverse to the opposite bank. From some of the lower branches she took a handful of the stalks carrying cones and made her way back across the stream. Back on the camp side of the water she set the stalks down. Tugging some of the horsehair from one of her plaits, she used it to tie her cone bundle into a woody bouquet. Standing at the water's edge with her offering, she asked Ceridwen, Goddess of the Moon and the Underworld, to assist Sieghild in his journey through the afterlife, wherever it may be. Tossing the bouquet into the water, she watched it bob along the undulating bed of the stream.

The image of a face winked on the moonlit surface of the water. Brithwen blinked and took a second glance, shocked to see a vivid representation of Wulfgar staring back at her. She recalled some of her mother's words, "When horsehair tells of who to wed". No, it could not be. She would ensure it was not so. Brithwen felt betrayed by this world full of illusions, where reality twisted and hid itself from view, playing hide and seek with your eyes, luring you into its falseness. She could not even summon a wry laugh, remembering Anwen's instructions to let the wolf into her life. Wulfgar had revealed himself only too well in his true form. He possessed the sheer muscle energy, the light stalking paws and the long, sharp fangs of his namesake. And yet, this afternoon by the stream he had sat beside her as if a faithful dog. He only bared his teeth when she had thrown angry words in his direction. She refused to admit she had misjudged him and harboured doubts of his intentions. She had no evidence to support his claims of Sieghild's dying words, and felt unable to press Leofgist or Trunhild for any knowledge they may have.

Brithwen summoned her crystal tunnel in the hope that by placing Wulfgar somewhere ahead on her journey it would help bring about a solution. Aware she had previously refused him privilege within, Brithwen regretted that she would have to redress her former decision. She settled herself more comfortably and readied herself to add Wulfgar. She placed him to one side, ahead of Sieghild's progress. Since Sieghild's death, each time she opened up her tunnel he was walking slightly ahead of her, never looking back. She wondered at first if he was merely keeping her company. It could be that Sieghild was trying to lead her in the right direction, guiding her along her path. His death did not negate his assistance to her.

Wulfgar's image met up with Sieghild's in the tunnel and the men took one another's forearms, drawing each other in for a firm embrace. Bizarrely, Sieghild stood aside and for the first time faced Brithwen in the tunnel. He gestured with his left arm to Wulfgar and stepped away, walking slowly backwards, as though presenting his friend to her. Quizzically she watched and waited for the whole event to unfold. Wulfgar remained still, gaze fixed on Sieghild. Eventually Sieghild disappeared around a bend in the tunnel that she had not seen before. In a panic she psychically followed him, speeding up as she rounded corner after corner in the crystal tunnel, unable to catch up with him.

Acknowledging that Sieghild no longer resided in the tunnel, Brithwen returned to her original location where a motionless image of Wulfgar awaited. He turned slowly and began walking towards her, speeding up to a run. His torso hunched lower, the fur cloak he wore spreading to cover his entire body as he became a real wolf racing towards her. Braving her fears from her nightmares, Brithwen held on until Wulfgar's front paws left the ground and he lunged for her. She drew herself out of trance, settling her gift back down into the earth. She did not know what to make of Sieghild's gesture. Either he blessed their union and the oath was real, or else he meant for her to approach Lord Wulfgar to help save Prenhwychas. Both would mean talking to their headman, however painful it may be and whatever the outcome.

Lady Night slung her black cloak over the moon and stars, and the still darkness overwhelmed Brithwen. She had done too much. All light seemed to have left her world, more than she had imagined possible since Sieghild's death. That she could have saved him, or at least warned him and given him a chance, was a burden she would have to carry forever. To have her life tied to the wild wolf warrior's would be an eternal punishment. Hot tears ran from dead eyes, though she had no strength to sob, and she collapsed to her knees.

Wulfgar stood at the tree line, watching Brithwen. He had gone to her tent and found her missing. He did not need to consider for long where else she may be, and had been right in his assumptions. He arrived in time to see her drop to the floor in an ungainly heap, and paused, allowing her solitude while her offering disappeared downstream. He understood why she had come here. After a brief moment he ventured forward, not wanting to leave her alone for too long. Removing his cloak, he draped it over her shoulders. It was a cold night and she was out in only her undertunic. She did not move or react to the warmth of the cloth or his presence. Gently, Wulfgar lifted her under the arms and raised her to her feet, but she faltered and he caught her in his arms. Wincing from the pain in his shoulder, he continued, returning her limp body to her tent. Lowering her inside, he tried to pull his cloak around her as best he could so she would keep warm. He moved away then hesitated. Motionless and only just breathing, she had her eyes open, lifeless. He recalled thinking that when he found her, he would wrap her in his arms and take away her pain. He had tried and failed. Unable to look upon her grief a moment longer, he left for his own bed.

Thegn Tortsig and Chapper had settled themselves outside their lord's tent for a midnight discussion. Wulfgar seethed at their insolence, which grew as he neared them and caught the subject of their conversation.

Tortsig spread his hands. "Eadmaer had never given us cause to doubt him. Sure, we all knew the story of Wulfric and Maerard."

Chapper nodded, adding, "I never liked the man, but I never thought he would betray us the way he did."

It had to stop. Wulfgar had had a gut-full of talk. They should have been satisfied that war had been declared on the Angle Boars and that they would soon be seeking out Eadmaer and his kin for slaughter. Wolves would kill pigs and it would end. No one acknowledged his appearance and Wulfgar gave each man a mental mark against him for the dishonour. He would remember who they were when he next plotted who would take the front of the shield wall.

"Whatever we may have known about that man we must forget," Wulfgar told them, glaring until they both stood. "Now he is a son seeking revenge for his father's murder. I, above all of you, know that torture. I alone know Eadmaer now."

Tortsig hushed his companion before he could intervene. "He changed when he reached this land."

Wulfgar dismissed nods of agreement with the wave of an arm. "This land has changed us all. We are, none of us, free from her hex. Know this when we next meet battle. Now be gone."

Chapper moved first, though Tortsig lingered. Wulfgar waved a guard over, one of two posted outside his abode, and this encouraged the thegn to leave. Wulfgar screwed his face into a snarl of contempt. He should not have had to add muscle to his orders. Dissent, it seemed, remained. It would need beating out of the Wulfsuna by force.

Enclosed in the meagre sanctuary of his battered and slashed tent, Wulfgar tried to empty his mind from all that had weighed him down that day. The heaviest weight was Morwyneth, now Brithwen, an impossible vision to remove from his thoughts. Their conversation by the stream remained with him. Drunk from the sound of her voice, he could not erase the way she had uttered his noble address. Every time she had said "My Lord" his desire had been ignited, Thunor's hammer bruising his soul into submission.

He slumped onto his bed, aching hands rubbing his face and sliding into his hair, elbows resting on his knees. His father had mentioned someone who would bring peace. Despite his hunger for revenge, he craved peace, and beyond all else he wanted Brithwen. The fates of battle lights he knew; the dance of swords and axes he could perform in his slumber. His fear of the nix, however, loomed like an otherworld giant. To possess her would be the greatest challenge he had ever faced; for her to come to him at her own will, the greatest sacrifice he could imagine anyone could make. After today, he knew it could never be. He dropped his hands, raising his face to the sky, visible through the torn roof.

"Mighty Woden," he begged, "bring me the peacemaker."

Stars blinked at him between passing cloud. He felt the Father of All, his power pouring down like a mother's milk and nourishing him. He closed his eyes to taste the gift of the gods, lips parting. Woden sent Brithwen's voice, an echo from that afternoon. "My Lord." He opened his eyes, chest heaving with a burning pain. He tore at his tunic, ripping the garment from his body as heat pierced his torso. It felt akin to the nix's magick she had worked beside the stream when healing his shoulder. His hands scratched at his flesh to rid himself of the sensation. Red scars criss-crossed his chest and abdomen from his fevered clawing, and finally he could stand no more.

"Frigg." He yelled the name of the goddess, grasping his hair in tight fists. "Cure me of this nix. Take away my pain."

The peacemaker is here. Frigg herself delivered the whispered message like a punch in the gut. Wulfgar fell backwards, stumbling round his bed and feeling desperately for the back of the tent to steady himself.

He fought for breath, choked by his experience. The gods did not tread lightly when they answered. He had known it so, though had never truly experienced it. With shaky hands he felt his body. The burning heat had left him. The peacemaker was here. Why had Woden sent him Brithwen's voice when he had asked for the peacemaker? He shook his head, eyes widening. No, it could not be. Burned by so many betrayals since arriving in this forsaken land, Wulfgar rejected the connection. He needed sleep. He would dissect it after sunrise. Good fortune favoured daylight. He would pay no more heed to night demons, teasing his mind.

Dawn broke too early for Wulfgar, whose sleep had been mauled by more nightmares: of the nix and of failed battles against Eadmaer. He hoped the fortune he had wished for would indeed arrive with the light. He could stand no more failures, on his part or anyone else's. He stank of spent sweat and spilt mead; a waste for the drink had not touched his lips. He called for a thrall and ordered water for washing, clean clothes and his cnapa Lorri to locate and clean or repair his war gear strewn around the tent.

Lorri arrived prior to his lord's washing, which Wulfgar had not expected. Since the Battle of Bathumtun and Frobe's demise, Lorri's punctuality had improved. He was keener, more attentive, and it pleased Wulfgar. The lad was becoming a young man. Lorri found everything Wulfgar had thrown astray the night before and gathered it into his arms. He did not speak and gave but a few cursory glances to the slashes torn into the tent exterior. Staggering, ungainly under the weight of it all, he left as the thrall appeared with water and clothes. The thrall, an older man Wulfgar knew well, set clean clothes down gently on his bed, taking care not to spill the bowl of water in his other hand. With no expression, he lifted the small table Wulfgar had upturned the previous night, settling it onto a level patch of ground. He sat the bowl of water in the centre of the table and bowed at Wulfgar on his way out.

Washing, burying his face in handful after handful of cold water, Wulfgar trusted his prayers had been answered. Rinsing away doubt, he cast his mind back to the night where he had asked the mighty Woden to bring him the peacemaker, and Frigg had told him the peacemaker was among them. Wulfgar did not know who they were and prayed the light of day would honour him, would reveal the peacemaker to him. He washed the rest of his body, dried and dressed.

"Lord Wulfgar, a scop has requested audience with you," one of the guards announced.

"A scop?" he answered.

"Yes, My Lord," came the reply.

Wulfgar looked in the direction of the wagon village, eyes trying to burn through the fabric of his tent. He wondered whether a weaver of the old sagas would know of the existence of the nix, and if so, what he could tell them about her. He needed to know if she were a gift or a curse. If she were the latter, he may have to sacrifice her to Tiw in order to bring them victory against Eadmaer, and to appease the more sceptical among the Wulfsuna. He was not certain he was capable of such a deed. He stood and left his tent, the daylight scorching his eyes. He shielded his face with an arm, squinting across camp.

A tall, thin figure in grey limped towards them. Women and children waved welcomes, which he returned with a flurry of hand gestures or circles, drawn in the air with his long staff, its many talismans rattling as the stick twirled his greeting. The bearded tale-weaver reached Wulfgar, staring directly into the headman's eyes before lowering his head in a shallow bow of acknowledgement. Wulfgar examined the newcomer, whose vestments were more rags than clothes, worn to holes in places by rocks and bracken, or stained from walking muddy roads in the pouring rain.

Wulfgar's eyes narrowed as the old man lifted his head. "Welcome, Scop."

He bowed a second time and answered in Seaxan, "I thank you, Lord." He did not merely know their words, the accent was genuine also. "You are a Seaxan." The tale-weaver smiled at him and Wulfgar asked, "Where is your homeland?"

The old man shrugged. "It matters not. I am old and have been away a long time."

"By what name shall we know you?" asked Wulfgar.

The scop grinned, revealing yellow teeth and highlighting the myriad lines across his face, ingrained from so many smiles. "I be Dudley, Lord."

"I am Lord Wulfgar. Join me, Dudley." Wulfgar motioned to his tent where the guards dutifully stood aside, holding open the entrance.

Inside, thralls had been busy clearing away the washstand and dirty clothes. The hearth fire breathed new life and wooden benches had been set out, draped in skins.

"Bring food and drink so we may break our night fast," Wulfgar ordered one of the last thralls to leave, then said to Dudley, "Please sit."

The scop obeyed, releasing his physical efforts in a deep sigh. He smiled at Wulfgar, who took the opposite bench and observed his guest in silence. Flames leaped in the hearth fire, throwing shadows across the tent behind them. Here they sat; one, a warrior with only two decades to his age, and the other an aged bard, long and white of beard. They were as distant in age and experience as Wulfgar had been from his father, Wulfric. Smoke billowed skywards, turning and twisting like fates between them.

A guard announced the thrall bearing refreshments and Wulfgar admitted them. He motioned for the thrall to offer the tale-weaver a portion of the ale, bread and ewe's cheese from the platter and to lay the remainder on the table. He could not eat until his mind was settled. He watched as the old man ate heartily, quenching his thirst when he had emptied his plate. He looked about Heahstan's age, though time had not been so kind to his bones. Perhaps the demons of the night had been playing with Wulfgar after all. This scop could be the peacemaker.

"From where have you travelled?" Wulfgar enquired, curious to know where the tale-weaver had been singing his sagas.

Dudley wiped his mouth on his sleeve. "Entertaining the Wealisc and hugging the west wolds."

"The Wealisc?" Wulfgar's mind returned to the day they had found the nix and he shifted his seating. "How far into Wealas territory have you been, old man?"

Dudley appeared indifferent to Wulfgar's agitated condition and merely smiled broadly. "Aberhabren, My Lord."

That was west of the mouth of the Saefern, which lay not far from the Ceastre of Gloui, and not far from their current location. A spider of thought began to weave her web in his mind, linking moments.

"When were you at Aberhabren?" he asked.

"For the festival of Hlaefmass, My Lord. The locals call it Lughnasadh."

Wulfgar considered the possibility that the nix had originated from Aberhabren and could feasibly know Dudley. They had suspected the nix to be a lure sent by Eadmaer. Although Sieghild had quelled the idea, the scop's arrival might point to the secondary phase of a deadly plan, birthed by the Angles to trap them or source their location. To know for certain, he had to keep the scop with them until he could verify his suspicions. Wulfgar smiled and smacked his thigh.

"Will you weave your tales for us this evening? It has been too long since I heard a good saga."

"I would be delighted, Lord Wulfgar," Dudley replied, standing with the headman and marking his leave with a bow.

"Guard." Wulfgar called one of the men inside. "See that the scop is given a place of comfort to perform his songs, and send me my ealdorman."

chapter sixteen

Fosse Way,
Middle Wolds South-East of Gloui

Wulfgar's ealdorman came quickly, intrigue of their visitor evident in his face. "Who is he? Is he a messenger from the Angles?"

Wulfgar laughed, holding up both hands. "Whoa, Leafy, steady boy. No, he's a scop, though I have reasons to suspect he may know the nix."

"Morwyneth?" Leofgist shook his head, scratching a cheek covered in an untidy beard.

"Until we can be certain he has not been sent by Eadmaer to trap us, we must keep watch over this tale-weaver." Wulfgar clasped forearms with Leofgist, reminding him of their blood swear. "Brithwen must not attend the festivities or know the scop is with us. Take Heahstan into your confidence with all of this, and do not let the scop out of your sight."

He smacked Leofgist on the back, the ealdorman squeezing his arm tightly before parting on a smile. Wulfgar knew he would carry out his duty well. He had concerns, but they pertained to the nix and whether she would do as she was told. She had been ordered to stay out of sight before and not heeded a word, instead finding herself a captive in a foreign slave market. Sieghild had been there to save her. He would be unable to save her this time.

That evening, Dudley gathered the camp for a rhyme of the season, as he had done at Aberhabren, and proceeded to weave old tales from inside one of the tents. As headman, Wulfgar sat through all the songs of sagas told as others came in small groups to hear of wisdom and heroism, death and victory, love and strife. When all who wanted to had heard their fill of the scop's stories, Wulfgar and Dudley were left alone. In the silence that fell between the men, Wulfgar thought of all that had brought them here. Life was not as he would have wished it to be. With each bend in the road, Woden tested his resolve, poking a spearhead into his back to force him along a path he did not want to tread.

"There is one saga I have not sung tonight," Dudley began, waiting until Wulfgar met his gaze over the fire, "for the hero walks among us."

The statement woke Wulfgar from his lamenting. "What saga is this?" he asked, lifting his mead cup to his lips.

"The Wolf Spear Saga," Dudley replied, the timbre of his voice rife with mystery.

Wulfgar's mead cup paused mid-air. "What of it?"

"You do not know the saga?" the scop began, drawing a circle on the ground with the end of his long staff. Wulfgar shook his head and the old man continued without having looked up.

"And yet your own name carries it, Lord Wulf-Gar." Eyes pale from age and fading sight glistened in the firelight.

Wulfgar put down his cup, tired of having his attempts to sample the contents interrupted by the tale-weaver's questions. "Yes, my name means wolf spear. I am the son of a wolf, of many wolves. By name or tribe, we are all Wolf Sons here."

Dudley straightened his back and closed his eyes, breathing deeply. On opening his eyes, he took several scorched twigs from the base of the fire and laid them on the ground, forming two runic symbols representing Thunor and Tiw, the Gods of Thunder and War respectively. With his finger, Dudley traced the protruding triangle of the Thunor rune and brought a single finger to his nose.

"Wolf," he said, glancing at the headman.

Wulfgar nodded that he understood the scop's suggestion of the wolf's muzzle in the shape of the rune, and realised he was going to hear the saga whether he wanted to or not. Dudley continued.

"Noble beast that never rests, hunting always, forever wandering the dark veil of night. The Great Devourer." A finger followed the upward-pointing arrow of the Tiw rune. "Spear, sharp as thorn to all who near it, bringer of pain and death."

Beginning with a deep hum, Dudley led into the song of the saga in a low voice. Wulfgar felt the potency of the words as they filled the air between them, floating like the unsettled spirits of long past mortals. They whispered, each one of them an eerie warning. It spoke of a daughter losing her mother and a son losing his father, of seers and one named Wolf Spear. He had lost a father and he was named Wolf Spear, though as quickly as the song had drawn him into its magick, nagging doubt arrived to drag him back again. It could all be a clever hex. As the scop's voice trailed off, he tossed the twigs back into the fire, sending blue sparks darting into the air. Wulfgar stood, hand running through his hair.

"It is but a tale, old man," he told Dudley, frowning.

"Did you not hear the words, Lord Wulfgar?" Dudley asked, opening his mouth to repeat them. Wulfgar waved a hand and walked away from the fire.

"Yes, yes, when a son loses his father. I have lost my father and I am called Wolf Spear. It means nothing. It is a tale."

The scop rose unsteadily, leaning heavily on his staff, a hand outstretched in a plea to the headman. "It is a powerful saga. One you would do well not to ignore if it has found you."

Wulfgar emitted a sharp laugh. "Found me?"

The tale-weaver refused to give up, leaning forward on his staff, expression tinged with warning as he whispered, "You can say truthfully you do not know a seer? One who has lost a mother and draws on the earth for their power?"

Sieghild and the strange sickness he had experienced when they landed on the island broke into Wulfgar's confused mind. He recalled comforting his friend on the riverside at Lindum when the earth's power had gripped his body. Sieghild had been crazed by the strange pain. He had also lost his mother. Wulfgar released his hair and faced Dudley.

"I know of one," he told the scop.

Dudley straightened, a confident smile tugging thin lips. "They are your seer."

Wulfgar laughed. "But you said a daughter loses her mother. This was a man and he is dead."

Dudley stamped his staff hard into the earth and walked away from the fire, pacing and mumbling incoherently. He reached a hand up to fondle the charms tied to his staff, kissing one of the carved sticks that dangled from worn string. He returned to the fireside.

"You know of no woman who shares this same pain? A woman who has lost her mother?" Dudley demanded. Wulfgar realised he could no longer disregard Brithwen and her possible part in his destiny. Messages from the gods were severe enough. To incur their wrath through ignorance could prove fatal. He nodded and lowered his eyes to the fire.

"I know of one, yet I do not know if she has lost her mother."

The scop moved to stand beside him, a warm hand seeking his shoulder. "You must ask her. If so, she will be your seer and the saga has found you."

"And then what?" Wulfgar asked, remaining unsure as to whether he wanted to be found by a saga so apparently feared.

Dudley giggled like a small boy, curling his arms into his body and jigging excitedly. "She will see the way that you cannot. She will find your destiny and bring you victory in your endeavours."

Wulfgar took hold of Dudley's cloak in one hand. "You mean she could help me defeat Eadmaer?"

Dudley shrugged. "If that is your destiny."

Wulfgar glared at the old man, shaking his cloak as fear battled with passion. "If it is this woman, and she has the eyes to my future, I am unsure if I can trust her."

Seeming to ignore the fist hanging off his garments, Dudley grasped Wulfgar's wrist with his free hand, eyes widening. "You must. Or else the saga will remain unfulfilled."

Wulfgar released Dudley's cloak and peeled the man's hand from his arm, stepping back to gaze at the fire for a while. If the old man was right and the nix was his seer, it would mean working alongside Brithwen to track down Eadmaer and the Angles. He felt confident the Wulfsuna could find Eadmaer without the help of a seer, particularly one who plagued his dreams with erotic temptations and for whom his body hungered every waking hour. However, nothing had gone to plan since they had arrived, and who was to say what further misfortunes awaited them.

"Must every Wolf Spear obey the saga?" he asked, needing to know the consequences if he chose not to.

Dudley replied, "It is not something to be obeyed, Lord Wulfgar. It is a path to a journey only you can decide to make."

Wulfgar met the old man's eyes. "Then others have not fulfilled it and met no evil?"

Darkness fell across Dudley's features. "Many have ignored the signs, those foolish enough to believe they could find a better way. You are no fool, Lord Wulfgar, and your journey has already begun."

Wulfgar shook his head, fighting against his belief in the cobbled ramblings of this old bearded tale-weaver. No, they were not ramblings. They were the first words to make sense to him since Sieghild had died. Succumbing to the stirrings in his gut and loins, Wulfgar inhaled deeply, praying that what he was about to do would lead him to his intended fate, and more importantly keep him and the Wulfsuna alive. Dudley responded, as though knowing his thoughts.

"You would not be a mortal man if you did not fear the seer. Use that fear to your advantage. Turn it into a power rather than letting it rule you as a weakness."

"I shall send for her." Wulfgar turned to call a guard, almost colliding with one entering.

"Lord Wulfgar?" The warrior's eyebrows lifted in surprise.

"Bring me the nix," Wulfgar demanded.

"But, My Lord," the guard spread his hands, "she is already here."

Wulfgar looked round to the scop sharply, Dudley releasing a soft laugh and partially distracting him from the guard's explanation that followed.

Continuing, the guard said, "She asked to speak with you. I came to tell you she awaits you in your tent."

To the guard, Wulfgar replied, "I come," then facing Dudley added, "she knows."

Dudley used Wulfgar's own words against him. "She has the eyes to your future."

Outside the night air had become cool, the first day of Holy Month beckoning autumn. Leofgist nodded to Wulfgar in the half-dark, proving he had been true to his orders and would not relinquish his watch on the scop. Walking back across the damp grass to his own tent, Wulfgar attempted to straighten the thousands of strands of chaotic thought tangled in his mind. He could not begin to know what the nix would say to him, though he knew that if she proved to be the eyes that saw his future, he wanted no one else to glimpse his destiny. Most of all, he did not want Eadmaer to be privy to what lay ahead for him and the Wulfsuna. To prevent her eyes from showing anyone else, to keep his destiny safe, he would have to keep the nix close by.

The fire in Lord Wulfgar's tent was low. It had burned down, long forgotten and not renewed. Feeling the chill of the evening, Brithwen pulled her soft head mantle further round her face. She had worn the garment to evade prying eyes through camp. Thegn Heahstan had been good enough to listen to her plea and escort her to their headman's abode, and she had not wished to be recognised. She swayed, giddy with sickness which she attributed to her lack of sleep and inability to eat, her slumber plagued by the recurring nightmare of a wolf's attack. She placed a tentative hand on her throat, recalling the beast tearing her to pieces. The stench of the animal's breath had not left her and she found it painful to swallow. She feared she had spent the night issuing agonising cries, her screams real and not confined to her dreams.

Waiting for their lord in the dark, dank tent, Brithwen began to wonder if her idea would work. She needed to persuade Lord Wulfgar to turn the Wulfsuna west before By Ceastre. She could not allow the opportunity to pass without trying to save her village. She needed to know Huweyn was safe, that he had secured his leadership since her expulsion. It would be dangerous to detour. It would allow the Angles time to lessen the distance between them and bring battle sooner. It was a large risk and

Brithwen doubted Lord Wulfgar would take it. However, for Huweyn and for Prenhwychas, she had to try.

Men's voices in hushed discourse outside alerted her to Lord Wulfgar's arrival. She heard him thank Heahstan and ask the thegn to remain close by. A shiver captured her body as fear ran through her. Brithwen held on to what bravery remained, knowing she had to be confident to deliver her request. It would not be easy. She would be facing a man who hated her for what she was; a man who had almost cut off his best friend's hands for betraying him, and threatened to remove hers also. She gained strength from the memory of him weeping over Sieghild's body and how the wild warrior power had left him by the stream.

She faced him as he entered, dropping in a deep curtsey, head bowed. When nothing but silence greeted her, she rose unsteadily to her feet. He wore a blue tunic, gold embroidered hems complementing his hair, and brown trousers. His head tipped to one side, considering her, and he glanced at his brown cloak, which she had returned to him, thrown across one of the benches. He gestured to the bench nearest to her, moving to the one opposite.

"Come, sit," he said.

They both lowered themselves slowly. Brithwen, aware that recent events between them had been strained, preferred the false politeness. It allowed her distance from her emotions, which threatened to consume her.

Lord Wulfgar rubbed his palms up and down his thighs, finding it hard to keep his eyes on her. "What brings you?" he asked.

Protected by the dimness of the interior, eyes shielded, Brithwen found the confidence to begin. "I come with a proposition, My Lord."

He cleared his throat, eyes narrowing. "A proposition?"

"Turn west before By Ceastre. Follow the river Wyndrysh through the cut in the uplands. It would take no more than a day, two at the most."

A deep frown settled over his grey eyes, blond curls teasing his brow. "Turn west? For what?"

"My village, Prenhwychas, lies beyond the high plateaus. I wish to return."

He regarded her for a moment, the frown dispersing and a hand slowly fondling his short beard. The hand moved up into his hair, tugging at the roots while his teeth sank into his lower lip. Swiftly his hand dropped to his side and he stood, stepping briskly away. With his back to her he released a short, exasperated sound.

Over his shoulder, he asked, "You wish to go home? You want me to release you?"

Sorrow threatened to bury Brithwen's heart as she feared his refusal. "Please, I must return home to save my village from an attack by blue painted northmen. Will you allow the Wulfsuna to help?"

He faced her. "If I do, what then?"

"We can continue north, to face the Angles."

His eyes became bright, regardless of the low light, as though he had been illuminated from inside. They widened into ice-blue globes that roamed her whole body before arresting her with an intent gaze.

"I see. Blue northmen? Do you speak of Pictii? How did you learn of this attack?"

"I have foreseen it. The vision was a gift from Spirit to warn my village. It struck fear into their hearts and they turned their fear against me. It is why I was cast into the wilderness. It is how you came to find me."

She watched him tugging at leather ties on his iron wrist guards, shaking his wrists when he became conscious of his actions and pacing the tent. He strode over to a wooden chest and threw back the lid. For a moment he eyed the contents, arms twisting agitatedly at his sides. Bending down, he retrieved a scabbard, grasping the hilt in his left hand and freeing the blade. Brithwen tensed, unsure of his intentions. Holding her breath, she regarded him turning the sword over and replacing it in the scabbard. With a thumb he caressed a design on the handle and set the weapon gently back into the chest.

"It can be done," he told her, closing the lid of the chest.

"It is agreed, then? You shall turn the Wulfsuna west?"

He adjusted his wrist guards again and walked away from the chest, a hand sliding into his hair. He looked back, and Brithwen was intrigued by his obsession with the chest. After so long without confirmation, Brithwen prepared to prompt him.

"I agree," he faced her, expression shrouded by shadows, "for a price."

She did not know if it was the dying hearth fire or Lord Wulfgar's words that had caused the tent to become icy cold. She had nothing to give him, only herself. She stiffened, even more wary of his interest with the knife in the chest.

"A price?" she enquired.

He lifted his chin. "A bargain always has two sides."

She searched deep into his eyes, through to the spiritual heart of him, seeking answers. They were hard to find. Honour fed his intentions, whatever they might be, and her probing brought forth the word "horsehair", which she dismissed. Reaching up to fondle one of her plaits, she realised she would have to agree to a bargain.

"Name your price then, My Lord."

He returned to search in the heavy wooden chest, and Brithwen prepared to give her life for the safe delivery of Prenhwychas from blue northmen. Closing her eyes, she straightened, awaiting cold steel through her chest. Fumbling sounds preceded shuffling feet and a cough, and Lord Wulfgar spoke.

"Forgive me, Brithwen. I have not offered you a drink."

She opened her eyes. He sat on his bench, clutching a piece of black fabric or hide, two cups and a jug. Taking one of the cups he offered, she held it while he poured her a drink. It was mead – the drink of nobles. She bowed to thank him for the honour of sharing such a drink with her.

"Here." He passed her a pelt as black as a starless sky.

She smiled politely. "I am warm enough, thank you."

He thrust it at her a second time, insistent. "It is to signify you as nobility."

When she did not receive it he threw his cup into the dead fire, mead and ash flicking up the hem of her gown. He waved the pelt at her, nostrils wide as his breath became heavy.

"If you become my wife, you will be treated with respect and have the protection of my whole army."

She could not believe her ears. She did not want to be his wife, and she was not flattered by the show of power in mentioning his army.

"That is your price?" she asked, rising and reeling once more from sickness.

His eyes did not leave hers. "It is."

She breathed deeply, trying to erase nausea and find a way through her predicament. "Very well. On one condition," she informed him.

He laughed bawdily, holding up a thumb and forefinger. "There are only two sides to a bargain."

She waited, hoping that silence would assuage him and give her a chance to consider what the condition would be, for she had not been prepared for his proposal. His expression became serious. He licked his lips and glanced at the black pelt in his hand.

"What condition?" he asked her.

"That it is a union of convenience, a statement of trust between Prenhwychas and Sachsen. No more."

His grasp on the black pelt grew tighter as he pressed it into his abdomen, wild eyes roaming the ground feverishly. His mouth hung wide, breath quickening, and he turned his back on her. Her last and only offer, Brithwen prayed he would accept it, although his response disheartened her. Following a long pause, in which time Brithwen had sufficiently regained her composure from her sickness, the lord faced her. His powerful shoulders hung low as those of a beaten hound, his eyes distant and his soul hidden.

"So be it," he muttered, extending his arm to offer her the pelt once more. "Will you wear the fur, Lady Brithwen?"

She felt her cheeks flush at the mention of her title, and could not look at him as he approached, draping the pelt around her shoulders. His hands lingered, his warm breath teasing the skin on her face. Hiding behind her, he seemed to regain his strength, revealed by the confidence in his voice when next he spoke.

"Although it is merely a marriage of convenience and not of...flesh, there must be a ceremony and celebrations. It must appear a true union to the tribe."

Not of flesh. His words brought forth her sickness and she fought with what strength she had left to remain steady on her feet. He had uttered them in such a way, as though he craved the union of their flesh despite having agreed against it. She waited for Anwen to bring her warning of her actions, though her mother did not appear in sight or sound. She recalled her vision at the stream, when the horsehair in her plaits had revealed Lord Wulfgar's face in the surface of the water. Horsehair had told her who she would wed. When she had been learning to use her crystal tunnel, Anwen had told her to let the wolf in. Brithwen ran her fingers over the ebony fur.

"What fur is this?" she asked.

Lord Wulfgar's breath caressed her cheek. "Wolf."

Before she could react to his answer, he hailed the door guards inside, gesturing to her. "This is Lady Brithwen. I am to take her as my wife. Give her access to this tent at any hour."

Her astonishment must have illuminated her face as brightly as the midday sun on a summer's afternoon. Lord Wulfgar stood in front of her and smiled, taking her arms in his hands. His grip was firm and warm.

"You can come and go as you please. This is your home when in camp."

Whether he had meant for his words to reassure her or command her, Brithwen refused them, stepping away from him and furrowing her brow. "I shall not be sleeping here."

His smile faded from his lips, though continued to sparkle in his eyes. "As I said, this marriage must appear a true union to the tribe. We must make sacrifices to avoid discontent among the Wulfsuna."

Lord Wulfgar's sacrifices were unclear to her. By having her sleep in his tent, she would be akin to a prized piece of war gear or a valuable relic, leered at and drooled over. This left little certainty that he would not attempt to touch that which was forbidden. Her sacrifices, however, seemed as clear as a running brook. She would have to spend each night with the "Wulf", with both his eyes and those of the entire camp upon her wherever she may be. Another large smile lit up his face and he raised a bearded chin.

"I shall address my people at midday and you will stand beside me."

Guarded commodity or humble prisoner, Brithwen knew she had to accept her fate if it meant saving Prenhwychas. Besides, resistance might cause him to withdraw his agreement. Dropping in a deep curtsey, she bowed her head to reply.

"Yes, My Lord."

Leather-clad legs walked over and he crouched beside her, gently taking her chin between his thumb and forefinger. She let him lift her face to meet his and waited for him to speak. He probed her dark blue eyes, drinking deeply from what he glimpsed therein.

"Please," he begged softly, "call me Wulfgar."

Weak from her relentless nausea and giddy from the knowledge that she may at last save her village, Brithwen cursed internally for being drawn into his gaze. She was the wielder of magick, the all-seeing seer. He had no right to cast a spell on her. He was a wild wolf warrior, a fearsome beast incapable of a gentler demeanour, or so she had thought.

Relenting, she whispered, "Wulfgar."

Sparks ignited amid pale grey eyes as she uttered his name. It would be a difficult marriage of convenience. She was steadfast in her convictions, however. It was all for Prenhwychas. After that, she could not foresee the future. She knew not what the fates would bring. Perhaps, in time, that would change. These were the final moments of her current life. From noon, their wedding would be announced and all would know her as Lady Brithwen. She craved the familiarity of the wagon village and the chance to absorb all that had occurred. She stood.

"I beg leave of you, My Lord, Wulfgar."

Crouching below her he paused, his hand in mid air, bereft having lost contact with her. He blinked, erasing emotions he had allowed to invade his features, and stood abruptly. He gestured to the doorway, eyes averted.

"As you will."

Brithwen tugged the wolf skin from her shoulders and smuggled it under her cloak, dashing across camp. It mattered little who saw her wearing it, though it represented someone she had not yet become. She had already forsaken Morwyneth, whose demise lingered fresh in her mind. Brithwen's life had only recently begun. All was new and unwieldy. She would hold on until the very end before relinquishing another identity.

And so at midday, the headman gave the announcement and henceforth the Wulfsuna knew her as Lady Brithwen. Wulfgar's speech had been brief and carefully worded. Brithwen thought perhaps he skimmed over the formalities in order to make haste to the union of flesh he had spoken of, hinting at a wanton disregard of the intention of their wedlock. Soon after, a flurry of activity arose throughout camp as preparations began for the noble wedding. In the company of all the free women, Brithwen ate her maid's meal: her final food as a maiden. Gifts were bestowed and each woman stood to impart a piece of advice on her entry into marriage. They called her *Leof Hlaefdige*, Dear Lady, and Brithwen struggled to accept the title, especially when used by her closest friends. Constantly, she reminded herself of the saving of Prenhwychas.

chapter seventeen

Fosse Way,
Middle Wolds South-East of Gloui

While Brithwen was having her maid's meal, a feast had been laid for Lord Wulfgar. Ale featured prominently, each free man toasting their betrothed lord's health and then one another. Not limited merely to the first drink, the toasting became progressively louder and more bawdy as the evening drowned in a cacophony of ale-merry men. Wulfgar, his thirst already quenched from Brithwen's agreement to be his wife, raised his cup for each toast, though did not consume all his ale. Allowing the ale to touch his lips but not his tongue, he spilt more than he drank. Towards the end of the night, it proved no hardship to fool his companions with a convincing drunken stagger. They cheered and whistled when he finally left them, for they believed he was returning to his tent to prise the virginity from his bride before being wed the next morning. It would not be so. Having denied anyone access to his tent since the feast had begun, Wulfgar had made a separate bed for Brithwen. He would not forswear his oath to his best friend. He had promised he would care for her.

Listening to the rowdy singing dissipate as he wandered back to his tent, he knew a noble wedding was exactly what the Wulfsuna needed. Filling his loins with a wife was a precursor to filling his enemy's gut with a blade. It showed power and authority; that he could command whatsoever he wanted, reminding the tribe of who led them. The gamble was not over yet, however. He had very little confidence in Brithwen remaining with him once she had returned to her home, and the fate of the Wulfsuna depended on their success against her foreseen Pictii attack.

To an empty and imaginary hall, the clatter of iron long gone, he asked aloud, "Woden, what have I done?"

Following tradition, Brithwen would have entered the marital abode first, accompanied to the entrance by another married woman. The men's feast, secluded in a nearby coppice with a fire and spit-roasting boar, allowed the women to pass freely without disturbance and out of sight. He had left a small fire burning so it would be warm for the night. He closed his eyes, losing himself in an image of her reclining on the bed, asleep and alluring.

Crude grunts and raucous laughter punctured his idyllic daydream and scared a pair of crows in a nearby oak. As they took flight, frantic wings thrashing branches, Wulfgar looked round. It seemed Leofgist and Tortsig had come to see him safely to bed. They meandered in wide swerves, shouting incoherently with wild gesticulations. He played along with them, though when they insisted on accompanying him inside, he assured them he was capable of entering alone. Tortsig served him a heavy slap on the back and he fell through the ox-hide entrance. Outside his companions laughed at his misfortune and were swiftly sent on their way by his guards. Face-down on the earth, Wulfgar remained motionless for a moment to be sure they had gone. Once satisfied, he quickly sat upright, swivelling to face Brithwen.

"I think they've gone," he whispered, grinning broadly.

Partially hidden by the dividing wool curtain he had hung, she sat on the edge of her bed, the front of her over tunic loosened. On a low wooden stool beside her bed she had folded her cloak and mantle. She shook her head from side to side, backing up along her bed. He surmised from her response she assumed he was drunk. She looked exhausted. It had been a long day. Wanting to alleviate her fear, he stood and approached her. She retreated further, her back connecting with the tent. He halted at the foot of her bed, observing her, head tilted to the side.

"Hey, little woman." He crouched down, elbows on his knees. "I am sober."

She screwed her nose up. "You smell as though you swam in ale."

"I admit I spilt a few cups." He grinned broadly. "But I spilt none into my mouth."

She appeared to relax a little, though continued to watch him closely as he removed his boots and threw them across the room. He shrugged out of his over tunic, which he tossed onto his bed before sitting on the end of her bed.

"Did you eat well, or were you tied in knots?" he asked, curious because he had felt that way.

"I admit, I ate little," she told him, all the while her eyes fixed on his every move.

"I have some foods if you can eat now?" He motioned to a platter of bread and fruit he had instructed to be set on a small table. She shook her head. He shrugged, rising to his feet.

"No matter, it will be there for morning." He smiled again, hoping to receive one in return, but he was not so fortunate, so added, "Sleep well."

After a pause, she replied, "You also" and he noted the subtle omission of any name or title. It pained him that she was unable to speak of him aloud. Unsure if fear or hatred was the cause, he decided it was best to think no more of it. After all, this was her first night, and perhaps all he should expect was that she was here. His side of the wool curtain, Wulfgar pulled off his under tunic and socks, leaving on his trousers and vambraces. Collapsing onto his bed, he closed his eyes and exhaled loudly, letting go of all the day's tensions. As they ebbed away a delicate scent pervaded his nostrils, distracting him. He opened his eyes. *It was her.* It was Brithwen. The sweet scent of her filled his tent. He would never sleep now. He rolled away onto his side, though it did nothing to erase the tantalising aroma. He took a skin in his teeth and bit down fiercely, silently cursing himself for inviting her into his living space. Images from his nightmares returned to tease him. He turned onto his back, covering his nose with an arm.

Brithwen slid down and lay on her bed, listening to him shuffling around as he settled. She would wait until she was sure he was asleep before she undressed any further. A blanket had been left folded at the bottom of her bed and she pulled it over herself. Determined not to sleep and to be on constant watch in case he should approach her during the night, Brithwen lost her fight. Sleep claimed her almost instantly.

A ray of pale, wispy sun found the smallest parting in the tent tarps and burst through across Brithwen's face. She stirred, warm beneath her blanket, and felt tension on the cloth. Blinking away slumber, she opened her eyes.

"Wulfgar!"

A mischievous grin crept across his face as he lay in repose next to her, leaning up on an elbow. "Good morning."

"How long have you been there?" she asked, trying to heave her blanket higher.

"Not long," he replied, "since sun up."

She knew that meant a few hours and pursed her lips at his audacity. Remaining under her blanket, using it as a shield between them, she eyed him warily. She wanted no tricks, despite it being the morning of their wedding.

"Will you please leave so I may wash and dress?" she asked, perturbed by his incessant grinning. "We have a wedding to attend."

"You talk as though you were entering a sentence of service."

"It is indeed a sentence of service," she challenged, levering enough spare blanket to sit up. "I am offering myself as part of a bargain to ensure the safety of my village."

Wulfgar sighed, the smile finally wiped from his face. "Ah, yes," he waved a finger under her nose, "but you are not offering your body, simply your word."

She lifted a defiant chin. "That is of no consequence."

"Not to you, darling Brithwen," he chided, "though it may be of great consequence to another."

With that, he left her and went to dress. It took him a long time and she considered he may be wearing additional attire for the ceremony. As at Sieghild's funeral, he would no doubt take the opportunity to exert his leadership by flaunting his best regalia. A while later he left the tent, looking well attired, without looking back at her. At last allowed some privacy, she shed her blanket and threw it onto Wulfgar's bed, along with the rest of her bedding. If he spoke the truth, it was imperative that they keep up appearances. She pulled the wool curtain down in time to acknowledge a female thrall at the entrance, who brought water for her to wash. The woman came with a fresh under tunic for her as well as several of her gifts from the previous evening. One that immediately caught her eye was a deep red over gown and accompanying it was an under tunic, edged in a golden yellow thread.

"I know that hand." Brithwen smiled, thinking of Godelina. Her companion nodded in confirmation and helped Brithwen into the garments. From another gift, the thrall unwrapped two round gold brooches, each with a garnet at its centre encircled by a repeating knotwork design. The thrall held out a fine gossamer head mantle in black and set it aside while she re-braided Brithwen's hair. A pair of new leather shoes and her own leather belt completed her outfit. Before departing, the thrall showed her a small bowl of crushed berry juices with which to stain her lips before the ceremony. She also explained that Cwenfleda had agreed to be her bride's maid.

Alone once more, Brithwen felt her nerves begin to dig into her stomach. Her own day of reckoning was here; the chance to see whether a Seaxan pact was steadfast and true; whether a wolf could keep a bargain. She was unsure, but knew she had to see it through. She busied herself, selecting a crust of bread from the platter Wulfgar had had set out and pouring a small cup of ale from a jug. The fermented aroma of the hops smelled putrid to her, and on tasting the ale she felt sure it had spoiled and avoided it. Left with dry bread and a few meagre berries, her appetite soon disappeared and she replaced half the crust on the platter.

When Brithwen thought noon would never arrive, an animal horn sounded and her heart leaped in her chest. It was calling the tribe to the marriage rite. A guard heralded Cwenfleda's arrival outside. Brithwen drew in a large breath to prepare herself. The moment had arrived. There could be no going back. She went over to the table and applied the berry juice to her lips with a small animal hair brush. Next she carefully slipped the black mantle over her head, adjusting its fit. The door guard prompted her politely and she knew she had to emerge, for Cwenfleda would become nervous too. About to leave, Wulfgar's voice echoed in her ears: "It is to signify you as nobility". She fetched the black wolf-skin cloak from the bench where she had left it and draped it round her shoulders. She lifted her chin and thought of Prenhwychas; in particular, Huweyn.

To herself, she whispered, "May the goddess watch over me" and announced to the guard, "I come."

As she stepped into the daylight a low sun hung in the white sky, large and deep orange. Cwenfleda stood before her in a gown of pale green, like sage, clasping a bouquet of hawthorn. They walked slowly and silently down to a rounded dip in the landscape chosen for the ceremony. Brithwen's breath caught in her throat as they cleared a raised earth area and came into view of the dell. The whole tribe had assembled around the outer slope, cascading down to the centre of the dip where Wulfgar stood in front of a large stone altar with Leofgist.

So much had happened in such a short morning, Brithwen had forgotten the fleeting image of Wulfgar leaving her earlier. He wore full regal dress once again, as at Sieghild's funeral, but without his helmet. His trousers and short-sleeved overtunic were pale and underneath he wore a blood-red undertunic with long sleeves. He wore a long fur cloak made of almost pure white wolf skin, secured with a large round silver brooch matching the silver pommels of his sword and the silver mouth and chape on his scabbard. Around his hip hung his seax in its horizontal leather scabbard, as well as three other ornate daggers slid vertically into the leather belt. He was every part the headman.

Behind the stone altar stood Heahstan, his immense hands clasped gently in front of him and his long white beard brushed and silvery in the sunshine. As the women approached he threw both hands in the air to signal silence to the crowd. Wulfgar's head shot round. As he caught sight of Brithwen he froze. She focused her attention on the altar as Cwenfleda led her through a gap in the circle to stand on Wulfgar's left. The few yards felt like miles, and Brithwen was glad to arrive. Heahstan began, his voice deep, lilting and hypnotic.

"Before Frigg, Goddess of Love, do we gather for this rite of marriage. A union of two who shall become one, a bond for as long as love shall last." Heahstan turned to Brithwen, holding out his right hand. "Wish you, Lady Brithwen, to become one with this man?"

There was no going back. "Yes," she responded, her gaze never leaving Heahstan or the altar.

Heahstan withdrew his hand and turned to Wulfgar, holding out his left hand to him, demanding, "Wish you, Lord Wulfgar, to become one with this woman?"

Brithwen held her breath, waiting for Wulfgar to answer. When he did not, hushed mumblings spread through the crowd. Desperate to know what hindered him, though hesitant to face him, Brithwen slowly turned her head. Raising her eyes from the altar, she met with Wulfgar's intense stare. She gave a sideways glance to signal he should respond. He remained a statue, apparently caught in the sight of her.

Heahstan repeated, a little louder, "Wish you, Lord Wulfgar, to become one with this woman?"

Wulfgar, as though suddenly drawn from a trance, replied, "Yes", his continuous gaze unwavering.

A shiver ran through Brithwen's body as she watched him give his oath. This was very real for him, no matter what bargain they had spoken of. It was then she realised the severity of the commitment she was making in the name of a bargain, and the earth became unsteady beneath her feet. She swayed, and Wulfgar threw a protective arm around her back, steadying her. Cwenfleda dashed forward to remove her bouquet from her arms. Another flow of hushed voices rippled through the crowd. Heahstan motioned for them to hold their hands across the altar. Wulfgar took Brithwen's arms and sat them crossways over his own. Heahstan made an announcement while tying their hands together with a length of embroidered linen.

"Above are the stars, and like a star may your love be constant. Below is stone, and like stone may your love be firm."

He took a cup crafted of thin pottery, filled it with wine and handed it to the bound couple, who held it between them to drink the contents. Brithwen drank first, leaving almost all of it for Wulfgar. The spoiled ale lingered in her mouth and she could not consume more than a small sip. Wulfgar, however, sank the remainder of the wine and led her in smashing the cup on the altar.

Heahstan bellowed, "No other may share what they have together. They leave behind one life and begin anew. All here witness, in the eyes of Frigg and Saxnot, God of Family… Lord and Lady Wulfgar of Sachsen."

The crowd erupted into a stupendous cheer, throwing pieces of seasonal foliage into the air, chants of "Wulfsuna" bouncing round the dell. Brithwen, briefly distracted by the celebrations, was taken by surprise as Wulfgar pulled her forward and kissed her fervently on the lips. The roar of the crowd grew tenfold in response and Brithwen hoped Wulfgar had enjoyed his moment, for it would be the last. Unable to fight him in public, she submitted, albeit too eagerly for her own liking. When Wulfgar released her she made as though the binding was too tight and Heahstan undid the cloth. She looked round at the crowds making off for the marriage feast and went to follow them. Her husband had other ideas, grasping her tightly round the waist and hoisting her above his head.

With her hands on his shoulders to steady herself, she looked at others. Wulfgar was whooping and shouting, holding her in the air like a trophy he had won. Cwenfleda was in tears. Leofgist was whooping with Wulfgar, like a pair of children in a game. Like a strange dream, no one seemed to sense the falseness of it all as she did. Thankfully, Wulfgar could see her wilting and returned her to the ground. Wulfgar's arm settled round her waist and, when they were separated by jostling crowds, his hand tightly grasped hers. At first she felt like a slave on a rope, a tethered dog longing to be free. However, several times he squeezed her hand and glanced sideways. Whether he meant to reassure her or was simply fulfilling his protection part of their bargain, she was grateful.

The feast consisted of another roasting pig and a cake of hot spices, fruit and mead, the latter being the drink of newly wedded couples for thirty days, or one moon, from the ceremony. The Wulfsuna settled into copious eating and drinking. Brithwen enjoyed the marriage cake, one of the few foods she had been able to consume in recent days. Its sweetness followed the roast pork well and she had managed a small serving of mead. When the music and dancing erupted the camp came alive, people swirling in their best garments: reds, browns, greens, purples and greys, flickering glimpses of coloured cloths mimicking the flames of the nearby fire. A strange heat grew within Brithwen and she shed her mantle and black pelt, the music and voices calling to her inner rhythm. Brithwen found her legs and leaped up to join others in a flowing dance of pirouettes and outstretched arms, bending and bowing like a tree in a breeze.

Before Wulfgar had time to react he had lost Brithwen in the throng, catching fleeting glimpses of her as she moved lithely past the flames. He had not been apart from her since the ceremony, but now allowed himself the privilege of viewing her from a distance. He watched her move rhythmically, her heart hearing every beat of the drums and her feet never seeming to touch the earth. Like a nymph she floated over the surface of the soil, casting her spell on everyone she passed. It was then he noticed he was not the only male enraptured by her image. Further down by the fire Trunhild sat alone and paid her keen attention, as did many others. As though a spear had shot him through the heart, Wulfgar felt anger overtake him. How dare they cast their eyes upon her that way. Stilling himself, he realised with closer inspection they were in awe. Digging deeper into the eyes of the crowd, it was not men alone that gazed upon her with respect and wonder. Many females pointed to her, picking out features like her skin by touching their faces with light fingers and nodding to their friends in appreciation. Warm smiles passed like a giant swell around the gathering each time she danced their way, and she was waving at them as she did so.

Wulfgar smiled, reflecting on his earlier jubilation when the marriage had been finalised. She had been so light when he had lifted her into the air, and still his lips tingled from that kiss. Although their lips had touched previously, it had not tasted so divine. It was not the berry juice on her lips. The gods had intervened. Yet each time he looked into her eyes, he saw immense sadness. She could not reciprocate for her heart belonged to another. He realised he wore the same formal attire he had at Sieghild's funeral and hated himself. What a cruel man she must think him. A heavy hand slapped him on the back. Heahstan stood over him, ale cup in hand which he raised to his headman.

"May the gods be with you, Lord Wulfgar."

Wulfgar raised his own cup to Heahstan and nodded acknowledgement. It was the first time he had noticed his eldest thegn using his noble title. It pleased him, and he would let Woden know his gratitude when next he sat in reverence to the Chief of the Gods. Heahstan nodded in return and moved silently back into the crowds. *May the gods be with you.* It had not been so much a wedding blessing as a prayer. Heahstan's fearful opposition to the nix had been well heard among the Wulfsuna. The thegn had agreed to do the ceremony for his lord due to the oath Wulfgar had sworn to Sieghild and the promise that he would keep a close eye on his new bride, lest she prove to be the river-witch they suspected. Wulfgar looked back to the fire and Brithwen dancing, wondering whether it was love he felt growing, or the beginning of a deadly hex.

And so, there arrived a time in the evening when no one knew how late or early the hour was, nor how much alcohol they had consumed. Many had forgotten where they usually slept, while others already slept, scattered around the camp fire. Wulfgar had long since given up on his drinking, instead watching his wife dance round the dying fire. He stood and stretched, looking for her when next she passed by. He sauntered down to the fire to greet her, calling out to her though she did not answer.

Laughing, he watched her prance another full circle round the fire, catching her by the arm. Her eyes were dark pools that looked straight through him to the trees beyond the dell.

"Brithwen. Brithwen?"

Giant orbs of pure black reflected his image back to him. She was not with him, but with her gods. She had been dancing elsewhere, chasing spirits around the flames. He wondered if she had done so to forget the madness the day had brought them, to pretend she had not given her life away to this marriage with him. She spoke, her voice deep and unfamiliar to him, and he feared it.

Lost in the arms of one, I seek another,
And already I am fated.
No sooner dead, than here,
Cold and isolated.
When will I see him?
When will I feel him?
When will my suffering end?
Lead me to the one who will make amend.

Wulfgar was less troubled by the words she had uttered and more concerned with how to release her from the dream vision. He could imagine she had been lost in Sieghild's arms, and he hoped he was the other of whom she spoke. However, he was resolute he would abide by his refusal to take her unwillingly. He had to bring her back though. He would not leave her tied to the spirits. Folding her in his embrace, he cupped the back of her head and kissed her softly. Dazed and bewildered, she came back from her vision.

"I lost you for a moment," he said, wiping beads of sweat from her face with the back of his hand.

She nodded, eyes closing involuntarily, revealing her weariness. She had eaten little before leaping up to dance and had not had the stomach to feed the previous night. He kept an arm on her waist and led her back to their tent. The day had been long and they could both use some sleep.

The door guards were thankfully awake and sober. Inside, however, the tent was cool as no fire had been lit. Wulfgar had ordered everyone to be in camp for the celebrations so no thrall had been to lay firewood. Brithwen started to keel over, and he caught her and laid her on his bed. Already, her head on the skins, she was nearly asleep. He removed her leather shoes and belt, wanting her seax as far from him as possible after the incident by the stream, and threw them into a corner. He removed his

211

pelt, war belt, boots and overtunic, placing them on his chest and sitting beside her.

Her face, flushed crimson from the fire, concerned him. He pondered removing her wool gown to make her more comfortable. He always felt more comfortable in his undergarments. He glanced at her seax. The night he had crept to find her in her tent she had worn nothing but her undertunic. His loins ached as he remembered her milky skin in the moonlight. He leaned over her, unclasping both brooches, and tugged the gown off her a little at a time. Ordinarily, they would both have removed all their garments and shared more than sleeping space.

Wulfgar found himself reflecting on when he had last bed a woman. Sometime before they had left Sachsen, he realised. She had been a thrall whose hands had always managed to catch his clothes as she passed each morning to light his fire. Finally she had done just that, lit his fire. His body reacted, remembering her plump little arse and how his gripping hands had left red marks on her pink buttocks. He sighed fondly at the memory. This was no ordinary marriage; they were no ordinary husband and wife. For all the ceremony and celebrations, there would be no joining of flesh.

Sliding the wool gown off her legs, Wulfgar undressed down to his trousers and even removed his vambraces. Lying next to her, he watched her sleeping for a while. When she stirred, rolling onto her side, he felt the weight of sleep upon him. As he settled his body behind her she leaned against him, sighing pleasantly. He draped an arm over her thigh, which she fumbled for in her slumber and moved to her abdomen. He recalled the night they had found her in the woods, draped over Sieghild, both fast asleep. He buried his face in her hair, inhaling her sweet scent and stifled tears. He had her in his arms. If only he could tell her how much he missed his friend, she would know they shared the same pain. He let sleep claim him, for he was capable of nothing more.

CHAPTER EIGHTEEN

Wulfsuna Camp,
Middle Wolds South-East of Gloui

The morning found them unmoved and entwined. Brithwen woke first feeling the warmth of another and briefly thought herself back in Sieghild's arms. She rolled over, smiling at the man who lay next to her in the shadows of dawn. Pale blond hair tumbled across a bearded face and her cheeks burned. With each beat her heart ached, tears stinging her eyes. Nevertheless, she gently teased Wulfgar's hair from his face, resting her hand on his cheek. His eyes fluttering open, he smiled and covered her hand with his own. Lifting her hand to his mouth, he kissed her palm and paused. Discomfort seemed to claim him and he released her, rolling to sit on the bedside.

Rejection burned into Brithwen's heart. She did not understand the swift change to his demeanour. Perhaps he had noticed her grief and this made him uncomfortable, or else he had awoken imagining he lay with another. She swallowed the rest of her tears, wiping her face dry with shaky hands. He stood, remaining with his back to Brithwen, and found his clothes. As he picked up the trousers he had worn at his wedding, a sprig of rosemary fell from the waistband. Brithwen leaned across the bed and picked it up. It was dry but still pungent.

"Why did you wear this?" she asked.

He spoke without facing her. "It is to honour Frigg, the Goddess of Love."

Her stomach rolled. "Love?"

He murmured after a long pause, "We are to keep up appearances, are we not?"

He dressed quickly, taking care not to make eye contact with her, and did not linger, departing their tent in silence. Appearances? She did not believe him. No one would have seen it hidden in the waistband of his trousers. She shrugged, smiling at his punctilious nature, and inhaled the menthol aroma of the rosemary. Senses refreshed, she searched the tent for her clothes. Her dancing had led her into a dream last night, filled with memories of her mother, Sieghild and Huweyn. She could not retrace how she had left the festivities for her lord's tent, though she must have made it back somehow, and she clutched the cloth of her undertunic, for neither could she remember undressing.

Dismissing her forgetfulness as a result of the visions, she arose and found her garments scattered nearby. A thrall had brought in water for washing earlier that morning, most likely while they both slept. Brithwen set her clothes in a neat pile on the bed and turned to approach the bowl and water. She tripped, ungainly, over a cold, hard object and bent to investigate. Leather-backed and covered in iron splints, they were instantly recognisable as the imposing wrist cuffs she had seen their lord wearing. She set the pair on his wooden chest and finished her toilet.

Outside it was a wild morning, gales brewing and the trees tossing their leaves in abundance. The cool, dry air was a welcome relief from the searing heat and thunder storms of the past few weeks. Brithwen asked a guard to find her a seat to watch the camp being packed up. It appeared they were moving on today and it pleased her. In a few days she would be back in Prenhwychas. The guard brought her a stool and she sat down to view the proceedings.

Wulfgar, in good voice, hollered at various groups, co-ordinating people in several directions at once. The central fire was being cleared away. As before, people gathered up the ashes and coals that remained. Animals, tethered to graze, were rounded up and attached to their relevant owners' wagons. The few tents were systematically dismantled, skins and hemp tarps first, then wooden posts and supports. Inside them, the contents had already been removed and the hearth fires cleared. Leofgist, meanwhile, organised the wagon village with a handful of men, ensuring all wagoners had left the area as they had found it. Cwenfleda walked over, waving and smiling, and began talking as she drew near. One of the guards hindered her approach with a spear across her path, instructing her scornfully to use the proper address.

"No address is needed." Brithwen offered a hand to Cwenfleda, but the guard did not remove the spear.

"It is required," came the terse reply.

"This is not necessary." Brithwen lifted the spear and offered a hand to Cwenfleda once more. Cwenfleda took Brithwen's hand and bowed graciously.

"Good morning, Lady Brithwen."

"Please rise," Brithwen begged, drawing her friend up and to her side. "This is a pleasant surprise. Have you come to talk a while?"

Cwenfleda smiled. "I have come as your handmaiden, to help you pack for the journey."

The half-hour spent listening to the latest gossip from the wagon village reminded Brithwen of Cwenfleda's capricious nature. She announced her involvement with the young man from the beer wagon, though Brithwen saw through her friend's efforts to disguise her jealousy.

"You slept here last night." Cwenfleda's statement came after several long glances at the marital bed.

Brithwen smiled politely, lips tight. "Yes." Cwenfleda's hopes of marrying the headman had vanished on account of a muddy wandering Wealas the Wulfsuna had stumbled across and taken in like a lost dog. This Cwenfleda's lord had chosen over her, "woman of beauty". It mattered not that he had no interest in return. Brithwen knew the discomfort would be a long time passing. Regardless of her handmaiden's feelings, Cwenfleda had packed a neat chest and stayed no more than was necessary once her chores were complete.

"May I be excused?" she asked, eyes darting to the entrance.

Brithwen smiled. "Yes. Give my blessings to your family."

Cwenfleda waved, giving no indication she would do so. The distance her position had given her disheartened Brithwen and so she decided to take a walk. As she left the immediate vicinity of the tent, one of the guards stepped in beside her, matching every step and turn she made. Could she go nowhere alone? Thralls and guards lingered in her life even as she lay in slumber in bed with her husband. She made for the beech coppice by the stream and sat on a fallen log.

"Do you find this pleasant?" she asked the guard, picking up a cone and enjoying the familiar woody aroma. "Have you smelled these before?"

The guard did not respond. She tossed the cone on the ground and glanced back at the busy camp clearing their wares. She saw her lord marching over to his tent, no doubt to oversee its removal.

"Will you not talk with me?" she asked the guard.

He shot her a sideways glance and stiffened his stance. "Lady Brithwen, we do not have permission to engage with you."

She frowned. "You cannot talk to me?"

The guard made direct eye contact, shook his head negatively and cut his gaze. She stared into the stream, its soft rippling progress pleasant on the ears. Her last visit here had been a farewell ceremony to Sieghild. With each passing day she wondered if she would ever forget him. She recalled seeing Wulfgar's face in the surface of the water and hearing the spirits whisper "When horsehair told of who to wed". How true that prophecy had been. She sighed heavily, her thoughts falling into the water.

Her guard's scabbard clanked against his spear as he stood to attention and Brithwen withdrew from her memories. Wulfgar marched toward her, shoulders hunched and head lowered like a wolf on the attack. She met his eyes and recoiled from him in fear.

"Come," he instructed, ignoring her terrified expression and pulling her after him by the arm. He had her fast, his strong hand clenched just above the elbow. She felt the tingling in her feet, but pushed the power back down into the earth for there were several onlookers. He walked at speed, but not as fast as Sieghild had that day at the market when he had dragged her into the woods and she had managed to keep pace. Inside their now empty tent, Wulfgar unsheathed her seax and tossed it away before she could respond. He was protecting himself. He still feared her. He faced her and she held up two palms as a protective barrier against any violence.

"Ah no, little wife," he chided, "not this time."

Using both his hands he knocked her arms down and took her by the waist, tossing her back onto the damp floor. Winded, she sat long enough to realise he had not followed her and did not intend to hurt her. He folded his arms, face scornful.

"I hear you dismissed one of the guards for requesting a formal address from one of your subjects."

"It was merely Cwenfleda…" She began.

"They are your subjects also now. You forget yourself. How am I to protect you if you do not allow my men to do their job? Not everyone is a friend. Even within the Wulfsuna, there are those who would have me dead and see another lead."

Brithwen gazed at the ground. He shared his predicament with Huweyn. It seemed foreign lords were no more safe than their Brytonic counterparts. It scared her into wondering how much danger he was in from his own people and how much danger she was now in as his wife.

"I did not know," she said meekly.

He continued, his anger not abating, "There is much you do not know, and I would not have you know. Your life is in enough danger. We turn west for Prenhwychas today and I know not the whereabouts of Eadmaer, who by now is likely to know I am on his tail seeking revenge." He thrust a pointed finger at her, moving forward in a single large step. "Anyone who approaches you, *anyone*, is to give formal address and be observed by the guards."

Brithwen remained silent, grateful for his protection though feeling undeserved of the way he expressed it. He lowered his arm, chest heaving from his rage. He flexed his left arm, wincing. She remembered the night by the stream where she had stabbed him in the shoulder. It was the same arm: the arm he had used to drag her back here. As her eyes rested on his shoulder, she noticed he glanced over to her seax and she wondered whether he remembered too.

She smiled at him. "Yes, My Lord."

He tossed a hand. "There is no need for that. You are my wife, not my thrall." He bent down and held out a hand. "I have asked you to call me Wulfgar."

He had extended his bad arm, out of habit no doubt. When she did not move to take it, he frowned. Lowering his arm, he winced a second time. She shook her head at his stubbornness and patted the grass beside her.

"Sit," she commanded.

With raised eyebrows, he joined her on the floor, his face full of question. She knelt over, placing her hands on his shoulders, exerting a soft pressure to ease him back. Ignoring the flickers of desire she glimpsed in his eyes, she slowly undid his tunic. She ignored too the flickering within her own body, a sign of something her body yearned for and not her heart. Finding the wound, bare and in need of treatment, she chided him with a shake of her head.

"You have not dressed this wound enough," she told him.

Breathless from his fast-beating heart, he replied, "I have had a thrall attend my arm. The shoulder will heal."

"You use it too much. Use your right."

His voice deeper than usual, he said, "I am not so good with my right."

She gave him a wry smile. "I shall dress it for you with an ointment."

As she went to rise he caught her wrist firmly. "Wait."

"Why?"

"Please, I bid you, wait."

Passion burned in his eyes and Brithwen decided she would have to shield herself from them, for each time she was witness to it, the nightmare of the wolf returned and quenched her desire. She could not defer from their marriage of convenience until Prenhwychas had been saved. Whatever her body wanted, it was in memory of another man's touch. No more than a physical memory.

"Why?" she asked again.

His eyes darkened. He had raised an invisible barrier between them, an emotional shield she had intended to make use of herself. It seemed he too struggled to retain their alliance without the union of flesh.

"If we remain here a while, those that witnessed me bringing you back will believe we have…"

"To keep appearances?" she offered, then added, "If it will assist in you retaining a hold on your leadership, I will comply. For how long should we wait?"

His cheeks flushed and he ran a quivering hand through his hair, biding time. She smiled, taking amusement from his discomfort.

"I need to know how long to sit here."

He pulled her over him, her stomach landing across his torso, firm hands tickling her sides. Laughing, she attempted to wriggle free, but he raised his knees trapping her in a vice between his thighs and chest. She kicked playfully, arms flailing. He smacked her rear and dropped his legs, rolling her away. Spinning over like an unrolled rug, she squealed as she came to rest, her back lying over his shins. She wiped hair from her face, giggling and breathless. She sat, conscious that he observed her closely, the smile gone from his mouth but not his eyes.

"Thank you. I…" she began.

In one lithe movement he faced her, an arm at her back as he leaned over her. She sank into the grass, eyes wide. Resting on his left arm, he cursed under his breath as more pain seized him. She raised a hand to his left shoulder, concern creasing her brow.

"I should dress it."

"Sh," he whispered as he lowered his head.

Brithwen thought her heart would break her ribs as it hammered loudly in her breast. She did not want him to ruin the jovial moment they had shared. If he imagined he could persuade her to give her body to him, he was wrong. Within a breath of her lips, he paused. With all the will in the world, she could not make him look at her. No magick could tear his eyes from her lips. His eyes closed, so slowly, blond lashes flickering and settling on tanned cheeks. His head turned and he buried his face in her neck, his short beard grazing her soft skin. She closed her eyes, relaxing as she realised an embrace was all he yearned for. A moment later he lifted his head, a weak smile tugging the sides of his mouth. He stroked the end of her nose with a finger, making her smile.

"How was that for you?" he asked her.

She could not answer, only smile.

He eased himself up and stood, massaging his shoulder. "I think that is about the right amount of time. I thank you."

"I should thank you." She rose to her feet and retrieved her seax, replacing it in its scabbard.

"For what?" he asked.

"For keeping to our agreement," she said, stepping forward and kissing him briefly on the lips.

She departed swiftly to find ointment for his wound. He deserved some gratitude for remaining true to his honour. He could easily have overpowered her, and knew only too well she would have defended herself violently.

Wulfgar closed his eyes, lingering in the feeling Brithwen's lips had left on his mouth. Drunk from her, his body jolted from memory of his dreams of her. "Take her as your own" Sieghild had made him swear. His fear had left him. Either love had bound him to this woman, or else the nix held him in a fierce hex that kept him blind. He wanted to take her, but he would not break an oath. He inhaled deeply, filling his chest with hope, and went to face his people.

Stepping into the daylight, he was met with raucous clapping from Leofgist and his thegns. He held back an anger rising in him, one he had not felt before. He did not want them to applaud him for having taken his wife, though knowing he had cheered fellow men for the same, he buried his resentment. He waved a hand, grinning.

"Don't you men have work to do?"

Heahstan, arms folded, replied, "We are waiting to take down what's left of this pitiful tent you call home."

"You were a little busy." Osmund winked.

Leofgist approached, grinning broadly and calling over his shoulder, "Lorri, collect your lord's war-gear."

The cnapa sniggered loudly as he scurried past, head down. Wulfgar rolled his eyes, looking for Brithwen though trying not to reveal it. Heahstan strolled over and leaned in to whisper, "She is down by the stream collecting herbs, My Lord."

Wulfgar was about to deny the truth, mouth open, when Leofgist's voice halted all words.

"I thought you slept in these, My Lord."

The gathered men ceased their jovial discourse and Wulfgar spun round. Leofgist held out both hands, an iron vambrace in each. Wulfgar glanced down at his naked wrists. He never removed them, except for washing. They had been a war gift from his father after his first battle against the Geats.

"Only when he doesn't have a good woman in his bed, Leofgist." Heahstan winked and the men laughed loudly.

Wulfgar took the vambraces from Leofgist and shouted, "Come then, dismantle my tent. Rally your men, for we head west." He shrugged the wrist guards over his hands, pulled them tight with the leather straps and tied them off. Leofgist lingered with Heahstan. Wulfgar nodded back to the dispersing thegns.

"I want my wagon moved again and as few men to know about it as possible. Leofgist, make it comfortable for my Lady Brithwen." He faced the older man. "Call council for me."

Heahstan nodded curtly. "My Lord."

"Who shall I ask to move the wagon?" Leofgist asked.

"You and Lorri do it. There are few I trust lately." Wulfgar patted Leofgist on the shoulder and strode off to find Brithwen.

Riding at the front of the convoy alongside Leofgist, Wulfgar silently asked Woden to safeguard Brithwen. They rode west, towards the wolds and in search of Prenhwychas. Council had been difficult and divided. Most of the thegns had given their full support, despite many who had previously shown a distrust of the nix, including Heahstan. The majority emphasised the possibility, however, that the Wulfsuna could encounter Eadmaer before, after or even during defence of Prenhwychas: a village to which no one held allegiance. To most it was a favour to a Wealh, and, although several knew Brithwen was actually Morwyneth, they may not have amended their view of the nix, even if she had married their lord. When they stopped to feed and water the tribe and its animals, Wulfgar called on his wife. It seemed she had heard some of their council.

"Who is Eadmaer?" she asked as he climbed in beside her.

He raised eyebrows at her and finished settling himself, offering her the plate he had brought filled with mutton and bread. "Good afternoon," he bid her, and continued when she smiled, "Some of the thegns were limitanei: mercenaries helping defend Rome against the Pictii."

"Heahstan?" she asked, tearing a piece of bread in her teeth.

"Yes. Heahstan and my father Wulfric, Sieghild's father Aelfsieg and Eadmaer's father Maerard. They were at Gloui and Vindolanda." He took some mutton from the plate, chewing the end. Brithwen set her bread in her lap, thoughtful.

"I know not all of you returned home. Trunhild told me his father remained on the isle for he had married a Brytonic woman."

"As had Sieghild's father, though he took her back to Germania." Wulfgar watched as memories sailed across her eyes. "Now we have returned to find settlement together. I have come to honour my father's dream."

"What of your mother?"

Memories of his own invaded his mind, threatening to dismember his composure, tearing his heart to shreds the way he had torn at the tent. He tossed the half-eaten mutton back onto the nearby plate and drew his knees up, resting elbows on them.

"We had to leave my mother. She was too sick to travel, like many others we left behind." His back stiffened. "Eadmaer murdered my father after we landed. If I do not hunt him down, Eadmaer will kill me."

"I am sorry. I did not know." She turned away, grief claiming her too much to be merely empathy for his own. Sieghild he knew she had lost, though there were perhaps others.

"How could you know?" he told her, lifting a hand to rub her back and hesitating, resisting the urge and allowing his hand to drop.

She faced him, wiping away tears. "Why does he want to kill you?"

Wulfgar released a sigh. "My father killed his father. Maerard did not want to leave Bryton. He wanted to ally to the Pictii and invade your land – land my father had defended for twenty years. They fought and Wulfric killed Maerard. Since then our people have been at peace under a truce agreed between my father and Eadmaer's mother." He met Brithwen's terrified gaze. "I don't believe Eadmaer ever forgave Wulfric. I believe he intends to join the Pictii and attack."

"My vision, Prenhwychas," she murmured.

He nodded. "This morning, my scouts reported Eadmaer is recruiting Pictii, promising them payment in land conquered if they fight with him."

"I understand now," she told him, taking one of his hands in her own.

"Understand?" He tilted his head to one side.

"Why we must be vigilant. I shall do as you have asked. I shall not challenge the guards again."

She released his hand and he made to leave, pausing on the edge of the wagon. The tale-weaver's words haunted him, daring him to know the answer. He needed to know if she were truly the seer fated to find him.

"And you, what of your mother and father? Do they live?"

She turned away, eyes gazing out of the wagon. "My father lives, I hope."

In the following silence, Wulfgar did not know if he would receive a full answer and felt compelled to prompt her. "And your mother, is she still with you?"

Brithwen smiled fondly, bringing her eyes back to him. "She is with me...in spirit."

She tensed in his tight embrace as he wound her in his arms. He had needed to hide his face from her for fear of revealing his thoughts. The tale-weaver had spoken the truth. Brithwen was his seer, sent by a saga to find him, a wolf spear, and fulfil his destiny. He kissed her gently on the top of her head and disembarked hastily, calling Lorri to bring his chestnut mare. He mounted and cantered down the convoy, intending to check all was in order. His concentration waned, however. It had been twelve days since Sieghild's passing, when he had sworn to take Morwyneth in his arms and comfort her. Finally he had achieved that, although he remained uncertain for the moment whether it had eased their pain or opened up a new wound.

They traversed the uplands, following the river of wind and rushes, where small hamlets folded into the steep sides of the valley, homes to fullers, weavers and sheep farmers. Dry stone walls trickled down the fields like streams of amber. The air remained humid, though Thunor did not strike his hammer and send the dark clouds rolling. Instead, the weather hung over them like a warning. Late in the day the landscape strangled the road, the wagons slow over the narrow and stony tracks. Saddle sore and replete with complaints from the tribe, Wulfgar sympathised with his people and ordered they should rest for the night.

Leofgist, who had been riding at the rear with half the armed warriors and thegns, joined him. "Is all as you wish it, My Lord?"

Wulfgar, aware his ealdorman most likely referred to the placement of his wagon and the dispersal of men and weapons, inhaled through his teeth. "I could do with a jug of ale."

"That goes without saying." Leofgist grinned. "And I would join you."

"Lord Wulfgar." Heahstan's raised voice, tinged with concern, made both men turn. The thegn strode purposefully past the jagged line of wagons and men, wiping sweat from his forehead with his forearm. Wulfgar glanced at Leofgist who reciprocated, and they waited for him to speak again. Out of breath and fidgeting with his war belt, the old man bowed briefly.

"My Lord," he began hurriedly, "the scop has vanished. No one saw him leave. Shall I have the guard beaten?"

Wulfgar leaned a hand on his horse's rump as he twisted to look back up the convoy. "Where's my wife?"

"Fear not, My Lord." Heahstan raised a hand to still him. "I have come from her and she bides fine. I have ordered extra men to stand guard, though given them no explanation."

Wulfgar felt his gut settle as panic ebbed. "Do not punish the guard. Move him to another post."

"My Lord." Heahstan retreated on another swift bow, hurrying away.

"I've never seen him run," Leofgist said, smiling. Wulfgar managed a brief grin, though his thoughts were elsewhere.

CHAPTER NINETEEN

Uplands of the Middle Wolds,
South of the River Wyndrysh

Brithwen had not welcomed another day tossing in the wagon. She had seen nothing of her husband since his brief embrace the evening before. She had heard him talking with friends until the moon was high, and assumed he had risen early, for he had not been there when she awoke. With no distractions, Brithwen's anticipation of reaching Prenhwychas became anxiety. With no way of knowing whether the Wulfsuna, or indeed she, would be welcomed, and by whom, the confines of the wagon were soon unbearable.

Nightfall came early and Brithwen jumped down from the wagon. A guard queried her departure and she waved a hand in front of her face, insinuating she was overcome by the humidity. She did not lie. The warm air smothered them and Brithwen felt it more than usual. Amid the excitement of the past few days she had not kept an eye on the moon. Her bleedings were possibly overdue, which would explain her light-headedness and sickness. As a child, she recalled Anwen had told her the women in her family had sporadic bleedings. In addition, she had not been eating well. Compared to her desperation to see Huweyn, however, it was merely an irritation. She looked ahead. Beacon Hill stood tall, a dark and silent silhouette against the arrival of the stars. Used for warning of enemy attack, she was glad to see no fires burned upon it. They had not yet been seen.

Wulfgar's voice cut through the quiet. "Make camp."

To be so close to Prenhwychas and yet so distant seeded a yearning in Brithwen's stomach. She understood the needs of the Wulfsuna were a priority, though she could not ignore her own personal longing to see her home once more. She had to know that Huweyn was safe. Wulfgar arrived, leaping down from his mare and tossing orders at his cnapa and four guards. Without acknowledging her, Wulfgar climbed into their wagon. Bewildered, Brithwen followed. Her husband had already removed his battle-gear when a guard lifted her in and dropped the hide down to enclose them. In the near-darkness, Brithwen crawled over to the sheepskins and straw to find Wulfgar lying there.

Fortunately, she had not intended to engage him in lengthy conversation. Nonetheless, she felt rejected and hoped his behaviour had not changed because they were nearing Prenhwychas. As she settled beside him, he made no move to touch her. He smelled faintly of horses, and underneath a strong musky odour she found comforting. A strong male scent, it reminded her of how she had felt in the protective company of Sieghild. She longed to curl against him and lose herself in his warmth. Instead, sleep claimed her and, haunted by conflicting emotions, her dreams took her on a spirit journey.

She found herself seated under beech trees in an unknown wood. Her eyes closed, she focused on the wind rustling through the leaves and the branches above her, dappled light dancing on her eyelids. The grey wolf, which on previous nights had torn her to shreds, paced steadily towards her, the placing of every paw a calculated move. It paused to growl revealing sharp white teeth, and she smiled as best she could, tentatively holding an outstretched hand towards the beast in friendship. The growling ceased. After a pause the wolf continued until it was within a few feet. Her heart pounded in her ribcage; the deep resounding heartbeat of the wolf in complete unison with her own: erratic and fast.

Equally in fear of her, the wolf hesitated within a snout's reach of her hand. The ends of her fingers tingled in anticipation of the touch of its fur. She tried to elongate her fingers to reach it. After an agonising pause, the wolf rested its head beneath her straining fingers and she laid her palm between its huge ears. The long fur, incredibly soft, belied the fearsome outward appearance of the beast. She lost her fingers in the grey pelt, inhaling deeply and uttering a name in one long whispered breath.

"Wulfgar."

A low, husky voice replied, "Yeah?"

Confused that a wolf should speak to her she attributed it to the voice of Spirit, but again a voice spoke.

"What?"

Startled, Brithwen woke from her dream and turned to find her husband looking into her eyes. "Wulfgar," she exclaimed.

"Yes, little wife?"

"I was dreaming," she told him.

"I see," he replied, rolling over slightly. "Was it a good dream?" His voice had a low timbre, perhaps due to tiredness, she thought.

"I think so," she said.

"In truth?" he asked, sounding surprised.

"Yes," she replied.

He reached over, taking her in his arms and kissing her warmly on the lips. Brithwen, safe and warm, felt no need to refuse him and, when he nestled her head under his chin, she returned to a dreamless slumber.

Sun burst into the wagon like flares leaping from a blazing fire, the air sharp. The winds had settled almost to nothing and a robin sang joyously in a tree close by. Brithwen stretched and yawned, finding herself alone. She had had the best night's sleep she had experienced since leaving Prenhwychas. And they were almost upon it. A little more than a month had it been since her feet had touched the soil of her birthplace; since she'd joined the Wulfsuna. A month as a Seaxan and now the wife of the tribal lord. She was one of them, in dress and speech. Her own linguistic skills had surprised her though. Trunhild was an excellent teacher and she had practised often with Sieghild and Cwenfleda. However, she felt another magick lurked beneath it all. There had been many times where she had simply known the words. Something, or someone, guided her. She knew she lay alone before she moved. If they were to arrive at Prenhwychas today, there would be important plans to oversee. By break of day they would have been visible from Beacon Hill. Once a fire had been lit upon the hill all would know, and a not altogether friendly reception would be awaiting them.

There would be mixed feelings about their arrival. She had heard Huweyn talk of the foreigners, the Seaxans. In the past, waves of warriors had invaded the east; a bunch of Eadmaers pillaging and taking whatever land their feet found. Rome had severed ties and left the people of Bryton to their fates. It seemed easy for people to forget those who had fought for Rome, taken her coin and protected her territories, as Wulfgar had told her; easy to forget twenty years. Brithwen remained confident though. She knew Huweyn to be a reasonable man. He would make his own judgement, if he had managed to retain power in her absence.

When the guard allowed her passage to see to her toilet, true to her suspicions a fire had been lit atop Beacon Hill. On her return an indiscernible figure blew a cattle horn repeatedly in four compass directions, its long lamented notes dissipating into the distant wolds. On the nearest slope to the convoy, Brithwen saw a farmer collecting in his flock of longhaired sheep, hurrying them up the hill with a long stick and whistles. Leofgist rode over to her in full battle dress, his thin face partially concealed by his helmet.

"Back inside, Lady Brithwen," he ordered. "Drop the skins and stay hidden. Lord Wulfgar bids it for your protection."

He rode off and two of the guards assisted her into the wagon. And so it began: the binding agreement and reason for their marriage of convenience. She listened and waited. The convoy did not move, though warriors harried and she heard Leofgist giving orders. When the hide entrance lifted on her wagon, she screamed.

"It is I, Lady Brithwen," said Estelflead, climbing inside.

"Why are we not moving?" she asked.

Estelflead's eyes searched the vicinity, her response vague. "We are awaiting the return of scouts who went ahead. Where are your mantles?"

Brithwen motioned to her chest and Estelflead found the soft, dark mantle she had worn for her wedding. "I bid you, wear this. Lord Wulfgar has asked that you hide your face as best you can. The wagons may be searched by your fellow countrymen so that they are satisfied we hide no villains."

Brithwen complied, draping the fine cloth over her head and lifting the front across her face, securing it at the side of her head with a pin Estelflead gave her. Over the top she added the thicker, lighter-coloured mantle, allowing it to hang around her face and shoulders. Already wearing her green cloak, she lifted the hood which cast a shadow over what remained visible of her face beneath. Estelflead hung her black wolf pelt on her shoulders, which she held in place with a brooch.

"Speak only Seaxan," the older woman instructed her. "It may be hard when you hear your own tongue, but you must persist."

Brithwen nodded, too scared to talk. The cattle horns were still baying in the distance and shivers ran up Brithwen's spine with each note that echoed down the valley. A flurry of horse hooves told her the scouts had returned. She heard Wulfgar questioning them and hurried responses from the two men. There seemed to be no sign of ambush; no sign of anyone. The villagers were in hiding.

"We move," Wulfgar bellowed, and the wagons began to jostle over the stones.

Memories of conversations in her own language filled Brithwen's mind and she closed her eyes tight, believing it would make them cease. It did not. She thought of Sieghild, and Trunhild who had taught her Seaxan, but earlier conversations they had shared in her Brytonic words filtered through. She could not forget. Again she heard Wulfgar.

"We ride, men."

As her thoughts turned to him, to all their times together thus far, her mind filled with Seaxan alone. They had shared no other language. To survive this return to Prenhwychas she would have to focus on Wulfgar. He was the wolf who would help her. She let him into her mind as she had let him into her life by agreeing to be his bride. Returning to face the hungry she-wolves responsible for her expulsion, Brithwen had brought her own pack leader. If they dared even to raise a curled lip, he would stand in their way. As they neared the hill, the cries of the beacon caller rang out across the hamlets, telling all who could hear him of the approaching strangers. The single drawn-out cry chilled her to the bone, for she was now one of them.

"S-A-E-S-O-N!"

Brithwen imagined in Prenhwychas and other places men rallying to find weapons, women hiding children and animals. Huweyn would be calling his elders to meeting and closing the gates to their hill dwelling, sealing all inside, or sealing their fate. Again the caller threw the single word into the open air, long, loud, sinister. She closed her eyes, asking the goddess to bestow her with courage and foresight. In Seaxan she reminded herself of her title of nobility, repeating it over and over, ingraining the words into her mind.

Wulfgar had set up his men to protect the wagons. He rode at the front flanked by Leofgist and Heahstan, with Thegns Osmund and Geldhere behind them, respectfully. A score of warriors followed on foot, preceding the five civilian wagons. Aft of those rode the ale and cook's carts flanked by the second score of warriors, followed by Thegns Ianbert, Trunhild and Tortsig with a line of armed thralls at the rear. They were almost fifty Wolf Sons, and Wulfgar prayed it would be enough.

The wagons made the bumpy journey to the base of Beacon Hill, where a small party of less-than-welcoming men had gathered, clutching scythes and forks. Leofgist waved an arm and the first score of Wulfsuna formed a crescent shield wall in front of their lord and his thegns, standing fast with angons leaning at ease. One of the locals hesitantly stepped forward and introduced himself.

"I am Clodri, the tucker. What is your intention?"

As had been previously arranged, Leofgist gestured to Osmund who translated. Wulfgar listened and gave Osmund his response in a low voice, barely turning his head to speak to the Brytonic thegn behind and to his left.

"Tell him we are the tribe of the Wulfsuna, two months out of Germania. We come to protect Prenhwychas."

Osmund relayed what Wulfgar hoped were the correct words, and repeated Clodri's reply. "He asks at whose request do we come?"

Wulfgar glared directly at the tucker. "Morwyneth of Prenhwychas."

A lengthy discourse erupted between Clodri and the others. They huddled round, arms on one another's shoulders and hands cupped over their mouths. When they parted, Clodri addressed Wulfgar, who waited eagerly for the answer from Osmund.

"Morwyneth is no longer of Prenhwychas. How do you know of her?"

Wulfgar shifted in his saddle, unease settling in his backside. "Tell them we found her in the wilderness and she asked us to save them."

Osmund's translation instigated surprise, shuffling of feet and hurried whispers. Clodri put a hand up to silence his fellow men and looked down the line of wagons.

"She returns with you?" he asked.

"No," Osmund replied, as Wulfgar shook his head at the natives.

The tucker and his band seemed satisfied, but Clodri said, "You may proceed to Prenhwychas, but first we must check for villains."

On hearing Osmund, Wulfgar nodded to Leofgist who led the way, waving Geldhere to follow at the rear with a handful of warriors. The Seaxan wall parted, a tide of shields receding to allow Clodri and his men passage. The villagers trod uneasily past the rows of upheld spears, foreign eyes squinting at them from behind metal faceguards. Before they neared the first wagon, Wulfgar shouted to Leofgist.

"Ealdorman Leofgist, remind them of whom resides in the first wagon."

Osmund dutifully trotted his horse over to Leofgist, for he did not know who sat in the first wagon. Leofgist muttered inaudibly and Osmund nodded curtly, facing an expectant Clodri who had been detained by the four guards that had remained to secure Brithwen inside.

"Go with respect to the first wagon. A lady resides within," Osmund instructed.

As Clodri drew near and one of the guards drew back the ox-hide entrance, Wulfgar strained to see the back of his wagon and his wife hiding inside. He prayed to Frigg she had done as Estelflead had asked of her. Wulfsuna surrounded the villagers, hands on weapons. In his own language, Clodri bowed and gave a greeting. He took a quick peek and backed away, bowing respectfully, moving swiftly onto the next wagon. Wulfgar had been unable to see Brithwen from where he sat. She had said nothing and he silently sent her his gratitude. With any luck, the villagers would not see her again.

Leofgist and a handful of warriors escorted Clodri and his men along the remainder of the convoy. It did not take long as Clodri and his men soon tired of their inspection. They were farmers, not warriors. They had less skill and fewer weapons, and probably knew full well the Seaxans could overpower them. Wulfgar felt a pang of disappointment, for he had

had men hide in the rear wagon, ready to leap out at the first sign of attack. He had wanted to see that. Thegn Osmund spoke and Wulfgar caught the end of the translation.

"Granted to proceed with our escort."

In a tight group, Clodri led his band ahead of the Wulfsuna. Leofgist settled his ride back alongside Wulfgar.

"They know little of battle," he told his lord.

Wulfgar smiled. "Yes. They allow nearly fifty armed foreigners to ride behind them."

Clodri observed them with odd backward glances, nervous at the banter being conducted in a strange tongue. Leofgist laughed.

"He believes we are plotting against them."

"Maybe we are," Wulfgar replied, unable to resist a loud, deep laugh.

Clodri remained wary of them even as they reached the gates of Prenhwychas. Guards in uniform, almost reminiscent of Roman Legio and carrying spathae, met them several yards out from the closed gates. Bowmen stood, ready-aimed at the visitors, on wooden towers either side of the entrance. Leofgist rode behind Clodri as he strode up to the guards and an announcement passed through to someone behind the gates. A response filtered back to Clodri who fed the request to Osmund.

Osmund waved a thumb towards the gates. "The leader and two men may approach, no more."

"Be cautious, My Lord," Heahstan warned from his right.

Wulfgar grinned. "I'm glad I wore my father's helmet."

Hidden behind the full face mask, Wulfgar glanced at the opposing force. He waved Leofgist over and imparted orders for another shield wall, angons lowered, and any bowmen they still had to flank the wagons. With weapons clanging against wood, warriors fell in as assigned by their ealdorman. Wulfgar watched the men on the towers, bows taught as arrows aimed at him and his companions on either side.

"Steady," Heahstan muttered, as though their opponents would hear his whisper and behave.

"I know what I'm doing," Wulfgar replied, and continued, "By the way, I didn't thank you for moving Trunhild."

Heahstan nodded. "I'm not sure he liked it, but he went. You do not want a man you do not trust sitting right beside you. Ianbert is loyal. He will watch him back there."

"Are you ready, My Lord?" Leofgist asked as he steadied his horse next to Wulfgar.

Wulfgar turned round and caught sight of Brithwen, peeping out from the wagon. He lowered his gaze, hoping she would go back into hiding. With his gut twisting into knots, he glanced up and found she had done as he had hoped.

"I am ready," Wulfgar told Leofgist and moved his horse forward. "Come, Osmund. We will need you."

The gates of Prenhwychas opened and, with trepidation written across their faces, what appeared to be three village elders met Clodri. One was a man of faith in brown wool garments; the second and third wore a long Roman peplos over their native tunics. They seemed neither completely Brytonic nor completely Roman. However, they spoke as Morwyneth, as Wealas and not in Latin, and Osmund translated.

The man of faith stepped forward, welcoming them with two upturned palms. "*Croeso.* I am Gwidol, the preacher."

Wulfgar nodded for Osmund to respond. The thegn held a hand out to his lord.

"Lord Wulfgar of Sachsen, Headman of the Wulfsuna."

Gwidol beckoned his two companions closer; they conceded with hesitation. "Permit me to present Vendognus nepos Lollia Scrivus, our professor and man of scripture, and Turpilos nepos Ourdilat Judex, our man of ledgers."

Osmund turned to Wulfgar. "There is a man of faith, a scribe and a man of ledgers."

Wulfgar frowned, though no one could see it, and replied tersely, "So there is no leader to greet me?"

Osmund shook his head, his expression revealing he knew the consequence.

"Ask them where he is," Wulfgar demanded.

"We beg pardon." Gwidol bowed low in response to Osmund's enquiry. "He is absent on commerce in the north-west, but certain to return by this eve."

The man identified as Turpilos intervened, "Please permit us to welcome you in his name and prepare for you a banquet to consume in his company and ours."

Wulfgar did not trust any settlement that could not produce their leader. He began to understand Brithwen's concern for her village. Nodding to Leofgist that he concurred, silently Wulfgar decided to wait and see if they could produce this leader or whether it was a delaying tactic hiding other intentions. All men gestured as was their own custom and parted company.

As the gates of the village closed, Wulfgar said to Leofgist, "Is it me, or do these people have too many names?"

Leofgist shook his head. "They were too polite. I don't like it."

Wulfgar shrugged. "We will know tonight. Either we feast or we fight."

Wulfgar sent Leofgist on ahead of him to instruct the tribe to remain in their wagons until told otherwise. There were to be perimeter guards as in camp, who would be set up a safe distance from the gates of Prenhwychas. If there was trouble brewing, Wulfgar didn't want to be camped right outside it. When the wagons arrived in a clearing, out of sight of the prying eyes of the gate towers, Wulfgar hailed Lorri who had been following him. Dismounting, he handed the reins to his cnapa and removed his helmet. He sauntered over to his wagon, cooled by an autumn breeze lifting his hair. Brithwen hung out the back, smiling. He tossed his head in a nod of acknowledgement.

"*Eala*," he called.

Her smile filled him with joy, and he fed hungrily on her apparent eagerness to see him. As he drew near her eyes were all over him, examining every part of him. He paused when he reached her, rubbing fingers through his sweat-drenched hair. Had she been a normal wife, he would have pulled her to him and kissed her. But he could not, for she was not a normal wife. He noticed she settled back slightly, eager herself and remembering what they were meant to be. He cut their gaze and rolled his helmet across the floor of the wagon.

"Good day, little wife," he said, checking her expression.

Her cheeks burned garnet, like her lips, and her silence revealed her betrayal. He grinned, removing his baldric and war belt before shrugging out of his byrnie. Crossing his arms, he grasped the hem of the chain mail and bent over, wriggling free from the weight. It slithered to the ground and he heaved it in beside Brithwen.

"I am yours until sundown," he announced. "I must attend a feast with their leader tonight."

Excitedly, she cried, "Huweyn?"

Puzzled by her familiarity, he frowned. "You know him well?"

She went quiet briefly, and then whispered, "Yes."

He guessed she thought she had revealed something she should not have. He removed his outer tunic, watching her reactions as he spoke.

"We have not yet met your leader. We've been told he will return for the feast."

"You do not believe them?"

He climbed in, Brithwen's eyes following his every move as he closed the entrance over and settled himself beside her on the sheepskins. "I shall wait until my own eyes can tell me the truth."

In a whisper, she asked, "What truth do they see?"

Her intimate question stirred a memory in him. Feeling sure she knew every nuance of what he saw in his mind, Wulfgar allowed the imagery to unfold, his gaze unwavering with hers. Amid the battle with the bandits, Wulfgar ran across the battlefield. Sieghild pulled his axe from a dead bandit and started a run towards him. Readying his own axe above his head, Wulfgar threw it and watched it spin past Sieghild. As it passed the ealdorman, he turned and saw it sink into the chest of the bandit that had been pursuing him. Wulfgar jolted as he felt the cold steel as though it were real, tears stinging his eyes. He tried to tell himself it was not his pain, but the memory of someone else's. The ground met his knees as he saw himself collapse in the dream, a sword protruding from his chest. Ahead, Sieghild was tearing across the open field, crying out his name. As the dream faded, so too did the pain of the sword from his body. From Brithwen's eyes, he knew she had seen the truth he wished he had seen that fateful day – he should have died on that battlefield, not Sieghild.

In a low voice, he whispered, "They see Sieg. They see him when I wake, they see him when we talk, eat, when we go to bed..."

He dropped his gaze, calling on Woden to bolster his heart so he could carry on. Brithwen raised a hand, which she then withdrew. He lifted his head once more, filling his chest with air, inhaling strength. Her eyes were filled with his pain and her limbs ached to comfort him, but she seemed unable to do so. He found his voice, though it shook with emotion.

"They see my friend." He choked back tears. "He is always in your eyes: my friend."

"My leader, my friend," she whispered.

She knew the phrase. His eyes danced between her blue depths and the rest of her face, searching, scanning. He heard Sieghild, felt the dying weight of him again across his legs.

"*All she is feeling – it will be in her eyes. Look nowhere else.*" Afraid to touch her, he begged Frigg to aid them in their pain, for Brithwen appeared to share the dilemma. She lifted one of his hands and pressed her moist lips into his hot palm.

"Sieg was right," he breathed, leaning closer, "all you are feeling – it is in your eyes. I see it now. I need look nowhere else."

He lay his head in her lap, where she cradled him as he succumbed to all the despair that lingered within him. She ran her fingers gently through his hair, and he knew then he was no longer afraid. She was not nix. She was Urtha, the Norn of Fate, come to save him.

chapter twenty

Wulfsuna Camp,
Outside Prenhwychas, Wealas

The call of the meal cart signalled it was midday. Brithwen stirred under the weight of her husband, who had fallen asleep crying in her lap. The warmth and comfort of his company had caused her to sleep also. As she moved, Wulfgar stirred and sat abruptly, wiping half-dry tears onto his sleeves. His gaze was averted, and Brithwen assumed the incident had embarrassed him. She had seen his pain at Sieghild's loss during the funeral, when she had been privy to his sobs over the body which no one else had heard, though she had not known how deep the grief had settled within him, or that he would share this knowledge with her. Watching him shift awkwardly beside her, she cupped his elbow in her hand.

"Wash your face in the river," she said. "Refresh yourself after a morning in the arms of your wife."

The look he gave her revealed he wished it had been so, and for once she did not blush. With a simple smile, she nudged his elbow. He slid to the edge of the wagon, pausing as he held back the ox-hide.

"Are you hungry?" he asked, his voice hoarse from his spent emotions.

She nodded. "Yes, I should like something. Thank you."

With a childish grin, he jumped down and wandered off. She heard Leofgist's voice and the pair engaged in boyish banter. The sound of their laughter diminished as they headed for the river, and Brithwen sank onto the bed, arms across her abdomen. She had not expected Wulfgar to collapse with grief. She felt older than he, having been able to escape the grief and not fall victim to its tight grasp. Sharing his dream on the battlefield and knowing he wished he had died that day, not Sieghild, gave Brithwen hope. Knowing her gift, Wulfgar had prevented her from knowing him; kept her spirit eyes blind to his feelings. What had transpired this morning proved his trust had grown and he was no longer afraid of her. She likewise had lost her fear. The wild-wolf warrior was tame beneath her touch and she felt safe. All that remained was to know if Huweyn was safe.

The ox-hide drew back, signalling Wulfgar's return. He slid two plates across the floor of the wagon and jumped up to secure the entrance open. Brithwen sat up when he came to sit, hanging his legs out of the wagon. She rubbed her thighs, trying to stretch her limbs that ached from almost two days of sitting.

"I should like to take a walk," she told him.

"That would not be wise," he began.

"I have been confined here for over a day and a night," she replied. "Please, I bid you, let me out for a moment."

He scanned the vicinity, lips compressed tightly while he considered. Finally he looked at her, jerking his head to motion her out.

"Come," he said, holding out both arms to take her by the waist. "Wait."

She froze, perched on the edge having swung her legs down, not daring to turn her head for fear of who may be approaching. Wulfgar lifted a hand and tugged gently at her mantle, pulling it to cover more of her face, focussed intently on what he was doing. Brithwen held her breath. She no longer feared Wulfgar, but she feared her own emotions. They were close, and the scent of him roused her senses, making the hair prickle at the nape of her neck.

"We could see too much of you, little wife."

He smiled, large hands grasping her waist as he lowered her to the ground. Her feet touched the soil, though he did not release her, leaning his torso into her and pinning her to the vehicle. She lifted her face and glimpsed the look he had given her moments before. Their marriage of convenience did not agree with him, and Brithwen admitted she was beginning to feel the same. She braved a glance behind him. Wulfsuna mingled outside their wagons, surreptitiously scrutinising their lord and his lady. He pulled her closer to him, as though trying to draw her attention back to him, his arousal pressing into her abdomen. He held onto her like a bird that might fly away.

"There was much to say," he said, the rasp lingering in his voice, hoarse from spent sobs.

She was instantly reminded of the night by the stream, where she had stripped naked and vowed never to be taken by anyone. She begged her heart to cease its pounding, which threatened to deafen her.

"A little less now," she replied.

"How do I thank you for this morning?" he asked, carefully watching her reaction.

Brithwen thought carefully before she replied. Aware of the current instability of the Wulfsuna, and also that of Prenhwychas, she knew their public conduct had to reflect a strong leadership. Wulfgar had told her as much when he had proffered their wedlock.

She smiled, dizzy from what she was about to suggest. "It may lift the spirits of the Wulfsuna to see their headman kiss his new wife on leaving his wagon after a morning with her."

Wulfgar's eyes leaped with excitement and his hands clenched her body more firmly. He paused. She waited. His eyes began to dart sideways, as though attempting to view the onlookers without turning his head. Brithwen felt the confidence leaving him as his hands relaxed their grip. Knowing she alone could save him from the torment, Brithwen wound her arms behind his neck, tilting her face up to his.

Closing her eyes, she whispered, "Kiss me."

He needed no further invitation, and Brithwen released a small squeal at the potency with which he carried out her request. His beard burned her soft skin, his mouth hot with passion. Not enough to have her waist fast, one hand dropped to her buttocks while the other reached up her spine, pulling her more fiercely into his embrace. Dependent on his hold, she relinquished herself to the emotions she had been denying. The kiss ended and he threw her up into the wagon. Wide-eyed, she watched as he slid the plates of food out onto the ground, released the ox-hide and jumped in. On his knees in the dim interior, he laughed and she giggled nervously.

"Do not think, answer," he said. "How do you feel?"

She shook her head. "I do not know. Happy?"

"Forsooth?"

She nodded.

"You can go on like this? Taking a small piece but never consuming it all?"

She became aware of what he meant. "It was an agreement."

"Yes. It was an agreement. Now it is a marriage."

She dropped her head, her hands twisting in her lap. He waited for her to meet his eyes before continuing.

"I am truly grateful for this morning." The smile had left him and he sidled up next to her. "I am. And I want to honour Sieg, but only if you are with me."

She could still feel his kiss upon her, lingering and affecting her whole body. She had asked him to do it. It could not be unbound. They had begun a journey.

"I cannot. Not yet."

"Yet?" His eyes lit up. "Then it is possible. You would have me? Kiss me back and tell me then you cannot wait."

She would not alter her promise to quench his lust for her, or hers for him. Prenhwychas and Huweyn's safety came first. She touched his face with her small fingers.

"When we have saved Prenhwychas." She smiled. "Wait with me. Wait for a better time."

She watched him tear down his weapons of emotional blackmail. He had to learn there was more than the lust for flesh. There would be time for him to fulfil his oath to Sieghild. She was his wife in name. Their love could wait.

"I shall argue it no more," he said, lifting one of her hands and kissing her knuckles.

"I offer you this and this alone, for now," she said, giving him a tender kiss.

He swayed as she withdrew, telling her, "I thank you for your token."

"It is more than a single gesture." He cocked his head to one side, frowning. She elaborated. "My token has no limit. I can kiss you and you can kiss me, but there will be no joining of flesh."

His voice dropped to a whisper. "I shall take this token as a gift from you. And it shall be a kiss, and no more. On my mother's life I shall save Prenhwychas in your name, Morwyneth."

Pain stabbed her heart at the memory of who she had been. "You called me Morwyneth."

"It is who you truly are."

His hand found the back of her neck, easing her gently to his open mouth. It was an exchange soft like feathers, a merging of two gentle streams. Entwined in his breath of an embrace, Brithwen lost all sense of time as they held onto the experience. One kiss became many, Wulfgar folding her over onto his body then rolling her to the floor to cover her with his. When lips were swollen, Wulfgar moved his kisses to every soft ounce of her face and neck. The everlasting whisper of lips on skin slowly washed away their carnal desires and left behind the firm foundations of the seed of their love.

A whole day in the arms of her husband, completely clothed but emotionally satisfied, left Brithwen feeling content but weary. They were both reposing on the sheepskins, their arms around each other, faces close. Wulfgar occasionally nuzzled her cheek and neck, dropping the odd kiss on her pink skin.

"I must leave you, little wife." He sighed his regret.

"I wish I could go with you, though I know I must remain here." It was, after all, his duty, and he would discover what had become of Huweyn. He released her and ran hands through his wild hair, plaiting it.

"You have wandering hands," he winked at her, "and I no comb."

Brithwen sat up to rearrange her own clothes, her mantles and cloak now strewn on their bed. He dressed quickly, for Leofgist had roused them with a gentle tap on the side of the wagon and waited outside. Wulfgar did not wear his byrnie. No doubt it was impolite to dress for dinner as though one was going into battle. Once fully attired, Wulfgar paused. Lifting a hand, he stroked her cheek and then he had gone.

As Wulfgar leaped down from the wagon, Leofgist winked at him. He rolled his eyes. He was busy remembering how Brithwen's hands had moved over his scalp and imagining those same hands moving over the rest of his body. His need to depart had saved him from temptation's lure.

"Heahstan waits for us," Leofgist told him, gesturing to the thegn standing a few yards away, arms folded across his giant chest.

Wulfgar called, "Heahstan."

His thegn nodded. "Lord Wulfgar."

Wulfgar shook the day from his shoulders and prepared for business. Heahstan wore his serious face. The three men stood, all looking at one another. No words passed lips and Wulfgar sighed heavily. He hoped it was a short meal so he could return swiftly and kiss Brithwen until he had expelled the passion loitering between his legs. He folded his arms to match Heahstan's stance.

"Well?" he demanded, knowing they had something to tell him.

Leofgist began hastily, "When you were kissing Lady Brithwen I think I saw Trunhild lurking in the undergrowth."

Wulfgar lifted his eyebrows. "So there was not one, but two of you prying on my lovemaking."

"We cannot help but pry if you conduct your lovemaking in public," said Heahstan, and then as an afterthought added, "My Lord."

Wulfgar nodded at Leofgist. "Keep a closer watch on him. Can you trust anyone else?"

Leofgist shrugged. "Maybe Osmund, though he is a Bryton."

Wulfgar thought about it. "Very well. What do you think Trunhild's intentions were?"

"I do not know, My Lord," Leofgist replied, fumbling with the hilt of his seax.

Heahstan finally dropped his arms to his sides, stance relaxing. "Whatever they were, he and everyone could see you wore no seax."

Wulfgar grinned cheekily. "Should I wear that to bed with my wrist guards?"

Heahstan's face puckered as he said, "Have it to hand, My Lord. How would you have us approach?"

Returning to the imminent task ahead, Wulfgar considered the wooden ramparts, two men high, surrounded by a ditch several feet deep. In the event of them coming under attack from within the settlement, no Wulfsuna could scale the fortifications. If the battle methods of the Brytons were similar to their own, initially bowmen would release an arrow shower. Wulfgar turned back to Heahstan.

"Have a line of men ready a wagon's length from the edge of the ditch. They can provide a shield wall should Prenhwychas attack."

"And bowmen, My Lord?" asked Heahstan.

Wulfgar pointed behind them. "Under cover of that tree line."

"Who shall you leave in command?" Heahstan enquired.

"Geldhere," Wulfgar replied without hesitation.

"I shall attend to that, Lord Wulfgar," Leofgist announced, making to leave.

"Wait," Wulfgar instructed. "Fetch Osmund. We shall need him."

Leofgist nodded and went to impart his lord's orders to Thegn Geldhere and collect Thegn Osmund.

"Will that be enough?" Wulfgar asked, once again examining the fortifications.

Heahstan's smile lifted his long beard. "We are beyond Burrium and Gobannus, deep into the land of the Silures. We fight with the men we have, and if we lose we will feast at Woden's table."

"Do you believe it will come to that?" Wulfgar asked, trusting the old thegn's judgement though praying he would be wrong.

"It is a large *rath*, as they say here. Their leader is wealthy and there will be plenty of men of fighting age beyond those fences. Our kinsmen have harried these shores for over a decade. They hold no trust where we are concerned."

Leofgist rejoined them and the gates of Prenhwychas opened. They revealed the man named Turpilos, whom they had met that morning, standing smiling beside an older man. Wulfgar assumed the latter to be the previously absent leader. Although his hair wore the silver of old age and wisdom, he had once had dark hair. His eyes were round and soft, his stance confident though relaxed. Heahstan accompanied Wulfgar ahead of Osmund and Leofgist. They halted shy of Prenhwychas soil. The new man held out a hand, eyes scanning all three of the Wulfsuna before him.

"Lord Wulfgar?"

Wulfgar thought he recognised the tilt of the mouth as the man smiled. A light touch from Heahstan's hand on his arm encouraged him to respond. He took the outstretched hand of his host.

"I am Huweyn Oran filius Hwychas. Welcome to our home."

At Osmund's translation, Wulfgar replied, "We thank you, Huweyn Erran Flius…"

"Huweyn." The leader laughed, bidding them inside with a large wave of his arm. "The shackles of Roma are hard to lose. Names, however, can be dropped."

Watching Huweyn as he listened to Osmund repeat the leader's words, Wulfgar knew he had seen that expression before. Troubled by the familiarity of the man's features, Wulfgar delved into the far recesses of his mind, trying to remember. They meandered through the village where residents gathered outside their homes to regard the visitors with mistrust. Women sheltered small children behind their skirts while brave young boys rushed forward to feel the Wulfsuna's clothing or weaponry. Heahstan waved them away like flies after honey. Behind the many thatched roundhouses, some as wide as long halls, groups of working men stood abreast with their tools. They could have been recalled from the fields to greet the guests, though could just as easily be an organised army ready to attack.

Prenhwychas sat atop a steep hill, or *bryn*, Huweyn's handsome villa at the pinnacle of the settlement, watching over its inhabitants. Like the scales of some great sea monster, five-sided slate tiles covered the roof, a grey spine stretching the length of two ships. As they neared, lavish Roman-style gardens enticed them towards a verandah on the south side of the building. They entered, following Huweyn and Turpilos through a rear salon where weapons hung as elaborate ornaments. Under the Empire, they would have been forbidden to keep and use such weapons. It seemed Rome's absence had been long enough for Huweyn to feel confident in displaying them, albeit in a back room. The Wulfsuna remained alert as they walked through a corridor where walls were festooned with godly images, and finally to a large communal hall.

Flames billowed up from the wrought iron baskets of several braziers round the edges of the room. In one half of the hall a long table, dressed with a generous feast of rabbit and boar, drew all eyes. Huweyn gestured they should wait while he consulted with his fellow kin gathered near the feast table. Wulfgar gazed at the erotic artwork across the wall beside him where naked goddesses held in the arms of muscled warriors flowed seamlessly into portrayals of holy men at the feet of a crucified man.

Huweyn called, and Osmund said, "Gentlemen, come."

Tearing his eyes from the wall, Wulfgar noticed the two other men whom they had met that morning and a red-haired woman. Huweyn reintroduced Gwidol the preacher and Vendognus and invited everyone to take a seat. Wondering why a woman joined them, Heahstan nudged Wulfgar and huffed in his ear, not bothering to hide his disgust at the break in formality.

"She doesn't look like a thrall to me."

Huweyn laughed, rubbing a finger across his nose. "Ah, and the lady beside me is my good wife, Acgarat."

While Osmund translated, Heahstan leaned in to whisper again, "She looks like a twig with hair."

Straining under the urge to laugh, Wulfgar grinned broadly at his host and waved a hand across the table, announcing, "A great feast, Huweyn."

Wulfgar glanced at Heahstan, who shook his head. Wulfgar knew, even without Heahstan's confirmation, women did not sit at a warriors' table, and yet he dared not challenge his host. He tried to quell his thegn's growing discontent with a dismissive wave he hoped had been discreet. Servants appeared from the shadowed recesses of the room to pour wine, and Wulfgar used the opportunity to examine the guests. Turpilos hid behind his goblet, only his shifting eyes visible over the rim. Vendognus remained silent, adjusting his goblet and platter on the table over and over. Meanwhile Huweyn chattered needlessly, Osmund recounting the leader's endless commentary of how the food had been prepared and what weather they were having. Fear ran through them, as sharp as a battle-light into flesh. Wulfgar locked gaze with Acgarat, herself busy scrutinising the Wulfsuna, her small nose wrinkling at the sight of him. He grinned, settling his back into his chair. Woden guided his instincts, and the Chief of the Gods did not like this woman. Wulfgar smelled trouble. Heahstan poked him in the shoulder, alerting him to Osmund relaying Huweyn's speech.

"Allow me to extend my apologies for my absence upon your arrival at Prenhwychas. The swell of the Afon Habren has caused much disruption of late and trade at the old fort at Gloui has diminished since so many have moved on. I have had to take my trade to the harbours on the west coast. I was returning from trade with the Menapii when you arrived."

Wulfgar shook his head and waved a hand, negating Huweyn's apology, asking, "Have you lost all trade with Rome?"

Huweyn responded swiftly, "No. The Romans enjoy fine cloth and none is finer than that from the central uplands on the Isles of Bryton. Our birrus Britannicus is much sought after."

Wulfgar's mind continued to chase down the memory of the smile reminiscent of Huweyn's. The elusion frustrated him. He knew that turn of mouth. He reached for his wine, the blood-red liquid contained within a red-gloss pottery vessel. Mythological scenes adorned the exterior.

"These cups are from Gaul," he said.

Huweyn nodded and finished chewing his food. "Yes. When I travel south there are many craftsmen from your homelands. I am rather fond of the style."

Lifting a large slice of boar meat from a silver platter, Wulfgar had his dining interrupted by Acgarat. He ignored Heahstan's grunt and waited for Osmund to talk.

"I am told you are here to save Prenhwychas," Osmund said, his eyes relaying surprise that she had dared to ask the question.

Wulfgar nodded, leaving a long silence while he tore at his meat and swallowed it with a generous mouthful of wine. Not satisfied with his gesture alone, Acgarat spoke again.

"From whom?"

Huweyn interjected, "My dear, does it matter?"

Wulfgar looked at the men of Prenhwychas, the supposed council to Huweyn, in turn. Either Huweyn wanted to silence his wife's inquisitiveness, or his elders had not imparted all they knew. His suspicions grew. Wiping the grease from his beard across his sleeve, he glared at her.

"From blue northmen. From Pictii. We come at Morwyneth's bequest."

Huweyn twitched, losing grip on a pheasant leg that clattered onto his plate.

"Morwyneth?" replied Acgarat, voice high as her eyes flashed to Turpilos. "She is no longer with us."

Wulfgar decided to forsake his meal, leaning back in his chair. "As we told Clodri, we found Morwyneth in the wilderness. She told us of this attack."

"And you believed her?" Acgarat did not hide her incredulity. Wulfgar glanced at Huweyn, who now rested his elbow on the table, rubbing his temple with his fingers. The remainder of the guests had ceased to eat and Turpilos choked on his wine.

"In my land, it is foolish not to believe one who speaks directly with the gods," Wulfgar told her.

The eyes of the villagers flickered round the table to each other and Huweyn. Their leader sat motionless, his thoughts lost in his wine. An uncomfortable lull settled on the room, Wulfgar aware that Heahstan had already removed his peace ribbon from his sword hilt and that Leofgist's hands hovered uneasily at his seax.

"Morwyneth." Her name was a breath expelled softly from Huweyn's lips. "Does she travel with you?"

Wulfgar frowned. "Did your council not inform you? Did Clodri not tell them?"

Huweyn lifted his head and looked straight at Turpilos. "Tell me what?"

Heahstan gripped his leader's thigh but Wulfgar shook his hand off, suggesting his thegn stand down by placing the back of his hand on the man's chest and replied, "She returned to the wilderness."

Barely waiting for Osmund to finish, Huweyn asked, "Did any of your people come to know her?"

Elements of Huweyn's expressions nibbled incessantly at Wulfgar's mind the more he saw of them. Why would he be so concerned over one missing villager? Wulfgar began to wonder at Morwyneth's role within Prenhwychas. Feeling it would do no harm to explain, Wulfgar gave him an answer.

"She befriended my former ealdorman."

"Is he with you?" Huweyn shifted, hands moving to the arms of his chair as though readying to stand. Wulfgar shook his head and merely gestured to Osmund who replied for him.

"No. He was killed in a battle."

Huweyn sighed, lowering his head. "I am sorry."

When Huweyn looked up, Wulfgar felt Thunor's hammer beat his chest. He had seen those eyes before. He knew that deep blue gaze, the setting of the mouth. Brithwen's eagerness to know of Huweyn's safety was no longer a mystery. Neither was Huweyn's interest in a village peasant. There could be no other explanation. He was her father.

Acgarat spoke out again. "I fear you have made a wasted journey," she told them, her narrow eyes and bony cheeks bearing little resemblance to Brithwen.

"By no means," Wulfgar retorted. Although she had to wait for Osmund's translation, she felt his tone for she stiffened in her seat. "We hope to meet another enemy nearby."

She tossed her coiffed head, reminding him of Cwenfleda. "Oh?"

"We hunt an Angle leader to avenge the death of our last great lord," he leaned across the table, voice sinister, "and we hear he is recruiting Pictii."

Turpilos broke his silence, false bravado fooling no one. "Ha! The Pictii would never come this far south. Why would they join barbarians?"

"Yes," Acgarat agreed, tugging silk closer round her shoulders. Wulfgar knew well the expense of the eastern fabric from the markets and wondered how much of Huweyn's fortune she had squeezed out of him to acquire enough to wear as a shawl.

"We have this knowledge on good authority," he told her, tiring of the woman's intrusions.

"Whose?" she challenged.

"My own men." Wulfgar slammed a clenched fist on the table, unable to shackle his anger much longer. Gwidol stepped in to avert further confrontation.

"Perhaps we should try another wine?"

Wulfgar grabbed his cup and set it down loudly on the table. "Good."

Jaded smiles filled the faces of all around them, and Huweyn said calmly, "He who restrains his anger overcomes his greatest enemy."

Wulfgar drained his cup of its contents and regarded his host. "Wise words."

Huweyn smiled. "I am afraid not mine."

Leofgist and Gwidol laughed politely, though the rest sat quietly, observing one another. After a second serving of wine, Gwidol amused them with witty anecdotes. Wulfgar watched and listened, as he had learned from Sieghild. Stilted glances and fidgeting hands told him something was amiss. Over the joviality, Huweyn caught Wulfgar's eye and the headman leaned over to better hear the leader of Prenhwychas, waving for Osmund to join them. The young thegn left his seat and stood next to Wulfgar's chair.

"Perhaps you would care to see my garden? Would you take a walk with me?"

When Wulfgar heard the words from Osmund he nodded at Huweyn, calling Leofgist over to them. His ealdorman approached and bent down at Wulfgar's request so his lord could murmur quietly in his ear.

"I am taking a walk with Huweyn. Make sure no one else leaves this room while we are gone."

Leofgist straightened. "Yes, My Lord."

Following Huweyn back to the southern salon through which they had entered, Wulfgar was grateful for the fresh air as they reached the garden. The feast hall had become stifling and the company unwelcome. Huweyn sat down upon a stone seat, running a hand through a nearby herb shrub, releasing its scent into the night. Realising there was to be no walk, Wulfgar leaned against the painted exterior and admired the stars.

Huweyn whispered to him, "Do you speak my words?"

Wulfgar cast a glance around them, ensuring they were alone. Conflicted by Huweyn's obvious desire to speak to him in confidence and the fact that his reply would reveal a truth he had kept his whole life, he hesitated. Sieghild had taught him in their youth to speak his mother's native tongue. They had used it surreptitiously as a code between themselves, though never in public. Wulfgar relented, too eager to discover what Huweyn wanted to tell him.

"Yes."

"How was Morwyneth when you found her?"

The question was unexpected and further sealed Wulfgar's opinion that this man was indeed her father.

"She had a fever, though recovered well." He omitted the fact she had been bound like a prisoner for colluding with one of his men and for fear she was a river-witch. One thing neither Sieghild nor Brithwen knew was that he had demanded daily reports of her condition. Had she died at his hands it would have unsettled the tribe and, regardless of his own fears of her, he hadn't wanted her to die either.

"Did she tell how she came to be in the wilderness?"

"She told me she had been expelled from Prenhwychas."

Huweyn stood and gripped Wulfgar by the arm. "I had no choice. They would have killed her. When she left, I wanted to feel victory that they had not taken her life. I felt only pain for losing her."

Wulfgar looked towards the village entrance, thinking about Brithwen sitting in their wagon beyond the gates. Briefly reliving her touch from that afternoon, he yearned to hold her again, to bed her wholly.

"Who are they?" he demanded, facing Huweyn once again.

Huweyn's hand dropped from his arm, face solemn. "I had to let her go. I would have lost everything."

Wulfgar sniffed derisively. "House, clothes, expensive wife?"

"No." Huweyn stepped away, gazing out at his garden. "They would have killed her had she stayed. The village would have suffered if I had lost my position."

"She is your daughter."

"You know?" Huweyn staggered into the stone seat, a hand searching behind him as he sat unsteadily.

"When I saw you tonight, I knew."

"Say nothing," Huweyn pleaded.

"Who was responsible?"

Huweyn shook a sorry head. "I do not know. We rounded up the women who attacked her, but they would not reveal a name."

Wulfgar recalled the day they had found Morwyneth on the roadside, soaked and dishevelled, hair roughly cut. He could only imagine what these women had done to her and it sickened him.

"Do as I say," Huweyn pleaded. "Stay a few days and move on. I am sure we will not suffer an attack. If we do it will be fated. Besides, I have no will left without my daughter."

Wulfgar wanted to tell Huweyn that his daughter was alive and well, and married to the Lord of the Wulfsuna. He wanted to embrace Huweyn as the father of his wife and ask for his belated blessing on their union. It would not be possible, however, or safe. Heahstan's imposing figure in the doorway hailed the Seaxans' departure for that evening.

"We should return, My Lord," his oldest thegn advised as Osmund and Leofgist appeared behind him.

Wulfgar extended an arm that his host took strongly as he offered Osmund a farewell for translation. "We thank you and bid you well."

CHAPTER TWENTY-ONE

Wulfsuna Camp,
Outside Prenhwychas, Wealas

They wandered down Bryn Hwychas toward the gates, all eyes poised for possible threats that might be lurking amid the houses. None appeared. Animals stirred and hushed voices filtered out from the homes as they passed. A wind grew around them, treetops lurching and leaves hissing, disturbing the otherwise silent surroundings. The gates were opened for them and closed swiftly afterwards. Nearing the camp, Heahstan excused himself, bidding good night to the three young men.

Osmund gave a small bow to Wulfgar, and said, "I thank My Lord for his trust in me and hope I proved worthy of the task I was given."

Wulfgar held out an arm, which Osmund clasped firmly. "You were worthy. I thank you."

Patting Leofgist on the back, Osmund left for his bed, and lord and ealdorman looked at each other. Wulfgar sank onto the ground, settling himself on grass beside the limestone road, and beckoned Leofgist to join him. Resting arms on bent knees, Wulfgar turned to Leofgist.

"Do you remember the oath you swore to me?" He continued once Leofgist had nodded, "I have a burden I must share."

Leofgist shuffled closer, hugging his knees to his chest. "Very well."

Picking up a piece of chalk and turning it in his fingers, Wulfgar asked, "I wish to know your thoughts on the feast this evening. I have some doubts as to the sincerity of our hosts."

"I share your concerns, My Lord." Leofgist leaned closer. "All but the woman feared to speak their minds."

Wulfgar tossed the chalk. "It feels wrong, here." He thumped his gut with a fist.

"Shall I order scouts into the village?"

Wulfgar tilted his head, weighing the idea. "No. Trust between the Wulfsuna and Prenhwychas is thin, and spying on them would surely break it. Have guards on watch all night and we will talk at sunrise."

"Very well, My Lord."

Looking in the direction of his wagon where his wife waited for him, Wulfgar whispered, "I do wonder if we have entered into a promise we will be unable to deliver."

"All we can be is our best," Leofgist assured him. "The Wulfsuna shall never be conquered. We shall triumph, for Woden is with us."

Wulfgar smiled at Leofgist's unwavering belief in his tribe. "We shall indeed be our best, though I fear this village is fated by its own evil, whether the Pictii arrive or not."

"Whatsoever evil arrives, I swear none shall harm you or your kin, My Lord," said Leofgist, placing a hand on his chest.

Wulfgar sighed and offered a small smile. "I thank you," then his mind turned to another problem. "Speak you still with Trunhild?"

His ealdorman shrugged, shaking his head. "Only if we need to when working."

"And socially?" Wulfgar pressed.

"Never. He disappears when his chores are done and does not eat with the men."

Wulfgar glared at him. "Consider your loyalties well. I had Heahstan remove him from his duty today for I fear he is against me."

Leofgist dropped his head, sighing. "It was expected. When I saw him hiding, watching you and Lady Brithwen…"

Wulfgar raised his eyes to the sky, as though the stars would provide an answer. "The root of a great disease has grown within him from the day I sent him to tell Morwyneth of Sieghild's death."

Leofgist shook his head. "You have only to ask, My Lord, and I shall swear an oath again and again to you. I have taken Osmund into my confidence, for he too is troubled by his fellow thegn's behaviour." He offered the arm they had originally sealed their oath with in blood. Wulfgar took it and wrapped his other hand around Leofgist's arm. Their grasp lingered in the dark stillness of night, eyes meeting across the seal they both recalled.

"I shall do as you command in all we have discussed," promised Leofgist.

Wulfgar could merely nod his appreciation, intensely aware that if Sieghild was alive, he would be sharing this moment with his best friend. For however worthwhile an ealdorman Leofgist was, he could never replace the friendship Wulfgar had had with Sieghild. He watched Leofgist walk away. He disliked asking Wulfsuna to spy on one another, but his survival and that of the union of the Germanic and Brytonic halves of the tribe depended upon it.

A large moon hung above him in the cloudless sky. He silently asked Woden, Chief of all the Gods, to impart wisdom upon him. He asked to be guided through the forthcoming few days and to be sent Tiw, God of War, as his shield should Eadmaer appear. He hoped this was enough. Dragging himself reluctantly to his feet, he headed for his wagon. He craved slumber, though knew Brithwen would be waiting, eager for news of the feast with Huweyn. Four guards remained outside the wagon, the two at the rear entrance straightening as he neared. Through slats in the side of the vehicle he saw a small light burning. Its yellow glow fell onto the limestone as one of the guards drew back the ox-hide for him as he climbed inside.

Brithwen leaned forward, tugging the mantles off her head, revealing tousled hair. "Did you meet Huweyn?" she asked, eyes alight with curiosity.

He moved the lamp into the far corner of the wagon to allow room to undress, replying, "I did."

She smiled, eyes sparkling like the stars he had admired. Undoing her brooch, she shrugged out of her cloak and gown and lay back on the bed, tugging a wool blanket up to her waist. He started to remove his war gear and leather vest.

"Who else did you meet?" she asked.

"A preacher and two other men in Huweyn's council."

She giggled. "I like Gwidol. He is funny."

Wulfgar grinned. "And fat."

She fell silent, contemplative. "How was Huweyn?"

"In good health," Wulfgar told her, pulling his tunics over his head, "though he was full of fear."

"He is not safe?" she asked, sitting up, hands twisting the blanket into a knot. Lightning flickered in her blue eyes, her shoulders raised, hands clenching into red balls. Outside a gust of wind blew up around the wagon, swaying it from side to side. Wulfgar slammed hands to the floor to steady himself, glancing warily at his wife.

"Taranis," she hissed as thunder rolled above them. By the gods, she had called on Thunor and been answered. She cried "Taranis" louder as another thunder clap rippled overhead.

"Brithwen," Wulfgar called, receiving no response. Taking her by the shoulders, he felt his body lurch with a sickness as she pulled him into her vision. He soared above the roundhouses, diving down to search each in turn as though hunting for something or someone. People slept, argued, cradled infants to breasts or made love. Having exhausted the homes of the villagers, Brithwen took them to Huweyn's villa. In the south salon, Acgarat and Turpilos were locked in a passionate embrace. Wulfgar screwed his eyes shut, willing his hands to release Brithwen. With a gasp he fell backwards, leaving Brithwen alone in her vision once more. He wondered why, if she could travel by spirit, she had not used her gift before to see Huweyn's wellbeing for herself. He soon realised as she collapsed, half-conscious and exhausted from her exploits, limbs shaking.

He joined her on the bed, folding her to him and scorning her. "This is no way to use your gift, little wife. Such power and advantage is good in battle, when your enemy is on the field."

"Power and advantage were no help to Sieghild," she murmured, eyes barely open, limp in his arms. He spat a profanity into his shoulder.

"He used his advantage to save me, and the bandit used his advantage to kill Sieg. Fate moves in many directions."

Her face broke into pain, tears spilling from her eyes. "They will kill Huweyn."

"I will protect him," he promised, though he knew not how.

"What if you are too late?" she asked, voice faltering. "I have many things to say."

Wulfgar took her by the wrists, holding her fists to his chest. "I too have many things to say. How can I ask for your father's blessing if he is dead?"

Brithwen's breath caught in her throat and she opened her eyes wide. "You know?"

He wiped her tears aside with his thumb. "I know."

Her gaze wandered. "If you know, so may many others."

"It is possible," he confirmed, releasing her. "Have strength, little wife. We shall be ready for them."

She retreated to the far corner of the bed and Wulfgar did not follow. He removed his boots and slid beneath the blanket next to her. Turning, he killed the flame in the lamp and lay back against the sheepskins. Under the cloak of darkness, Brithwen whispered to him.

"I thank you for saving me from my own anger. I felt I could not stop."

Wulfgar closed his eyes and swallowed hard, his voice deep with emotion. "I told you I would protect you. That includes protecting you from yourself."

"You are my watcher," she told him, recalling a conversation with Anwen from what seemed an age ago.

"Yes. My heart and mind watch over you every moment of the day and night, even when I am not with you." He felt her go still for a moment beside him and realised the portent of the words he had spoken. He had admitted something he had not even allowed himself to acknowledge. He was revealed in that single phrase.

Quietly she said, "I feel that and I am comforted", and after a brief pause "Wulfgar?"

He licked his lips. "Yes?"

"Did Huweyn tell you he was my father?"

"He had no need to. You share the same eyes and smile."

She released a small sob and he heard her raise a hand to cover her mouth. Feeling her emotion fill the space between them, contrary to his earlier desires he did not want to kiss her until his passion subsided. He simply wanted to be with her. He rolled onto his side, careful to avoid disturbing her. After a while, when his breathing had relaxed, she sidled up to him, resting her head onto his chest. He thought perhaps she imagined him to be asleep. She draped an arm across his torso and he closed his eyes. She was with him and he loved her. He cared for nothing else at that moment.

Brithwen woke to a light tap on the back of the wagon, a dawn call from one of the guards. She nudged Wulfgar, who continued sleeping. She rubbed her nose against his upper arm while running fingers of one hand up his thigh. As a second tap came. Wulfgar sat sharply, rubbing the heels of his palms into weary eyes.

"I come," he said.

Warm light filtered in through the wagon sides and birdsong beckoned a new day. The sun had barely risen above the world. Why they had called so early for him she did not know, though assumed they had made certain plans following the events at the feast last night. He rolled onto his knees, hands searching for his clothes. Pulling his tunics over his tangled hair, he took his padded vest, pausing to gaze at her, a smile raising one side of his mouth.

"It is the day of Tiw, the day of justice," he told her, slipping into the vest and securing his war belt around his waist.

Brithwen refused to acknowledge the fear that crept into her heart. The Wulfsuna were here at her request, to save her father and her village. Whether they were saved from painted savages or saved from themselves remained to be seen. She had to trust in Wulfgar to carry out her wishes.

Outside, a guard announced, "Ealdorman Leofgist, My Lord."

"Yes." Wulfgar tossed the word over his shoulder and grabbed his boots in one hand, preparing to leave. Brithwen clutched his sleeve and he stopped, his smile fading as he read her concern.

"May your gods protect you," she said.

He gazed deep into her eyes, motionless, and she waited for him to

251

reply. Muscles in his face twitched, fighting against the words he struggled to find. He blinked, releasing himself from his trance, and lightly brushed her cheek with his fingers, gone all too soon, or so she felt. Brithwen watched the ox-hide swing to and fro.

She heard Leofgist greet him and Wulfgar suggest they move away from the wagons to talk. Brithwen dressed urgently, knowing there was no time to waste. Any precious items she wanted from her home had to be sought immediately. With Wulfsuna occupied in their defence of Prenhwychas, it should be easy to slip in through one of several secret places she knew. All that remained were the guards outside the wagon. While plotting to experiment with her gift so as to cause a disturbance that would distract the guards, Brithwen thanked her gods when the warriors were called away. The fates were working with her.

She slipped from the wagon, adjusting her linen mantle on her head, and dashed into nearby trees. Her heart leaped about her breast, sound was muffled by the pounding in her ears. She sank her back into a tree trunk and inhaled deeply, releasing her fears with her breath. Moving through the wooded coppice to the rear of the settlement, she saw the tiny gap beneath one of the vertical planks in the ramparts. She slid into the ditch, picking her way carefully through protruding wooden stakes and climbing the embankment to the base of the rampart. The gap, formed by a broken plank and a dip in the earth made by children and animals, proved enough for Brithwen to slide through.

A low wall which skirted a field greeted her, and she found a break in the stone. She crawled in, heading for an area of dense shrubbery in which to conceal herself while she took a look around. The shepherds had not yet arrived in the fields, though they would soon enough. Beyond the shrubbery stood several roundhouses, most of them occupied as villagers ate their first meal, smoke pluming from the roofs. Taking a quick glance, she lifted her gown and ran to her home.

The aroma of soured milk infused her abode, the goats' milk she had collected on her last morning here curdled and rancid. Nothing had been disturbed. No one had entered, except perhaps wandering chickens. The hearth fire, a grave of cold stones and ashes, had not been lit in her absence. She approached her small table where a half-empty cup of milk had been abandoned. She held it in her hands, recalling how her world had lurched uncontrollably that morning as she had been dragged into her very first vision.

Her gift tugged at her and she felt it swell from the ground up through her feet. She let it take her, dark clouds consuming her once more. The screams of dying men and clashing iron met with the stench of spent blood. Accepting the familiarity of the vision, Brithwen did not flinch when a face emerged from the darkness. Not blue and painted as before, this face was half-man, half-boar, baring yellow teeth. The vision released her and she dropped the milk cup, clutching her abdomen as her stomach churned several times. She closed her eyes, inhaling deeply, waiting for the sickness to abate.

It released her and she opened her eyes, her hands reaching out for the scattering of small carved objects strewn over the table. Set aside were a bone cow and a wooden crow with which she had divined prior to her expulsion. She collected the well-worn figures, softened by the myriad times hands had rolled them to the floor, and dropped them into the accompanying cloth bag. Her only other remaining possession had been handed down, woman to woman, over many generations. Dropping to her knees, Brithwen opened her bench chest and tossed out the contents. Taking hold of a small strap of leather at one side, she lifted a secret compartment in the base of the chest. With careful hands she lifted her mother's dress from its confined resting place, admiring the knotwork embroidery around the neck and cuffs. Un-dyed wool crept over the shoulders and down the bodice of the lavender gown, sewn into tangled foliage of oak leaves, holly, acorns and mistletoe.

In the field behind the houses, Brithwen heard one of the calls used by the Wulfsuna. She stood in a hurry, folding the gown over her arm and tying the cloth bag to her belt. When she heard the "tic-tic" sound outside her home she held her breath and dared not move. They had heard her fumbling inside and the warrior was announcing he had found someone. She attempted to return the appropriate call without success and so intended to flee. A firm pair of hands found her and she looked up at the iron mask glaring down at her.

The man released her, bowing. "Lady Brithwen."

He signalled the two men with him should remain as he guided her back past the shrubbery and over the stone wall into the coppice. He made a hand signal she knew to mean nobility, for she had seen them form the gesture on Wulfgar's arrival. She saw her husband's back as he received the news his wife had been found and recognised the hunch of the shoulders. He would not be happy with her. His helmet dipped and turned as he scowled at her. When she arrived he turned fully, shaking his head.

"I should be the only noble out here," he scorned, his anger diffusing swiftly as he saw the remnants of her previous life she clutched to her bosom. Knowing he would not chastise her further, she smiled at him.

He frowned, head tilting to one side, and he came forward to feel the embroidered gown she held.

"You returned for your things," he said, eyes never leaving the cloth.

"Yes."

"Your home, is it in a good position? Can you see Huweyn's villa?" His eyes raised to see her nod and he beckoned the warrior who had brought her to the woods. "Take us to it."

He winked at her and left.

chapter twenty-two

Wulfsuna Camp,
Outside Prenhwychas, Wealas

Wulfgar, penned into Brithwen's home with Leofgist and a handful of Wolf Sons, instructed men nearest the door to keep watch on Huweyn's villa for signs of movement. Scabbards and elbows jostled for room in his wife's modest former home. Her life had begun here, he thought, without knowledge of him or the Wulfsuna. Looking round, the barren interior gave up little to provide insight into his wife. Leofgist stumbled, knocking him into the low bed and he felt a dagger slip in his belt. He sent a hand to it.

"Sorry," Leofgist whispered.

Wulfgar shook his head, mouthing, "No matter."

Glancing down to secure the dagger he noticed a tiny wooden object resting on the floor beside his foot. Squinting to identify its shape in the dim light, he reached down for it, steadying his scabbard with his free hand. Rolling the talisman across his palm, he felt his heart still. He closed his fist around the carving of the pregnant woman and slid it into the coin purse that hung from his belt.

"Do you see anything?" he demanded in a hushed voice. His men shook their heads. Wulfgar clenched his jaw. Following Brithwen's vision of Huweyn's wife Acgarat in an embrace with Turpilos, he had decided to act. He did not trust these people, Huweyn aside, and would not have the safety of the Wulfsuna endangered by a village squabble. As his men had already voiced in council after his wedding, they could encounter Eadmaer here or soon after, possibly allied to an army of Pictii. Considering that, it could have proven difficult to persuade his thegns on merely a seer's vision. However, with Heahstan, Osmund and Leofgist at his side, he had been able to relay the discontent they felt at the feast, and council had agreed to act.

He intended to force Acgarat to confront her husband with the truth of her betrayal, which Wulfgar felt certain was not purely for passion. At the feast, he had seen her lust for power, and if Brithwen's vision was true, Huweyn's wife had been responsible for Morwyneth's expulsion. Heahstan and Geldhere in the meantime were rounding up the members of Huweyn's council. Hearing a whistled call, Wulfgar knew Heahstan and Geldhere had Turpilos, Vendognus and Gwidol. He responded with his own whistle and rallied his men.

"Acgarat is mine. Leofgist, you find Huweyn in his feast hall and remain with him. We go."

They had waited until the village men had left for the fields and women had begun their chores. Having already been invited into Prenhwychas the previous night, they trusted that the villagers would assume they had been granted entry when the gates had been opened for the farmers that morning. Wulfgar, Osmund and Leofgist checked their surroundings and slipped into the open, unnoticed. Walking sedately up to the villa, they meandered through the garden as they had done the night before, nodding politely to anyone who saw them. The remaining men attempted to reach the rear of the villa unseen, trailing back through the coppice so as not to cause alarm.

Wulfgar's decision to send scouts at sunrise had been a good one. They had told him Huweyn had already risen and was attending to his accounts on the ground floor, while Acgarat slept on the first floor. They reached the front entrance and Wulfgar gestured for Osmund and Leofgist to enter there. Leaving the two thegns to announce themselves to the servant who answered their knock, Wulfgar walked round to the verandah and the rear salon. Stepping inside the cool building, he smelled the enticing aroma of warm bread filtering from the main feast hall. Having not yet quelled his hunger, Wulfgar inhaled at length, savouring the smell. To the side of the salon Wulfgar viewed a set of stone steps and took them. He crept up the single flight to the first floor, where a gallery corridor ran along the back of the villa. A young female thrall came out of one of the rooms with a silver tray. He rushed to her, snatching the tray so she would not drop it and pinning her to the wall, a hand over her mouth.

"Say nothing and you shall live," he said in Brytonic. Her eyes bulged and she nodded. He released her, handing back the tray and patting her swiftly on the backside. The girl hitched up her peplos and ran down the stairs. Faced with three doors, Wulfgar halted, eyes and ears straining for movement and sound. A pungent perfume escaped from the centre door, which stood ajar. He strode confidently into the room, closing the door behind him, quickly searching for pieces of Acgarat's own clothing to bind her. Approaching the sleeping witch, he knelt on the side of the bed and gagged her roughly with a length of silk. Acgarat woke with a start, trying to scream and kicking at her bedclothes. Wulfgar overpowered her, snatching her feeble wrists in his large hands and tying them in front of her. She made to retreat across the bed, thwarted by Wulfgar's grip on her ankles sliding her back over the bed towards him.

"Be still, bitch," he ground out in a throaty whisper, white teeth flashing at her through his beard.

Acgarat gave him a look of horror and did not move. Wulfgar issued a vindictive laugh, tying her ankles and straddling her with his legs. She had a kick like a pony and he planned to avoid injury. He wanted to scare her, to weaken her, so later she would talk. Bending over her, he rested his hands either side of her head and lowered his body. Acgarat squealed behind the silk gag, squirming and tossing her head. Waiting for her to cease once more, he spoke.

"Lady Acgarat, I would rather bed a boar."

Taking pleasure in her contorted features, Wulfgar swung her over his shoulder like a deer carcass and carried her downstairs. Hopefully, Leofgist and Osmund would be entertaining Huweyn, and Heahstan would soon be arriving with the village elders. Turning into the feast hall with his captive, Wulfgar smiled when he saw everyone present. Heahstan's and Geldhere's men held Turpilos, Vendognus and Gwidol in chairs, while Huweyn sat unmolested with his accounts, guarded by Leofgist and Osmund.

"Ah, everyone is here," Wulfgar announced cheerfully, as though meeting a gathering of friends.

"Explain this barbaric intrusion," Huweyn demanded with a hint of fear, watching as Wulfgar deposited his bound wife on a chair.

Wulfgar strode up to Huweyn, taking a mouthful of wine from the man's goblet, and said in Seaxan, "I am calling a meeting of the elders."

Vendognus interrupted Osmund's translation. "Where are our wives? What have you done with them?"

"Yes, your wives." Wulfgar stared at a writhing Acgarat. "Your pretty little harmless wives."

A hush fell on the room and Wulfgar's confidence grew with each word he spoke. Even Acgarat attempted to sit regally on her chair while tied like a festival spit roast.

"Good little wives, who conspire to overthrow their husbands while they are away trading with the Menapii. Sweet little wives, who bed other elders while their husbands barter with the mountain men of the west."

Turpilos tried to break free, two Wulfsuna wrestling him to the ground. He glared at Wulfgar, who removed the silk from around Acgarat's mouth. Turpilos scowled at her.

"You whore, you told him?" he cried.

Aghast, she replied, "No, you fool. Though now there will be no doubt."

257

"Acgarat?" Huweyn rose unsteadily from his seat. "You would do this to me? Is this true?"

Acgarat's rolled eyes preceded Turpilos's outcry. "I pledged my love to you."

"Turpilos too?" said Vendognus, battling the iron grip on his arms and losing. "She said she would see me in Huweyn's seat."

Huweyn sank into his seat once more, head in his hands, weakened by the news. Wulfgar raised his eyebrows as he wandered round the hall, examining the gathering of guilty parties.

"I think you will find, Huweyn, your wife has been very busy, though I admit I did not know about Vendognus."

Vendognus shifted uneasily. Turpilos tried to spit in his direction and shouted at Acgarat again, "You whore." Acgarat ignored the insults, aiming her daggered stares at Wulfgar instead.

"This sweating barbarian tried to rape me. How do you know so much?"

Wulfgar ceased pacing and faced her. "Morwyneth."

The name brought all eyes in the room onto him and Wulfgar knew it would soon be over. It had been easier than he had envisaged. The fortifications of Huweyn's settlement were ten times stronger than the stability and loyalty of his own council.

"Did that slut's daughter send you here for revenge?"

Huweyn winced at his wife's defamatory description of his lover and child. Wulfgar shook his head slowly while he waited for Osmund to repeat the words in Seaxan.

"Only I seek revenge, and not with you. With another. Morwyneth asked us here to protect the people of Prenhwychas."

Vendognus scoffed aloud and waved a hand at the warriors surrounding him. "You call this protection?"

Turpilos added, "Those painted men of the north will not come."

Wulfgar paused before he replied, ensuring all were listening. "Even if the Pictii do not come, it seems clear Prenhwychas needs saving from its own inbred disease that eats away at her from within. Either way, I am here to save this village."

Huweyn lifted his face, gaunt and grey. "You may be right, Lord Wulfgar. I believe Prenhwychas does indeed need saving from itself. I only wish Morwyneth were here."

As Osmund finished relaying the statement, Wulfgar's eyes narrowed and he glanced at Acgarat. "Yes, if only Morwyneth were here. She could tell you how Lady Acgarat bred fear among the women of Prenhwychas so they would oust a young seer into the wilderness."

"Liar," Acgarat spat, leaving her seat only to be restrained by a warrior after a single gesture from Wulfgar.

"Or did you hope they would kill her?" Wulfgar asked, ignoring her outburst and not waiting for Osmund's translation. Weighted down by a pair of giant hands on her bony shoulders, Acgarat seethed in silence. Her husband fell back in his chair, a shaky hand hovering near his lips. He glanced at his elders. Turpilos, who remained pinned to the floor, had resorted to laying his face on the tiles, eyes closed. Vendognus tried to hide sheepishly under lowered lashes.

"Did you men have a hand in this?" Huweyn asked them.

"No, My Lord. Oh Huweyn, forgive me," Vendognus pleaded in vain.

"Yes," Turpilos said into the floor.

"Shut up, you fool," Acgarat screamed at Turpilos, stamping a foot.

Feeling the time had come for the final scene in this strange saga, Wulfgar called to his ealdorman, "Leofgist, you know what to do."

The Hwychas exchanged puzzled glances as Leofgist departed, accompanied by two Wulfsuna. Wulfgar drew up a chair and helped himself to a large red apple from a bowl on the long table. Reclining, one leg over an arm of the chair, he bit a chunk from the apple and slowly chewed. When Wulfgar was eating the last half of the core, Wulfsuna voices heralded the regal arrival of Lady Brithwen. Leofgist appeared in the main entrance and formally announced her as two guards escorted her into the main hall.

"Dear Lady Brithwen, wife of Lord Wulfgar of Sachsen, Headman of the Wulfsuna."

Wulfgar picked apple skin from between his teeth with his tongue and smiled, walking over to Brithwen and extending a hand to his audience. "Elders of Prenhwychas, my wife." He held a hand out to her, which she took, looking round at the faces in the room. She was cocooned beneath mantles, the hood of her cloak and her black wolf pelt as he had instructed Leofgist to demand of her. He did not want her identity revealed until the moment was right. She glanced warily at him and he squeezed her hand. No one had addressed her yet and he turned to them, brow furrowed.

"What say you?" he asked.

Acknowledgements rippled round the hall from all the men. Acgarat kept her silence. It was time. He tugged gently on Brithwen's hand, encouraging her near so he could whisper in her ear.

"Remove your mantles," he said. She refused, shaking her head and stepping back. He caught her by the waist, trying to assuage her fear with a gentle smile, clasping her hand to his chest.

"*Ic bidde thu*, Brithwen. Let them see who you have become. Have strength."

She relented with a small nod and he stood aside so that everyone could view her fully. She removed her hood and released the outer mantle from her face, head bowed while she removed the second mantle. When she lifted her head, the linens dropping with her hands, there were gasps. Gwidol spoke for the first time.

"The child lives," he declared, signing the cross.

Acgarat hissed, "She is no child. She is a weaver of evil powers."

"What do you care?" Turpilos challenged, allowed to rise from the floor at last. "You have no love for God yourself. You did not fill the minds of those women with lies and fear in the name of God. You did so because you wanted to remove Huweyn. We all wanted to remove him."

Vendognus added, "Now a horde of Seaxans have descended upon us, out of your own personal hatred for one innocent child."

Huweyn looked at Acgarat in despair. "How could you?"

Acgarat clenched her fists. "I was sick of you pouring your pity on that wretched girl. You never loved me as you did that crazy witch who bore your child. I had to do something."

Huweyn's face became shrouded by anger. "It was not pity, it was love. Something you know nothing of, it appears. You encouraged a rebellion to expel my daughter, threatened a civil uprising through religious panic, all for your own jealous ends." He turned away from her in disgust.

"She is your daughter?" Gwidol asked.

Huweyn nodded. "Before I married, Anwen was my mistress. I loved her so, but we kept our love secret for we knew it would not be wise to reveal it."

A look of realisation dawned on Gwidol's face and he smiled. "You have your heir, My Lord."

Huweyn walked over to Gwidol and squeezed his shoulder before turning to Turpilos and Vendognus. "Gentlemen, consider yourselves no longer of Prenhwychas and no elders of mine. Lord Wulfgar," he glanced over his shoulder, "may I call some of my own men? I wish to place these villagers under arrest."

"Ealdorman Leofgist," Wulfgar called, "assist Lord Huweyn in his request."

"Yes, My Lord," Leofgist replied, dutifully disappearing in search of Clodri and his band of amateur warriors.

Huweyn came over and stood before Brithwen, though keeping his distance out of respect. Father and daughter exchanged loving glances, but neither moved nor spoke. Wulfgar took his wife's hand and addressed Huweyn in Brytonic, no longer concerned if his secret was known.

"Lord Huweyn, I ask for your blessing."

The surprise on Brithwen's face as he spoke her native tongue was sweeter to Wulfgar than the figs he had eaten at the harbour market. He revelled in what fun he might have later, when she had more time to confront him on it. He gave her a wink and she smiled.

Huweyn took their hands in his. "Of course. What better than for my darling daughter, an unsung noble, to find love in the arms of another of equal stature." Brithwen hurled herself into Huweyn's arms and he held her close. "So many years hiding. Your mother and I should have found the courage to fight against them all. I cannot believe I denied you all this time."

"We were still together," she muttered into his tunic.

"Until wrongful banishment, my child." Huweyn stepped back to observe her. "But no child are you now. What a fine woman you have become."

Clodri and his men returned with Leofgist, and Huweyn excused himself, instructing the tucker to take Turpilos and Vendognus into custody. Wulfsuna mingled with Hwychas, Heahstan wiping his brow at Wulfgar in mock relief. Wulfgar grinned. He had succeeded in restoring power to Huweyn. He had saved Prenhwychas from one danger.

A high-pitched cry reverberated round the hall, drawing everyone's gaze. Acgarat had hobbled to the table and used a knife to cut her ankles free. Her banshee scream preceded her lunge at Huweyn, stabbing him in the back. As the leader of Prenhwychas fell to the floor, Wulfgar felt Brithwen's hand on his chest, pushing him out of her way.

Contrary to Wulfgar's initial thought, she did not run to her father's side. She unsheathed her seax and hurled it at Acgarat, where it embedded in the woman's neck. Blood splattered over white skin and pale clothes, and the woman landed heavily on the tiles. A loud whistle caught Wulfgar's attention and he looked up to see Heahstan beckoning him to leave. Seaxans and Hwychas jostled in the fracas, the imprisoned traitors trying to flee in the confusion. Clodri struggled to quell the panic in those of his men who had not seen Acgarat kill Huweyn. Two of the villagers insisted the Seaxans were responsible and were intent on avenging the murder.

Wulfgar turned to Leofgist and shouted, "As they say back home, fish and guests smell at three days old. It may be time to leave?"

Leofgist yelled, "Withdraw."

While Heahstan and Geldhere fended off the revolt within the hall, Leofgist and Osmund raced to open the entrance doors at the front of the villa. Wulfgar searched for Brithwen. She had gone to collect her seax and walked calmly towards him, wiping the blood from her blade onto a piece of Acgarat's clothing. Re-sheathing her weapon, she met his wide-eyed stare.

"We should take Huweyn," Wulfgar began, although he was fearful the fighting in the hall would soon spill out into the rest of the village.

"There is no time." She took him by the hand and started to run. "I live for you now, husband."

Wulfgar glanced over his shoulder to see Leofgist and Osmund battling to close the entrance doors against a wave of angry villagers. Without information to advise them otherwise, the people of Prenhwychas had assumed the Seaxans had come to wage a battle against them. Brithwen tugged on his arm and dragged him through to the rear salon and a side door near the staircase. The side door brought them out near outbuildings for grain storage. Aware they were isolated and a fierce battle could ensue at any moment, Wulfgar prayed she knew where she was taking him. They weaved in and out of buildings and patches of vegetables, Wulfgar wondering how long it would be before villagers found them and turned on them. He saw no other thegns or Wulfsuna, and had to dispel a fear he and Brithwen were the only survivors. Reaching a stone wall, Brithwen crawled through a hole and he followed. On the other side, she ran to a damaged section of the ramparts he had not seen and scrambled under.

"Come," she called.

Dropping onto his stomach, dry dirt flying into his mouth, Wulfgar slid under the fence. For a moment his baldric caught on a shard of wood and he struggled like a caught fish on land. The leather belt worked free and he scrambled to the brow of the ditch, rolling down and colliding with the base of a stake. He grunted, seeing no more than Brithwen's gown disappearing over the grassy mound. He climbed out of the ditch and ran after her. She had her skirts in both hands, her wolf pelt half-hanging from her shoulders. They passed the entrance gates and turned up the road towards the wagon camp.

Alerted by the commotion and battle cries of their fellow Wulfsuna from inside the village, the tribe were hitching oxen and horses and turning their wagons. Tortsig and his men ran up and down the convoy, banging fists on the sides of vehicles, shouting for urgent withdrawal, and Ianbert rode out to Wulfgar with his mare. Brithwen had slowed, breathing hard and pulling at her pelt and cloak, hot from her exploits.

"Take Lady Brithwen to the wagon," Wulfgar cried, catching the reins Ianbert tossed him.

Ianbert rode over to Brithwen, tossing long blond hair off his face as he offered her an arm with which he hauled her onto his lap, calling out to Wulfgar, "We are trapped in this valley. The only way out I see is the way we entered."

Settling onto his saddle and quietening his horse with a rub on her neck, Wulfgar considered the route. "Take it," he said, for he knew no alternative.

"No," Brithwen intervened, "I know another."

"Show us," he told her and rode after Ianbert.

Following his wife's directions, trying to map the way in his mind to retrace it, Wulfgar prayed all the wagons were on the move. He hoped Leofgist, Heahstan and Osmund had escaped alive with their men and would be waiting with the wagons.

"Have we gone too far?" Brithwen asked, her voice faltering in fear.

"No. It is wise to ride ahead and ensure our way is clear." He smiled. "Let us return."

All his thegns were waiting for them, Leofgist the most relieved his headman had survived. Heahstan informed him it had not taken long to break free from Prenhwychas. The villagers had been too involved in fighting one another, and those they did encounter had little combat experience. Wulfgar informed them of what he and Ianbert had ridden ahead to view.

"Brithwen's way is clear and looks to take us up onto the plains. Keep us south-east."

"Very good, My Lord," said Leofgist. "Thegn Heahstan is riding at the rear with his men. Geldhere and Tortsig will flank either side of the convoy. Ianbert, will you ride at the front with me?"

"Certainly." Ianbert nodded.

Leofgist continued, "I have secured your wagon at the centre of the convoy and added extra guards, My Lord."

Wulfgar grinned. "Good. I shall ride with you."

Leofgist cast a glance at Heahstan, replying, "My Lord, I feel you would be better protected if you rode with Lady Brithwen."

"What?" Wulfgar asked incredulously, and caught Brithwen looking at him, her eyes large blue orbs fixed on him. He realised he was no longer a lone warrior. He was Headman of the Wulfsuna with a wife to care for. Brithwen had seen her father murdered and had killed someone, possibly for the first time. He could not leave her alone and yet he needed to lead the Wulfsuna.

"There is no need for my lord to accompany me. I shall be fine," said Brithwen. Wulfgar wanted to thank her with many kisses. She knew his need to be with his men, to be seen. He would indulge her with his company when night fell.

"Very well, Lady Brithwen," said Leofgist, motioning for Ianbert to deliver her to the wagon.

"Wait," Wulfgar commanded, perhaps too sharply, and sidled his horse alongside Ianbert's. Brithwen smiled in anticipation, recognising the expression in her husband's eyes. She leaned forward enabling Wulfgar to slide a hand round the back of her head and pull her to him for a kiss. Ianbert dipped his head, cheeks flushing. Satiated, Wulfgar released her.

"Now you may take her," he told Ianbert.

The convoy began to move, thegns and their men arranging themselves as had been agreed to protect the wagons. Finding comfort in the familiarity of riding at the front of the convoy once more, alongside his ealdorman, Wulfgar held no sadness at leaving Prenhwychas. He had not favoured coming because of what he might have lost here. He had never been certain Brithwen would leave with the Wulfsuna once reunited with her father and her own people. Huweyn's death, however sad, appeared to have sealed a decision in her mind. She had pledged herself to him a short while ago and at the same time owned him. What man could ask for a better wife? Not merely a wife – a warrior; a breathtakingly beautiful woman who would someday bear him children; a strong woman who could make him a great leader; an intelligent, wise woman of immense power and foresight. He felt humble and in awe.

As a grey day sank into a sober night, they rode out of the valley and into the uplands. Their position now preferable, being able to view the landscape in full and see prey approaching, Wulfgar considered the future. Eadmaer would not wait forever to hunt him down. Eventually he would lose patience with his childish game of hide and seek and would come for revenge. Wulfgar concluded that if he wanted to finish what had begun in the marsh fens, he would need to find Eadmaer first.

In the beginning he too had wanted revenge, at any cost. Sieghild had persuaded him it would not quench the loss of his father and that Wulfric would not have wanted it, so he had set aside his own desires. "You are bound by the bonds of your ancestry," Sieghild had told him after the Battle of the Fens. Familial bonds are so called for a reason and can very rarely be broken; blood binds indelibly. At most those bonds can become damaged or frayed, and love of those bonds is all that will heal them. But, thought Wulfgar, you cannot ally to all you love at the same time. Despite his love and respect for Sieghild, at his friend's funeral, when he had realised the rest of the Wulfsuna also wanted Eadmaer dead, he had had to relent. He gazed at the uninterrupted spread of darkness, the cool air punctured by the cry of a vixen.

"Leofgist?" he said.

"Yes, My Lord?"

"Send scouts to locate Eadmaer."

chapter twenty-three

The Uplands,
South Wolds

Brithwen had not expected Wulfgar to return to the wagon. He would want to be with his men, to oversee the tribe's escape to safer ground and demonstrate his strength as their headman. Grateful that he had consented to her request to come to Prenhwychas, she now realised how dangerous it had been to bring Seaxans into her homeland. She recognised also the absolute trust Wulfgar had in her and her gift by assenting to her wishes. Such faith demanded she should return that trust and she vowed to do so at the next opportunity.

Thankful for the solitude, she took a moment to contemplate her situation. Since leaving Prenhwychas she had dreamed of seeing Huweyn again, imagined conversations in her mind and wondered what she might say to her father if she met him again. Reunited briefly, there had been little time for words before Acgarat cut him from her physical life. They had, however, freed Prenhwychas from the rotten element that had threatened its leader. What fate awaited her village, Brithwen did not know. She could have used her gift to divine its future, but chose not to do so. She had become a Seaxan and her destiny rested with Wulfgar. With Huweyn dead, nothing existed in her former home that would entice her back.

She had no hesitation, though, of opening up her crystal tunnel to see her father take his first steps on his spiritual journey. The soles of her feet tingled pleasantly as she welcomed the blue light into her psychic vision, eyes closed to the wagon. Dudley waved to her, beckoning Huweyn and escorting her father along the translucent path. At first she feared the scop dead, although appearing in the tunnel did not necessarily denote death. Time would tell her if her fears were founded. She opened her eyes, arresting them in the dimness of the wagon. Exhausted, she sank onto the sheepskins and tugged a wool blanket around her, falling into sleep too swift to dream.

Cold air invading the wagon woke Brithwen. The convoy had halted and she heard raised voices near the front. Dudley lingered in her thoughts like the last stubborn leaves of autumn, and on hearing the cry of "Wealh" her chest tightened. Without cloak and mantles, caring not who saw her, she climbed out of the wagon. Strangely, no guards barred her as she hurried along the disjointed line of vehicles through the meagre remains of wildflowers that lined the chalk road. Harebells and corn marigolds strained towards the weak sun failing to break through gathering clouds. They were traversing an upland meadow. Icy breath against her cheek compelled Brithwen to run faster, hoisting her gown over the long grass. Wulfgar called her from his horse as she ran past. She could pay him no heed. At a gathering of people being ushered back by a mounted Leofgist, Brithwen stopped.

"Brithwen," Wulfgar called her again and she glanced back. "Wait."

She waited. He rode down to meet her, dismounting and taking her cold hand in his warm one. Leofgist, now aided by Osmund, moved the onlookers back. As their lord and lady approached, the crowds parted to let them through. Directly in the path of the wagons, a large figure lay curled in the grass, a sack cloth bundle held tight in his embrace and across his body a long staff draped in a collection of charms. So it was true.

"Dudley," she whispered, emitting a sob and leaning into her husband's embrace. Wulfgar pulled her head into his chest, his hand cupping the back of her head.

"The tale-weaver."

She withdrew from her sorrow, recalling how he had said they may meet again one day in a meadow. "He is at peace. Blodeuwedd has him in her eternal embrace."

Wulfgar squeezed her hand, making her look up at him. "Is there something you must do?" he asked. She offered a weak smile, grateful for his consideration.

"I have done all I need."

"Should we bury him?"

She gave Dudley one last glance. "No. The Queen of the Meadows has him. Let her return him to the earth in her own time."

With Brithwen's hand still in his, Wulfgar instructed Leofgist to move the wagons around the tale-weaver keeping a suitably sacred distance. Telling Lorri to give his horse to Osmund so he might assist the ealdorman, Wulfgar returned with Brithwen to their wagon. They walked in silence, which continued once they had climbed inside their portable home. Eyes dry to her grief, Brithwen knew of no words that would serve their situation.

"Would you like me to stay?" Wulfgar asked tentatively.

She smiled, sensing his need to return to his duty. "No, there is no need, truly."

"As you wish, little wife," he said, pausing to examine her, tracing the backs of his fingers across her pale cheek. "So many have you lost. You are stronger than I."

Brithwen caught his hand in hers, eyes widening at the bravery of his admission. "You are strong in other ways. Your honesty is a gift."

He laughed, eyes breaking away briefly. "Honesty is the knife with which we carve our paths. Sometimes we cut ourselves or others in the process."

Brithwen nodded, acknowledging they both shared emotional scars. She lowered her eyes to his shoulder, placing a hand over the wound she had inflicted upon him; a physical scar of their emotional journey. Wulfgar shifted, easing away from her touch, breaking swiftly into conversation.

"Leofgist says it is desolate because you can see nothing for miles." He looked towards the entrance behind which lay the windswept upland. "It is high here and open for sure. At least an enemy will be well visible."

"You say that as though you are certain Eadmaer will come," she replied.

Wulfgar sighed. "He will, I have no doubt."

As though hidden in her mind behind her cosseted thoughts of Huweyn, the altered vision Brithwen had experienced on returning to her home came back to her.

"I must tell you something."

Wulfgar took her shoulders in his hands, kneeling up. "What, little wife?"

"Back in my home I again had the vision where I first glimpsed the threat of the Pictii."

Wulfgar settled on his heels, eyes dropping. "So they are still coming?"

"No." She took his face in her hands so she could gaze into his eyes. "It was different. Instead of Pictii, I saw a man with the head of a boar and yellowed teeth."

"Eadmaer." He exhaled, losing his balance and bracing himself with a hand on the sheepskins. "In Woden's name, the tale-weaver spoke the truth. You can see my destiny."

Brithwen let her hands wander down his neck and torso, clasping his hands. "I see many destinies, though not often my own."

Wulfgar rested a hand on his purse, inside of which he had placed the pregnant talisman, eyes wandering back in the direction of Prenhwychas. "I must go," he told her, face sombre.

She released him and he climbed down from the wagon, his feet barely reaching the ground before a guard called for Leofgist. Within moments his cnapa had brought his horse. It seemed the Wulfsuna remained vigilant in safeguarding their headman.

At noon the convoy paused for a welcome meal and a break from travelling on the rough limestone. Cook's wagon drew to the side of the road and people left their vehicles to stretch their legs or tend to animals. Children hid beneath the wagons or raced from one end of the line to the other. A weak sun had managed to filter through the thick cloud blanketing the sky, and the brightness of the weather filled Wulfgar with warmth. On learning of his wife's new vision he had hurried to speak with Leofgist and Heahstan. Both thegns felt confrontation with the Angles unnecessary considering the civilians they were transporting. They admitted, however, that Eadmaer would pay that no heed. He would come regardless and they would have to be prepared.

Standing with Leofgist by Cook's wagon, where the cabbage soup and strips of cold mutton were fast disappearing, Wulfgar watched the ealdorman pull at his baldric, his head twitching with each and every sound. Curious as to the cause of Leofgist's discomfort, Wulfgar struck up a conversation, hoping to weed it out of him.

"Will you eat with me?" Wulfgar asked.

Leofgist shook his head. "Thank you, My Lord, but I must find someone."

Wulfgar shrugged, in no mood to chase the man down, and fetched a hefty portion of soup and mutton, which he sat on a rock to eat. Two infant boys with wooden swords mounted an attack, one stealing a piece of his meat, and he waved them away, laughing. His own appetite replete, he returned to Cook for a portion to take back to Brithwen. He knew she would forget to eat, hidden inside the wagon with her thoughts on her lost loved ones. Laden with a full bowl of soup, Wulfgar headed back to his wagon. After no more than a few paces, a hand on his arm drew him to a standstill.

"I thought I would never find you alone, *Lord Wulfgar*." Trunhild used his headman's noble address as though it sickened him to say it. Wulfgar remained silent and motionless, trying to locate Leofgist in his vision without making any obvious moves with his head that would alert Trunhild. In a whispered rasp, Trunhild continued.

"I know what you have done. I know you have poisoned that pure girl's mind with empty promises of saving Prenhwychas. Did you believe you would find Eadmaer there and have your revenge, or was it a ruse to divert us from hunting Eadmaer in Yr Gogledd?"

The soup bowl began to burn into Wulfgar's hands and he wanted to hurl it into Trunhild's face, though he knew he had to stall Trunhild in the hope Leofgist would find them. "She knew there was a chance Eadmaer would be with the Pictii. Leofgist has told me you want him dead as much as the rest of us."

Trunhild's grasp on his arm tightened. "You believe you are leading us all to glory, when in truth you are sending us all to our deaths. I hear the leader of Prenhwychas met his death. It is a wonder no Wulfsuna were killed, prying into another's business."

Wulfgar laughed. "We went to save them."

"I'm glad you did not come to save our village," Trunhild spat phlegm onto the ground near Wulfgar's boot, "or else I would not be here. I do not trust you and my men will not fight for you."

Wulfgar turned towards him, though did not meet his gaze. "We shall see about that when I call council."

Trunhild released a short, bitter laugh. "You think you hold sway in council? You are a fool," he said, moving to block Wulfgar's passage. "I shall see to it they all know you put the Wulfsuna in danger for the love of the nix."

The area around them had become strangely silent and devoid of activity. Wulfgar's back prickled with agitation, but he chose his words carefully.

"What do you want?"

Trunhild dribbled like a hungry hound as he relayed his intentions, breathless with excitement. "I want to see you squirm on the end of a battle-light and feed your entrails to hungry dogs. I want to see you torn apart by your own council when they learn you have more trust in a river-witch than you do in your own men."

Seething, Wulfgar demanded through gritted teeth, "Why?"

Trunhild's breath caught in his throat several times, his eyes bulging from their sockets as a fever rose in him. "Many times since we met have I wished you had cut my tongue from my head that day we arrived at Lindum."

Wulfgar recalled how he had forced Trunhild to bow before him, threatening to cut his tongue out lest Trunhild answer him. "Why?" he asked again.

Trunhild's face contorted at the memory that ran through his mind as he said, "Without my tongue, I could not have carried out your order and told Morwyneth of Sieghild's death."

Wulfgar kept his eyes forward, anger searing through him, an unquenched heat ready to engulf him. Tensions about the possibility of battle were already high. He could let nothing jeopardise council. Trunhild, however, was not the same man he had met at Lindum. His eyes were wild with a terror bred from mistrust and hatred. The pounding of horse's hooves alerted them to the arrival of Leofgist, breathless and grey in complexion. The runt scurried away, calling out over his shoulder.

"You shall hear from me again."

Leofgist steadied his horse beside his headman. "Are you unharmed, Lord Wulfgar?"

Looking at the bowl in his hands, Wulfgar replied with a grin, "I'm fine, but the soup has gone cold."

"Please forgive me, My Lord. I had Osmund watching him, but when you invited me to eat, Osmund had told me he had lost sight of Trunhild." He leaned over. "What did he want?"

Wulfgar grinned wryly. "My life. I need to hold council, but do not want Trunhild present. Can we do that?"

Leofgist pondered before replying, "Tell me who you want to attend, My Lord, and I can invite the men for a drink." He winked.

"Ah." Wulfgar nodded, winking back. "A drink. In that case, as many of my thegns as you can without rousing suspicion, and have Trunhild occupied elsewhere."

Leofgist summoned two guards to escort Wulfgar back to his wagon and cantered away. Suitably accompanied, Wulfgar continued his walk. He had sworn to enter a battle only with what he had taken with him, though he never imagined it would be a bowl of cold soup. Reaching the wagon, he called for Brithwen.

"Little wife?"

Her face peered out from behind the ox-hide and Wulfgar felt Frigg thump his chest. He had to tell his woman he loved her, soon. He held the bowl out to her and she took it from him, moving further inside to allow him in. The guards checked the interior and dropped the hide over the entrance. Wulfgar sat with his knees drawn up, ankles crossed, smiling. He would not tell her about the incident between him and Trunhild. There was no need to concern her.

"How did you know I was hungry?" she asked, sipping the tepid liquid eagerly from the bowl.

He winked. "A husband knows these things."

She kept her eyes on him as she drank her soup, tears welling in them. He frowned, reaching up to take the half-empty bowl from her and setting it aside. She lowered her gaze. With a firm thumb and forefinger, he took her chin and kissed her hard and swift. He drew back, dismayed to find he had not erased her sadness.

"You are all I have left," she wept.

He pulled her to him abruptly, pressing his mouth on hers. He had not forgotten her sweetness. Satiated, he cradled her in the crook of his arm, stroking her wet cheeks.

"I belong only to you. You have all of me," he said.

Her crying ceased and she offered garnet lips to him, eyelids closed over the blue drowning-pools. He rubbed a thumb over her mouth, aroused when her lips parted on a breath escaping at his touch. He slid his hand to the nape of her neck, pressing her mouth into his. One of her hands wound into his hair, and again he wished he could feel them over his entire body. He wanted to taste the flesh upon all of her; every ounce of pale, delicate paradise.

"Lord Wulfgar."

Wulfgar grunted in response to the guard's call, burying his face in Brithwen's neck. He muttered an expletive and thumped the floor of the wagon with a fist. Sitting up, he slid Brithwen off his limbs, raking a hand through his hair. Knowing his lust still burned in his eyes, he met her gaze, wanting her to see all he felt for her. As Brithwen reclined on the bed, Wulfgar ran the back of his hand across his mouth, struggling to tether his desire while savouring what scent remained of her on his skin.

"Lord Wulfgar?" the guard called once more. Wulfgar rasped his response through gritted teeth, his eyes never leaving his wife's.

"What?"

"Ealdorman Leofgist has need of you, My Lord."

He pressed his lips together, inhaling deeply, swivelling onto his knees and sliding from the wagon.

"I come,"

His feet sank into a carpet of self-heal, disturbing a butterfly collecting nectar from the delicate purple buds. The sun had strengthened, stretching the heavy clouds into fine sinews. Looking round, he did not see Leofgist. However, Lorri had come to call for him and held a hand out. He followed his cnapa over to where his ealdorman stood huddled with Thegns Heahstan and Osmund. The latter gathered his black hair into a low tail at the nape of his neck, securing it with a piece of string.

"You needed me?" Wulfgar asked Leofgist, who broke his conversation with the other men to acknowledge his headman.

"Yes, My Lord."

Leofgist went on to say he had been informing Heahstan and Osmund of the threats Trunhild had made upon Wulfgar a short while ago, and the arrangements he had made for their discreet council. Wulfgar could only half listen as he fought to resist images of Morwyneth naked by the stream, insisting he take her body; her demand that he kiss her in front of his people outside their wagon; her offer of countless kisses as a token of her sincerity to submit to him once they had saved Prenhwychas. She had asked him to wait until the moment they were now living. He looked back to the wagon, imagining her sprawled on the sheepskins and blankets. She had seemed prepared to give herself to him back there; maybe without intention, though he had felt sure of it. There could be no better time to honour the oath he had sworn to Sieghild. She was his wife and, so help him, he could keep himself from her no longer. Let Frigg and all her battle maidens try and stop him.

Leofgist's voice buzzed in his ear like an irritating fly that would not cease. "My Lord, you should really tell Thegns Heahstan and Osmund what Trunhild..."

Wulfgar held up two palms, shouting, "Sieg!"

An awkward hush fell among the four men, their eyes darting between them. No sooner had the name escaped his mouth than Wulfgar knew what he'd done and regretted it. Leofgist continued, skilfully moving the conversation past his lord's error.

"You should tell us what Trunhild said to you, My Lord."

Wulfgar lifted the side of his mouth, as much of a smile as he could manage, and patted Leofgist on the back. "Thank you. Yes."

Osmund interjected, thrusting his sturdy chin at Wulfgar. "You should know, Lord Wulfgar, not all are in agreement with Thegn Trunhild."

Wulfgar nodded. "That is good to know, Osmund."

"What did that weasel have to say?" Heahstan asked, folding his arms.

Two male thralls appeared carrying stools and ale barrels for the men to sit on, arranging them in a crescent amid the meadow grass. A woman brought a jug of ale and cups, pouring each of them a drink to hydrate their discussions. Settled on a barrel, Wulfgar replied, "He made several threats, one of them against my life."

Heahstan growled disapprovingly. "He has brought his own death upon him with that alone."

As the others nodded, Wulfgar said, "Yes, though no one heard it but I. He also threatened to tell council a falsehood about my reasons for going to Prenhwychas: that we are no better than the Angles and went to rape and burn that village. He said I put the Wulfsuna in danger for the love of the nix."

Heahstan shook his head. "I have heard no utterance from the men."

"Nor I," Leofgist added.

Osmund held out a hand. "At the most, Trunhild has only persuaded a few: those who would not fare well in battle such as the old."

Wulfgar downed his cup, accepting a refill from the female thrall. "Trunhild accused me of using Prenhwychas as a diversion to avoid hunting Eadmaer in Yr Gogledd. He says there is no trust. You say there is. Who is right?"

"I have spoken with Geldhere and Ianbert. They are with you," Heahstan said, glancing at Osmund. "Know you of any more?"

Osmund rubbed hands along his thighs. "I am unsure of Tortsig."

Heahstan expelled air. "Worry not. He is a coward. He will align with the stronger side. The thegns will lead at council, and Tortsig will be among us."

A buzzard shrieked above them, circling high as it searched for prey in the lush meadow. The men's thoughts rested on the sky, their thirst for ale quelled by the weight on their minds. Wulfgar considered all they had discussed. If everyone but Trunhild stood firm, the Brytonic thegn would find himself alone against them all. A man with his back against a wall had no alternative but to fight, and to fight harder. Unable to fathom what Trunhild might do in that situation, Wulfgar recognised the need to prepare for it.

"Knowing he stands alone, Trunhild may take further action. He said I would hear from him again," Wulfgar warned. "He may reveal Lady Brithwen's identity. Will that be a danger?"

"My Lord?" Osmund glanced at the other men, eyebrows raised and mouth open. Leofgist straightened on his stool.

"Not to you, nor Lady Brithwen. Those of us that know are with you. Those who do not know..." He shrugged.

Heahstan leaned over to Osmund and muttered to him, "I'll tell you later, son", and to Wulfgar, "Whether she is named Morwyneth or Brithwen, she is the daughter of a Brytonic lord and is my headman's wife. You have united the two halves of the Wulfsuna by your union with that woman."

Wulfgar released a small laugh, gazing at the grass, turning his ale cup in his hands. *If only they knew.* Heahstan waved a thrall over to order more ale and mead cakes he had apparently overheard had been baked by one of the women.

"I can breathe easier then?" Wulfgar asked, smiling.

Leofgist grinned. "If Sieghild were here, he would tell you so."

Once again Wulfgar broke his gaze with his fellow men, shaking his head slightly. "I am truly sorry, my friend. His name lingers at times."

Leofgist rested a hand on his headman's shoulder. "Sieghild's memory lingers with us all."

The woman returned with a jug of ale and the mead cakes, two of which Heahstan was quick to pilfer from the plate she offered round. He shoved one whole into his mouth, spitting crumbs into his white beard.

"As good as my mother used to make," Heahstan said and, lifting a full ale cup, added, "To a successful council at sunset."

Nibbling the edge of a mead cake, Wulfgar digested the words of his ealdorman and eldest thegn. Those that already knew Lady Brithwen's identity accepted the fact she had once been the nix. Those who did not know would have to acknowledge her as the noble she was and would be opposing their own headman if they chose not to. There should at least be sympathy from the Brytonic Wolf Sons, knowing their lord's wife to be one of their own. Leofgist had already told Wulfgar that Trunhild had removed himself from all social aspects of tribal life. He had become a *wolfhead*, an outlaw. Lone wolves, devoid of a pack to run with, never lasted long. He hoped it would be so of Trunhild.

With one crisis partially concluded, one other remained and she awaited Wulfgar in their wagon. Burning from an intense fire inside of him at every thought of his wife, Wulfgar knew it would be folly to return to her prior to the council meeting. He slapped Leofgist on the shoulder, grinning.

"Will you challenge me at sword?"

Leofgist raised eyebrows and smiled. "Yes."

Thank Woden, thought Wulfgar, or else I would go mad.

Sunset came early, reducing the apprehension. Wulfgar handed his tunic to a waiting thrall and doused his face and naked upper torso from a bowl of water, watching Heahstan gather the thegns. There would be no one else attending council on this occasion. Once again the sky would be the roof and the warriors the walls of the imaginary mead hall that Wulfgar dreamed about building. The men and the fire were real, their gestures and voices giving life and breath. The sword duels with Leofgist had given Wulfgar a blood-thirst temporarily stemming his passion for Brithwen. He required a warrior lord's mind for council tonight. Dancing with swords had enabled him to prepare his word hoard, and he thanked Woden in anticipation of his success. He shook water from his face, running both hands through his hair and plaiting it. The thrall handed him his tunic, which he shrugged into, and his war-belt. He walked over to where another servant had rolled a fallen log into position facing the horseshoe of thegns waiting.

Pausing to gaze at each man in turn, Wulfgar stepped onto the log and announced loudly, "Give council."

The thegns delivered their names and rank in turn, then all fell silent. No sound filtered between the partially leafless trees, only glances. Leofgist regarded everyone and looked to Wulfgar.

"We abide," he told his headman.

"I will not," Trunhild declared, taking a step forward and staring down his fellow council members in defiance. "Lord Wulfgar, you dragged us here, at the whim of a river-witch, to fight with farmers and meddle in affairs we should never have become involved in. Meanwhile, Eadmaer and his Boars lie in wait in Yr Gogledd."

Geldhere swung round, a hand moving to grasp the hilt of his sword. "How dare you call our dear Lady Brithwen a witch. Remember to whom you speak."

Trunhild scowled, opening his mouth to speak and was beaten by Heahstan's steely reply. "Do not dishonour yourself in council with cheap talk, Trunhild."

Shaking the older thegn's rebuff from his shoulders, Trunhild pressed on. "It is the truth. She is Morwyneth, the Wealh we found on the roadside."

Ianbert squeezed Geldhere's arm, encouraging him to release his grip on his sword. Successful, Ianbert faced Trunhild, arms spread wide. "It matters not to me who she was. She is now the wife of my headman and I shall honour her as such."

Wulfgar watched the lone wolf begin to panic, seeing his argument receding fast like a tide in a storm. Trunhild paced the line of thegns, inspecting each of them, hunting for some faint remnant of support from kin. None was forthcoming. He stopped in front of Osmund, the only other remaining Brytonic Wolf Son.

"Osmund?" he whispered.

Osmund glanced away, closing his eyes briefly before looking at Trunhild, sighing heavily. "Yes, she was Morwyneth, daughter of Lord Huweyn. A Hwychas. A noble, Trunhild."

Trunhild swung round to face Wulfgar, eyes wide. "A noble?"

It seemed the seer had not shared everything with Trunhild, and Wulfgar gained strength at seeing the thegn stumble as he received the truth. Wulfgar jumped off his log, in front of Trunhild within two strides, glaring down into the weaker man's eyes.

"And she remains a noble as Lady Brithwen," he said calmly, watching tics erupt on Trunhild's face. "Yes, I did take the Wulfsuna to Prenhwychas at the request of Morwyneth, but this council has not been called to spread hearsay about my wife." He threw his arms in the air, addressing the whole council. "Hear me."

All thegns but Trunhild cried in unison, "We abide."

Wulfgar fought back a smile, walking in a circle to compose his features before continuing, "We came to make this land our own, to settle and raise families. Not all among us are warriors. We are a tribe with women, children and elderly. Many people are carrying their livelihoods with them. But this will all be for nothing if the Angles find us."

"What say you?" Ianbert asked, grinning broadly at the prospect of what his headman might say. Wulfgar allowed his own smile to break free.

"We must find Eadmaer before the Angles find us."

"If we are a tribe filled with women, children and elderly, how can we fight a horde of Angle Boars?"

Wulfgar waved his arms, trying to encompass the entire upland in one gesture, pacing, unable to stand still. "There are many warriors among us. Those young in blood can go and seek the wild hunt, be greeted by Hel and her fire maidens, or live, having quenched their battle-lust, and build businesses, families and wealth for the Wulfsuna." He shook a fist. "Once we have killed the threat to our peace, we can find settlement and live without fear."

"We are with you, Lord Wulfgar," Ianbert cried, raising a clenched fist in the air.

Geldhere bowed. "We vow our everlasting service to you, My Lord."

Wulfgar laughed, staggering in jubilation from the response of his thegns. Leofgist held his sword aloft, grinning broadly, joined by Geldhere. Tortsig, glancing at them, shrugged and waved a hand in the air to signal his agreement. In response, Wulfgar thrust a clenched hand up, shaking it in celebration. Giving a snort, Trunhild left council. Wulfgar did not care. He met Heahstan's gaze, which was fixed on him without expression, the old man's arms folded across his chest. Wulfgar dropped his arm to his side, his face sobering. The thegns fell quiet, weapons and voices lowering as they followed their headman's eye to their eldest member.

Licking his lips, Wulfgar said, "What say you, Thegn Heahstan?"

Heahstan slowly unfurled his arms and hung them by his side. He reached for his sword hilt, flipping the peace ribbon to free the handle and drew the blade from its leather scabbard. He paused, the patterned iron pointing to the ground, glinting in the firelight. Wulfgar flexed his hands, his wrist muscles taught against his vambraces. When Wulfgar began to doubt Heahstan's loyalty, the thegn swung his sword high, filling his chest.

"*Wulfgarsætan Cyning*," he cried.

Council erupted as every thegn joined Heahstan in his cry of "King of the Wolf Spear settlers". Wulfgar's body jolted, pounded by Thunor's strength as it emanated from the words shouted by his kinsmen. He had done it. He had become a real headman. He no longer held fear of men heeding his word. From out of the red burning end of day, Wolf Sons emerged to hear the chant, their voices swelling the cry. As more dark figures gathered to add their call, Wulfgar recognised a silhouette running across the grass, drenched in the last garnet glow. Brithwen halted shy of the crescent of thegns, hair blowing free in a cool evening breeze. She clasped her hands together, lifting them to her lips, shaking her head. She could not believe what she saw. Laughing through tears, she lowered her hands and rested them on her abdomen. Wulfgar touched the leather pouch inside of which he kept the pregnant talisman he had found in her home at Prenhwychas. He wanted her more than ever. He wanted her to have his child.

chapter twenty-four

The Uplands,
South Wolds

The night breeze tugged at Brithwen's gown and hair, urging her nearer to him. Lost to the merry-making that had begun around them, Wulfgar felt his heart surge as she walked closer. He dropped his head, watching her from beneath lowered lashes, chest heaving from the anticipation. "Run," he silently bid her, "run." She smiled, grabbing her skirts and running through the long grass, fracturing the blazes of light thrown out by the fire as she passed. His breath almost left him as she reached him, arms wide. He caught her by the waist, hoisting her above him as he had done at their wedding, spinning round as he lowered her into his embrace, kissing her firmly. Her warm hands grasped his hair in her fists, pulling him to her. When she released him he stood her away from him, hands owning her hips.

"Did you hear them?" he asked, tasting her sweetness on his lips.

"Yes." She stroked his face, tear-filled eyes roaming over him. "*Cyning.*"

Heahstan and Leofgist appeared beside them, and Brithwen was first to acknowledge the thegns. Wulfgar relinquished his wife from his gaze and faced them also. He knew the time for action was upon them, while the Wulfsuna's hearts were alight with the promise of revenge. He looked at Heahstan, whose eyes were red from emotion.

"Send scouts north tonight to hunt for Eadmaer."

"It is done, Wulfgar Cyning." Heahstan left quickly.

"Shall I assist?" Leofgist asked.

"No." Wulfgar grasped him by the arm, settling Brithwen against his hip. "You are my second sword."

Leofgist nodded, made mute by the well-spring of his feelings, extending his arm scarred from their blood-swear. Wulfgar released his wife to clasp forearms, the gesture reminding both men of the initial oath. With his other hand, Wulfgar grabbed Leofgist's shoulder and smiled. Sieg had gone. He had to leave his old friend in that grave by the lake, Sieg's warrior spirit riding off on Harsteda to join Woden, and make another bond. It could never be the same, although he knew there could be no other.

"My ealdorman, my friend," he said.

Leofgist blinked away tears. "I thank you, My Lord."

"I have plans for the morning. For now, go and drink to our victory." Wulfgar squeezed his arm once more.

Wiping wet eyes with the heel of his hand, Leofgist let go of Wulfgar's arm and bid them goodnight with a nod, dashing off to the ale cart which had been wheeled out for the celebrations. Thralls were bringing more wood to enlarge the fire that had been laid for council, and people gathered in small groups to warm themselves and consume their ale. Wulfgar turned in search of Brithwen who had wandered off and been folded into the darkness. In the distance a fox barked and the eternal flurry of water over pebbles hinted at a nearby stream. Gazing into the dark blue expanse of night, glistening with stars, Wulfgar came to understand his wife's affinity with the land and its magick; how she knew every leaf, every fruit and understood each animal and their cry. He felt the ground speak to him, its pulsing life-rhythm flowing through his feet like the roots of the mighty world tree, Yggdrasil.

His eyes tried to find her in the dark, small fragments of her lit by the growing fire. She was singing. He paused in his approach, breath catching at the siren sound. Long drawn-out syllables, soft or rolled in the throat, sang a lament, though not in Seaxan. For a while he listened, eyes closing as the song captured him. Her song ended on a long-held note that flew away over the uplands and unfurled to the stars. As the last remnants of the intoxicating sound ebbed, Wulfgar opened his eyes and looked back. He had not been the only one under her spell. The merriment round the fire recommenced, men and women shaking the hex from their heads and returning to their drinks. Urtha, Norn of the Fates, had woven their destinies. Wulfgar joined Brithwen who smiled, but did not speak. She took his hand, taking a final look at the persistent ribbon of red lingering across the land as the sun bid farewell. Tugging on his hand, she led him towards the wagons.

The orange glow of candlelight flickered through shafts of wood in the wagon, and Wulfgar imagined her leaving it lit in her haste to find him when the chanting broke out. Four guards acknowledged their headman and his lady, one of them peeling back the ox-hide so they could enter. Facing outwards at each corner of the wagon, they regimentally marched to a further distance by several strides as Wulfgar assisted Brithwen inside.

Sitting on the edge of their plump bed, which seemed to have been renewed with more straw and clean blankets, Brithwen removed her boots and unclasped the brooches on her gown. Her beauty a distraction, Wulfgar turned his back on her to undo his war belt. Glancing over his shoulder, he saw she had already removed her gown and risen to her knees, lifting the hem of her linen undergown over her head. His breathing increased and he feigned a cough to disguise it, returning his concentration to his war gear. His sword and daggers clanged as he arranged them in a corner with shaky hands and grasped the bottom of his tunic, tugging it over his head.

Kneeling bare-chested, he rolled his tunic into a tight ball while he decided where to rest it. They had been married for five days and in that time neither of them had undressed fully. Peeping round at her once again, he eyed her settling beneath a blanket, expectant eyes blinking slowly at him, lids heavy with affection. He emitted a small laugh and threw the scrunched tunic over his war belt, running a hand into his hair. His fingers caught in the plait and he tore at the three strands with both hands, pulling his damp hair free. A leader of men, a fearless warrior with many a slain victim stained on his hands in blood, yet he had no bravery before her. He felt sick with the shame should she witness the power she created in his body, which had already begun to throb. He burned to have her and could not spend a night beside her naked flesh without quenching his desires. He fumbled under his tunic for his seax and hurled it at the back of the wagon, where it embedded in the salt-worn wood with a loud thud. Brithwen screamed, propping herself up on her elbows.

"Is all well, Lord Wulfgar?" a guard demanded, tapping the vehicle near the door.

Wulfgar ran a hand into his hair, staring at Brithwen, tongue sliding across his lower lip. "All is well," he replied. He waited, listening for the guard to return to his post a little way from the wagon. Brithwen's face held questions, brow creasing as she tried to fathom the reason for his actions. He held her gaze, head shaking from side to side.

"Wulf?" she prompted, her use of his shortened name adding to his passion.

"I can kill men, hunt beasts," his eyes darted round the wagon, trying to find some distance from her in their confinement, "yet I am a weak man before you."

She sat up, clutching the blanket to her bosom. "What?"

He met her intense gaze, laughing. "Do not."

She smiled, "Do not what?"

He held a palm out to her. "Your sweet smile drags me to you, a ship's rope around my heart." Pressing a fist to his chest, he added, "You say my name and Frigg stabs my gut with a death-light, and I am slain by love." When she did not reply he continued, voice cracked with all his pain, "I must know if you will have all of me. I swear, in Woden's name, if you take me you shall have me until Hel does drag me to my grave, or for as long as Frigg makes magick between us, or until the hand of war seeks me out for Woden's Great Hall."

He waited on her word, praying she would ask for no more. All he had, he had given to her. He watched her slender throat as she swallowed, pressing a palm to her heart. She peeled back her blanket, swinging her legs off the bed and sliding over to kneel in front of him. She was as pure as he remembered her being by the stream. As though sensing his thoughts, she placed her hands on his shoulders, the fingers of her right hand sliding down to caress the scar she had given him that night.

Lifting her lips within a breath of his, she murmured, "I want all of you, if you will have all of me."

He closed his eyes briefly, inhaling her scent and allowing her statement to consume him. When she began to untie his trousers he gathered her in his arms, sinking down onto the bed with her. His gaze roamed over her, wanting to absorb every milky smooth facet. He cupped her face with a hand, a smile flickering across his mouth as he felt tears spill onto his cheeks. He had her. He had all of her. Brithwen smiled, taking his hand from her face to rest it on her heart.

"*Ic luf thu,*" she whispered.

Wulfgar slid his hand down over her breasts to her waist, watching every ripple of pleasure from her as he replied, "I love you, little wife."

He claimed her parted lips with his mouth, revelling in the long-awaited sensation as her hands found every ounce of his flesh, roaming over him, her seer's gift causing his body to hum beneath her fingers.

Wulfgar woke to a cold morning and his wife prostrate across his lower torso, a shoulder free of the blanket that lay over them. He watched her, waiting as slumber left her also and she raised sleepy eyes to him. They had shared their love and their bodies several times before sun-up, and yet he wanted her again. Hauling her up with hands under her arms, he kissed her fervently, trailing fingers up her neck and into her hair. The guards would soon call for him. He growled and buried his face in her neck. She giggled.

"I want you," he mumbled into her flesh.

"I also want you, but day breaks," she said, taking fistfuls of his hair and lifting his head so she could view him.

"Once more," he begged, watching laughter play in her eyes, "or I shall never know last night was real."

As sure as the sunrise, a guard called for him through the ox-hide. Wulfgar rolled Brithwen onto her back, straddling her and taking her mouth once again. Dragging himself from the warm sweetness of her, he pulled on his trousers and boots. As he was about to leave, Brithwen caught his arm, smiling.

"You may want these," she said, waving his vambraces at him.

Chaos greeted Wulfgar when he left the wagon. Some Wulfsuna were making fires and eating where they had parked, while livestock grazed among them untethered. Others were hastily packing wagons and arguing over which ox belonged to whom. Leofgist and Osmund were half-dressed, running between people and wagons, trying to placate a gathering of angry Wolf Sons. Wulfgar exchanged a quizzical glance with the guard who had hailed him. Waving away the thrall who arrived with his wash bowl, Wulfgar put two fingers in his mouth and gave a loud whistle that ceased all activity. People halted with bread hanging from their mouths and bundles of belongings in their arms.

He raised his arms. "What goes on?"

"Lord Wulfgar," Leofgist ran over to his headman, his tunic and sword scabbard still in his hand, "you must come and see this."

Wulfgar followed his ealdorman, Osmund falling in with them along the way, as Leofgist took him to one of the wagons nearer the rear. He glimpsed Ianbert on his horse, readying to gather some men to arrest the confrontations and hopefully restore order. Leofgist stopped by a wagon, pointing to rough carvings on the side. The old wood bore two words in deep grooves, each letter half a thumb high. They read *tha Eforas*, the Boars.

"Are these fresh cuts?" Wulfgar demanded, body twisting to scan the open land for any clues.

"Yes, My Lord," said Leofgist, "new this morning according to the owner."

Wulfgar looked at the carvings then back to his wagon, where he and Brithwen had been making love all night while an Angle Boar made the marks no more than three wagon lengths away.

"Find Lorri. I want my horse, and you, Heahstan and Osmund mounted to ride out with me as quick as you can dress."

He marched back to his wagon, fitting his vambraces onto his wrists on the way. No wonder the Wolf Sons were restless. There had been Angles, or at least one Angle, unseen in camp last night. How easily could they have attacked the Wulfsuna where they slept? He shuddered at the thought, realising Eadmaer and his men may well have learned new tricks during their time with the Pictii. He decided he would have to consider a new way of fighting. If Eadmaer brought Pictii with him, chances were they would have been educated in the way of the Angles. He reached his wagon and jumped inside to grab his clothes and weapons. Brithwen had fallen asleep face down on the sheepskins, her backside bare of a blanket. Wulfgar covered her over and jumped out, dressing where he stood.

Lorri had found Wulfgar and brought his chestnut mare by the time Leofgist and the other thegns arrived. Not prepared to take any chances, he was wearing all his armour, as were the rest of the men.

"We are going for a ride," he told them, tugging on the reins and leading them off at a canter. Following him northeast along an uneven limestone road, the men settled their horses into a walk, two abreast. After a quarter of a mile, Leofgist spoke up.

"Where are we going?"

Ignoring Leofgist's question, Wulfgar turned in his seat to address Heahstan riding behind him.

"Can we find an area to hide the more fragile members of the Wulfsuna?"

Heahstan chewed the request over behind his beard, saying finally, "There is a wood near here, by a sheep town."

"Find this wood," Wulfgar instructed, gesturing that his eldest thegn should lead the way. Osmund waved an arm at Heahstan as he rode past.

"There are many sheep towns around here."

Heahstan glared at Osmund and sucked on his teeth. "But only one by a wood where you can hide half a tribe of people."

"What is your plan?" Leofgist asked Wulfgar. Wulfgar ran a hand across his mouth, trying to organise his own thoughts so he could relay them coherently to everyone.

"We will need to fight differently. The Angles and Pictii may have shared tactics. If we can hide the less able, we can build a false wagon camp with warriors inside the vehicles and a headman's tent filled with fighting men."

Heahstan shook his head, saying over his shoulder, "You cannot build a shield wall in a wood."

"We will have to try, or fight another way," Wulfgar told him.

Wulfgar allowed Heahstan but half the morning to locate a road the thegn vaguely remembered which would lead them to the sheep town by the wood he had suggested they use. Wulfgar wanted to waste no more time with only four thegns at camp, one of whom was Trunhild. Should Tortsig be swayed it would pit him and the runt against Geldhere and Ianbert's men, and cleave the Wulfsuna in two. It would be a bloody break, and one that Wulfgar wished to avoid with Eadmaer all but upon them.

With thanks to Ianbert, they returned to a calm tribe packed and ready to move. Geldhere and a handful of his men greeted them as they rode into camp, informing the headman no one had seen Thegn Trunhild since he abandoned council the previous night, even though a small search of the surrounding area had been undertaken. Wulfgar disliked the taste that sprang to his mouth upon hearing the news. He considered his first thoughts about Trunhild had perhaps been true: that the Brytonic runt had allied to Eadmaer and intended to lead the Wulfsuna into a trap. If Tiw watched over him, the scouts would bring word of it.

Using Aelfsieg's map, Heahstan roughly charted the way and agreed to join his headman riding at the front. Leofgist and Osmund would follow with a score of marching men. Behind them would be the wagons and a second score of men on foot, with Thegns Geldhere, Ianbert and Tortsig spread between them. Arrangements for the arrival at the wood were set before they departed in order not to waste time when they found the location. Sentries were to be posted out of sight along the roadside in advance of the scouts' return, and Tortsig had ensured every able-bodied man and woman bore arms. Once they were in the wood, creating the trap and hiding the infirm would take time. Ianbert had taken it upon himself to gather a group of the youngest and least experienced warriors. These he had charged with the task of creating a diversion, should the Angles attack before the Wulfsuna were prepared, drawing the enemy towards the experienced fighters hidden within the camp.

Wulfgar settled quickly into the rhythm of the road, his mare a familiar comfort for he knew her manner and handling. She refused a firm rein and preferred a confident leg command to which she responded instantly. And she hated walking. One feast night, drunk on ale, he had promised her one day they would gallop until neither of them could breathe and collapse exhausted beneath an oak tree to chew grass and lie in the sun. For the moment, however, she would have to bear his teasing tugs on the reins, reaffirming the pace.

He had noticed a change in the tribe's response to him since his pronouncement as *Cyning* in council. His thegns heeded his wishes and were eager to share ideas as always. However, warriors and civilians seemed more aware of him moving among them. People spoke to him who had not previously and thralls seemed more amenable. Wulfgar recalled how jealous he had been of Sieghild's ability to take command at Lindum, and swelled with pride at his achievement.

It took the rest of the day for the Wulfsuna to reach the wood near a small sheep-farming town. On arrival, Wulfgar ordered his men to carry out what had been decided on the edge of the uplands. That dusk would soon be upon them was of no consequence. The Angles could attack any moment. Leaving men posted to lie in wait for the return of the scouts, they took the wagons into the wood. An accessible track led partially into the trees, though not for long. Soon warriors were hacking at undergrowth or forcing back branches in pairs to allow the vehicles to pass. Roots of trees threw the wagons about, inadvertently unloading people and supplies or trapping the wheels. When it looked as though their initial idea would have to be abandoned, a clearing beckoned. They would have to pack the wagons tight against the surrounding trees, but it would be possible to form a crescent of vehicles set about a central fire opposite which they could erect a modest headman's tent.

Remaining mounted while his thegns prepared to direct their men on foot, Wulfgar hailed Leofgist with a wave of his arm. "Oversee the wagons and tell people to remove only what they need." He searched for Heahstan and found the thegn standing beside him. "Where do we hide the ill and old?"

Heahstan lifted an arm. "South of here."

"Show me," said Wulfgar. Heahstan marched directly into dense forest once more, Wulfgar having to bend and weave around low branches while riding after him. Twenty or so paces south the forest floor descended into a steep dell: a deep bowl in the ground. It had not been visible on the approach, and any who came upon it without light or at speed would be likely to fall in. Wulfgar rode to the edge and peered down into the leaf-laden cradle in the earth.

"The sides are not too steep to traverse." Heahstan demonstrated, treading slowly to the base of the dell and looking back at Wulfgar. "The frail could be aided. And it is south of the camp, so Eadmaer should find the wagons before he finds this."

"You have done well," Wulfgar praised him. "We shall call it the pond. Bring Tortsig here and he can organise who should come. I want you with me."

Heahstan nodded. "Very well, My Lord."

They returned to the camp in the clearing. Thralls had collected wood and lit a fire at the centre of the crescent of road-beaten wagons. If Woden answered his prayers, Wulfgar hoped this would be the final resting place for what remained of the *Hildwaeg*. The majestic vessel had served them well, both on water and on land. She deserved to sleep and be remembered in saga songs around the fire in his mead hall.

Wulfgar dismounted and handed his mare to Lorri. Young women, children and the frail gathered by the wagons, clutching sparse belongings as warriors rifled through the interiors of the wagons, preparing to occupy them. Old men and women of pallid complexion stared back at him, some only possessing a warm blanket. A small girl, no more than eight years old, cradled an infant sibling in her arms which were barely long enough to hold the child in swaddling. Her enormous brown eyes blinked at him. In the throes of blood-rage he knew he would think of her, for when all seemed lost she would bring him the strength he needed to kill one more time. If it was for nothing else, she alone would be the reason they were facing the Angles. The future of the Wulfsuna depended on her survival and that of the child in her arms.

Midnight almost upon them, Tortsig and half a dozen warriors collected the civilians for passage to the pond. The young girl's eyes remained on Wulfgar as she trudged after her family. He smiled and felt pain in his heart when she responded. He looked away, his gaze finding Brithwen. She wore a gown of lavender with strange but beautiful foliage embroidered at the hems, her chin-length hair free, without mantles or horsehair plaits tied in. Her eyes seemed to hold a new light in them, the likes of which he had never seen.

"My Lord." Leofgist appeared at his side.

Wulfgar smiled at his ealdorman. "Tell me."

"I have sent pairs of men to hide in the hawthorn and dogwood, and there are warriors in every wagon."

"Where will we be?" he asked.

Leofgist pointed to the headman's tent. "You and Lady Brithwen will be with me and Thegn Heahstan in there."

Wulfgar turned, surveying the camp. "What of the other thegns?"

Leofgist counted the men on his fingers. "Thegn Ianbert is guarding the south side near the pond with Tortsig. Geldhere and Osmund have men between the road and camp."

"This is it," Wulfgar said, grinning.

Leofgist smiled back. "It is, My Lord. May Tiw be with us."

Brithwen drew her knees closer to her chest, nuzzling her face into Wulfgar's side. He rested a hand on her back, his thumb caressing her through her clothes, and pulled at his war belt to move the seax scabbard further from her face. His firm touch roused her inner desires, which she fought against. There was no time for romance for they were not alone. Wulfgar sat talking with Leofgist and Heahstan by candlelight, strategising and plotting all feasible outcomes of the Angles' attack. She had imagined they would have exhausted all words by now, though they appeared to have supply enough to talk all night. The tent smelled of wood smoke, men's sweat and the cabbage broth they had all consumed before retiring. Meanwhile, the scent of polished leather and grease from their byrnies lingered from their earlier preparations for battle.

Destined to remain awake, Brithwen gave thought to the recent change in the vision she had first experienced at her home in Prenhwychas. Believing the attack by blue northmen would befall that village, she now wondered whether it had ever been meant to happen. With what she knew now to be her true fate, here with Wulfgar and the Wulfsuna, it was possible she could have foreseen Pictii warriors as a precursor to Eadmaer's betrayal of the Wulfsuna. Therefore, the vision becoming the face of Eadmaer made sense as they headed into battle with the Angles. Dudley and Anwen had been correct in their predictions that a wolf would enter her life and she would help someone find peace. Listening to her husband's deep-throated whispering soothed her. He had shown no resistance in allowing her to remain at his side in camp. Thinking he would have preferred her to hide in the pond with most of the other women, she had been pleased with his response when she had asked to stay. "You are my eyes," he had told her, "I need you with me."

A guard's whisper alerted them that the scouts had returned safely, and shortly afterwards the two men joined them in the tent. Both tired and dusty, one of them bearing a knife wound on his right cheek, they were eager to share what they knew. From the bird crest torques on their arms, Brithwen knew them to be Ianbert's men.

The wounded man spoke first. "It is true they have made an alliance with the king of the Clann mhic Ailpein in the north. He has gifted Lord Eadmaer with several men."

"Do you know where they are now?" Wulfgar's hand left Brithwen's back as he handed the man the jug of ale he had been sharing with his thegn and ealdorman.

The warrior drank copiously and, once quenched, replied, "North-east of us by less than half a day."

The second man eyed the ale jug, adding, "We listened to them boasting beside their campfire. They have travelled from a place named Peanfahel."

Wulfgar gestured that both men could share the ale and turned to Heahstan. "Less than half a day. We are more than ready for these motherless *hildisvinas*."

The second warrior ceased his drinking to rest a hand on Wulfgar's arm. "My Lord, the Angles may be less than half a day, but we killed a Pict south of the Boar camp."

Heahstan grunted. "They could be planning to send the Pictii to us first to inflict as much damage as they can, to weaken us."

Brithwen sat up, unable to relinquish herself to slumber when such horror had been revealed. Wulfgar glanced round at her, his pale eyes searching for evidence her seer's vision held an answer. She felt nothing and shook her head at him. He faced all the men, banging a fist into the ground.

"We are still ready."

Chapter Twenty-Five

North of the Middle Wolds and River Wyndrysh,
Wooded Camp Near the Sheep Town

Wulfgar hung his head over a pail of icy stream water on a small table, hands resting on the wooden rim of the vessel, shoulders hunched. None of them had slept in the warm, damp confines of the tent. How could they have following the scouts' return delivering the news that Pictii and Angles were but a few hours from them? Wulfgar had wanted to bed Brithwen to soothe their fears in the light caresses of one another's bodies. Instead, he had plotted the forthcoming battle down to the last slice of blade; the final severed limb of the enemy; the last drop of Angle blood. He knew full well, as did Heahstan and Leofgist, that the fight would not be woven as they had planned last night. The Wolf Spear Saga ran through his bone house, its strength fortified when his loins joined with Brithwen and brought their fates together. Destiny remained all that could deliver them alive from the death-dance awaiting them.

Cupping his hands, Wulfgar sank them into the pail, tossing the handfuls of water over his face and scrubbing his tired features with the heels of his palms. Shaking his head, he opened his eyes, stepping back a pace at the sight before him. The squat man, mud and stubble grazing an otherwise bald head and face, glared at him through eyes blood-red from lack of sleep.

"Trunhild," Wulfgar murmured, wiping wet hands on his trousers to aid his intentioned grip on his seax hilt.

"I have been waiting for this moment," said Trunhild, spitting the words through clenched teeth. Wulfgar glanced at the sword the thegn held at him, the point of the blade a pace away, and considered how fast his opponent might be if he drew his seax in response.

"Why did you leave?"

As unexpected as Trunhild's return was, Wulfgar knew the longer he kept him talking, the more likely the chances another would stumble across them and intervene. With all the heightened security Leofgist had organised, it was impressive the Brytonic runt had made it this far unmolested by guards.

Trunhild waved the tip of his blade up and down, shaking his head. "When I heard council, I knew I would not be welcome."

Wulfgar ran his right hand through his hair, surreptitiously resting his left hand on his seax hilt as he did so. "All are welcome. Council is for discussion. Not all must agree to remain Wulfsuna."

The thegn released a mocking laugh, blade lowering briefly. "I do not want to remain Wulfsuna. I never did. That tribe left when your father returned to Germania. I am Bryttas."

Wulfgar tightened his hold on his seax. "Then why have you returned?"

Trunhild's eyes flickered from side to side, his feet shuffling as he raised his sword level with Wulfgar's face, eyes overcome by madness. "To cut you from this world."

Watching the shorter man quiver on the spot, possessed by his betrayal, Wulfgar wondered why no one had yet found them behind the headman's tent. People's conversations pealed through the morning mist that crept across the forest floor, the first stirrings of Wulfsuna. Sorrow filled Wulfgar's heart. One moment of duty had disposed of the man's dignity, turning him against those that nurtured him.

"I have only to shout..." Wulfgar began.

Trunhild's breath caught as he interjected, "I am fast", though his feet did not move.

Wulfgar, having used the comment as a threat although he could not be certain anyone would come, made his intentions clear to Trunhild. He withdrew his seax and grasped the throat of his battleaxe resting in his war belt. Trunhild's face contorted in rage. Wulfgar kicked the table, sending the pail of water spilling over Trunhild, and drew his axe. The thegn leaped backwards, raising his sword arm and emitting a roar. Wulfgar readied both blades, preparing to block Trunhild's sword blow with his axe haft. Trunhild jumped over the fallen table, squinting in light reflecting from a sword. Leofgist, two hands on his hilt, swung his sword down in an arc. Trunhild ran into the slice, which opened his gut protected by tunics alone. Trunhild turned to the ealdorman he had not seen, legs folding, sliding off the death-light into a squirming mass of blood and innards ruptured by agony. Wulfgar stared at Leofgist, whose face hung heavy with disdain for his victim, white knuckles gripping his sword as Trunhild's life oozed down the blade's blood-gutter.

Having heard the commotion, warriors appeared led by Heahstan. The old man locked eyes with ealdorman and cyning in turn, marching forward and drawing his sword. Holding it aloft in both hands, blade down, he drove the weapon into Trunhild's chest. The thegn died instantly, eyes wide.

Heahstan abandoned his sword in the cadaver and faced Wulfgar. "Never leave a man in agony if there is a swifter way to Woden's Hall, especially if he is one of your own men."

Leofgist looked up. "It was I, Thegn Heahstan." And then, regarding Trunhild, he added, "I never imagined my blade would slay a fellow Wulfsuna."

"Many years has it been since we last killed one of our own," Heahstan murmured and pointed a stern finger at both men. "Mark it well and hope never to repeat it in your lifetimes."

"He intended to kill me," Wulfgar told Heahstan, "and Leofgist saved me."

Heahstan nodded. "Then it is death for treason served upon Trunhild." He grabbed a guard by the sleeve. "Let it be known by all."

As the man left to carry out his order, Wulfgar asked, "Should I hold council?"

Heahstan shook his head. "No. We knew of Trunhild's threats," he glanced down at the body, "though I never believed he would act upon them. Bury him and bury your pity with him."

Heahstan strode into the woods, leaving Leofgist and Wulfgar with three men. Wulfgar sheathed his seax and slid his axe back into his belt, sighing heavily. The prospect of killing kin had not rested well with him. Thankfully Leofgist had saved him that anguish, though he did not envy his ealdorman. He waved to the three warriors.

"Bury him as discreetly as you can," he told them, and turned to Leofgist. "You were there for me, friend."

Leofgist lifted soulful eyes to his lord. "Yes."

Wulfgar reached a hand out to clasp him by the arm. "And you were there to kill Sieghild's murderer. You do me the same honour."

Leofgist blinked slowly. "But you live, My Lord."

Wulfgar shook him fondly. "It is not forgotten."

They courted silence a while in mourning for a fallen friend, the air around them thick with the sounds of men readying for war. Whetstones rang out against blades, horses whinnied and men grunted from clashing foibles as they rehearsed for battle. Wulfgar released Leofgist's arm.

"How did you find us? Did you hear him cry?"

Leofgist stared at Wulfgar for a moment, blinking past a thought that had gripped him. "No, My Lord. Lady Brithwen told me to find you, that she had seen death surrounding you."

Wulfgar's stomach clenched. She had seen his fate. Leofgist let out a small laugh. "It took all of my will and Osmund's firm arms to stop her coming herself, My Lord. I gave her my word I would find you in time."

"And so you did." Wulfgar smiled also, slapping his ealdorman's shoulder.

Leofgist gazed through the trees, his line of sight following the path the men had taken to remove Trunhild's body. "I could never have foreseen this."

"I did." Wulfgar paced beneath the wind-hewn trees. "I knew at Lindum. He hated me before we met. He never wanted to bow to a foreign headman."

"I cannot believe that." Leofgist followed him, coming round to face him.

Wulfgar exhaled and grinned. "Believe it or not, there was distrust in his heart a long time before I sent him to tell Morwyneth of Sieghild's death."

Trapped by the pond under the stern eye of Thegn Osmund, Brithwen gasped with relief when she glimpsed her husband wandering through the trees. She hoisted her gown and ran to him, slowing as she neared and caught the pain in his eyes, the weight of an immense sadness pulling at his shoulders. Her gratitude that Leofgist had been true to his word vanished when she sensed Wulfgar brought with him an uncomfortable burden. Refusing her outstretched hand, he looked away from her, eyes briefly closing.

"Wulf?" she whispered.

He faced her, jaw firm and a deep frown across his brow. "There has been an execution for treason."

"Treason? But who…"

"Trunhild," he cut her short, dashing a hand aside as though to eradicate the matter from further discussion and turning his back on her.

"Poor Trunhild," she said, her empathy inciting Wulfgar.

"Poor Trunhild?" He confronted her, his eyes ravaging her as he struggled to understand her compassion. "He tried to kill me."

She gazed around them, conscious they were under scrutiny and knowing it would do no good for the tribe to see their headman, their *cyning*, erupt in public prior to such an important confrontation. She lifted her skirt, walking over stumps and bracken deeper into the wood, knowing he would follow her. She paused beneath an oak that challenged lesser trees surrounding it, dominating the earth and air it occupied. Wulfgar sauntered over, his stubbornness making her smile.

"Understand me," she said before he could raise his voice at her again, "he taught me Seaxan, helped me see Sieghild, told me…"

She had no need to finish her words, for she could see Wulfgar knew. That one moment of duty had sealed the thegn's hatred. She placed her hands on Wulfgar's byrnie, trying to meet his wavering gaze. Wulfgar relented, locking eyes with her, hands sliding into her hair.

"Heahstan told me to bury my pity with his broken body. I have done this," he told her, words stiff as he fought emotion.

"Pity yes, but not compassion," she said, smiling. "He was a caring man, a generous man, shackled by the wants and needs of a warrior lord many miles across the ocean."

"I know he did not wish to be Wulfsuna. I know the fire of his hatred of me burned brighter when I sent him to tell you of Sieghild's death, but," he cradled her face closer to his, "my sorrow vanished when he came for my life. He chose his side and I mine."

He caressed her cheeks with his thumbs and lost his fingers in her hair, tugging her to him for a deep kiss. She covered his hands with her own, sending her magick through them and into his arms. His chest heaved several times as she soothed his anger, his angst flowing out of him with each breath. As he withdrew from the kiss she allowed her power to subside. With heavy lids he observed her.

"I want you," he whispered.

"I know," she said, smiling once again. "There will be another time for love."

One side of his mouth lifted in a faint smile. "I understand."

"Good," she said.

"No," he took one of her hands "I *understand*. Had I been Trunhild, a thegn living as a lord of my own small tribe, I too would be unwilling to bend to the wishes of a man who was a stranger to my land. I would have fought to hold onto my way of life. I would have fought harder than Trunhild."

She tilted her head to one side. "Yes, I believe you would have." After a pause, she added, "I love you."

He examined her face, his smile fading as thoughts found him. "I think I loved you even before I knew you." She felt her face flush, remembering her encounters with him since the Wulfsuna had found her on the roadside. His insinuation was that even then, when he had hidden behind his helmet and bellows of discontent, he had wanted her through all his fear. And yet he had allowed Sieghild to have her.

"And if Sieghild had lived?" she asked.

He slid an arm round her back and pulled her to him. "I would have spent a lifetime wondering about you."

She considered the many twists and turns of her existence since her expulsion from Prenhwychas, and whether their fate had already been written. Dudley had found her in time to divert her into the path of the Wulfsuna, Sieghild saving her from death at her own foolish hands. Even Sieghild's removal from life could have been a part of destiny's purpose: to send her into Wulfgar's arms.

She reached up and kissed him. "So would I."

Heavy footsteps through the undergrowth revealed Leofgist, his face still gaunt from his encounter with Trunhild. Brithwen felt Wulfgar's hold on her tighten inadvertently as he looked expectantly at his ealdorman.

"They are near?" he asked.

Leofgist shook his head, saying, "Yes, but Pictii not Angles. Fresh reports tell us Eadmaer has sent his blue painted allies ahead of his own warriors."

"We were right," Wulfgar said, leaving Brithwen so he could pace as he thought.

So was I, thought Brithwen, reliving the vision of the painted warrior looming in the darkness that fateful morning at Prenhwychas. She had indeed foreseen these Pictii, who were to attack the Wulfsuna and not her village.

"There is more." Leofgist's face twisted in anticipation of his lord's dislike of what he was about to tell him. "They come not from the road. They come from the south across land."

"Through the wood?" Wulfgar's eyebrows lifted, his head swerving round towards the civilians hiding in the dell. "Then they will find the pond before they find our men. Eadmaer must have sent scouts further than we anticipated."

"My Lord," Leofgist swallowed to quench a dry throat, "do you think Trunhild met with them?"

"You think his betrayal ran so deep?" said Wulfgar, glancing at Brithwen. She gave no reaction, not wishing to complicate her husband's already difficult decision. All their efforts had been designed to protect the tribe from an attack from the road, to trap them in the fake camp and reduce their numbers. South, beyond the wood, open grassland sloped into a valley lined with trees and large shrubs at the foot of tall, distant hills. A war-band could easily lie in wait below the brow of the sloping land having crept unseen through the hidden valley. Both men had fallen silent, gaze fixed on one another. Leofgist's failure to respond seemed to confirm his opinion that Trunhild would have been capable of such betrayal. A muscle twitched in Wulfgar's cheek and once more he glanced in the direction of the pond before facing Leofgist.

"Build a shield wall behind the first line of trees ahead of the pond. We will wait for them and cut them down."

Leofgist raised eyebrows, shifting from one foot to the other. "But Heahstan said you cannot build a shield wall in a wood."

Wulfgar set one foot forward, pointing at his ealdorman. "I'm your headman and I'll tell you what you can and cannot build."

Nodding so fast Brithwen thought his head would roll, Leofgist stammered, "Yes, yes, My Lord." Brithwen turned to Wulfgar who was watching Leofgist disappear into the trees, seething from some inner anguish. "What is it, Wulf?"

He spun round, eyes down and searching as though the answer lay on the ground, fists clenching. "I did not foresee this."

She held out an upturned palm. "We cannot know why the gods deprive us of such knowledge. They only show us that which we need."

He lifted his gaze, sliding a dagger from his war-belt and handing it to her handle first. "Take this and remain at the pond."

Brithwen accepted the eight inch engraved blade with wolves chasing each other's tails around the deer horn handle. "It is beautiful."

"It is the death-light I hope will bring Eadmaer his final breath. It was my father's." He stepped closer, cupping his hands beneath hers. "If the tale-weaver spoke the truth and you can see my future, you will find Eadmaer before I do."

A white orb strained beneath a veil of cloud shrouding the autumn sky. Like a green ocean, the grassland bent in great swathes as the wind caressed the landscape. Lorri's hand on his arm made Wulfgar turn as the cnapa handed him war-face. The youth patiently held his lord's wolf-head shield and spear, observing in silence as Wulfgar rolled the helmet between his hands in quiet contemplation. Men's coughs and murmurings drifted around them like whispers from the trees themselves. Wulfgar swivelled to view the sturdy shield wall behind him. Almost forty good men stood in three rows, and he prayed to Woden, Chief of all the Gods, it would be enough. Leofgist, Osmund and Geldhere protected the pond with only five warriors, while Ianbert and Tortsig hid in the false camp with another five men and a handful of youthful reserves. The reserves were fresh to battle and would soon be a worm feast if Eadmaer's best warriors found them.

"Will this work?" Wulfgar asked Heahstan, who was guarding a space for him in the front row.

Heahstan's chest puffed out as he scoffed, "We will know soon enough."

Behind the thegn, Chapper sniggered, sharing a broad grin with Skinner to his right. "Only the gods know, Lord Wulfgar. We men have to wave our seaxa and grit our teeth."

Skinner elbowed Chapper in the ribs. "You may want to grab your balls when those painted savages appear."

The men's bawdy laughter echoed through the branches above them, every man's courage renewed by the hilarity. Humour devoured their fear and bred strength in their limbs. Wulfgar laughed, settling war-face onto his head and fastening the chin strap. Conscious he had once made a vow to face a battle however it found him, today it would find him in all he possessed so no blade could find his flesh. His best grey wolf pelt adorned his shoulders over his byrnie, war-vest and tunics, vambraces secure over his wrists. He took his shield and spear from Lorri.

"To your place," he told the young man, stepping into the wall on Heahstan's left and turning to face the lush emptiness.

Soon after, as sun breached the forest and amber shards broke through the trees setting alight the fern-lined floor, they came. Men and women, faces and torsos scarred with crescents, circles and beasts, leaped from behind trees and shrubs. Screaming their war-cries, the Pictii brandished weapons, their fearsome dance a precursor to a death-cloud of arrows.

Wulfgar yelled, "Stay firm," dropping to one knee in line with his fellow men as they bolstered the wall against the deadly arrows, heads bowed behind shields. "Send arrows."

Heahstan echoed his command to ensure it had been heard by those warriors at the far left and right flanks. Fighting from within the wood, the bowmen were positioned to the sides of the wall, as close to the edge of the tree line as possible to allow a good arc. They launched their retaliation. The sounds of arrow showers overlapped, interspersed with the pelting thuds as the flying weapons met shields, helmets or limbs. As agonised cries rang out, Wulfgar seized the moment to rouse the Wolf Sons. He stood, Heahstan and several warriors joining him, and raised his spear above his shield, yelling the tribe's name.

"Wulfsuna! Wulfsuna!"

The wood reverberated with angons and pommels against shields, a deafening roar of defiance. The Pictii responded, charging the slope and repeating their war-cry. Arrows ceased and the Wulfsuna, including their lord, launched angons, the javelins soaring longer than usual, following the descent of the hill. The surviving enemy were not deterred and Wulfgar drew his axe, waving it forward.

"To *sweord*," he called, leading the wall in an advance, his breast swelling with pride as all men followed.

The Pictii rushed them, screaming; tattooed warrior-men and maidens in skirts and pelts with finely turned blades and cloaks pinned to one shoulder with circular brooches. At a distance they had appeared as blue savages, wild and untamed. Within a blade's touch they were noble warriors, no different to the Wulfsuna. They had intricately made weapons and wore garments of high worth.

Battle-lights clashed, men screamed and the stench of the fight erupted. Lorri skewered a man on his upturned spear and struggled against the weight, the haft sinking into the ground. Wulfgar fought off one man, shoving his shield boss into the enemy's face and smashing his features into a bloody mass. A second lunged at Lorri, landing on his shield and trapping him beneath. Wulfgar called his cnapa's name, bringing the young man to Skinner's attention. Skinner intervened, gripping his seax with both hands and driving the blade into the back of the Pict's neck. Blood sprayed Skinner's face, and he spat it out.

"Ugh." Skinner shook crimson from his head. "I thought these sons of bitches were blue all the way through."

"They brought their bitches with them," Chapper shouted, waving his sword at a female warrior carving her way into the wall. Heahstan released a deep belly laugh and Wulfgar grinned, turning to bolster Cook and Thegn Ealdwig's son Bruneald as more Pictii forced the wall. To his left he heard Osmund shouting instructions to Shepherd and Alemanson to fend off enemy who had broken through the first defence.

"Room for one more?"

Wulfgar glanced round at Leofgist. "Always."

"Osmund has gone left and Geldhere is to the right," Leofgist told him.

Swiping left to cut a gash in a Pict's chest, Wulfgar realised the three thegns protecting the pond were now in the battle. "Who guards the pond?"

Leofgist fell into Cook, who fell against Wulfgar, all men grunting from the forced contact as they fought to right themselves. Leofgist staggered back, tightening his grip on his seax, catching Wulfgar's gaze.

"Five warriors and Lady Brithwen," he replied.

As Wulfgar paused, briefly hit by fear, a cry from the distant hills signalled a Pictii retreat. Painted northmen and women dispersed back across the grassland and out of sight. The Wulfsuna caught their breath and assessed their dead. A man sobbing caught all ears and Wulfgar swung round, trying to find the source. He grabbed Bruneald by the shoulder.

Without verbal request, Bruneald said to him, "Barker has lost his son. He took a blade, his face peeled from his skull."

"And I hit the painted whelp with my head," Shepherd admitted, pulling back his shoulders and demonstrating the move.

The Wulfsuna's respite was brief. Their fearless attackers came in a second wave, smaller than the first though still as ferocious. Wulfgar, hungry for Eadmaer's demise, would have to quench his blood-thirst with a few more Pictii. Wulfsuna raised their faces to the sky and howled in unison, hilts raising merry Hel and all her maidens on scores of shields. Straddled by Bruneald and Leofgist, Wulfgar dealt fatal blows to the enemy alongside his companions. The altercation was swift, however, Pictii withdrawing moments later.

Wulfgar inhaled the smell of blood and pine-needles. Enemy bodies scattered the edge of the wood, the tattooed carnage only occasionally interrupted by the unlucky corpse of a Seaxan. Wulfsuna celebrated but Wulfgar knew their victory was momentary. It was not over. Having sent his Pictii allies in to weaken them, Eadmaer would be readying *tha Eforas* for the final battle. Leofgist grabbed Wulfgar's arm, removing him from his thoughts.

"My Lord, we have one of them."

Wulfgar frowned and followed his ealdorman towards the right flank of the wall. Warriors had encircled a tree. The men parted for their lord, revealing a Pict held captive against the tree by Skinner.

"One to throw back to sea?" Skinner offered to his headman, holding a blade beneath the man's throat while two Wolf Sons held his arms.

Wulfgar looked at the man, about his age with long, dark hair scraped into a tail and a generous beard adorning a resolute chin. He glared, showing teeth as he growled like a dog. There were some cultures where warriors would rather take their own lives than be sent cowering back to their people. This man's eyes told Wulfgar if he was freed, he would fight all men around him to the death. The Pict spat in Skinner's face and strained on the grasp of the two men holding him, pushing his throat onto Skinner's blade, holding Wulfgar's gaze as he gurgled and wretched. Skinner let go of his dagger and stepped away, eyes wide. Wulfgar had no need to see more.

"Send him to his gods," he ordered. "He does not want to live."

Skinner shook his head. Wulfgar searched the throng of warriors for volunteers. Heads bowed and feet shuffled. Wulfgar strode forward, pulling Skinner's dagger free of the Pict's throat and slicing the man's neck. Giving his back to the corpse collapsing as the two Wolf Sons released his arms, Wulfgar shook his head at his men.

He shouted into the trees, "Know your enemies well. Know not only how they wish to fight, but how they wish to die and respect their gods. It is what you would ask for yourselves." To Leofgist, he added, "Remove our dead."

"What of the enemy?" Leofgist asked.

Wulfgar looked down at the body by his feet. "No. Leave them so Boars may find them and be warned of their fate in crossing Wolves."

Cheers erupted, though Wulfgar ignored them as he departed, Leofgist hurrying in his wake. Striding towards the pond and Brithwen, he called to Leofgist over his shoulder.

"Did we lose many?"

"Half a dozen or so. Not many."

Wulfgar glanced at Leofgist, frowning at his ealdorman from beneath his helmet. "Too many for the numbers we have. Those in camp are pups dressed as men."

"The Angles sailed with as many men," Leofgist replied, running to keep up with him.

"Yes," Wulfgar nodded, "but as far as I know the Angles have not fought four battles since landing."

Brithwen stood by the pond with other women, ensuring the wellbeing of the young and infirm nestled in the dell. Two days they had waited for the Angles, sheltering in the wood from the wind and rain. Such waiting bred an unfulfilled anticipation of confrontation, consuming her husband with anger. She had consoled him by saying Wulfsuna would not be tired of waiting once the enemy arrived. When the Angles did finally arrive, the Wolf Sons would be prepared and hungry for conflict. Her efforts, however, did little to placate Wulfgar until the morning of the second day. She had received a prediction of Eadmaer's coming, which would be by night, and Wulfgar had shed his anger.

Brithwen vowed not to be taken prisoner. She would fight. With her husband dug deep into the wood, it fell to her to take charge at the pond. She felt sure there must be some way of protecting those within it. The hiss of rustling leaves from the surrounding trees reminded her of the incident at the harbour market in Caernwealas where she had bent the trees and thrown Sieghild to the ground. She had the power to move nature, and the pond was encircled by tall pines. If she could bend them over the depression in the earth it would be almost impossible for anyone to enter.

"Stand clear of the pond." The frail and unprotected looked up at her from inside and she comforted them. "Stay low and still."

Placing herself behind the first row of trees surrounding the dell, Brithwen secured her stance. Closing her eyes, she inhaled deeply and released her breath, calling on her gift. Mother Earth sent her power up through the soil and into Brithwen's feet, rocking her body as it flowed into her. Willing the trees to move, Brithwen opened her eyes when she heard and felt nothing in response. It had not worked.

"I cannot do it, Mother."

Anwen's gentle voice whispered, "You can."

Brithwen splayed her fingers wider, trying to pull her gift into her hands. "I do not understand. I did it before."

"Remember that time and your gift will remember too." Brithwen recalled her salvation from the slave market, Sieghild running her into the woods. She had refused to follow and her gift had risen, albeit unwanted, bending the trees.

Brithwen heard the smile in her mother's voice as Anwen said, "I knew you would remember. You were with another, the same as you. The power was greater in his presence."

"Another Bryton?" she asked, unsure that alone would increase her gift.

"Another seer, my child." Anwen's words were a blade through Brithwen's memories as her mother continued, "You know it to be true. He had the gift, though he had not realised."

"If only he were here now," Brithwen wished aloud.

"It could not be. There can be only one seer for every Wolf Spear."

In that single phrase, Anwen had confirmed Brithwen's earlier thoughts about Sieghild. There could not be two seers in Wulfgar's journey and so Sieghild's life had been taken by the gods to fulfil the saga. If she had ever doubted the potency of the saga, she would no longer. Holding her hands out to her sides, palms facing forward, she once again attempted to draw her energy from the ground. Focussing on Sieghild's image in her crystal tunnel and using the combined powers of her ancestors embroidered into her gown, she felt her gift surge through her like never before. Branches of trees rattled briefly and fell silent. She kept trying, a few warriors pacing backwards several steps, locking fearful glances with fellow Wolf Sons.

Her petite frame convulsed, a gale hurling itself from her hands and flying around the pond. Everyone screamed and clutched one another in fear. Brithwen gradually brought the wind under control, endlessly circling the first line of trees around the dell. Trunks began creaking and bowing inwards, leaning their branches down across the depression. Like a roof, the trees pitched in and over, forming a natural cover on the pond. Straining, some trees had their roots pulled partially from the ground. As the tree tops met, their branches interwove to connect them permanently. The wind ceased and Brithwen became still. Her palms burned from the experience, unharmed but hot from the process. She caught her breath back from the exertion as cries of joy suddenly filtered up from within the pond. Her people spoke to her for the first time and she blushed at their gratitude.

"We thank you, dear Lady."

"May the gods bless you, Lady Brithwen."

The scent of well-worn leather filtered past Brithwen in a faint breeze and she half-turned her face, eyes closed, to inhale it. She shivered, not from cold; perhaps from the experience of her gift and the love of her people; she was unsure. The warm frame of a man met her back and she inadvertently sank into him, inhaling the leather again, mingling with his body heat. As she felt his arms wrap around her, she sighed, grateful for the comfort.

"I thank you," she breathed fondly, her eyes resting on the pond.

A head lowered, bringing lips to her ear, and whispered, "I thank *you*, Lady Morwyneth."

The unknown warrior had left her side before Brithwen could even recover from her shocked gasp. She swung round reaching an arm out, expecting the man still to be within her grasp. He was not. He was some distance away now, his back to her as he ambled through the forest; she thought to call out to him. As though anticipating her request he turned, catching her gaze and holding a finger to his lips. Silent tears ebbed from her glassy eyes; a thousand painful cries and haunting dreams all revisiting her at once as she looked upon him.

Sieghild smiled and disappeared into the mystery of the wood.

chapter twenty-six

Wulfsuna Camp,
Wood Near the Sheep Town

Wulfgar sat huddled inside a wagon with Leofgist, Heahstan and two warriors, poised for a signal to warn them the Angles were near. The end of the second day of waiting was almost upon them, moonlight falling through gaps in the fabric billowing over their heads. The Holy Month had brought the north winds with it, and the sun had begun to lose his strength during the day. Soon the leaves would turn and fall. One and a half months had elapsed since the *Hildwaeg* had delivered them to this land in the name of his father's dream. Following the Battle of the Fens, he had spoken with Sieghild on the jetty of how they had intended to find land to settle on and good women to wed. Wulfgar dug a hand into his purse, pulling out the small wooden carving he had found on the floor of Brithwen's home. He rolled it in his curled palm, contemplating the pregnant female figure; a representation of fertile Mother Earth. He had found the good woman. All that remained was to kill Eadmaer and settle the Wulfsuna in a new land. Wrapping the talisman tight in his fist, he prayed to Woden to deliver them victory and to Frigg for the gift of a son.

Coded whistles of the Wulfsuna rang back, telling camp that the Angles drew near. Wulfgar's lungs filled with the cold breath of reality. Like a wolf on the brow of a hill observing its unwitting prey, so Wulfgar's chest heaved at the prospect of the battle.

"Here come the *hildisvinas*," murmured Heahstan.

Wulfgar nodded. The Angles were indeed as fearsome as Ingui's *battle-swine* and it would be prudent for every man to pray to Woden to deliver them safely through battle, or else take them to his mead hall in warm welcome. Faint taps on the side of the vehicle confirmed they could disembark. As silent as the still night, Wulfgar and his party climbed out and crouched down. A ripple of hand signals ran from Wulfgar to the tree line as he asked for an estimation of the enemy's distance in paces: a dozen. Wulfgar tossed his chin up at Heahstan, who threw fingers in various directions, fanning the men out as they had planned.

Pulling his grey pelt more securely over his shoulders, Wulfgar progressed towards the enemy, head and shoulders hung low. Aiming to ambush men moving down the flank of Eadmaer's approach, he circled wide, leaping knowingly over roots and fallen branches. Since Brithwen's vision he had spent two days familiarising himself with the wood, running through it and charting its obstacles in his mind; he had fallen many times, and hoped the Angles would too. He smelled and heard the Boars before he saw them, stalking them from behind dense hawthorn, holding his breath. He saw one, two, three men and knew he could take them. They strode upright through the forest, weapons drawn, confident their night advance would be a surprise. One by one, Wulfgar made them his victims, using his seax and rolling round tree trunks or leaping out from shrubs. He slit two throats, and one man, likely a thrall as he wore no mail, he stabbed in the back.

Not far from him, Leofgist provided his second sword as he had sworn. Wulfgar held up two fingers, telling his ealdorman the number of remaining flank men on their side. He motioned for Leofgist to take them while he moved in closer. A baby's cry echoed from the pond and all things froze. The flutter of birds' wings and an owl's hoot broke the death of night in response, and Wulfgar halted a curse on his lips as he heard enemy feet shuffling to reorganise. Seeming not to care if they were heard now, the Angles issued men in the direction of the noise, and Wulfgar saw the whites of Leofgist's eyes in the dim light.

Four Angles ran past them, unaware of the Wulfsuna hiding in the bushes beside them as they sent hands to hold their scabbards, jumping logs and brambles. Wulfgar leaped into pursuit, striking the last man in the side of the neck with his axe blade and clobbering the next on the back of the head with his axe pole. The third warrior peered over his shoulder, a tree root claiming him before he could call out. With a quick glance, Wulfgar left the fallen Angle for Leofgist, who followed through the trees, and pursued the last man. A familiar whistle made Wulfgar dive to the ground and roll away as Heahstan's long arm appeared from behind a tree, brandishing his axe. The blade smashed into the nose plate of the Angle's helmet, forcing the iron into his face as the axe heel tore a gash in his cheek. The force of the blow lifted the warrior off his feet and sent him hurling against the earth, shoulders first. Standing in readiness to finish the man's life, Wulfgar stepped aside for Heahstan who ran from hiding and cut the enemy's head from his shoulders. Wulfsuna whistles and battle howls filled the forest. The Wolf Sons were coming and they wanted the Boars to know.

"You should head back to camp, My Cyning," Heahstan said, chest heaving from exertion.

Wulfgar nodded. "Come with me."

With Leofgist and Heahstan's men, they returned to the false camp. In their absence, Ianbert and Tortsig had ambushed enemy men who had entered the headman's tent, unaware of its lethal contents and that of the wagons surrounding it. Slowly, they were dragging the Boars from the dense wood and reducing their numbers, though they knew not the full amount of men they faced. The Wulfsuna had known the Angle numbers aboard the *Saehunta*, but who could say what friends they brought with them. The Pictii might have returned with them, or other allies Eadmaer may have made north of the Humbre. Like a siren, the forest wailed with the sounds of clashing metal, broken bones and the cries of men.

Wulfgar looked to his thegns, their clothes and faces already battle-worn with blood spatter and cuts. "We have to join our fellow Wolf Sons before the Angles breach the pond."

"What of another attack from the road?" asked Ianbert, whose nose appeared broken though he did not seem to care. "We will be surrounded if we do not leave men here to thwart them."

Wulfgar dashed his axe aside. "No. We do not have enough men. It is a chance we must take. Who is with me?"

All men raised arms and Wulfgar led them back through the forest, chasing down the far flank of Angles and those who had survived the battle in camp. When all they came upon were Geldhere and their own kin, Wulfgar feared the worst.

"Have they made the pond?" he demanded, voice brusque.

"No, My Lord." Geldhere handed his bloodied sword to his cnapa, gesturing westwards. "We met ten Angles back there and lost two into the woods who we were chasing when we heard you. Osmund holds the pond still, as well as I know."

Wulfgar cast his eyes south, where Brithwen, Osmund and a few men were all that remained to protect the future of the Wulfsuna. He grappled with his chin strap and ripped war-face from his head, shaking blood and sweat from his hair.

"Something is wrong," he murmured, swinging about to face the direction of the road.

"What is it?" Heahstan asked.

Wulfgar waved his helmet at Heahstan and Leofgist. "We three defeated seven Boars between us." He turned to Geldhere. "You say you met ten and killed eight of those. And Ianbert?"

The thegn replied as his lord fixed eyes on him. "We killed maybe a dozen."

Face contorting into a snarl, Wulfgar stared at Heahstan. "We were three score men when we set sail from Germania, the *Saehunta* carrying the same. I do not think all *tha Eforas* are in this wood."

Wulfgar's words reminded him of Sieghild's observation on the jetty before the Battle in the Fens. Not all Angles had disembarked to join them. *He should have known.* Eadmaer had reserved warriors for another attack.

"Eadmaer is picking us off a few at a time, reducing our numbers and spreading our warriors through the wood." He gestured to Geldhere. "Return to the pond and watch for attack from all directions. Take Tortsig and a few men."

"What of us, My Lord?" Leofgist asked.

"Remain here and set up a northern defence. I need to see Brithwen." He held a palm up at Leofgist who had made to follow him. "No."

Hurtling through the trees with Geldhere and the others, Wulfgar prayed he would be the first to see Eadmaer, though he knew it could be fated otherwise and was glad he had gifted Wulfric's seax to Brithwen. Tasting sweat and others' blood on their lips, the wolves howled, shattering the eerie stillness they disturbed, crushing furled bracken. The great devourers had come to feast on the dead. Even they had been fooled into thinking the battle was over.

Brithwen called for Wulfgar through the trees before he saw her, as though she knew of his coming. "Wulf, I need to speak with you."

"And I with you, little wife," he replied as he cleared the last of the undergrowth behind the rest of them and came into her view. "Some of them are holding back. Do you know why?"

She ran to him, halting short of him. "I have had no vision, though a strange sensation troubles me."

"Something you have had before?" He frowned.

She shook her head. "Never. I cannot see, but I can feel..." Her voice trailed off, but Wulfgar had already heard her fear.

"What do you feel?"

"Eadmaer," she whispered.

"You can feel how he feels? Is he wounded? Is he worried?" He splayed a hand, guessing through her silent stares. "What?"

She lifted the back of a hand to her mouth, stifling sobs. "I do not know. I cannot tell. What if I become his eyes and he can see all of us here and know what you are plotting?" She darted her gaze around them at the few remaining warriors and the pond. "Dear gods, I have become the beacon for evil, shining light on the weak."

"Can you share your gift this way?" Wulfgar closed the distance between them, knowing she could not move, setting his helmet down and cupping her elbows.

She stared into the woods, eyes frantic like a trapped hare. "Send me away. Shield my eyes, tell me nothing…"

He grasped her arms more firmly and whispered, "Brithwen, look at me. Look at me." The wildness left her as she turned to face him, and he said, "Break it."

She released a long breath and closed her eyes. When Dudley had told him she would be his eyes, he had warned the old tale-weaver of the danger. He tried to quell doubts clouding his mind that marrying the nix would now be his undoing and his fellow Wulfsuna had been right. A moment later she opened her eyes and Wulfgar knew she once again had control of her gift.

"It is done," she told him.

"Where is Eadmaer?" he asked, eager for his destiny now that she had recovered.

She closed her eyes briefly, her voice distant and strange. "He comes in two long lines," she said solemnly, "as a tide of waves would meet the shore. He has a score and twelve men." Wulfgar watched her eyes flutter open and saw the darkness of the seer's vision leave them.

"Thank you."

The distant sounds of shields and spears clanking alerted them all to the return of the Angle Boars. Wulfgar bent down to retrieve war-face, sliding his head into it and fastening it tight.

"Lord Wulfgar."

Leofgist's call came as no surprise to Wulfgar who had envisaged his ealdorman would not heed his wishes for long. "Leofgist." He turned, throwing his arms out, fingers touching to form a V. "We shall fight like cattle horns."

The Wulfsuna would move through the wood like a giant arrow, splitting the Angle tidal wave Brithwen had described. It would divert men from both tribes in among the trees to fight man-to-man. Having fewer men, they would live longer that way. They might even win.

"Osmund." Wulfgar waved the thegn over to them. "Create a crescent shield wall with your backs to the pond. Be ready."

"We are but a few men," Osmund replied, gesturing to his handful of warriors huddled in a group.

"No," Wulfgar countered, grinning, "you are Wulfsuna. We wolves eat boar for breakfast and it will soon be light."

Osmund shook his head, smiling, and rejoined his men to organise the wall. Geldhere and Tortsig, meanwhile, were already doing likewise in two other directions. Wulfgar looked at Leofgist hovering like a hungry buzzard, and gave his attention to his wife. She had found a smile and it pleased him. He took her face in his hands.

"Remember, my heart and mind, they watch over you."

He enveloped her in a passionate embrace, wanting to take the taste of her with him into battle. The desire made him feel as though he had stolen Woden's heart, the power of the Chief of the Gods pounding behind his armour.

Brithwen swayed as she watched Wulfgar leave, his kiss having resurrected her gift and brought forth a fleeting vision of a boar's head, its tusks glinting in moonlight. She wrapped her arms round her abdomen. He did not look back. He had said he would watch over her and he had. When she needed focus and protection from herself he had arrived. It was as though the Wolf Spear Saga possessed a power that brought them together whenever they needed one another. She lifted her face to the moon, giving silent praise to Brigid. The light of the goddess had allowed her to see the truth and to drape a gossamer sleeve over the illusions that had descended in a thick fog, obscuring her seer's vision.

The Wulfsuna around the pond were restless, shuffling and flinching at each miniscule movement coming from within the wood. Growls and men's screams punctured the air nearby, and Brithwen grasped the carved hilt of Wulfric's dagger. The wolves were hunting the living, not satisfied with the dead. The resounding clash of men fighting and dying at their meet of weapons grew louder.

"I cannot wait here," Osmund declared, breaking from his crescent and tapping warriors on the shoulder to accompany him. He locked gaze with Brithwen. "I am joining our cyning. Do not stop me."

Brithwen shook her head. "I would never hinder a warrior in joining his king. Go if you must."

Osmund drew his seax and pointed the blade to Tortsig, whose eyes bulged. "Are you with me?"

Tortsig licked dry lips. "Yes."

Retreating from the edge of the clearing towards the pond, Brithwen looked on as Osmund and Tortsig disappeared into the trees with eight men. She glanced at Geldhere who was reorganising those left into a circle around the pond. Like living standing stones, they braced to meet imaginary foes, blades and shields poised. Her belly twisted, an unease she could not quell. She considered it could be her fear of losing Wulfgar, as she had lost Sieghild; that, or the threat of facing her nightmare on four legs, now roaming the woods in search of torn flesh. With a yelp, she was flung to the ground. Pain tore at her stomach, stronger than she had experienced with her first vision in Prenhwychas. Hands grasping at the cold soil, she struggled to keep herself on her knees.

"Lady Brithwen." Geldhere ran to her, stooping to help.

Her vision began and she cried, "Leave me!"

Breath strangled her in short gasps and she shuddered from the earth energy coiling through every pore, opening her seer's sight. Her forehead felt aflame with a fire-softened blade pushing through her skull. Sobs wracked her and the vision found her. She was running, running fast. Trees sped past and she could feel bone in her hand, which she assumed to be Wulfric's seax. The sound of battle grew louder, echoing in her ears. Wulfgar, he was...

Released from her vision and the accompanying pain, Brithwen stood. She took Wulfric's seax to the hem of her gown, ripping the cloth to a knee-length tunic. Sliding Wulfric's dagger into her belt, she faced Geldhere, who had remained by her side, and lifted his axe from his war-belt, stealing into the trees like a hare. The wood folded her into the night. Her breathing laboured and erratic as she avoided raised tree roots and fallen logs, she ran fast across the fern-lined bed of the forest. Objects flew past her, blurred by her haste, though an image remained level with her. Something was keeping pace. Fending off her fears, Brithwen glanced sideways at the grey wolf accompanying her, its long tongue draped out of the side of its mouth. It was breathless like her; hungry like her for the final outcome. The wolf veered off into the night, trailing the bloody scent of the fallen. Words from Dudley's stories at Aberhabren took over her mind and she understood. Written in the saga prior to her birth, told for generations but rarely lived, this was the moment; this was her namesake.

Wulfgar was alone with some dead Angles for company, crouching under a fallen tree overrun with moss and brambles. He tried quietly to scratch an itch beneath his cheek guard. He had lost sight of Leofgist somewhere in their advance. He knew not where his ealdorman or other Wulfsuna were now. Their cattle horns had done as he had intended and broken the centre of Eadmaer's wave of Angles. Wolves had split the Boars in two and pushed east and west, dispersing them into the forest. He could hear the battle continuing without him and realised he could be beyond it, perhaps almost back at the false wagon camp. Without shield, axe and seax, he had his sword alone for any remaining fight. He wished his friend were with him at that moment. Sieghild had always bettered him at sword. Sighing, he knew it could not be so. They would meet in another time, when the Chief of all the Gods would serve them mead in his hall. A single pair of feet trod over twigs and pine needles, coming to a halt a few feet away. Not yet, he thought.

"Wulfgar." Eadmaer's voice was chillingly familiar.

"Eadmaer." Wulfgar tossed his name into the night, rising out of hiding to face his opponent who towered over him in a cloak of wild boar skin, the head of the dead animal draped over his helmet, a menacing hood of wild eyes and tusks that glinted in the moonlight. "The Pictii did not stay long. Did you not give your new allies enough gold?"

Eadmaer chuckled in the half-dark. "They are busy harrying further north. I met their king and informed him of our mutual interests. He sent me enough warriors to trouble you until I arrived."

Grinning, Wulfgar replied, "I had thought that to be true."

"I knew the Pictii would not defeat you." Eadmaer waved his sword at him. "I know the Wulfsuna are fearless warriors, strong and blade-ready, and none fight harder than you."

"At least I fight fair," Wulfgar replied, subtly moving a foot to ready his stance and tightening his grip on the hilt of his sword.

"When is a fight ever fair?" Eadmaer laughed at him.

Anger tore at Wulfgar's features. "In my mind it is not a fair fight when you need two men to hold a man down for you to strike him in the heart."

"Yes." Eadmaer wandered as though on an afternoon stroll, his tone light-hearted though his words were as heavy as boulders. "How does it feel to hold onto revenge for one's father? Has it eaten you from within? Has it broken your back, boy?"

"You will find me no boy, Eadmaer." Wulfgar straightened, hungry to wet his blade with the man's blood.

Eadmaer turned, sword arm set. "I was a boy when Wulfric murdered my father. I only wish I could have made you suffer a lifetime, but I am not a patient man."

"Then let us end it," Wulfgar offered, flexing his free arm, vambraces winking back at the moon.

Eadmaer grinned. "You bear the name and the skin of the wolf, young Seaxan. Let us see if you bear the teeth."

Wulfgar had already set the blade of his sword at a tilt to receive the first down blow from Eadmaer, and his shoulder muscles locked to steady the weapon as his adversary swung up and over in an arc, crashing upon him like a tidal wave. They turned and twisted, dipped and folded, their duel a dance with swords. Wulfgar could feel his left shoulder giving way beneath high blows from Eadmaer. He had not had full strength in it since being wounded by Brithwen. Being older and a head taller, Eadmaer had experience over him as well as strength, and Wulfgar feared he would lose before long were it not for his swiftness. Using all he had ever learned from Sieghild and more he had learned since, Wulfgar unleashed all he had. The shorter warrior, Wulfgar sliced at the older man's shins. However, hefty iron splinted guards hid beneath bearskin wadding and thwarted his attempts to bring the Angle down.

Dodging the shield boss Eadmaer swung at his face, Wulfgar pivoted. Taking his hilt in two hands, he rammed his pommel into the rear of the shield, forcing Eadmaer to release the hand guard. The shield skimmed the ground, tossing up needles and dirt, and Wulfgar jabbed his pommel into Eadmaer's side. The Angle grunted, his step faltering allowing Wulfgar pause. The face of the child at the pond slipped into his mind, bolstering his reserve. He drew in air, the sweet scent of the trees and stench of rotting bodies filling his nostrils. Eadmaer, heaving for breath beneath his heavy animal cloak, bared his ghastly teeth. Wulfgar lifted his shoulders as he filled his chest to bursting and released an almighty howl. His nemesis grinned, emitting a short laugh at the antics of the young warrior.

Eadmaer moved to advance and halted as an eruption of howls, of men and beasts, ruptured the wood, scattering birds and nocturnal wildlife. Wulfgar charged the few paces between them, roaring until his throat hurt. Wide-eyed and forced to block a cut aimed at his thigh below his byrnie, Eadmaer stumbled, but was all too ready when Wulfgar came again. Quick to sense Wulfgar's left shoulder was weakening, he threw a barrage of high blows onto the headman's sword. Hounded by downward slashes, Wulfgar felt muscle tear in his back and shoulder. Putting faith in Woden and the thick pelt over his byrnie, Wulfgar turned his back on Eadmaer to avoid the final swing. Eadmaer's blade collided with Wulfgar's shoulder blade and caught his helmet, jarring his head. His sword fell from his grasp as he buckled under the blow, sinking to his knees and growling from searing pain. Nevertheless, his cloak and mail had stood firm against the cut. He fumbled for his sword with his right hand, wanting to take Eadmaer with him if this was the end.

Undergrowth rustled and Wulfgar heard Eadmaer laugh as a figure leaped through the trees, brandishing an axe. Wulfgar glanced up to see Brithwen racing towards them. Lithe and light, she cleared the ground with the ease of a deer. Her gaze firmly set on Eadmaer, she rushed at the Angle, still several strides away, thrusting a single palm at him. Wulfgar knew she had summoned her gift. He felt Thunor thump his chest as her power surged through him, knocking aside plants and branches. Eadmaer's laugh was cut short as he flew backwards into a tree trunk, grunting loudly with the impact. Rolling onto his back as she dived over him, Wulfgar watched aghast as she hurled the axe, securing Eadmaer to the bark through the gut, and ran a seax into his throat on reaching him. The Angle leader hung like a drying carcass waiting to be skinned, a last lingering breath escaping his open lips. Wulfgar thanked Woden it was over and struggled to lift himself with one arm. Brithwen came to his aid. Once on his feet, he cupped his hands over his mouth, lifting his head back.

"Wulfsuna-a-a!" he cried on a lingering note, signalling victory.

The tribe responded from all directions it seemed, and when the Angles' calls of "Tha Eforas" received no response from their leader, cheers erupted. With the realisation of the battle's end came more pain and a head that pounded louder than Wulfgar's heart. He dropped his hands from his face and they felt wet. Brithwen dashed his hand away as he went to feel his cheek.

"You are covered in blood," she told him, ripping a section of his undertunic away to wipe his face, "and bruises. Have you been walking into trees?"

He smiled. "Maybe."

She dabbed at his left cheek, her eyes like midnight crystals. "I saw…"

He nodded and turned to look at the body. Wulfric's seax handle protruded from Eadmaer's neck. It had indeed been the death-light that brought Eadmaer his final breath. Wulfgar hobbled over to where his sword lay, aware he had an injured right thigh. Brithwen crouched for him and retrieved his sword, handing him the hilt. He pulled at the boar's head, trying to tug the whole skin of the beast from the Angle's back. It would not come. With his sword he cut the head free and faced Brithwen. He tossed his chin at her to join him, and she walked over.

"To show your victory." He handed her the dead animal head, frowning when she did not take it.

"I cannot take it," she said.

A confused smile joined his frown. "You killed him. You have the honour." He pressed the creature to her. She stared into his eyes.

"He died by your blade. You must have the honour for the Wulfsuna as cyning."

Linking her left arm through his right, she took them in the direction of the pond. They heard the Wulfsuna howling and laughing in jubilation; friends, husbands and wives calling for one another. Eastwards, a thin line of golden dawn was breaking into the star-ridden blackness. Sobering from the fight, Wulfgar acknowledged the pronounced limp in his right leg, thankful he had his wife to lean on.

"I may have taken a sword in my thigh," he announced.

"You have," she said, gaze fixed towards their destination.

"My head throbs like I've had a keg of mead." He blinked, trying to clear blurred vision.

Brithwen smiled. "There will be time for that."

chapter twenty-seven

Wulfsuna Camp,
Wood Near the Sheep Town

Light from torches that had been lit in the clearing danced through the trees to greet them. People were singing and shouting, expressing their joy at surviving the fight, while two animal horns sounded heartily and in disarray. Brithwen stopped shy of the last line of trees, ignoring her husband's tug on her arm. He waited. Men were helping their women from the pond, mothers passing babies and children up into the arms of their tearful fathers who scooped them into the air. She saw Alemanson run into Cwenfleda's arms, grasping her tightly to him in a passionate kiss. This break of day would be recounted for years to come, with songs and ale and music.

The clunk of iron against wood drew Brithwen's gaze to swords, spears, helmets and shields being tossed in a pile; the spoils of battle signifying the number and stature of the dead enemy. Beside the pile a wagon had been parked, she guessed either to cart the infirm back to camp or to gather the dead. Weight dragged her down and she grappled for Wulfgar as he folded to the floor beside her.

"Wulfgar," Leofgist cried, running to them and sliding his hands under his cyning's arms. Brithwen took Wulfgar's legs and they brought him out of the trees. As they were about to set him down on the floor, Wulfgar regained consciousness and struggled against them.

"No, I must stand," he murmured, waving the boar's head at them.

She looked at the ealdorman, who shrugged and hoisted Wulfgar to his feet. He was beaten by his injuries, but would not give in to them; at least not yet. The merry-making gradually dimmed to hushed voices as Brithwen and Leofgist assisted a wounded Wulfgar over to the wagon. Struggling to stand unaided, he gruffly refused an upturned barrel that Leofgist brought him, instead propping himself against the side of the wagon. He lifted the boar's head in his right hand, thrusting the piece of dead pig repeatedly into the air. The tribe yelled their name again and again, cheering and whooping. Brithwen smiled at the broad grin on her husband's face, despite his pain that she knew he hid. The Wolf Spear Saga had been told; they had lived it. It might always be with them, throughout their lives and into those of their offspring. Time would tell.

Wulfgar faltered, once again refusing Leofgist's assistance. He threw the boar's head into the wagon and stepped up onto the barrel with his good leg. Using his body weight for momentum, he managed to slide his right knee onto the lip of the wagon, standing precariously. Brithwen and Leofgist lurched forward expecting him to fall. He winked at Brithwen, making her smile, and found steady footing by leaning most of his weight on his left leg. For an age he regarded those gathered around him, and Brithwen wondered if he would announce the tribe were to move on come morning. They had defeated the Angles, though who could say if more would come from across the sea to avenge Eadmaer's death. Maybe even the Pictii king would want to take revenge for the clann-men he had lost fighting for someone else's cause. However, when Wulfgar called his ealdorman over, she knew none of those thoughts had been on his mind.

"How many have we lost?" he whispered down to Leofgist, who lowered his head a moment before responding.

"Not many, though Skinner and Tortsig were among them."

Brithwen swallowed her grief which had risen as a lump in her throat, placing a hand on her neck to quell emotion. Wulfgar bowed his head in reverence to lost Wolf Sons and fumbled with his right hand on his chin strap. After a second attempt he freed the leather from the buckle and bent his head, dropping war-face into his hand. Lorri had appeared by the wagon and tapped the wood to catch Wulfgar's attention. Brithwen almost sobbed when she saw her husband smile through tears at the sight of his cnapa alive and well. He tossed war-face into Lorri's hands and pointed to the sky.

"This night," he cried, his breath an ethereal mist in the icy grasp of early dawn, "we have chased war from our lives so that we may find peaceful settlement. Here, in this wood, let us take this green land to our bosom. Let houses and a great hall be built where our sons and daughters can hear great tales sung."

The Wulfsuna roared in agreement and Brithwen's head spun from the euphoria. She swayed, Leofgist catching her waist, setting her back on her feet. She smiled in gratitude, beginning to feel the chilled air round her bare legs.

"Are you alright, My Lady?" Leofgist whispered.

She nodded. "A little cold, that is all."

The ealdorman waved at Geldhere, commandeering his cloak which he draped round Brithwen. She smiled her appreciation at both men. Meanwhile,

315

having assumed their cyning had finished his speech, Alemanson and Cwenfleda crept into the clearing pushing the beer wagon, no doubt in anticipation of the celebrations that would follow. The cheering subsided and Wulfgar continued, the beer wagon halting abruptly.

"Let us share in the fruitfulness of this land and honour our Brytonic neighbours. Work wool, carve bone, shape metal and send your animals to graze and your children to wed. Bring new *bearns* to life." Brithwen saw him notice the beer wagon, which he openly acknowledged with a hand. "We shall feast for five days to honour those slain."

A surge of men ran eagerly to the beer wagon. Their cyning had decreed five days of festivities and for five days it would be so.

"Brithwen." Wulfgar's voice was croaky form his exertions and she almost did not hear him above the commotion erupting round them. She moved closer to the wagon, gazing up at him expectantly and asking the gods to make him take rest.

"Are you with me?" His eyes searched her face. She sank teeth into her bottom lip. Even now he had to ask if she would be staying with him. Even now he was afraid of losing her; afraid that, although she had shared her body and heart with him, she would leave because their agreement was over. Light from the torches danced like fire faeries across his pale eyes.

"I am with you, husband," she told him as sincerely as she could to convince him she spoke the truth. "Let us build a new life here."

He keeled sideways, Heahstan's bulky frame on hand to catch his exhausted and wounded body over broad shoulders. The thegn slid Wulfgar into the wagon and snapped his fingers at Ianbert.

"Get your cyning a bed made and fetch another wagon for the dead."

While Ianbert sent men with a horse to find another wagon for the dead, Heahstan and Leofgist wheeled Wulfgar a short way from the rowdy gathering. Wulfsuna arrived with blankets and hides, Heahstan climbing into the wagon to lift Wulfgar as they arranged them beneath him. Ensuring his cyning was as comfortable as he could make him, Heahstan jumped down and turned to Brithwen, putting a large hand to her elbow.

"I shall fetch Godelina. Have you need of anything else, My Lady?"

Dazed, Brithwen looked to the forest and back to Heahstan, stammering, "I… I must search for healing plants."

"Leofgist," Heahstan waved the ealdorman over, "go with her."

Away from the torches, the wood did not give up her secrets easily. The sun teased them, its glow now casting pink clouds above its arrival. Brithwen resorted to her gift to lead her, finding what she needed and gathering wood sorrel, winterbloom and devil's nettle. When they returned, Godelina had arrived, and the older woman smiled warmly. Over a small fire a pot steamed with boiling water, in which bobbed a linen posset of pine needles. On the upturned barrel, two onions had been cut into halves and Brithwen placed her assortment of plants beside them. A nearby torch threw light over Wulfgar, who remained unconscious in the wagon. His war gear, padded vest and byrnie had been removed and arranged neatly by his head.

Godelina waved to Leofgist, gesturing for him to give her a lift into the wagon. The ealdorman complied, though seemed to regret his offer as he struggled to heave her generous backside up with his shoulder, his face disappearing in her skirts and his hands grappling to free himself. After a struggle, the older woman was up. Brithwen removed Geldhere's cloak, draping it on the side of the wagon, and gave Leofgist a smile. He looked worried. She squeezed his arm and he blushed, hiding behind his hair and shuffling off in the direction of the beer wagon.

Brithwen strained over the end of the wagon to wait for Godelina to invite her to assist. Wulfgar's tunics were drenched in blood: his and that of others. Godelina took a small knife from her belt, proceeding to cut open his tunics. Mauve and yellow bruises covered his torso, either thick lines where blades had bounced off his byrnie or round spots perhaps from pommels or spear handles that had connected with him during battle. The older woman ran her hands over his chest and abdomen and slid them beneath his back, searching for further wounds. Satisfied there were none, Godelina moved to his right trouser leg where a large crimson stain and slash in the cloth gave no doubt as to the wound beneath. Tearing his trousers open, she revealed the gash in his thigh was smaller than Brithwen had expected from the amount of blood, high on the leg and not too deep into the muscle. Godelina grasped his leg in both her hands, raising it, twisting it left to right and bending it at the knee, inspecting it closely as she did so.

"Nothing is broken," Godelina said to Brithwen, waving her to lean closer and inspect the palm-length cut. "Ladle some water into that bowl on the floor and you can rinse the wounds."

Brithwen turned and found the small wooden bowl, inside of which rested two folded pieces of linen and a rolled leather pouch. "What is this?" she asked, lifting the pouch.

"My needles," came the reply, and Brithwen hastily handed the pouch to Godelina, poked the cloths into her belt and set to ladling the pine-scented water into the bowl.

Steadily sliding the bowl of hot liquid into the wagon, Brithwen hauled herself in on the opposite side to Godelina, kneeling on Wulfgar's left. She took the cloths from her belt.

"One for each wound," Godelina told her and she nodded.

The water was steaming hot, burning her fingers as she soaked the first cloth and wrung it out. She began on his face, uncovering the small dagger cut on his left cheek as well as several generous bruises, the largest on his right brow bone and lower right jaw. The shallow cut had already begun to seal itself. Discarding the cloth, she soaked the second piece of linen to bathe his thigh.

Wulfgar stirred, consciousness still far away from him, murmuring, "Morwyneth."

Brithwen stifled a sob with the back of a hand.

"He will live," Godelina reassured her.

Staring at her husband's pale sleeping figure, Brithwen replied, "I know. For that I am giving thanks."

They shared a smile and Godelina shuffled to the edge of the wagon, hanging over to pluck the onion halves from the barrel below. Inhaling deeply to free herself of her welling emotions, Brithwen set to cleaning Wulfgar's thigh wound, careful not to pull too firmly on the slit flesh. Setting aside the damp, bloodied cloths, Brithwen took two onion halves from Godelina, gently rubbing the cut sides over both wounds. The juices would ward off infection and promote healing. Anwen had used the same method on Brithwen as a child when she had cut her leg playing up the Bryn.

Once done, Brithwen nestled the onions on the dirty cloths. "Will you sew, Lady Brithwen?" Godelina asked, opening the leather pouch and removing a bone threading needle and some horsehair. Brithwen stared at the soiled linen and the torn skin of Wulfgar's thigh wound beginning to peel back and continuing to bleed. Tears claimed her, wrenching another sob from her tired body, and Godelina took her arms in firm hands.

"Morwyneth, will you sew?"

Brithwen met eyes with her, a tiny smile breaking tear-soaked lips, nodding. "I shall sew."

"You will need to force a hole in the skin before you draw the thread through. If he wakes we will need two strong men and a good stick."

Taking up the horsehair in shaky hands, Brithwen threaded the needle. Closing the two sides of broken flesh together with a finger and thumb, she lined up the needle for the first pass through. As the bone went into skin she paused for a reaction. Wulfgar merely shifted restlessly, his eyelids pinching and head rolling. She released the breath she had held tight in her chest, feeling her shoulders relax. She pulled the thread through leaving some to tie, and found a rhythm in puncturing the holes and sewing the stitches. Godelina sang one of her songs in a hushed voice, and Brithwen imagined herself back in the fifth wagon, watching the other woman embroider tunics and sew hides. When the sewing was complete, Godelina helped her tie off the horsehair then slid off the wagon, gesturing for the pile of linen and onions which she tossed into the fire, muttering a rite to the gods to ward off evil.

"I will fetch more linen. You make your ointment." Godelina handed her the pile of wood sorrel, winterbloom, devil's nettle and two stones. Using the stones to crush the leaves and release the healing oils from the plants, Brithwen summoned her gift, calling on Mother Earth to bless the blend. Shortly afterwards, Godelina returned with a long piece of linen to bandage Wulfgar's thigh, and also a lump of bread and cup of ale for Brithwen.

"I know you," Godelina warned, wagging a thick finger and smiling. "Do not forget to eat."

"Thank you." Brithwen smiled, grasping the hand Godelina held out to her and squeezing it warmly.

Godelina left them, ambling off into the throng of Wulfsuna singing and drinking round a larger fire some way off. Brithwen scraped her concoction on to the centre of the linen strip and wrapped it securely round Wulfgar's thigh. The dressing complete, she rinsed her hands in the remaining warm pine water then tossed the water out over the side of the wagon. It had been a long day, or two, and she had lost sense of time. She did not feel hungry, though knew Godelina would chastise her if the older woman found she had not eaten. She nibbled a few mouthfuls of bread, washing them down with small sips of the ale, the taste of which made her lips curl. Unable to consume it all, she set it aside in the corner of the wagon. A spare blanket sat folded next to Wulfgar's belongings and she shook it over both of them, lying down. Although morning was breaking, she wanted sleep. Closing her eyes, she was soon claimed in slumber's warm embrace.

The scent of a fresh fire woke Brithwen. She had slept well, and knew by the rise of the sun in the sky it was after noon. No longer by the pond, the camp had moved to the grassland where they had first seen the Pictii approaching. She sat up in the wagon, eyes wandering down the slope to the valley they now overlooked. People were milling around, women making bread nearby and a group of men dismantling a wagon. Beyond them, in the centre of open land, was the largest fire Brithwen had ever seen; larger than that she had witnessed at Aberhabren and larger still than the one for her wedding.

"We used the trees covering the pond."

Appearing renewed from his own sleep, Wulfgar sat on a high-backed wooden bench seat covered in sheepskins and hides, his right leg supported on a stool and a blanket across his lap. His voice was hoarse and weaker than usual, though his smile was strong.

"Will you sit with me?" He patted the skins beside him. Pulling aside her blanket, Brithwen scrambled out of the wagon. She tugged at her gown, believing the hem to be caught, and glanced down. She had forgotten she had cut it during the night. She waved her short dress at him, grinning.

"I am not very well dressed, My Lord."

"Things look good from here," he laughed, "but it is warm under my blanket." He lifted the grey wool, eyes gleaming as he watched her walk over, covering their legs with the thickly woven cloth and seeking out her left hand.

"I did not expect to wake here," she told him, grateful for the secret show of affection.

He smiled, gaze darting back to the wood. "No. I told them to bring us here. We have buried the enemy in the pond. It shall be their resting place for evermore, an unseen reminder of our struggle to find peace here."

"I hope they find peace also within whichever afterlife each of them sought solace." She tugged on his hand. "What of our kinfolk?" He met her eyes, thoughtful, searching.

"Their sacred remains have been laid to rest further east." He pointed down the grassy slope to their left. She sat up a little, straining to peer downhill into the midday sun to where his arm led and felt his breath on her cheek. She settled her back into the bench, slowly turning her face to him. His pale grey stare reached inside her soul.

"I did not believe I would see you again. I was ready for Woden's Hall when you found us." His hand gripped hers more tightly.

She recalled her anguish that dawn, fearing he would not survive his injuries. "This morning, I thought you were sure to meet your God. I am grateful you did not."

He released her hand, eagerly rummaging in his purse. "I have some things for you, for us." He withdrew a clenched fist, his other hand taking her right and turning it palm upwards. He deposited two items, retaining one for himself. Brithwen examined the wooden talisman and silver ring. The talisman she knew. It was one of her divination carvings. She released a little laugh. The ring she did not know and she fingered the design. A silver wolf chased its tail around a polished sphere of amber. She picked it up, turning it. It was much too large for her dainty fingers.

"Wulf, it is beautiful, but it will not fit me." She held it out to him.

"That's because it is mine." He grinned, waving a second ring at her.

"This one is yours." He slid the ring on to one of her fingers and offered her his hand for her to do the same. She complied, afterwards taking his face in her hands and kissing him. He moaned into her lips making her giggle, and slid a hand beneath the blanket to grab her thigh under her gown. As she squealed, he stifled her following laugh with his mouth, his other hand grasping the nape of her neck and tugging her to him. She took his hair in both hands and wiggled his head until he released her, whereafter he nuzzled into her throat, his beard tickling her skin.

"Wulf." She had intended for her tone to chastise him, though it escaped as more of a breathless gasp.

Outwardly lifted by their playful encounter, Wulfgar drew her attention beyond the fire where men were hard at work on a long rectangular platform. Other Wulfsuna had begun constructing small rectangular timber homes and designing *wyrt-tuns* not dissimilar to her kitchen garden at Prenhwychas.

"They are building my mead hall," he exclaimed.

To their right, a pair of ash trees she had assumed were for the fire had had their branches and bark removed. Two men were now working the wood with carving implements, plotting intricate designs.

"What are they doing?" She pointed to the woodcarvers.

"Those ash are to be door pillars representing Yggdrasil, the world tree connecting Urth's well to the home of the gods." Wulfgar pointed to the earth and then the sky. "We decorate them with gods and spirits of dead ancestors who will protect our dwelling."

Brithwen felt them akin to a vertical equivalent of her blue crystal tunnel, linking her with those already on their journey to the Summerlands, and an idea grew in her mind. "May anything be carved?" she asked.

Wulfgar stole a kiss on her cheek. "Yes. Why?"

She placed a hand on his face, meeting his gaze. "There are those I would wish remembered."

His smile left his lips, though a glint remained in his eyes. "It can be done," he murmured.

"Dudley, Huweyn..." She began.

Wulfgar covered her hand with his. "And Sieghild," he finished.

A wind stirred, sapping the warmth of the autumn sun, reminding Brithwen the world was moving into Geimredh, the dark half of the year. She contemplated how beautiful their new home would look cradled in ice when snow covered the land. It would not be the home alone that would be cradled. She rolled the wooden talisman round in her palm. Her bleedings were overdue by half a moon's turn and she would soon have to concede that the light of another's life burned in the vessel of her womanhood. The sickness and disgust of ale could be ignored no longer.

She licked dry lips. "Wulf?"

He placed a warm hand on her thigh. "Yes?"

"I am with child."

Wulfgar's breath quickened, his hands shaking and vibrating against his grasp on Brithwen's leg. His gaze flickered between his wife's belly and her face. Sliding hands round her waist, he hauled her onto his lap, ignoring intense pain in his thigh. He grinned at her and bent down to her stomach.

"Welcome to Wulfgarsaetan, little wulf," he whispered, joy numbing his wounds as Brithwen cradled his head into her body and his thoughts turned to how fate had brought them here.

Peace comes in many forms. To a young warrior, peace is the existence lived between battles. To a cyning, peace could be found in the mind. Since his father's slaughter at the Battle of the Fens, Wulfgar's mind had raged a battle of its own, demanding to know who he had become and why he had not foreseen Lord Wulfric's murder. Sieghild had still been with him, though, to quell the madness. After the Battle at Bathumtun his mind laid itself waste; became a barren terrain where his thoughts feared to tread. Each footstep, every breath, had been sheer agony to live.

When an ageing tale-weaver had told him he would find a peacemaker who would have the eyes to his future, he had not believed a saga could have such power. The nix had invaded his life and his nightmares. The all-seeing had sought him out and freed the wellspring of his mind with her hexes, like the norns beneath the great tree of life. She had driven the madness from his soul. Through her, he had seen the light of the gods and been blessed. No more would he doubt the boundless might of the Wolf Spear Saga.

He sat up, meeting Brithwen's eyes. "We shall name him Wulfsieg," he said and she nodded, smiling through tears. He had chosen Wulfsieg, meaning Wolf Victory, to refer not only to the heroic Battle in the Woods won by their tribe, but also to remember a special friendship between two wolf brothers. Wulfgar prayed to Woden to ensure Wulfsieg and his offspring would sire the future of Wulfgarsaetan on the soil into which they thrust their hands and blades, and perhaps sing songs in the mead hall of the brave Wulfgar Cyning. Their blood and sweat would stain and mark the land as their own, where one day a Wolf Spear would once again find a seer.

Acknowledgements

It is certainly true that a book is written by many people. The writer puts words onto paper, but there are many unsung influences that assist in creating a novel. First and foremost has to be my husband and secondly my family, who have been a constant support. I am also grateful to fellow writers whose creative community spirit keeps us all afloat on the ocean of ideas. Finally I must thank re-enactment friends whose advice has been invaluable to my research.

CPSIA information can be obtained at www.ICGtesting.com
Printed in the USA
BVOW07s1709210415

397079BV00003B/152/P